CROWN OF WINGS

JENNIFER CHANCE

OLIVERHEBERBOOKS

For the monsters who help you fly.

CHAPTER 1

The warrior should make a decision in seven breaths.

"One!" I gasp, pulling my long sword around in a wide, sweeping lunge, low enough to cause the four-foot-tall, flying weevishes to spin away, their chittering whoops and wheezes sounding so much like laughter that I narrow my eyes. Half a dozen of these flying spawn of the Seventh House's mighty sandworm monster bob around me, pushing me back—back on the narrow ledge. I can barely breathe with all the debris their leathery wings kick up, and I can't see all that well, either.

"Two!" I spit out, hacking my way forward the moment the smallest of the creatures exposes its underbelly. At the first slice of my sword, it screams and poofs out of this plane. I whirl in one motion, hauling my sword around in a vicious arc.

"Three...four." My aim is true, and the blood thrall from the first cut has made the remaining five creatures jittery and foolish. I take out two more, but as I spin around in the flow of water and wind, I catch sight of a rider high in the mountain pass above me, watching me in this abandoned canyon. A lone rider on a steed, wearing a cloak of...what *is* that color?

All this happens in the space of a breath, but it's a breath I can't spare. I miss the next screeching beast as I complete my killing arc, and I wince at the miscalculation. I've confronted these plague-born spawn before. If I don't dispatch the rest of them in, well, two more breaths—

But it's already too late.

I rush forward, slashing away at the fourth weevish, then the fifth, and they pop out of existence with satisfying screams of irritation. I'm not truly hurting them, of course, but by besting these weevishes on the battlefield I'm keeping them from their next stage of evolution—an evolution that has to be *earned*.

And this last weevish manages it. Even as I arc my sword high to slice a vicious stripe through the sixth, it convulses, jerking away from my sword as if yanked out of reach by an unseen hand. Then it explodes with a feral scream of glee, bursting out of its glistening carapace and morphing into a creature a third again larger than its weevish stage, lifting itself skyward with more powerful wings and lashing its multiple appendages out in all directions. These appendages have actual claws that drip poison, a precursor to the thick hide of its adult state, where the appendages draw back to become razor-sharp scales, the better to administer a lethal dose. I personally think the external claws do a good enough job on their own.

A second after the worm transforms, the shockwave strikes me. "Blood and *stone!*" Despite my best efforts to hold my ground, I'm knocked backwards off my feet, bouncing painfully across the rocky scree by the force of the weevish's transition. The flying worm soars straight up into the sky, convulsing in exultant joy at its evolution. It's forgotten me entirely, spinning off the muck of its discarded skin and showering me with a rainstorm of oozing flesh and gore.

Then it disappears entirely.

A far-off roar of deeply satisfied monsters reaches my ears—the weevish's mother? My own powerful Divh?—but their joyful, ululating cry is faint enough I know they are safely on their own plane, not crashing through the few remaining trees of this mountain pass. Too many monsters have done that already in the run-up to the Tournament of Gold, now nearly four weeks past. The mountain could use a rest.

"*Light*," I groan as their cries die off. I stagger to my knees, then upright. I flip my cloak open and wipe my sword clean before sheathing it anew, then drag a forearm across my grimy face. When my own Divh, Gent, brought me an entire army of enormous, otherworldly creatures at the close of the Tournament of Gold, I'd assumed my job would be merely finding enough warriors to bond to them. I hadn't understood that *all* unbonded Divhs would consider me their ambassador on this plane...including newly minted sandworm mothers who needed a warrior to help their babies transition from weevish to wormlet.

Hanging my head, I work my hands through my gore-soaked hair, slicking off the worst of the mess.

Then I hear the stamping hoofs, the heavy, gusting exhale of a nervous, but stalwart horse. The rider from the high pass.

I straighten and turn around in one movement, but though my hands are loose and at my side, I don't pull a blade—not at first. Never at first. The warrior doesn't betray his abilities when surprise might yet serve him...or her. Especially her.

Instead, my gaze rakes across the watcher, still at a distance where a bow or spear might serve but not a sword, and he has drawn no weapon either. He sits atop his horse a few lengths ahead of a second steed, barely visible around the narrow entrance to this ledge. He's not alone, then.

"I would have rendered aid, warrior, but you seemed to be in no need of it." The voice is strong and full—and not one I've heard before.

"I didn't," I call back, my gravelly croak no longer a grating affront against my own ears. I've gotten used to it, and in this garb —alone on this ridge—it's not such a bad thing to sound like a man. I may be the head of my own house, commander of a battalion of fierce and otherworldly monsters, but I'm still a woman alone against a brace of fighting men whom I don't particularly want to beat to death, even though I could. The Protectorate has need for fighting men, now more than ever.

Even men I do not know and cannot place. While before, I could have sworn I'd caught a bright and vibrant color of this rider's livery, it's now nowhere to be seen. He's hidden the colors of his house beneath a dull gray cloak, keeping them from my view.

Interesting.

"That was a remarkable thing, given that the numbers were well against you. Those were sandworm spawn? Weevishes, I think they're called? At least—they were. It's been some time since I have been to the southern plains. I expected, even hoped to be free to take part in the Tournament of Gold, but fate is a cruel mistress. I assume you took part? And more importantly, you clearly survived. That was a bigger challenge than usual, if the traveling bards are to be believed. I come to pay my respects to the new lord protector, having never had the pleasure of meeting the old one."

I squint at the warrior, hearing the mountains in his tone, the eastern brogue so similar to the way my own brother used to speak. But this is no boy. He looks to be of an age to me, and there are no men with Divhs whose lineage I haven't been exhaustively trained on. The only one close was Lord Orlof's son, a boy of maybe fourteen years, notable mainly because he was supposed to be my betrothed.

I grimace. Fortiss had been kind enough to send a runner to the Twelfth House, advising them of the events of the Tournament of Gold. And, too, that I wouldn't be coming to wed the son of that house.

I've never met Lord Orlof's son—I don't even know his name. I'm sure he's a good enough boy, though, and I'm sure, like most fourteen-year-old children, he has no real interest in being wed to someone he's never met. I hope the Lord Orlof isn't too disappointed, though...we'll have need of his son soon enough.

The Twelfth House is the smallest of all the houses in the Protectorate, and being a mountain house, its Divh is likely similar to my own Gent in his original form—an imposing creature, but not the goliath he became upon the death of my brother and my subsequent banding to him.

I rouse myself from my thoughts as the warrior continues to peer at me.

"You'll be heading to the First House then?" I ask him gruffly, once more keenly aware of the roughness of my voice. To my own ears I don't sound anything like a man, but I managed to convince enough people these past few weeks that it's easy to fall back into the cadence. And, again, I'm a single female alone on a mountain road. Even if he had heard of the wild story of Talia of the Tenth House who took up the mantle of her brother and fought in his place to gain a seat at the Court of Talons, this rider wouldn't assume I was her. Especially considering the layer of worm guts that's currently drying to a crispy exoskeleton over my clothes.

"I am," he says gravely, looking around the barren ledge. "You have a horse nearby? We didn't see one on the road come down from above, and there can't be any easy passage from the rocks below. Ride with us, if you've finished with your work. You can tell us the tales we have missed in our travels from the eastern borders."

"The eastern..." My brows go up as my brain finally catches up to the rest of my body. "You're coming to us from the Exalted Imperium? Are their agents headed this way? Their army?"

Despite my best efforts, my mind cartwheels through too many thoughts at once. It's been weeks since the Tournament of Gold, and my father has returned to the Tenth, thank the Light, his saddlebags filled with gold and his retinue swelled by a dozen fighting men. But they are new men, and our house—his house—is one of the smallest in the Protectorate, perched in the mountains overlooking the Blessed Pass.

It's the primary passage into the Protectorate from the Imperium, and I've only known one good man to ever come through it.

The warrior sits back in his saddle and regards me curiously.

"Who are you, that you know so much about the eastern borders? What house do you hail from?"

"Right now, we all fight for the First—and for the Protectorate." The words are rote, dismissive, but I have no desire to distract the man with my own story. I can't tell how much he knows, and what he thinks is not my business, assuming he thinks at all. Thinking is a rare gift among most soldiers I've met so far. "You're wrong about the path down, though. Having come so far into these mountains, it'd be foolish to go back up the way you came. How many riders are you? And how heavy are your horses laden down with packs?"

"Five. And we can fit through wherever you take us, but—"

I lift a hand to stop him, my mind still churning. Five, with no packs? What sort of scouting expedition doesn't carry provisions?

Not a scouting expedition at all, I suspect. An advance party, more like, barely a few hours ride ahead of a much, much larger company.

Blood and *stone*. Dismay rips through me, as the truth of my missteps are laid plain before my eyes. I'm alone on this mountain, and no one knows exactly where I went to help the sandworm offspring with their rite of passage. I'm no longer Talia of the Tenth, skulking about in the shadows, but a woman with my own house and people to protect. I still wandered off without retainers or a thought to my own safety.

I'm an idiot.

Forcing myself to focus, I whistle sharply, summoning my horse, Darkwing. The gorgeous beast snorts, stamps, then strolls out from behind a wall of rock, as if he was simply passing the time away from the fray of weevishes, trying to keep his coat dry. Truth to tell, my mighty warhorse can easily handle Divhs the size of mountains...but the small ones absolutely unnerve him.

Upon assuring himself that no more of the small creatures—or the much larger wormlets—remain, Darkwing picks up the pace and reaches my side a few moments later. With a muttered apology for sullying his tack, I swing myself into the saddle, shedding bits of dried weevish gore.

Then I turn back to the warrior. "If you follow me, we'll be off the mountain and into the forests of Maradeer in a matter of hours, making Trilion by sunset. But you'll have to ride in a single file until we clear the mountain itself. If any of your packs are too heavy, you'll want to reset them now."

"There won't be any need for that." He half turns in his saddle and looks back to the opening onto the wide ledge, then barks a command in the formal language of the Imperium. My eyes flare, though I keep my face steady beneath its mask of sweat and dust. I've heard that accent before. The priest of the Tenth House, Nazar, who has become my closest advisor, spoke with that same rich inflection when he first set foot in our home so many years ago. Over time, as he became accustomed to the rougher angles and patterns of speech at the Tenth, Nazar adjusted his language and tonality to fit it. But this man clearly has never felt the need to make such modifications.

One by one his small company of soldiers comes into view. And they *are* soldiers, I can see that at a glance. Not the biggest or strongest of men, but stern, sturdy, and heavily cloaked in dark gray. Gray makes sense for marauders or outlanders, as any recognizable color they had chosen to wear would have marked them as one of the royal houses of the Protectorate. Still, the wool of their capes is finely spun, the material rich and thick. And their horses are well fed, shiny creatures that have maybe been allowed to get a bit too fat.

That realization puzzles me, though I can't help expelling a soft breath of relief. Their extremely healthy state seems a little surprising for animals that have made the long trek from the heart of the Imperium, but at least it underscores my belief that these are no marauders. Even if they had just stolen these horses, they would have taken all the riches they could carry from whatever unfortunate house they plundered.

"Thin enough for whatever passages you'll be guiding us through?"

The warrior's words startle me back to focus, and I cut my attention away from the men and back to him. There are no insignias or flourishes to mark any of them as Imperium, but I suppose there wouldn't be. And now that I'm at a level with the warrior and not peering up at him, I make another realization too.

He's shockingly, ruggedly *gorgeous*, in a way both similar to and profoundly different from Fortiss. They both exude a warrior's attitude, practically oozing confidence and bravado. But where Fortiss's eyes are golden and his hair as black as obsidian—this man's eyes are a clear, brilliant blue. His face is square cut and chiseled, and his hair is a thick chestnut brown, pulled back at the nape of his neck, its full length hidden by the dropped cowl of his cape. Unlike Fortiss, whose muscled ranginess speaks of speed and stealth, this man's body is hard and heavy, almost too bulky.

He's as tall as Fortiss, I'll give him that. Based solely on the way he sits tall in his saddle, I'd put this warrior's height at well over six foot—a true warrior. It's too bad he's Imperium-born. Had he been raised in the Protectorate and if his blood were true, he would have commanded a Divh by now...probably a powerful one. Maybe I would have commissioned him to join my own growing stable of warriors, cloaked in silver.

Granted, I'd probably have to arm wrestle Fortiss for the man, given how sorely we all needed warriors in the wake of the disastrous Tournament of Gold. But that might not be such a bad thing, either. A little hand-to-hand combat with the newly minted lord protector *would* allow me to touch Fortiss again—to feel his skin against mine, to revel in the sharp crack of his laughter as I surprise him with a jab or feint, and maybe, just maybe—

What am I even thinking? Fighting the urge to roll my eyes so far back in my head I may never find them again, I favor the stranger with a curt nod.

"They'll be fine. The switchbacks are known as the Narrows,

and they're aptly named, but you should have no trouble with them. It's just a shortcut through these mountains."

"The Narrows," he echoes, smiling at the name. The sudden change of his expression causes a strange prickling of awareness to skate along my nerves, and I pull Darkwing around a little roughly, murmuring my apology as we start to move. I don't look back. Can't. Because if I did, I might see something in his eyes that would send my mind haring off down paths I have no time to tread.

"Stay close, but not too close," I say over my shoulder, heading for another crevasse in the rock wall at the far end of the ledge.

If the man replies, I don't hear him. Instead I push my thoughts out ahead of us, forming the image of Gent, my glorious Divh, my battle partner and the creature closest to my heart. I hear the faint sound of his returning roar, sounding a little too delighted for the fearsome creature that I know him to be. But I can't waste our connection. I focus my mind on the five men trailing behind me, praying that they're not even now drawing swords or bows. I make the pictures in my mind as detailed as possible and then imagine a second Divh, beautiful and fierce, a blue scaled dragon with an injured wing. Szonja is Fortiss's Divh. And even if our new lord protector has been far too busy to even spare me a glance these past few weeks, I need to warn him of the possible trouble I'm bringing his way.

"*We're coming,*" I think to Gent.

A long, crooning howl of joy echoing through my mind is his only response.

CHAPTER 2

B y the time we clear the mountains, it's mid-afternoon, but the clouds conspire to keep me from having a conversation with the traveling party by conveniently opening up on us just as we break out of the mountain path and enter the forest. The heavy canopy of trees keeps the worst of the wet off us and our horses, as do the men's heavy gray cloaks. I elect not to cover up, welcoming the occasional blast of heavy rain through the trees to sluice the worst of the weevish grit from my clothes and hair.

And, too, my cloak isn't made of dead gray wool, but a deep charcoal fabric shot with silver. The color of the Thirteenth house, which has no castle, keep, barracks, or even a barn to call its own. It's a house on the move and so am I...so my cloak can stay in my packs.

We are out of the forest and on to the final stretch as the rain pelts down over us, the skies finally clearing as we reach the outer borders of Trilion.

The city has shrunken dramatically in the weeks since the Tournament of Gold. Where before it sprawled outward, overflowing its boundaries to become a city ringed by tents, camps, and clusters of cart sellers hawking their wares to the tourists and fighting men of the tournament, now it has returned to its equally rollicking but more constrained size. A city of markets and inns, artisans and workers. Lord Rihad, the former lord protector of Trilion and all of the Protectorate, may have been a cunning traitor, but you'd never know it to look at the residents of his jeweled city.

As we wind our way down the cobblestoned streets, I'm struck anew by the vibrancy all around us—and wonder what the warriors from the Imperium think of the obvious displays of wealth and prosperity. Shops with carved wooden signs hang over the street, each advertising wares or services—a smithy with a hammer and anvil etched into its placard, an apothecary decorated with the outline of a mortar and pestle, and a glassblower's shop where delicate works of glass sparkle in the window, catching the early afternoon light. Square-jawed cobblers, nimble-fingered tailors, and sharp-eyed jewelers tout their wares through windows flung open wide to the rain-freshened air, and a stout bakery, its walls of dark timber and stone, sends out the warm scent of spiced cakes and fresh loaves to greet us.

My stomach growls loud enough to be heard all the way to the Western Realms. I'd forgotten how hungry I was.

We pass by tall, well-kept buildings that I barely noticed when I passed through this town the first time, broken and grief-stricken on my way to the tournament. Back then, I wanted nothing but revenge for my brother's death and a brace of fighting men to rebuild the Tenth House.

Now, I can study Trilion from a perspective that is worlds different. The stone guildhall, its doorway framed by thick wooden beams and an iron crest, marks the center of commerce, and even as we pass by, we can hear the shouts of those inside, arguing over...what? Contracts or prices? The flow of trade?

Have they any idea of the dangers that loom to the west? Or the apparent arrival of the Imperial armies from the east?

I set my jaw, my mind galloping ahead to Fortiss at the First House and all the problems that await us there. The people of Trilion have already forgotten the most pressing results of the tournament—that the defenders of the houses of the Protectorate have been cut in half, then in half again. A new cluster of warriors have risen from those ashes, but they are still new to their Divhs... too new.

They'll have to serve, though.

Just ahead, the town's courthouse rises above the other buildings, its steps polished smooth by generations of use and its columns capped with intricately carved stonework. Outside, a few townspeople linger, deep in discussion—merchants in thrown-back cloaks and rain-dampened hats, discussing grain shipments and seasonal fairs. There's also the watchtower, not too far from the town square, its walls fortified and manned by guards in the black-and-gold livery of the First House, their short capes of deep black already a familiar sight to me.

Looking at it through a newcomer's eye, other details tug at me. The townspeople walking the streets are prosperous-looking, I believe, though I've never been to the cities of the Imperium to compare. Still, Trilion has to stack up favorably, even if the wealth of my own house would not. Here the women wear linen skirts and fitted bodices dyed in rich hues—deep blues, greens, and scarlets —with well-spun cloaks pinned at their shoulders. Men stroll along in woolen tunics, each accented by belts of intricately tooled leather, with boots polished to a faint shine. Young apprentices in tidy tunics and breeches hurry between shops, carrying crates or bundles under their arms, eyes wide as they dodge horses and carts.

Other travelers, strangers to the town who somehow missed the tournament's pull or deliberately avoided that crush of people, pass by as well—weathered men and women from more rugged regions, dressed in cloaks of muted, earthen colors and boots caked in dust from the road. There are traders from the south, their clothing woven with bright stripes of yellow and tan, as well as travelers from the northern mountains—Fifth House traders, their bags bulging with unknown wares.

"What are they talking so secretively about, I wonder?"

The warrior's words startle me, but once I focus on the faces of the townsfolk milling around, I see what he means. They pause here and there to greet neighbors, but their smiles are either over-bright or tightly controlled beneath sidelong glances, their comments delivered beneath their breath. Some have heads huddled close in whispered exchanges, while others practically buzz with gossip I cannot quite hear.

"Well, the Tournament of Gold is only a few weeks past," I say carefully. "It was a sight to behold. Have you heard much about it?"

The warrior snorts with more derision than I expect. "Not nearly enough as I should have, that's clear."

I nod as if his response makes perfect sense, but I don't dare look at him directly—though I can't say exactly why. There's been an energy flowing off the warrior since we entered the town that strikes me wrong...it's equal parts angry and exasperated, and that doesn't quite tail with someone so new to the Protectorate. What stories has he been told?

It doesn't take me long to find out.

His gaze slants over to me, sharp and pointed. "You fought in the tournament, yes? Was it as deadly as people say?"

I grimace, the worst of my fears realized. So the Imperium's ambassadors *do* know that Rihad slaughtered some of our finest warriors in a bid for power and control. I suppose I would be angry about that too, though the Imperator has not seen fit to oversee its western-most lands in generations. To my eyes, their outrage is a little suspect.

Not for the first time, I'm glad I don't fight with words but only with the short and long sword. At least the art of war makes sense.

I choose to answer only part of his question. "It was a tournament that showcased the best warriors the Protectorate could assemble, and they came together in a battle that the bards will be spinning into gold for a hundred years on, I bet. But yes, it turned deadly at the end. Good men died, their Divhs gravely injured and lost to us—some, we fear, forever."

"Lost," he echoes, and though I yearn to defend, to explain, that's not my place. Something else finally occurs to me, as we clear the center of town and turn our horses toward the looming castle of the First House, high atop its mountain aerie, across the open plains. But before I can ask my question, he gestures to the other monstrous structure that dominates the horizon, this one farther out, beyond the marshes, where the earth is still packed flat. "They fought there? That's the coliseum for the Tournament of Gold?"

"It is." I nod, chafing against the slowing pace of our mounts, when all I want is to get my charge to the First House and escape this interloper's presence. But as we leave the official boundaries of the city and strike out across that path, my gaze is held fast to the coliseum, my vision clouded by the memories of the battles fought there—both inside the ancient structure and on the fields surrounding it. I can hear the screams still, the cries of both men and Divhs driven to take each other's lives, drowning in an all-consuming rage for blood and misplaced honor.

As I gaze upon the structure, my heart aching, a roar rises up from the coliseum, a howling squawk that's half screech, half trill, and all pure joy. Even as I stare, I see the tiniest speck shoot up from inside the open coliseum, like a pebble thrown up a mountain's height. No sooner does the speck reach the top of its arc and come plummeting down, then a Divh nearly two-thirds the size of my own colossal monster leaps to the top of the coliseum just long enough to use it as a launching pad before it catapults into the air. I recognize this Divh immediately, and my heart stops as his enormous, clawed paw reaches out and swipes the tiny speck from the sky, cradling it into his massive chest. Stunted, flapping wings unfurl and I blink. I know this particular Divh has the head of a falcon, but have I ever seen him *fly*?

In any event, he doesn't do it well. The wings seem to jut out from his heavy arms less for the art of flying than to help break the speed of the monster's divine descent. He hits the ground with a resounding boom, only to turn sharply toward us, his galloping, ungainly run equal parts horrifying and awe inspiring. No more than six ground-eating strides later, the Divh Marsh is upon us.

Except for the steed of the warrior beside me, the soldiers' horses nicker with fear and scramble back, scattering as the Divh plants his ungainly feet and leaps up again, just as he chucks his precious cargo to the ground with what even I can see is a practiced flick of his wrist. Then the monster winks out of existence with a bone rattling caw of joy.

Uttering his own howl of delight, the warrior Caleb tucks his body into a tight ball, rips through the sky, and crashes to the marshy plain. He rolls in several flopping somersaults before stopping barely a dozen strides away from us. No sooner does he rise to his feet than he draws the fingers of his right hand to his lips and utters a piercing whistle, so loud even Darkwing flinches. The warrior besides me grunts as he struggles to keep control of his own horse, who had staunchly endured the arrival of my ridiculous beloved friend and his ridiculous beloved Divh but wasn't expecting this new affront.

A moment later, however, the pounding hooves of a mare I know well fills the space between us, and Caleb's mount races to be reunited with her new master. The sight fills me with such unfettered joy that I don't think about what must come next until it's too late.

"Talia!" Caleb crows, as he deftly swings himself up in the saddle. He may only have one arm, but he's more deft with it than most warriors are with their full complement of limbs. "Didn't I tell you Marsh could leap straight out of the coliseum if he wanted to? Didn't I?"

"Talia? *Lady* Talia?" The words come out like a crack of thunder, and both Caleb and I wheel around, my short sword half out of my scabbard at the clear rebuke in the warrior's tone.

"The same," growls Caleb, rushing to defend me whether I need his help or not. "Champion of the Tournament of Gold, winner of the winged crown, head of the Thirteenth House. Which you should know since you're clearly riding with her, warrior or not. Who are you and where are you from?"

"Caleb..." I wince, feeling a headache coming on. I slide my short sword back into place and pitch my tone to as placating as possible. "These men weren't at the tournament. He and his men—"

"These men buried *Lord Orlof* two weeks ago, the old man still waiting for a promise to be fulfilled that he had negotiated in good faith," the warrior snaps. He stares at me fully now, and for the first time since he arrived at the top of the path, when he looks at me, I feel seen.

It's not an especially good feeling.

"Lady Talia of the Thirteenth House—a house I have never heard of—can I assume you are also Talia of the Tenth? Whose marriage to the heir of the Twelfth House would have united two mountain fortresses and maintained the strength of the borders of the Protectorate against the marauders from the east?"

"I..." I squint at him, fully at a loss. Who was this man? Some agent of the Imperium sent to aid the Twelfth House? And is Lord Orlof really dead?

But the man continues to stare at me, unyielding.

"I—yes," I finally manage. "Though it's of no account to you. Lord Orlof and my father arranged my marriage to his fourteen-year-old child and sent me off to fulfill the promise. Then my brother was murdered by an agent of Lord Rihad, and I came here instead."

"Came to Trilion," he sneers, his disbelief plain. "To fight in the Tournament of Gold as a *woman*."

"Came to find justice for my brother and fighting men for my house the only way I could—because my brother was *dead*," I spit back.

He doesn't back down. His blue eyes are sparking with fury which I absolutely do not merit. "A fair decision," he seethes. "But fairer still would have been the one that took you to the Twelfth

House, which is now the house you should cleave to by dint of the wedding contract."

A cold wash of certainty rolls through me, and far away, I hear the questioning trill of Gent, can almost see his massive horned head tilting on his distant plane, as if to better hear my response.

I don't disappoint. "A contract nullified by the fact that I am banded." I reach up to the collar of my waistcoat and yank it aside, revealing my reinforced sleeveless vest and the very, very obvious warrior's band that circles my upper bicep. "I would not have wished the shame of that truth to sully the standing of the Twelfth House."

His gaze darts to my arm, then returns, more slowly, to hold mine. His eyes burn with rage, surprise, and something else, something I can't pin down. "Then maybe you should have asked your betrothed his opinion."

Oh, please. "I *told* you, I—"

"Because I would have supported you."

My throat closes tight as if gripped by a vice, and breath completely deserts me as the warrior wrenches his cape over one shoulder, betraying the inky midnight blue of the Twelfth House. "Tennet, son of Orlof, first-blooded and firstborn. Contracted in the Light as your husband, Talia of the Tenth, now and evermore."

"But..." I stare at the man, barely able to form my words. "You're supposed to be fourteen!"

He smiles at me, all teeth. "And you're supposed to have hair down to your feet, laden with enough riches to feed our people for a year. It's a day full of surprises."

CHAPTER 3

"Tennet of the Twelfth House!" Caleb says brightly, gaze darting from my face to the warrior's beside me, who is most assuredly not the boy my father thought he was marrying me off to. "I tell you plain, your name has never appeared in any official roll of the houses of the Protectorate, nor in the line of first-blooded and first born."

He holds up his right hand to ward off Tennet's obvious question. "I know, because I made it my business to know two years back and more, in my studies to join the warrior class of the Second House. And yes, you're right. No self-respecting warrior would go about the business with only one arm, but it's not as if I started out that way. I simply had to make an adjustment along the path, as all great warriors do—as you did, surely, first-blooded and firstborn and all. Shall we ride? Lord Protector Fortiss will be eager to meet you and to feed you and your men after your travels."

This virtual torrent of words does me the service that Caleb's chatter has since the moment I met him. It gives me time and space to separate myself from the disasters of my own making and allow me to think.

"Warrior Tennet—no, Lord Tennet it would be, may the Light

receive your father's soul—this is warrior Caleb, banded in the great melee of the Tournament of Gold. Now he's in charge of training the new banded soldiers and their Divhs." I stop short of assigning my closest friend and staunchest supporter as a member of my newly formed house, but Tennet's quick, assessing gaze rakes over Caleb with...what? Dismissal? Calculation? I'm too churned up inside to know, but it's certainly not wholehearted acceptance.

Yet another mark against him. The man will be covered in blacking stone by the time we reach the gates of the First House.

Then again, Fortiss also was quick to dismiss me when we first met, that day in the forest outside the Shattered City. He saw me as nothing more than a bride-to-be on her way to her wedding, dressed for a life of passive, diligent service. From the hard set of his jaw, Tennet *still* sees me that way.

Well, Fortiss learned the truth quickly enough. I'd make sure this hulking brute did, too.

"It seems the scant information I have received about the Tournament of Gold has been neither complete nor fully accurate," Tennet replies, his words as neutral as a granite wall, despite his easy smile. "We should probably start with your explanation of what exactly happened here, these few weeks' past."

"Then we talk and ride." Now I wince at the gravelly rasp of my voice, though I shouldn't care what I sound like, only that I can be heard. Had my father's aim been any truer when he sliced my throat all those years ago, when I was but a girl of seven, I would have lost both voice and breath in one fell strike.

Plus, what do I care that Tennet eyes me curiously as I speak, his sharp eyes dropping to my imperfectly covered throat? Can he see the ugly, puckering scar that peeks out beneath the fringe of my too-short hair that barely brushes my collar?

He looks too long. Not with disgust—but not with indifference, either. My stomach twists as I long to shrink away from him. Does he consider me gruesomely damaged? No longer worthy of being his betrothed?

Betrothed! The word turns sour in my disfigured throat and, not waiting for the rest of them to move, I turn Darkwing roughly toward the First House and start out.

"Talk and ride, yes! Talk and ride. Two of my favorite activities in one," Caleb announces, deftly maneuvering his horse between mine and Tennet's, the two of them slightly behind me and to the left. I fix my gaze on the spires of the First House while he tells the tale of the tournament, as only Caleb can.

"This year's Tournament of Gold was destined to be life-changing well before it started, given the rewards Lord Rihad promised the warriors and their houses who turned out for it. Promises of rafts of soldiers to the winning houses, exalted seats on the Court of Talons, and his favor at every turn. We already had a fair number of combatants a solid two weeks out from the tournament, all of them setting up camp in the fields between Trilion and the coliseum, but Lord Rihad wanted more. It was a time for all houses to come together and represent the glory of the Protectorate, and all able-bodied warriors who could come, should. Begging your pardon, Lord Tennet. You verily had sound reasons for staying away, especially if your father was ill. May the Light receive him."

Though he's behind me, I can see Caleb in my mind's eye as he turns to Tennet, equal parts somber and full of welcome. I further imagine Tennet's sour expression as his response follows hard upon. "We received no such summons to the tournament, and it wasn't for lack of watching the passes for any riders with word."

"None at all?" To my surprise and frustration at my own impulsiveness, I turn in my saddle to gaze back at the two men—who couldn't look more different if they tried. Caleb's face betrays a curiosity equaling my own, while Tennet seems to only have grown more stoic in the intervening moments since he last glared at me. "My understanding was all houses were summoned well in advance of the tournament. Merritt certainly knew of it, my father as well, for all that the Tenth had no intention of competing in the spectacle this year. Merritt was too young."

"Too young," Tennet echoes, never mind that Caleb beside us is barely fifteen years old, and clearly this tournament wasn't his first. But Caleb isn't the first-born son of Protectorate royalty. "And yet, you are a year Merritt's junior, was my understanding—by your father's own description."

My gaze leaps to meet his and I see the challenge there, read it in the twist of his lips and the smirk behind his eyes. "And you're supposedly a boy of fourteen. It would seem the contract forged between our houses was formed on lies and strategy, Lord Tennet," I concede. "Doubtless more truths will come to light before we're done."

To my surprise, his smile deepens some, and something dark and fierce flashes in his piercing eyes before he schools his expression back to a mask of indifference. "Doubtless," he murmurs.

The tension between us is thick enough to bring down a charging stag, and Caleb's cheery voice sounds ever so slightly strained as he takes up his tale. I turn back in my saddle and ease Darkwing forward at a slightly faster clip.

"Once the tournament proper began, it seemed much as it always does—chaos, but controlled chaos, falling into the time-honored order of pit battles among the rank and file and exhibition fights of mighty Divhs to whet the appetite of the spectators. At night there was music and food and the camaraderie of a Protectorate who seeks a reason to come together and witness the glory of the warriors and their Divhs. Have you ever been to a tournament, Warrior...ah, Lord Tennet?"

Caleb either receives some sort of non-verbal response or determines that the good lord has no intention of divulging more information, for he immediately launches ahead, a baby shorebird flinging itself out of its protective nest to flap about in an unforgiving sky. "Well! It's a sight to behold. Warriors from houses across the Protectorate—not all, not all, but most—brought caravans of attendants, all of them setting up an unruly camp for weeks where goods were bought and sold, food and drink were celebrated, and music rolled across the plain. When these warriors met upon the battlefield, their Divhs fought with them and for them, mighty creatures that would take your breath away. Sand-worms, winged lizards, fearsome lions, great horned beasts with powerful arms and legs—every combination of creature you could imagine. They came and they fought."

We pass through the gates at the base of the mountain, beneath the sharp-eyed gaze of the guards at the top of the tower. I stare up at those guards with as much mental force as I can muster, fully aware that the heat of the day and the cessation of rain, coupled with how near we are to the end of their journey, has loosened the mood and circumspection of the riding party. The colors of their tunics are now plain to see, announcing them as Twelfth House soldiers.

I pray the moment we pass this station, the guard or one of his lieutenants will race to the top of the tower, signaling the watchers at the castle to warn them about their impending guests. There need be no concern or undue security that gets triggered—these men are loyal to the Protectorate until they prove otherwise. But given who is about to land on his doorstep, I suspect Fortiss will want at least a few moments to prepare a reasonable greeting, especially if Gent didn't convey my message from earlier to Fortiss's Divh, Szonja. I would've preferred some advanced warning myself.

Thank the Light that my father has returned to the Tenth House. The wedding contract he and Lord Orlof had forged was done so without any input of mine, of course. I didn't even know the boy's name to whom I was promised—he remained deliberately unnamed, according to Caleb, in any official records kept by the First House. But I would have remembered the name Tennet, if I'd ever run across it in any documentation on the Twelfth House. Theirs was a strange holding, as close to the eastern border as we are at the Tenth House, but tucked into far less hospitable terrain. The Tenth House was generally considered the official point of welcome for anyone traveling from the Imperium, whereas the Twelfth was only the destination of marauders bent upon slipping into the Protectorate unseen or unchallenged. Not that the Twelfth House deliberately welcomed them, of course, but from every snide comment I'd been able to glean from traveling bards, they simply couldn't do much more than look the other way.

I have a hard time believing that the square-jawed warrior who's listening so attentively to Caleb's ongoing patter about the Tournament of Gold would've looked the other way. He's as big as he is arrogant, like most every warrior knight I've met. So where in the Light has he been all these years? How is it that Caleb had never heard of him; my friend who's pored over every scrap of knowledge about every House, from the first through the Twelfth? How is it that my father fully believed that he was sending me to a *child*, a son so captured beneath the thumb of his father that I would be put in my place by the elder Orlof for years before taking over as the mistress of my own house?

Because mark me plain, my father wasn't interested in doing me any great service in marrying me off. He wanted to be rid of me, yes, and he had jewels to spare for my dowry, but the Twelfth House must have paid a bride price for me that was worth more to my father than the ornaments that he suffered me to carry on my person as I made the trek through the mountains.

I scowl. Clearly, I haven't given this wedding arrangement enough thought. What is it that the Twelfth House had to trade for me that my father would have thrown in a mountain of jewelry and still felt like he had gotten the better part of the bargain? Lord Lemille of the Tenth wouldn't have made the agreement otherwise, no matter how eager he was to be rid of me.

I don't even like thinking about my father, and doing so now puts me in an even worse mood as Darkwing strides so fast up the winding mountain path that he nearly breaks into a trot. When my father had finally quit the First House to return to his own fortress with a brace of fighting men and the consideration that Fortiss settled upon him for his trouble, I'd thought myself well and truly rid of him. Perhaps that belief was too quickly formed.

These thoughts are my companions all the way up the mountain until at last we ride through the village that fronts the First House. Unlike the reception during the Tournament of Gold, our arrival today merits barely a flicker of interest. There is actual living and work to do when the pomp and glory of the Protectorate's royalty ceases its demands.

Still, much like in the town of Trilion, there is also the faintest undercurrent of nervous energy riding along the conversations and sideways glances between the residents of First Village as we pass by. These people may not care about us specifically, but something remains very much on their minds. Whether it's the threat from the west or simply continued speculation about the long-term impact of the Tournament of Gold's deadly melee on the Protectorate, I don't know. Further, I don't want to know. Politics has never been a game I had the patience or discernment to play.

The moment we pass through the gates of the First House, however, my heart eases. Fortiss himself stands at the top of the sweeping steps to the castle, garbed in gold and black, his cape lifting with the breeze. There's a smile on his face as our company approaches, but when his gaze shifts to me, I nearly choke on its intensity.

He's changed. He's definitely changed. Something has happened at the First House in the few short hours that I've been gone. Something he almost certainly won't want to share with the newcomers from the Twelfth House.

I lean forward, my mind scrambling to figure out what has happened to him.

He looks the same as he ever has—tall, lean and well-muscled, with an arrogant twist to his mouth that echoes the smirk Lord Tennet wore so comfortably. As if the world had been fashioned as his handmaiden, willing to do his bidding at the merest word.

It's a right and a power I've come into myself, having been banded to a Divh, but I wear that mantle with far less grace. Something else to work on.

But I'm not mistaken, I think. There's an energy that suffuses Fortiss that's different than the man I left in the small hours of the morning, the two of us breaking our fasts over an early strategy meeting. He was determined to explore the endless scrolls that his predecessor had left behind, scrolls that whispered of the danger and the magic held beyond the Western Realms, scrolls that, presumably, also held some details about the extraordinary monsters that fought so ably and well, then consented to remain at our beck and call for centuries after. We know ridiculously little about how that agreement came to be, and we must understand it better if we are to command the Divhs to help us in the battle that looms large to the west.

Has Fortiss discovered more about the Divhs? Has he stumbled into some magic that the former lord protector hoarded away; magic that could help empower us against the threat we know is coming? Had he—

"Welcome to the First House, riders of the Twelfth!" Fortiss's call is so bold it shakes me out of my racing thoughts as he moves down the steps, stopping halfway to extend one arm, as if to offer the whole of his castle to his guests. "We offer you rest, hospitality, and camaraderie as we mark this glorious new dawn of the Protectorate."

"We'll accept it and leave you to your glorious dawn," Tennet announces, the heavy brogue of his voice bouncing off the walls of the courtyard. "But we're taking my wife back with us."

CHAPTER 4

Tennet's words bang around in my head like hail pounding in an ice storm, but I haven't come so far, or faced so much loss, to back down now.

"I'm sure we can arrange that, Lord Tennet." I angle in my seat and stare at the man, my words disrupting the sudden silence that's marked only by the quiet struggle of Caleb swallowing his tongue. "If you've come to find a wife, I'm sure there are any number of women in Trilion who would gladly take you up on that offer."

He clasps his hands over the pommel of his saddle, holding his reins loosely. "Fortunately, my choice is already made. Talia of the Tenth."

I bare my teeth at him. "What a tragedy that she no longer exists."

"Lord Tennet, Lady Talia," Fortiss cuts in, with such force to his voice that my blood seizes in my veins. I glance toward him, startled, and sense Tennet's gaze jerk from me to focus on Fortiss as well. Once again, our new lord protector looks the same as he did when I saw him last, not even a full day ago, but something has definitely changed.

Is it a good change, though? Or does the danger that seems to unfurl like an invisible cloak around Fortiss threaten more than it protects? I've thrown my lot in with his leadership, sought to preserve and nurture the tiny flame of connection that sparked between us...but do I truly know this man?

Oblivious to my concern, Fortiss charges on. "We are blessed to be able to welcome our guests with a household still flush with wine and ale from the tournament, never mind that it was a month ago. We welcome you and your men, Lord Tennet. Let's get you off your horses. Tonight's banquet will be a happy event, and you'll be pleased that some warriors of the houses remain to hear your stories and share their own. It's been some time since we've celebrated a first-blooded son of the Twelfth House at our table. Welcome."

At this last, he gestures to no one in particular, but clearly, it's a symbol that's been eagerly awaited. A tumble of five stable hands burst from the gates of the outer bailey, dashing across the courtyard to assist the riders. I swing off Darkwing before Tennet can dismount, leaving him to glower at me as Caleb deftly slides off his mare. I start to hand over my reins to Caleb—then check the movement and grimace.

He's no more a servant than I am. Not ever again.

Before he can stop me, I signal one of the stable hands over. I first hand him my reins, then pull Caleb's out of his right hand.

Caleb flinches back. "I can take care of her," he informs me, his eyes wide with surprise. As comfortable as he is with his new position as warrior when it involves his mighty Divh, he's nowhere near at ease with the idea of being treated as one. Well, he'd better get used to it. He'll be expected to attend tonight's dinner, even if he is lucky enough to be able to sit with Nazar and not at the high table.

There's been no call for feasting in the wake of the tournament, not with so many warriors injured and too many dead. We've also been grappling with the grim reality of Lord Rihad held in private chambers, awaiting the arrival of the Imperium. The former lord protector's plan to devastate the army of Divhs and leave the Protectorate crippled surely merits swift and harsh justice, but it isn't justice for us to mete out, but an agent of the Imperator.

Would that one sees fit to come all this way.

"If you wish." I shrug and gesture to where the stable hand is walking Darkwing toward the stables. My stallion still has his ears laid back. "We can follow them and make sure he doesn't bite anyone."

Caleb shoots me a lopsided grin. "Him or you?"

"I'm glad you're having such a good time with all this."

"I mean, you have to admit, it's entertaining." He glances back to where Tennet has finally decided to dismount, and I follow his gaze to assess Lord Orlof's son anew. His stiff stance is evidence either of his long ride through the mountains or, I suspect, a stick as wide as a club driven right up his—

"You know, you don't really have a face for gambling."

I jerk my gaze back to Caleb, and he chuckles, which does nothing to improve my mood. We've moved far enough away from the Twelfth House group that he continues in a low voice, the two of us maneuvering his mare toward the far end of the stables. She doesn't need to be stabled near Tennet's horses, especially if they're as foul-tempered as he is.

My temper has definitely soured as well. I feel trapped, hemmed in, flanked by the subtle and strangely powerful Fortiss on one side, and the bristling, bull-headed Tennet on the other. And I've come too far since leaving my father's house, endured too much, to ever allow myself to be trapped again.

I slant a glance toward Caleb. "You've never heard of Orlof having an older son?"

"That would be a definite no," he confirmed. "Then again, news on the ground about the Twelfth House was as scarce as it was about the Tenth. I knew about Merritt, and that Lord Lemille had had other daughters besides his son, but there definitely was no mention of the fact that the Tenth House's firstborn child was a female, and that she was a full four years ahead of her brother, not a year his junior."

"Yes, but there was a good reason for that level of secrecy. I shouldn't have been allowed to live as a firstborn daughter. It was only the pleading of my mother and my father's fear of offending the Light that he suffered me to stay alive until she got pregnant again, two years after I was born. And then my father was so certain that he would have a son that he announced plans for my death to her in exacting detail while he thought she was sleeping. She miscarried that same night."

"*What*?" Caleb chokes.

I grimace, but the story rushes out, as if I'd held it for so long, another moment was simply too much. "She certainly didn't want the miscarriage to happen—she was devastated by it. But she also never betrayed that she was awake the whole time during his hateful screed. Either way, he was sufficiently superstitious afterwards that it served to spare my life another few years."

Caleb stares at me, horrified. "I had no idea."

"Well, there had to be some reason why they waited another four years after that to try again. My father wasn't faithful to my mother during that time, of course. If he'd been able to have a male child by another means he would have done so. But finally, my mother grew afraid for my safety once again and approached him with all the trappings of a woman blessed by the Light itself. She said she had a vision that he would be blessed with the success of a baby boy if he would lay with her and preserve his firstborn child despite the mistake of my birth. He did so eagerly, and nine months later, my brother was born. I was nearly four by then, and already no fool. I understood that no matter what, there would be a boy born to my father. It was the only way my mother could ensure my safety."

"But how could she guarantee such a thing?" Caleb asks, with the wrinkled brow of an innocent. "Especially if all he'd been producing was girls up to that point."

"There were blessings, herbs, and tinctures involved, and there was also cold strategy," I tell him with a grim smile. "There were many babies born that month to the Tenth House women, a spike of fertility that would have made it into the tales of many a passing bard if any were allowed close."

"She'd made plans to...adopt someone else's baby?" he asks, aghast. Caleb may have been schooled in the art of combat and war, but clearly, he has no idea what it takes to be a woman in the Protectorate.

I shrug. "She did what she felt she needed to, in order to spare my life and the life of whatever child she gave birth to, boy or girl. And it worked. Merritt was born—legitimately, by all accounts—and my father never raised a hand against me after that unless he was drinking. I learned quickly enough to avoid him during those times. Except for when he sliced my neck when my brother was maybe a year old, I never faltered in my vigilance. As you can imagine, I was far more careful after that event."

"Blood and stone," he mutters. Then glances back over his shoulder. "Lord Tennet doesn't have a case though, does he? I mean, he can bluster all he wants about the marriage contract, but it's not binding...right?"

"It's not," I say with a confidence I don't feel. Still, I push on, as if by a sheer volume of words I can convince the Light that it's so. "Orlof contracted for the second-born daughter of the Tenth House, not the firstborn, first-blooded daughter with a warrior band on her arm. He wanted Talia of the Tenth, not Talia of the Thirteenth."

"Still..." Caleb holds up both hands as I slant a glare at him. "I'm just saying, maybe you should talk to Nazar about this, before Tennet puts his question to Fortiss or the councilors."

"The councilors." My lips twist in disgust, but the clutch in my chest isn't going away, and I know Caleb is right. "They're as close to useless as anyone I've ever met. They stood by for the last decade and more, letting Rihad nearly destroy the Protectorate. They threw Rihad in prison and then moved him to a nicer cell not a day later."

"I mean, he hasn't woken up since he fell on the battlefield," Caleb points out. "It's been four weeks, and he hasn't so much as twitched."

"But he hasn't died yet," I insist stubbornly, my voice dropping even more. There's magic happening here that's not of the Light, swirling and whirling around the First House. Fortiss has changed, I know he has, while Rihad..."He hasn't changed, Caleb. Fortiss took me to him two days ago. For a man who hasn't visibly consumed water or food for the last four weeks, he hasn't shrunken an ounce. His face is full, his skin warm, his sleep is easy. He might as well be taking a nap. How is he managing that?"

"Not from walking the Lighted path, that's for sure," Caleb mutters, and I make a swift, impatient gesture.

"Definitely not. I think he's in the plane of the Divhs, getting his sustenance there."

He blinks. "But you'd know that, wouldn't you? Wouldn't I? I mean, I haven't asked Marsh, but that never even occurred to me."

I shake my head. "Gent says Rihad's not there—or his Divh. He says that Rihad's scorpion died in that final attack in the melee, but that's all wrong too, from what I'm gathering from him. Rihad's Divh shouldn't have died, since Rihad didn't. But I can't quite understand everything he's trying to tell me. It's not like he talks in linear sentences."

Caleb snorts. "At least he talks. Marsh mostly communicates by pointing at things impatiently, trilling, and expecting me to understand. That said...I didn't realize Rihad's Divh was so broken in the melee. I mean, it disappeared, sure, but—"

"But a Divh doesn't automatically die when their warrior dies," I finish for him. By now we've reached the stalls where our horses have been stabled since the close of the tournament. I glance back to see that Tennet and his men have gone, leaving their horses in the capable hands of the First House workers. "Not unless they're mortally wounded. And Rihad's flying scorpion wasn't. Gent is sure about that. Only he's gone—absolutely vanished. And apparently, that means he's dead."

"And Gent has no idea why?"

"Oh, he has plenty of ideas, but they're all words I've never heard of. Like I said, it's tied to some kind of magic that Rihad played out before the melee even started, magic that's all bound up in the books and scrolls that Fortiss is poring over."

We turn back toward the First House, though my strides are shorter now, slower.

Caleb frowns my way. "You heard that resonance in Fortiss's voice, didn't you? I didn't make that up in my own mind. He sounded like Rihad when he wanted to get all lord protector on people. I thought it was just an affectation that he turned on and off like a bard would—a vocal trick to make his voice carry. But when Fortiss spoke just now, he had the exact same trick."

"Mhmm." I sigh, my head officially starting to hurt. "So you're thinking, maybe it's not a trick?"

"I mean...what if it is something tied to his lord protector status, and nothing more than that? He was officially blessed into the role, and we didn't see any of what went into that. Could he have been given special...I don't know, powers?"

I rub my brow, as if I can scrub all these thoughts away. "I have no idea. He's not supposed to have any. The power of the Protectorate is wrapped up in the might of its leaders and their Divhs. That's the way it's been since time immemorial."

"So says the woman who shouldn't even have a Divh," Caleb points out cheerfully. He claps me on the back. "But hey! If nothing else comes of Tennet's arrival, at least we're going to get a good meal of it. And since he's your betrothed and all—maybe you should put on a dress."

I shove him back—then stop short when there's another commotion at the front gates.

"Seriously, this is the most activity that's happened here in a month," Caleb says, slowing down to peer that way as well. "Are these more of Tennet's men? Maybe an entire troupe of bards to sing at your wedding?"

He laughs as he ducks away from my punch to his right arm,

but we both watch the initial brace of horses that trot through the gates, our vantage point keeping us from seeing much more than the scramble of people getting out of their way until Caleb and I realize the truth at the same time—

"They're wearing Tenth House green," Caleb blurts. "It's your *father*."

CHAPTER 5

"What are they *doing* here?" Caleb practically chokes on his own words as I pull him back behind a farmer's cart, which is piled high with enough fruits and vegetables to tide anyone from the First House over until the next full market day.

"I don't know, but what do I do now?" I glance quickly from the oncoming men to Caleb's face. "Should I go out and greet him? I have no standing in this house. I'm not part of—"

"Oh, blight," Caleb interrupts me, peering up toward the doorway of the First House. "Someone's told Fortiss. Here—onto my back. Get up to the first-level balcony, and act like you've been there this whole time."

"But—"

"They're all looking up there, you're over here, and we have this cart as protection. Come on!"

He drags me over to the wall of the First House and braces his legs wide, muttering a stream of curses as I step up onto his thigh, then his shoulder, then latch onto the thin stone columns of the balustrade and drag myself up. Caleb grabs one of my flailing feet and shoves it high, the extra push giving me the momentum I need to shove my way through the columns and onto the first-story balcony. I crouch in sudden panic as Fortiss calls out over the courtyard.

"Lord Lemille, well met. You honor the First House with your return." His voice is calm, strong, and maddeningly sure—like nothing could rattle him, not even the unexpected return of the man who gave me away like a bargaining chip...and then lobbied for my death. I should be grateful for Fortiss's steadiness. I am grateful. But it also makes me feel like I'm three steps behind, and I hate that.

"Lord Protector Fortiss." My father sounds far haler and heartier than the last time I saw him. I swallow my rising hysteria as I crouch walk to the far edge of the balcony. This late in the day, the area is hung with shadows, and I slowly work my way to a standing position, smoothing down my clothes. Bits and pieces of weevish gunk still hang from various creases, but I don't intend to get close enough to my father for him to judge my attire.

I draw in an unsteady breath as he keeps talking. "The Tenth House is secure with your men, and I thank you for it, but there is more work to be done. I have returned to offer my aid."

All this is shouted loud enough to be heard all the way to Trilion, but I understand the posturing for what it is. The men of the Protectorate shout when they could speak, fight when they could debate, and choke off their enemies when they could simply let them breathe and be.

Fortiss strides down a few steps, and only then do I realize he's not alone. My heart spasms so hard in my chest I nearly black out.

Tennet also stands at the top of the stairs. Of course he's beside Fortiss. Where else would he be? The two of them create the perfect picture of twinned power—one bold and brash, the other nuanced and mysterious. And now with my father to complete the trifecta of bristling authority, I think seriously about slinking back over the side of the First House, finding my horse, and fleeing to freedom.

I don't move, of course. But I think about it.

"And we welcome that aid!" Fortiss proclaims loudly. "It has been a good day for warriors giving their troth to the First House and the Protectorate. All are welcome here. Lady Talia, step forth."

Hearing my name so unexpectedly, I can do little more than stride forward to the edge of the banister. Fortiss raises his fist to his chest and bows over it to me, his gaze meeting mine.

The bow is formal. The grin isn't. And the look in his eyes... that's not for anyone to see but me. A whisper in the chaos swirling around me, reminding that he's with me.

He's with me.

I swallow down my confusion, glad I'm far enough away that my father can't see the blood rushing to my cheeks at this overt display of camaraderie. Fortiss is acknowledging me as a worthy member of his company, and his smirk deepens as I look up at him, as if he somehow knows how I managed to get up onto this empty plaza without going through any doors.

For just a moment our eyes meet, and I really *do* wonder how he knew where I'm standing. Through everything we endured in the tournament and the weeks since, Fortiss and I have forged a strange and unique bond, but it's a bond that was quickly wrought and remains untested.

I want to test that bond, though—need to. So, I manage an uncertain smile in return.

Then he has to ruin it.

"Lady Talia has also brought a new warrior to our house today; one I think you'll be glad to welcome as well. Lord Tennet of the Twelfth."

He turns with a flourish as Tennet descends the staircase from the doorway of the First to stand beside them. From my vantage point, I can pick out every difference between the two warriors. As I suspected, Tennet is nearly of a height with Fortiss, but his burly shoulders and thick chest make him seem bigger, coarser, while his wind-weathered face and thick brown hair are a striking contrast to Fortiss's smooth black locks and bronzed skin. Tennet looks like he could pummel rocks into submission, while Fortiss's body is built for speed and stealth. Both would be dangerous adversaries, but right now they're even more dangerous allies.

"Lord Lemille," Tennet calls out, and it's a testament to his bulk that he doesn't even have to raise his voice for it to career off the courtyard walls. "Well met. I confess I was expecting to see you under much simpler circumstances than these, but the Light clearly blesses us both. Perhaps now—at last—the contract—"

Outrage spikes through me at what I know—*know!*—Tennet is going to say, but for once my father's arrogance works in my favor.

"Lord *Tennet* of the Twelfth?" he drawls, cutting Tennet off. "Well met, indeed. It would seem we have much to discuss."

His tone implies that he plans to do most of the talking, He throws back his cloak and kicks his right foot free of its stirrup, then swings his leg around and dismounts smoothly. He shucks his gloves and hands them to another man, then mounts the stairs to where Tennet and Fortiss stand.

Through all this, he spares me only the slightest, dismissive glance, and I'm keenly aware of my position on this lower balcony as the three of them meet on the landing. Tennet bows to him with only the barest amount of deference and then surprises me by turning to Fortiss with a bright, easy smile.

"What other house lords are here, Lord Protector Fortiss? Or shall we continue directly to your council chambers to talk further?"

"Only Lady Talia," Fortiss shoots right back, and because I am looking straight at them, I can see the irritation this response generates across my father's face.

Tennet, however, only deepens his grin. "Oh, by all means she should join us—eventually. I'm sure she'll have much to say. She and I have already had such interesting conversation over the hours we've ridden together today."

His words teeter somewhere between insolent and mocking, and I barely keep from curving my hands into fists. I don't know what game he's playing at, but it's serving to antagonize everyone.

Which is undoubtedly his intention.

Fortiss nods curtly, then shoots me a glance with such barely controlled fury it practically scorches me into the stone wall. I manage not to flinch, but give him back my brightest smile. He blinks, then collects himself.

"Then it's agreed," he announces. "We'll get Lemille and you settled, Tennet, then we all can meet—but there's no rush. We'll allow you some time to shake the dust of your travels off. My stewards will fetch you in due course from your rooms."

He waves and two men I hadn't seen before emerge at the top of the stairs, trotting down halfway as Fortiss beckons the two lords to follow them. Tennet and Lemille willingly comply, and Fortiss waits until they're almost through the doorway before turning to me.

"Lady Talia? I'll summon you first. Be ready."

There's no doubt that the men at the top of the stairs hear him, but they stoically press on, their momentum carrying them into the First House and blessedly out of my sight. I press my lips together, struggling not to laugh as I nod formally to Fortiss.

This time, he doesn't seem to share my amusement. With little more than a scowl, he turns and continues into the First House.

I glance down at the courtyard, but Caleb, the traitor, is nowhere to be seen. I trudge up the stairs to the First House, but I have no interest in returning to my rooms right away. I can't slow down—and certainly can't stop. I stomp down one corridor, then another, my mind churning. Why has my father returned to the First House, mere weeks after he left? Is there any trouble at the borders? Has he decided he needs more support from the First, whether in men or supplies? And what in the Light must he be thinking about Tennet's claims...if he even believes him?

Maybe the two of them can spend the night yelling at each other, leaving the rest of us to dine in peace.

Every possibility assaults me, and none of them make me feel any better. I wind my way through the First House, my path finally taking me toward one of the manor house's impressive overlooks. I could use some fresh air, that's for sure. Who knows how long it'll take Fortiss to summon everyone to meet? I'll take these precious moments where freedom and possibility are still mine to command.

In this new world of lies and shadow, the only thing a warrior can truly command...is herself.

"Gent," I whisper as I reach the long corridor near the top of the castle and see the sunshine pouring in through the doors at the far end. I've been thinking about my gorgeous Divh since I saw Marsh hurl Caleb far up into the sun-warmed air. He's the only thing that feels right these days. "*Gent.*"

In my mind, he howls back, sending a surge of joy through me. I pick up the pace, angling for the wide overlook at the end of the corridor, a short leap away from the open sky. He'll appear the moment I call him into this plane, I think. He'll appear, and I will—

A hand snakes out from the shadows, wrapping around my right arm like a vice, jerking me off my feet. No sooner do I draw breath to scream, than a second hand clamps over my mouth, dragging my head ruthlessly to the side.

"Quiet!" a voice hisses in my ear.

A warrior makes her opponent her weapon.

CHAPTER 6

Moving with my assailant's momentum, I curl my hands around his forearm and leap sideways, launching up and out. My feet connect with the wall, and I take one, two steps, then leap, arcing out and around. Then I crash into him from behind, propelling him forward to the floor. It's not until I land heavily on his back that I realize who I just dropped, and I roll off to the side.

"Fortiss! What in the blighted path—"

I've underestimated his clear anger, whether at me or at my impressive defensive moves. He lunges for me and wraps an arm around my torso, dragging me across the hall and through a doorway. He all but hurls me into the center of the room and slams the door behind me.

"Will you *stop*!" I begin, trying to scramble away. But he's on me a second later, his body draping over me just enough to flatten me face first to the floor, while he grabs my head in his hands and clamps tight, smothering my ears.

I'm so startled I freeze, like a kitten picked up by the scruff of its neck, and he pulls me back into the curl of his body just enough that he doesn't crush the wind out of me. I'm overwhelmed by the sheer everything of him—the hard thud of his heart, the way his

41

skin smells of wind and sky, the rasp of his breath. My own breath locks up in my throat, and my heart hurls itself against my ribcage, trying to bang its way to freedom.

"Pay no attention to anything but my voice," he whispers urgently as my left hand flails ineffectively at his forearm, my right trapped beneath me. "Focus on my voice, only my voice. I'm telling you the secrets of winning a battle with a Third House fire lizard, and you're desperate to know, consumed with focus, and you care about nothing or anything but the words that I'm saying, their texture and weave, their weight and force."

He continues on, and still caught, mesmerized, I do as he say, relaxing in his hold and trying to breathe as quietly as possible. I listen to him pour words over me like he's ladling perfumed oils into a bath, the colors of them whirling and swirling together, then draining out to return to his hands and be poured out again.

Faintly, so faintly, I feel a pressure deep within me, first in the crown of my head, then my chest, then at the base of my belly, a spinning spiral of energy that swoops down my body and is gone. But Fortiss doesn't ease up with the torrent of words until my body loosens and I relax to the floor, lost in the endless flow.

Finally, he sags down over me, and in that moment, I feel the weight of him not as an enemy, not as a friend, not even as a comrade in arms...but as a man. The first man I ever truly thought might see me for who I was, who I might be. The first man whose flirtatious teasing shone a light down a dangerous path I yearned to follow.

Sudden awareness shoots through me, followed by a wave of prickling heat. Fortiss and I are no strangers to each other, after all. We've kissed—first by mistake, and then...well, then...

I desperately try not to move, not to do anything to ruin this moment like I did the last time. Because when we kissed in the caverns of this house, I wanted more—so much more. I wanted to feel the weight of him not just over me but inside me, to connect as closely as a man and woman could. I nearly got that wish, too, that fateful night...but I had too many secrets I couldn't share, and I was far too awkward to know how to get what I wanted without betraying who I was. Because I wasn't just an ordinary woman that night, I was a banded warrior and thus a heretic and an outlaw in the Protectorate. I couldn't reveal myself then—wouldn't.

But I did want him. Wanted *this*. And now, with Fortiss draped over me as if he just saved my soul from the blighted path, my body remembers every last drop of that wanting, that need. I may know well the way of the warrior, but I have no blessed idea about the ways of women when it comes to wooing a man.

Still, it seems like his body pressed against me, his lungs heaving, his breath hot on my throat is a really, *really* good start. My heart kicks into a fast staccato, sending my blood rushing through me with a winding, skittering need. I draw in a careful breath, praying to the Light that I don't embarrass myself, and whisper, "Fortiss?"

"Shhh," he breathes out, and my eyes nearly cross as the murmur lifts the hair across my neck to brush my chin. Forget laying with the man, he could just breathe on me and that would probably do the— "There. The spell is cast."

I freeze in his arms again, all desire flattened like a twig beneath a carriage wheel. Slowly, carefully, I shift beneath him, but his attention is fixed on the door we just entered. "The what?" I ask him quietly.

He glances down at me as if suddenly realizing I'm beneath him, but he catches on quickly. His eyes instantly warm, and his face eases into a rakish grin that a bare few breaths ago would have been the best thing I've seen in weeks. "Well, hello, Lady Talia," he murmurs, angling his body to the side to allow me to turn to face him. "This is unexpected."

I don't try to escape the circle of his embrace, but I tell myself it's only to keep him talking. Because the way of the warrior sometimes calls for baldfaced deception.

"What spell, Fortiss?" I ask again, meeting his golden-eyed gaze. "What are you talking about?"

All his previous urgency has ebbed away, and he chuckles. "You know, it never occurred to me that all I had to do to get you to stay still was to tackle you to the ground."

Another wave of warmth blooms deep in my belly, but I can't unhear his words. "Fortiss. What spell?"

"Mm." A crafty expression crosses his face, like he's just bested a warrior on the battlefield without his opponent even realizing it. "It's not what you think."

"Oh, I have a pretty good idea." I glare at him, suddenly understanding what he's done, and why he seemed so different on the steps of the First House. "You found something in Rihad's library, like maybe the book of magic he used to reach out to the demons in the Western Realms. You discovered other magic too, safer magic, and you thought you'd give one of the lighter spells a try. Only once you set that magic in motion, you realized that maybe it wasn't so safe after all, and you wanted an ally who wouldn't go bleating to the councilors that you'd just opened a box of snakes."

He blinks. "All right, it's exactly what you think. How are you feeling about it?"

"Annoyed. Get off me."

He complies, and I feel the loss deep in my belly, so I scoot back from him several feet, levering up to a half crouch. "You shouldn't be reading Rihad's books alone, Fortiss. You definitely shouldn't be trying out some of his pet incantations. This isn't of the Light."

"Maybe not, but it's magic that's been rolling around this house for hundreds of years, I just never knew it." Fortiss leans back against a chair, one knee up, the other extended out, as if this impromptu conference on the floor of some guestroom is perfectly normal. "Nazar helped me work out the language of the Western Realms—it's not so different from ours, did you know that? It looks different, but if you speak the words aloud, the next one comes easily to you. He says theirs is an oral tradition, and only the more powerful combinations must be written, because those, you don't speak unless you're intending something out of the ordinary."

"Like magic." I press my lips together, trying to beat down my own superstitions. "Nazar is a priest of the Light." *My* priest of the Light, it should be said, but this doesn't seem like the time to emphasize that point. Nazar came to the Tenth House when my younger brother Merritt was barely eleven years old, right on the cusp of stepping into his role as warrior of our house. As a priest of the Imperium, he sanctified the transfer of our Divh from my father to my brother and guided us all on our path in the Light. But there was far more to Nazar than I ever realized. Learning that he can speak the language of the Western Realms doesn't shock me as much as it should, but there still are rules about such things. "I can't imagine he's good with you walking down the blighted path on your own, and I also can't imagine him walking it with you."

He shrugs, his expression turning mutinous. "He warned me off."

"And you ignored him. Rihad would be so proud."

"I need to *understand*." The snap to Fortiss's tone makes me stiffen, and a sudden need to flee coils within me—alongside a need to stay, to explore, to understand this shift that's happened so quickly in the man I only met a month ago.

Even as I think the words, they convict me. How well do I really know Fortiss? I saw him for the first time skulking around in the forest outside the Shattered City, barely a quarter hour before my brother died. I didn't see him again until Nazar and I led a brace of road-weary, battle-shocked horses into Trilion a few days later. By then, I'd changed so much I wouldn't have recognized myself if I met me on the street—my hair hacked off, my arm scarred bloody by the banding of a monster in a ritual I barely understood, my men and brother murdered by unknown assassins.

Fortiss was everything I expected in a vaunted warrior of the First House—bold, arrogant, and beautiful. And when he'd thought I was the man I'd disguised myself as, my own brother, he'd treated me like he would treat any other warrior. When I'd worn the robes of a woman, he'd treated me like he would any woman. And I never once had stopped to think about who he really was, other than cobbling together a scant understanding of his background and reveling in a brief, precious connection to the Divh he finally bonded to.

I don't know Fortiss. At all.

And now he's the lord protector of this land, in large part because of me.

"Then you will understand," I say into the silence that's swelling around us, threatening to take on a life of its own. "But there's understanding, and then there's knocking me to the ground because you're afraid of me falling prey to some spell you've just unleashed using Rihad's unholy book."

"Well—I was in the middle of it when you sent word of the arrival of the Twelfth House warriors. Nazar has been warning me for days to expect a conclave of the houses to descend upon the First, demanding answers—but I wasn't expecting Orlof or... whoever this Warrior Tennet is. And certainly not your father hard on their heels. When I finally returned to my task, I had to finish the incantation more quickly than I wanted or risk the energy not having anywhere to go. And I wasn't in the best frame of mind."

He has the grace to look a little chagrined, but that doesn't make me feel any better.

Far from it. A fear strong enough to border on nausea has begun to take root in my stomach, and I have to fight the urge to press my fist into my belly to keep it from spreading. I glower at him some more. "What kind of powers did Rihad have?"

Fortiss rubs his hand through his hair. "Manipulation, I think, or that's the one he used the most. Those pages were heavily worn, the parchment thin as rose petals. And when you think of Rihad, it makes sense." He shifts his gaze to me. "You never met the lord protector outside the tournament, but he always gave the impression of being larger than life. He could walk into a room and fill it up just with his presence, no matter if it was the size of this chamber or the great arena of the coliseum. I'd always just assumed that he was gifted in the art of swaying men, and perhaps he was. But he also was aided by the spells in that book. People would be honest around him to their detriment. People would believe in him, defying their own logic. People would accept his orders, do his bidding, believe whatever he told them as if it were sent down by the Light itself. He was a great man, even when you inherently knew he wasn't a good man, but he was the lord protector, and so it somehow felt right and just."

"And now you find out that it's all lies."

"Not lies, exactly," Fortiss corrects me, and in that moment, he looks more tired than any man of twenty-five years should. "Rihad believed that he was given this power by divine right. He believed that he deserved it, and that he could rule equally well without it, just not as quickly. He was a man who needed speed on his side. There are other books, with other spells, including conjuring ones."

"The snake demons in the fire," I murmur. The first time I had been in Rihad's chambers, on the hunt for any clue as to who might have murdered my brother, I'd seen the creature he had summoned to him. A tall, wraithlike being whose body was made up of snakes. It didn't matter if it was a real creature or merely a representation meant to shock and awe—it had done the trick for me. I'd see that thing in my nightmares for the rest of time.

"And worse. So much worse that's coming for us if we don't go out to meet it first." He makes a face. "Except now my top Divh commander is being summoned back by her betrothed. So, forgive me, I made an adjustment to the spell of honesty I just cast that... could prove interesting. That which is hidden must be revealed—by everyone. Everyone is going to speak their whole truth. We don't have time for anything less."

I peel open my eyes wide. "*Fortiss*," I protest, my words a raspy squeak. *A spell of honesty?* "What did you do?"

The bells in the high tower chime over the last of my words, and he rolls to his feet.

"We'll be working that out with your father and your betrothed in my council chambers shortly, Lady Talia," he says, holding out his hand. "So, I guess we'll see, no?"

CHAPTER 7

I'm the last to arrive to Fortiss's quarters an hour later, partly by design, and partly because weevish goo isn't as easy to remove as you might think. My father turns as I stride in, his face hardening into a mask of deep resentment.

"Excellent," he announces, gesturing at me with a curt wave. "It appears I'm to be surrounded by deception and heresy in every direction, except for straight ahead."

He swings around to glare at Fortiss again as I take in the other members of our unlikely group. Tennet stands to the left of my father, and Nazar to his right. Fortiss stands as well, facing us by his large writing desk, while his council of seven men and one woman sit or stand behind him. It's not a formal setting; I suspect by careful intention. Fortiss wants to have a conversation, not to lay down orders. But the sight of so many open books on his desk fills me with unreasoning dread.

Not just the books, either. The man behind them also unnerves me—his composure, his fire, the way his golden eyes darken as they meet mine. I don't know what I'm more afraid of...that Fortiss's interest me is merely a result of the magic he's been dabbling in, or that it isn't.

"Why is the so-called priest of the Light here?" my father

demands of Fortiss. He jabs a finger at the nearest of the councilors. "You all, I understand. You carry the knowledge of this land, and it's knowledge we need. But this pretender isn't a member of the Protectorate. He's not even a true follower of the Light. He has even less right than he had before to take part in such conversations."

Well, then. It seems like Fortiss's spell of utter honesty is already off to a fine start.

I take my place to the right of Nazar, grateful for what little barrier he can provide between me and the man who's wanted me dead my entire life. The priest spares me a quick glance, regarding me down a long, slightly hooked nose with eyes that can drown the unwary in his steady gaze, and his lips twitch slightly at my bristling. He's a tall man of slender build, with hair that once looked like snow upon the hillside but now is showing irregular patches of gray. He's dressed in a long, shimmering robe of gray wool shot with silver; the color will eventually mark him as a Thirteenth House man. Once there's a Thirteenth House built, anyway.

"Lord Lemille," Fortiss begins, his voice heavy with exaggerated patience, but to my surprise, Miriam steps forward.

"With your permission, Lord Protector," she murmurs, and I can feel Nazar tense beside me. He's surprised as well, and a warrior who doesn't know his enemy is never in a good position.

Fortiss, of course, doesn't flinch. His calm exterior never cracks. But I watch him more closely now—not from distrust, but because I can't help myself. There's a part of me that wants to know how deep his steadiness goes. How far I could fall and still be caught.

Focus, I implore myself. I glance quickly to the others, but they seem remarkably...placid. Is that a good thing, given Fortiss's spell?

The council of the First House has traditionally represented the voice of the Imperium in all Protectorate matters. This group of eight worthy souls were Rihad's closest confidants, for all that they claim to have no idea of the darker dealings the lord protector engaged in under their very noses. Fortiss has questioned them all and been forced to conclude that they are telling the truth. Which demotes their perfidy to inattention and ignorance, at the very least, or to full-on stupidity.

Or are they craftier than that? The councilors cultivate the air of knowing more than anyone around them, especially Miriam, the lone woman who serves in their ranks. For all of Rihad's disdain for women, he had directed her into this role. In our scant dealings with each other, she's indicated no particular love for the former lord protector, yet she wouldn't be here without him. So, can she really be trusted?

Oblivious to my racing thoughts, Miriam offers my father a deferent nod. "The task has fallen to me to interview the priest Nazar and cross reference his claims with information that we've received over many years from the capital city Hakkir in the heart of the Imperium. In no way has he provided a single piece of false testimony of the events and actions of which we have separate confirmation, nor has he represented himself as an agent of the Imperium, only of the Light."

"He is *banded*—" my father cuts in sharply, but she continues as if he doesn't speak.

"It is a fact little known in the Protectorate—by Lord Rihad's decree and the decree of his father before him—that the Imperator, in his great wisdom, decided to break the band between Divh and warrior in all such unions across the Imperium. At the time of this decree, the priest Nazar was an honored warrior and submitted to the process. His Divh, however, would not fully release him. This was not an uncommon experience among tightly banded Divhs and resulted in great damage to his person."

On the other side of my father, Tennet grunts. When Miriam shifts her gaze to him, he glances from her to Fortiss. "May I speak?"

She smiles as if she expected this, and I narrow my eyes on her. Despite her white hair and lined face, Miriam is no doddering old woman. She's both steady and shrewd, her gray eyes unflinching and seeming to see everything at once.

Fortiss gestures Tennet to continue.

"You say this unbanding ceremony is little known, but we knew of it at the Twelfth. It's ancient history now, but when it happened some fifty years ago, there were many such shattered soldiers who came to the Protectorate. Some of them were fully unbanded but broken, shells of men who had lost their place in the world. Some, according to the old accounts, still had pieces of their band embedded in their skin where, as you say, the connection could not fully be severed. To a one, though, they had lost the ability to summon their Divhs."

He turns to Nazar. "Yet you could?"

At Fortiss's nod, Nazar shifts forward slightly so that he and Tennet can face each other squarely. I decide I can understand the value of a spell of utter honesty after all. I wonder how long it will last.

"I couldn't, no, despite all my efforts," Nazar says, his voice quiet but steady. "And for long years I tried to rekindle the connection—first in desperate sorrow, then in secret, as attitudes of tolerance shifted within the Imperium. I knew of other soldiers who had traveled to the Protectorate, hoping to find what had been lost. But no one, to my knowledge, ever did. I couldn't make such a journey, not at first, and instead I threw myself into the service of the Light."

My father scoffs in derision, but Nazar's voice doesn't waver. "It was one of the few paths available to warriors, as the Imperium remained uneasy about our past association with Divhs despite being assured that we could in no way summon them again. In time, we heard word of past warriors being hunted down, taken to the capital for interrogation. Those of us who turned to the Light were spared such attention."

"That tracks with our accounts." Tennet nods.

"Well, it doesn't track with ours." My father folds his arms over his chest. "That would have been in my father's time and his father's as well, and we have long entertained travelers from the Imperium. We kept records, too. None of them were skulking vagabonds, and only a handful were priests. None of those priests offered to stay for longer than a season before you."

He narrows his eyes, and his gaze shifts between me and Nazar. "Did you put her up to this?" he asks, his voice taking on new energy.

"Lord Lemille," Fortiss cuts in. "There is more that councilor Miriam needs to share. If your questions are answered, Lord Tennet?"

Tennet nods, rocking back on his heels a bit and resting his hands on his belt. He glances at me, and when our gazes meet, a crack of energy zips through me. His eyes instantly heat, and I force my own away. There's only so much honesty I can take at once, and I can sense Fortiss's sharp eyes on me as well. Between my father's loathing, Fortiss's subtle heat, Tennet's bold assumptions, and Nazar's amused scrutiny, I have a choice of staring at the wall or Miriam. The councilor proves the more interesting option.

More interesting than I expect, of course, given the spell of honesty to thrumming through the room.

Miriam draws in a deep breath, then slowly exhales, as if steadying her nerves for what she has to say next. "According to our recorded history, we were notified of the Imperial order to unband warriors outside the Protectorate a few months after it happened. We were given the right to continue with our existing unions, tied strictly to the houses, but were explicitly instructed long years ago not to create new warrior-Divh connections at any level."

"Wait, what?" I blink, my gaze shifting to Fortiss. "How is that possible? There've been new Divhs created at every tournament, and Rihad planned dozens more."

Forget Rihad. I'd been gifted with the ability to band an entire *army* of Divhs to new warriors. How could that be possible, if—

Fortiss fields this one. "The lord protector at that time, and Rihad since, elected to ignore that particular part of the instruction. Any such bandings were done without the knowledge of the Imperium and were certainly not advertised. Bards from every generation we're given enough gold to keep them quiet on that score, and fortunately, these were men with sufficient understanding to realize that any betrayal would eventually be discovered."

He waves across the jumbled pile of sacred texts. "Every lord protector has had the ability to inspire fear as needed. And the truth was, we couldn't afford to lose any opportunity to keep the connections between our houses and our Divhs strong. Because the threat of the Western Realms, while faded into distant history, exists as a threat yet today."

"Since when?" Lemille humphs. "This Tournament of Gold is all puffery, you ask me. This Court of Talons and its winged crown. All of it is lies and fancy stories, meant to scare us into submission."

He blinks, as if surprised at his indiscretion, but Fortiss only allows himself the smallest flicker of a smile while I try not to choke in surprise.

"Winged crown?" Tennet echoes. "Warrior Caleb mentioned that too. What is it, some prize of the tournament?"

"A prize, yes, but more a rite of passage." Another of the councilors speaks, his worn, scholarly face alight with enthusiasm as he reels off the history for us all. "The original winged crown was an artifact discovered by the first lords of the Protectorate and worn by General Mirador in the Great Conflict that resulted in the warriors of the Imperium bonding with the Divhs. It was lost in the years following that conflict, but its legacy lives on, its honor granted to each winner of the Tournament of Gold."

"So it's not real," my father points out. "You can't show it to us."

"The winged crown and the Court of Talons are honorary terms now, but they existed at the dawn of the Protectorate," Miriam counters firmly. "They're not lies. We forget the past at our own peril, Lord Lemille."

My father just humphs again and rolls his eyes. "And this threat from the west? Is that honorary too?"

"It was a dormant one for hundreds of years, but not anymore," Fortiss says, his voice turning hard. Maybe he doesn't enjoy the honesty he's spelled into this room as much as he thought he would.

He reaches over and picks up a sheaf of parchment pages. "There are multiple accounts of hordes of snake-like creatures coming down from the mountains surrounding the Eighth House to terrify travelers on the open road. Those attacks have been increasing over the past few years. What few accounts Rihad has of the dawn of the Protectorate here in the First House all tell stories of these snakes practically blanketing the higher reaches of the Meridian mountains, where the great pass to the Western Realms remains. These skrill, as the snakes were called, are the advance army of creatures the books reference only as the shadow hunters. We have ridiculously little information on all this, but these hunters operate and manipulate darkness to turn men against themselves. They're definitely of the blighted path, not the Light."

"Glad we established that poisonous, mind-altering snakes weren't here to be our friends," Tennet observes dryly. "In case anyone was wondering."

Fortiss ignores him. "We also know that generations of houses along the western borders have lived in fear of any sort of uptick of activity from the skrill. That sort of uptick—which is what we've apparently been seeing around the Eighth, for all that they didn't breathe a word except to Rihad directly—is a precursor of the return of the shadow hunters."

A brief silence settles over the room, cut short by Tennet, because of course it is. Like most warriors I've met over the past several weeks, Tennet tends to think with his mouth.

"Well, then, fair enough. We've got a legitimate threat on the western side of the country; one we need to launch an army to defeat. I understand we've a growing battalion of Divh-enabled soldiers here at the First, and I can spare some men for the cause, along with myself. I assume you can offer up a few soldiers too, Lord Lemille?"

He turns to my father, clearly catching him off guard. Lemille, however, has more to share. "Soldiers, certainly, but the western border isn't our only issue. The eastern one is also imminently at risk."

"What?" one of the councilors asks sharply, and Miriam steps forward. Fortiss and I exchange a quick glance, and the flash of camaraderie between us warms me, even as my nerves wind tight.

"What are you talking about, Lord Lemille?" Fortiss asks him.

My father spreads his hands wide. "Why do you think I returned here so quickly? I assure you it wasn't for your gracious hospitality. For generations, the Tenth House has employed a series of households within a five-days' ride of our holding, along the Imperial Road. Their job is simply to alert us to any force coming our way from the heart of the Imperium. Marauders, traveling gangs, that's one thing, and a challenge we are well used to solving at the Tenth. But when it comes to actual agents of the Imperium, some advance notice is always ideal."

"And they're coming?" Fortiss presses. "How many? And what is their manner?"

Fortiss turns to Miriam before my father can respond. "You sent what we discussed, yes? Only that?"

"Only that," she agrees, her manner firm. "We sent word of Rihad's transfer of power to Lord Protector Fortiss and requested agents of the Imperium to come to help adjudicate an issue of law. But we did not disclose anything more than that. The precedent of past generations has been to avoid courting too much interest from the Imperium, lest they start to covet more control over what is ours."

"Well, from the reports I'm getting, they're sending more than just a few magistrates and supplies for the journey," my father says, and now it's his turn to drop his hands to his belt. For just a moment I imagine him in his younger days, a man eager for the battle, ready to defend both house and Protectorate. His face flushes as he continues his report. "It's a battle party of about fifty soldiers altogether, along with what appeared to be functionary types unused to riding. They're moving slowly, almost leisurely, their caravan spread out over several days—far enough apart that they wouldn't attract notice unless someone was being paid to notice. I expect they will stopover in Rhienne and allow their numbers to consolidate, which will take perhaps a week, but no more. It's less than a day's ride from there to the eastern pass and into the Protectorate."

"How far away, then, are they now?" Fortiss asks.

My father shrugs. "From the Tenth House, I'd say two days. Add to that another two to get here, if they ride hard, four if they don't."

He smiles, and his expression is hard, but expectant. "So don't waste too much time on snakes from the west, Lord Protector Fortiss. You have barely more than a week to get your story straight about Rihad. And you'll need that same week to pull together what fighting men you can, in case the Imperium decides that they *do* covet what they see once they get here."

CHAPTER 8

We break up shortly after that to return to our own chambers until the great dinner feast. After so much *honesty* in such tight quarters, I'm not especially hungry. Still, I know from experience that, no matter how dire the news, warriors of the realm can *eat*.

By the time I stalk out of my sleeping chamber and into the sitting room allocated to me, Nazar's not only waiting for me, but Caleb is, too. I instantly detect a trap, and they don't wait long to spring it.

Caleb speaks first, waving his right hand at me. "You've got to be kidding me. No. Go back and try again."

I know exactly what he's talking about, but that doesn't make his censure any more tolerable. If Fortiss's honesty spell doesn't wear off soon, there's going to be bloodshed. "I'm the lord of my own house, Caleb. I am not going to show up at a banquet of warriors wearing a dress! No one else is, why should I?"

Caleb folds his arms in a huff, but the most telling response is, as always, the silence that billows around Nazar like an unfurling cloud. I pivot on my heel to glare at him. "What?"

Even when he's judging me, it's reassuring just to stand in the presence of the priest of the Tenth House. One day, hopefully, he'll serve as the priest of the Thirteenth House, should we ever have two stones to build upon each other. For now, however, I'm grateful that he decided to remain behind with me at the First, versus returning with my father to the Tenth. It might have been an easy decision for the itinerant priest, but it's one that may have lasting repercussions.

Nazar, for his part, puffs on his pipe, a whisp of sweet-smelling smoke curling up to accompany my rebuke. "You're a woman, Lady Talia," he informs me, not even trying to hide his amusement. "No amount of warrior clothing will change that."

"I know I'm a woman!" I grouse. "But where is it written that women may only wear dresses and gowns, while men may wear breeches when it pleases them and robes when it doesn't? Why could I not show up in a cowl and feathered headdress if it made me happy to do so? I don't need to wear a gown."

"You don't," Nazar agrees, with such easy capitulation that I already know I'm trapped for all that I cannot see the snare. "Who is in the feasting hall will be put in his place if you come out in the vestments of a man?"

"Well, Tennet for one. Since he is vying to ensure I return to the Twelfth House as his bride, he's sorely in need of being put in his place."

"And you would trust a bolt of cloth to do that work in your place?"

"That's not the *point*, Nazar—" I begin, but he holds up a hand to silence me.

"Who else? The lord protector? Your own men? Would they treat you with greater dignity and respect if you were wearing armor, and diminish and demean you if you stood before them in a gown and jewels if you wished to do so?"

"I don't wish to do so."

His hand descends in an easy wave. "That wasn't the question."

I scowl at him. "My men know that I'm a woman. And they have seen me fight."

"They've seen you call your Divh." He nods. "And command a battalion of no less than thirty others, who cleaved to you simply because you called them. What were you wearing when you did so?"

"Blood, mostly," Caleb puts in helpfully when I don't respond quickly enough.

"And then a heavy robe, no? Wincing from your injuries, standing beside Fortiss after you awoke for the first time when all the fighting was done."

"Fair enough. They've seen me in something other than battle gear, but this isn't battle gear. This is simply more comfortable and as formal as Fortiss will be—Tennet too, unless I miss my mark. I'm their equal."

"You're their equal whether you show up covered in gold or blood, I agree," Nazar says. "Who else will take their cues from your attire?"

I wave that off. "Nobody else that I care about."

"Are there any from the Savasci that remain behind?"

I snort. The rogue band of women fighters who had come to the Tournament of Gold to harry its competitors and steal what they might had become my adopted sisters, but the bulk of their party had returned to the Western Realms to see to their families and extended people and learn what they might about the threat that lay beyond the borders. Still, Nazar's right. A small group of women have remained, training with me in the hopes they will one day become banded warriors in their own right. "They'll be at the banquet, for sure. They like to eat."

"And what will they be wearing?"

"Whatever they want." I cross my arms defiantly. "They have dressed in gowns or breeches depending on their mood. Gowns allow them to blend."

He nods gravely. "And for them, blending is how they survive."

I understand the way of the warrior, and I can see the trap Nazar is about to spring on me. I can also see that it's not one from which I can easily escape. Still, I roll my eyes. "I know what you're doing."

"Well, I don't," Caleb protests as Nazar smirks around the tip of his pipe, the fragrant smoke still curling around him in equally smug wisps. "So what if they wear gowns to blend? They're not you. What they do and why they do it shouldn't matter."

"It doesn't matter," I agree. "But they wear gowns to blend—to survive—because for them, the smartest thing they can do is to blend. To bend with the prevailing wind, much like the servants on the floor and in the kitchens keep their gaze on their feet and their voices quiet. They *blend*."

I can tell the moment during my little speech when he understands. To my annoyance, though, he merely bounces up and down on his toes. "But you don't have to blend, because you're blessed Talia of the Thirteenth House, strong and fierce. You don't look like anyone up on that dais and you're proud of it." He grins at me. "So you're going to wear a dress."

I curl my lip in disgust. "I think I preferred it when you were confused."

Still, I turn on my heel and stomp back into my inner chamber, unsurprised when the door is opened again behind me to admit a wide-eyed maid. Dressing according to my station is a far sight more complicated at the First House than it was at the Tenth.

"Let me guess," I huff, as the young woman whom I've never met before bustles over to the large chest and pulls out enough rough silk to blanket the room. "Nazar already stuffed a gown in there, knowing I would change my mind. What's your name? I'm sorry I don't know."

"Alis, Lady Talia, and this won't take but a few moments," she promises. "Just hold your arms up...?"

The chemise is first, thrown over me and cinched tight with laces, its soft linen nicer than anything I've ever worn. I savor its light touch against my skin, because the rest of my ensemble seems custom-made to weigh me down. Alis produces an underdress of deep emerald green—a shade far darker than Tenth House green—shot through with silver. The dress's fitted bodice requires a second round of lacing, and then she lugs out the heavy gown of pure silver. The hem of this gown is heavy with green and gold embroidery, all vines and tiny flowers, and the sleeves...oh, the sleeves. They're ridiculously long, falling nearly to the floor, lined with dark green silk that shimmers as Alis lifts them onto my arms. "How do you expect me to eat without dragging these through the food?" I grumble, glaring at the offending fabric. "And how in the Light can I fight in this?"

Alis only smiles. "You'll look splendid, Lady Talia."

She's not finished, of course. She fastens a girdle of polished bronze links around my waist, and it sits low over my hips, its pendant hanging just slightly too long for comfort. My jewelry is next—a delicate golden chain with an emerald the size of teardrops nestled against my collarbone, and matching earrings that tug at my ears.

The final touch is the shoes—soft leather slippers dyed silver to match the gown. Simple, at least compared to the rest, but I know my feet will ache before the evening is through. "All this effort," I sigh, adjusting the emerald at my throat, wondering where Nazar conjured it up from, "just for me to annoy people."

Alis steps back, satisfied. "You'll annoy them so much they'll never forget you," she says, and I grimace at her.

"You heard that, in there? I'm sorry, I didn't realize you were already on hand.

"I was waiting just outside the door. Master Nazar wasn't entirely sure you'd allow yourself to be dressed."

"He wasn't?" That at least makes me happy. "Good. He shouldn't be so certain he can outmaneuver me."

"Never that, Lady Talia," Alis says firmly, her deft fingers pulling my hair back into ornate combs. The feel of feminine adornment in my hair unnerves me more than the rest of my costume combined. I squint at Alis as she fusses over me.

"You think I'm making the right choice? Dressing as a lady instead of how I prefer?"

She bites her lip for a moment, as if debating how honest she should be, though I suspect she, too, is under the lingering influences of Fortiss's spell. Still, I don't press her for a response. I know what it's like to be unsure of whether an honest comment would merit me a laugh, a word of ready agreement, or a slap across the face. No female servant of mine will ever be forced to speak when they would rather stay silent...or dress in a gown when they'd rather wear breeches.

Just as I decide that no answer is in the offing, she surprises me. "Yes," she finally says. "I do think you are making the right choice. I understand why all of these clothes would not be your first choice. They're heavy and awkward and they make it difficult for a woman to move. Doubtless that was the intention of whoever designed a gown so bulky it takes two men to carry it. But you look like who you are, Lady Talia. Just as you looked like a young man determined to win the Tournament of Gold when you first came to the First House and were singled out by Lord Protector Rihad— former lord protector, I mean."

I wince. "You were there for that? At the banquet? I'm surprised you remember me."

"You were kind—to your soldier knight." At my startled glance, Alis steps back, her face reddening. "I wasn't the only one who noticed. What I mean, though, is—you fully looked like you belonged that night, but wearing this gown tonight, after everything you've done, everything you've proven on the battlefield, and given how much Lord Protector Fortiss already values your insights, and how much the council already whispers about you in their closed chambers, you dressing like this, boldly and assured, is the best thing you can possibly do. As a boy warrior, you deserved a place at Rihad's table. But as the lady of your own house, you should dress like you own the table."

She meets my gaze with wide eyes as if she's surprised at her own candor, then wheels around to scurry out the door ahead of me. I stare for a moment longer, carefully cataloguing everything she's said—it's too much to understand now, but there was much in her little speech of vital importance—and not just the business of what I should be wearing.

Why has the council been talking about me? And does Fortiss know about it?

And who else is talking, whether here or throughout the Protectorate? The faintest thread of concern unspools, embroidering the edges of my thoughts. I no sooner clip it off in one place then it spins up in another. There's something important in Alis's casual comment…even if it's only the offhanded nature of it. Of course the council would be discussing me. I'm nothing like anything they've experienced in the Protectorate—nothing like anyone has experienced.

There's definitely a danger here.

I leave my inner chambers far more slowly than I entered them, careful not to overbalance myself, but if Caleb's startled huff of admiration when I step back into the sitting room is any indication, Alis has the right of it.

"Good?" I ask, and he grins, bobbing his head up and down.

"Absolutely good," he agrees, and he knows me well enough to say no more.

Nazar is nowhere to be seen, though I could use his counsel before I proceed into the banquet hall like a stuffed doll. I force Caleb to carry an extra two blades for me just to ease my mind. He strides down the halls to my left, chattering the whole way about who's still remaining at the First House, who's left just today, and how much he's looking forward to getting all the gossip he can about the Twelfth House from their retainers—the moment he gets them drunk. Which, from his keen eye, won't take long.

His words serve me the way they always do, easing my tension at least during the long walk. Still, by the time we reach the great hall, my resolve has all but deserted me.

"Caleb…" I mutter, and he reaches out and grabs my arm at the elbow, just below my warrior band.

"Let me tell you what else Nazar wanted you to know, before you walk in there. He was as surprised as you were that Tennet existed. There's absolutely no record of him in any of the official Protectorate records, nor in the First House annals of the Twelfth House. Much like your situation, it's not outside the realm of possibility that he's who he says he is, the firstborn unacknowledged son of Lord Orlof. But it's also possible that he was sent here on a mission to deceive, to set himself up as the son of a dead lord, a man at arms for a boy who is in no position to rule a house. A boy who could use someone like you to help him rule his house."

"Well, he's going to be waiting a long time for that to happen," I say, and Caleb squeezes my elbow.

"I agree, but it would explain a lot of things. Nazar says there's no way Tennet's an agent of the Imperium. He's not some forerunner of the army that's supposedly coming."

I glance at him sharply. "Nazar told you about that?" Honesty in this house certainly is proving useful.

"He did, and he's about chewed off the end of his pipe thinking about what it could mean. But no matter that he's not Imperium, Tennet may not be who he says he is. If, in truth, he's just a soldier who's been sent here to drag you off by your hair to force you to honor the marriage contract to Orlof's actual heir, I mean...that does make more sense."

"It does..." I wonder if Fortiss has put Tennet to the question already, while the effects of his spell are still in place. I would have.

Caleb waggles his brows at me. "I will say, we need to find a way to get his Divh to show up. That would be instructive don't you think, if he is actually Orlof's son? A Divh of a mountain holding should be large, but not too large, but if he's the Divh of a first-blooded and firstborn son, they usually grow them bigger for that. That said, I can't see a giant on the scale of Gent stamping around the mountains and not being noticed. We need to see that Divh, tournament or no tournament. And we can't wait till we actually have a genuine battle. I'm back at the coliseum tonight training, and some of the Divhs of the soldiers are impressive. What if Tennet's Divh is the size of an overfed cow?"

I snort. I'd pay good coin to see that. Maybe then I'd stop

noticing the way Tennet's voice curls around my name like it still belongs to him. "I can't tell you how happy that would make me, I'm not going to lie."

"You say that now, but we've had four weeks of holding our breath, waiting for Rihad's books to catch on fire in Fortiss's inner chambers. They haven't done that, but even Nazar is saying that Fortiss doesn't seem quite right, that there's some strange energy in the halls of the First House. That's bad. That has to be bad, right? That feels bad."

"All of this feels bad," I mutter. But I lift my chin up and sail into the room.

CHAPTER 9

The banquet is a disaster.

The food is, as always, exceptional—I've grown spoiled so quickly by the First House's largesse. I confine myself to eating only that which I can reach without effort—my glass of wine and the portion of my plate closest to me. I can barely breathe in this gown—I certainly can't eat in it. So, it's no hardship to do little more than sip at odd turns and smile serenely as Fortiss tells Tennet the tale of the tournament once more, while my father pointedly ignores me and corrects Fortiss at every possible turn when the subject turns to history before Fortiss's time.

Eventually, Fortiss invites the warriors in the hall to join us at the main table, and another hour goes by with the warriors taking turns discussing their role in the melee, as well as picking apart any word received back from the houses who lost so many fighting men. It's heartening, in its way—it seems that more fighting men are coming to the First House to band with new Divhs. For all the families who have lost great warriors, they seem ready enough to send sons or brothers.

No one sends a female, of course. Young women who hear of the unrest will have to bring themselves—and news of my own participation in the tournament has been relegated to whispers and the occasional accusation of a bald-faced lie. Not even the bards, as eager to stir up trouble as any group in the Protectorate, are trying to push the narrative of a woman commanding a Divh and meriting her own house. It's dangerous talk, apparently.

My mood grows fouler by the moment.

"And where's the former lord protector now?" Tennet asks abruptly, drawing my attention back to him, though I take care not to look at him directly. That takes some work, because Fortiss positioned me directly opposite the man. Intentional? Does he want me to see Tennet...or Tennet to see me? Or—Light help me—does he want to see what I'll do, caught between them both like this?

Carefully setting that question aside, I take another sip of my wine and scan the group before us as all eyes turn to Fortiss—none more so than my father's.

The new lord protector has been busy, too. For an event assembled in less than a few hours since the arrival of the Twelfth and Tenth House riders, we nearly have a quorum of representation of Protectorate might. Fully six houses are represented at the table. The First, of course, and the Second, whose stronghold is so close they might as well be an adjunct of the First, but also the Fifth and Ninth, and of course the Tenth and Twelfth. I could argue that I represent the Thirteenth as well, but on this night and at this table, I'm here for my fighting skill.

In a gown that would send me sprawling in a battle before I took three steps.

"Lord Rihad is safely confined to a suite of rooms first fashioned for high-level prisoners sent here from the Imperium in the first century of the Protectorate's rule over these lands," Fortiss says smoothly. "The lord protector is a hereditary role, conferred from the Imperium at the founding of our state. It's always flowed through this house or been conferred by the decision of the lord protector himself, should he not have the family to sustain the role. The actions this past month are right and true, but uncharted territory. The Imperium must weigh in."

"The Imperium hasn't seen a sunrise in the Protectorate for

over two hundred years," grouses warrior Berryl, a junior warrior of the Fifth who is now one of their few banded warriors. He's junior in name only—he's served long and well beneath the first-blooded knights of his house, and he's nearly twice my age. "We aren't beholden to their laws, or their decisions. Lord Protector Rihad declared battle against his own houses. The man is clearly mad. You were right to lock him up, but you would have been even more right to drop him on the battlefield."

A murmuring of agreement rolls around the table, then stops abruptly at my father's seat, as well as the dinner plates of the gray-cassocked duo who are positioned between me and Fortiss. Councilors Miriam and Dolor, of course, know better than to agree to anything—or disagree, for that matter.

Apparently unconcerned about the line of conversation, however, Miriam lifts her voice to be heard above the murmurings. "The actions of our new lord protector are right and true. You're not wrong, warrior Berryl. We haven't been honored by a visit from the Imperium for too long. I assure you; it's not for lack of trying. We send out riders at the turning of each season, seeking counsel of course, but above all advocating for the return of an Imperial envoy for which we would gladly give safe passage. In all the years I've served, we have never been taken up on that offer. We are left only with the approval of the Imperium to continue conducting matters as we see fit and reporting on the safety of the Protectorate and the strength of our borders."

Berryl scowls at this. "But surely now they would show interest. They must. Lord Rihad created a tournament that destroyed everything it celebrated. And if the rumors are to be believed, rumors culled from your own house, councilor Miriam, Lord Rihad was engaged in dark matters, matters that go beyond treason to the other destruction of us all. What say you to these claims?"

The man to Miriam's right fields this question. Councilor Dolor is aptly named, his pale face receding into his cowl, his skin a muddy gray that gives him the appearance of a man who has not seen the sun in decades. But he's a calm man, a cautious one, and his words flow over the table like an unctuous balm.

"I am one of the longest-tenured members of the council," he informs us gravely. "I've served since before Rihad took power some twenty years ago, himself barely more than a boy, ushered into the roll by the untimely death of his father. Rihad was always impetuous and headstrong, but he served the Protectorate. He observed all the dictates of the Light and the Imperium. The accusations you level are profound, warrior Berryl, and not for idle conversation around the table where anyone can hear you without the full context of what we speak."

"Then we move back to Fortiss's council chambers." Tennet's unexpected directive startles me, and my glance cuts toward him. He's waiting for me, and our gazes clash like warriors entwined in battle. It's only for a second, then I turn toward Lord Fortiss, who's also staring at me. It appears I'm of great interest in this conversation.

"There will be a time for that discussion, but I agree it's hard upon us," Fortiss says evenly. "All warriors present will gather after the banquet in my chambers. It may a conversation best suited to house lords, but they were called back to ensure the strength of their own houses. They have given me proxy authority to direct their warriors in battle."

Another ripple of interest circles the table, and it's one I share. Proxy authority?

My father voices the question on everyone's mind. "And if I hadn't returned, Lord Protector Fortiss, would you be directing any men from the Tenth as well? Because I certainly haven't given you authority."

"You have in the case of anything to do with preserving the Protectorate," Fortiss counters, his tone hard as granite. "In that, I have the right of rule."

"And all houses have the right to disagree, do they not?" Tennet argues, and Fortiss turns to him.

"A worthy stand for a warrior knight of the Twelfth House," he retorts, pitching his words to be deliberately but lightly mocking, with just enough emphasis that you can't say for sure that is his intention unless you know him. But of course, I do know him, at least that well.

He continues as Tennet's brows draw together. It seems Tennet is no idiot either.

"Fortunately, while some conversations are better suited for behind closed doors, this one isn't. We are pleased to welcome you to our table, Warrior Tennet, and more pleased still to hear your story. We have no record of your birth or upbringing, and we are saddened for the loss of Lord Orlof, which we still need to confirm. Is there, in fact, a younger brother in your household, a boy of fourteen? Do you have other brothers and sisters? Help us understand how you came to be the lord of a royal house without having ever visited the First House or, by all accounts, having left your holding at all?"

If Tennet is surprised by Fortiss's direct attack, he doesn't show it. He had to know that there would be an accounting, and one like this over a meal, in friendly conversation, is surely preferable to a grilling that no one views and from which there is no escape. If he had made these allegations during Lord Rihad's time, he might well have been wrestled to the floor and imprisoned until his story was proven out, even if it would take a full two weeks for riders to reach the remote mountain stronghold of the Twelfth House and then return.

And of course, Tennet is still compelled by Fortiss's spell of authenticity, even if that spell is now waning. So, this...well, this should be interesting.

I glance at him and once again realize he's staring at me. I hope my thoughts aren't so plainly written on my face as I fear, but the quirk of his mouth into a quick smile tells me different.

An uneasy warmth washes through me at that smile as Tennet returns his attention to Fortiss. "With Lady Talia fighting so well in the tournament, it seems you've already experienced the strategy of the mountain houses, Lord Protector Fortiss. We are small and left without the great defenses of the houses on the wide plains, or even the natural benefit of the open desert that gives the houses to the south some protection from their enemies by virtue of the fact that they can see them coming. The mountains can hide a multitude of enemies, and sometimes the best defense a house can mount are the stories that swirl up around it."

"But we have no stories about the Twelfth House," Miriam puts in, sounding genuinely curious. My father sits forward, too, his sharp eyes hard on Tennet's face. "Lord Protector Fortiss is correct. Your father hasn't left his home since his last tournament appearance nearly twenty years ago. By that reckoning, you would have been a young boy, but there was no record of a boy in attendance with Lord Orlof, or a wife or family of any kind. It was simply him and his attendants. He acquitted himself quite well in battle, advancing to the final stages of the competition. In those times, Lord Rihad had just come to power and was eager to impress all the houses as to his strength and dedication to his families charge of ruling the Protectorate. He gave Lord Orlof several fighting men, and gold to pay for goods in times of trouble. Or at least, that's what is written in the annals of that tournament."

Despite myself, I'm also fascinated by Miriam's words. It never occurred to me to look back at the old records of Orlof's last visit to the First House. I slant a glance toward my father. Did he know Orlof had a son at that time?

Tennet's reply cuts across my thoughts. "I can't speak to events of that tournament, as you say I was just a boy, and my father traveled frequently when I was a child, leaving a brace of guards to protect our home and my mother. He continued traveling after she died giving birth to my younger brother, who yes, still lives. My brother is afflicted by the same illness that took my mother's life, however, and he is not fit for fighting. But he is well, and safe."

"And you, a warrior of clear merit, never wished to compete in the Tournament of Gold?" Miriam asks.

Tennet's lips quirk derisively. "My father was keenly aware of the value of winning at the tournament when he did and how he did, and he also understood the inherent gamble of the tournament. Yes, you could go and win men and money for your house. You could also die or be injured to the point that you are of no service to your house...and then your Divh might be forfeit to your eldest son who perhaps isn't prepared to take on that responsibility. You may also draw the attention of the lord protector if you perform too well or too poorly, and attention often begets more attention. My father was fiercely proud of our mountain home and keenly aware of its status among the other Protectorate houses. He also had no love of visitors. No doubt you have that written in your records as well."

She waves that off. "Only the hearsay of the bards, whom he still entertained, though less and less over the years."

Tennet smirks. "The mountains to the east are dangerous for unwary travels, and while the Tenth House boasts a location close to the pass into the Imperium, the Twelfth House isn't so blessed. And so, we took the gold that Rihad gave us, and we traded it for hunting spears and farming implements that would be best suited for gleaning the fruits of the mountains. What we could produce that was beyond our means, we carried over the border to the Imperium and sold there. It was a far less difficult journey than making it to strongholds like the First House where we would be competing against so many better equipped houses than ours."

My father straightens. "You *what*?" he demands. I'm equally surprised, but grudgingly impressed at the Twelfth House's strategy. We should have been doing the same, truth be told.

Tennet glances at my father, unperturbed. "Our produce is good, our wine is better. I'd need to taste it to be sure, but I'd guess that some of the imported wine you bring from the Imperium is our label made over into the image of whomever we sold it to. But that's of no account. The story of the Twelfth House is one of industry and isolation, and it remained that way until my father signed the marriage contract to join our lots with that of the Tenth House. He died waiting for that promise to be fulfilled."

My lips press tight together, the heavy fist clutching my heart unwilling to move. Despite Fortiss's spell, I don't know whether to believe this man or not, but his story...almost makes sense to me. It explains why the Twelfth House had no need of Protectorate wealth beyond the seed money Rihad provided through Orlof's tournament rewards twenty years earlier. And in truth, though we are a simple holding, the Tenth House has also been largely self-sufficient. Father has seen no need to subject us to the tournament in all the years that I can recall. Merritt chafed against that restriction far more than I did, having never seen it in all his seventeen years, but...

So many questions bubble up, but Fortiss seems done with this line of inquiry. Even as my father leans forward, he cuts off the conversation. "Then we take you at your word, Lord Tennet, until we have reason to believe otherwise. We don't need to search for trouble in these challenging times. Welcome to the First House at long last, we have much work to do."

And he raises a glass of wine, then glances at it realizing as I do the truth. "Is it your vines we have to thank for our enjoyment this night?"

Tennet takes a measured drink—his first, I realize. "It just may be," he agrees with a smug smile, lifting a glass. "To the Protectorate."

I lift my glass to my lips, but this time I don't drink.

CHAPTER 10

We manage to finish out the meal without coming to blows and sit through two rounds of entertainment—first, a brace of bardly music, and then the First House's own performers—a medley of bells and strings and the pulse of drumbeats.

All of it sounds like a coming war to me.

By the time we finally quit our tables and Fortiss releases the gathered fighting men and villagers hastily assembled to round out this welcome meal, I'm ready to crawl out of my skin, let alone the mountain of cloth that seems to conspire to rob me of my breath and my will to live in equal measure.

"Lady Talia, Lord Lemille, and Lord Tennet. Councilors Dolor and Miriam. Warriors of the Fifth and Ninth. Let's adjourn to my receiving chambers." Fortiss's words carry a shiver of intensity that I feel straight to my bones. I cast a look across the room, where Caleb and Nazar are in what appears to be idle conversation, but I'm not fooled. Nazar leans casually over to Caleb, who grins and slides off the bench in one easy movement, dashing off toward the nearest door.

"A *second* meeting?" Miriam asks. She gestures around the table —there are only the two of them out of the eight councilors that appeared earlier. The rest were left to rest in their rooms or sent on other errands for Fortiss. "We don't have a quorum."

"Then how fortunate for us that we will not be determining any matters of state," Fortiss replies. His tone is light enough, but once again I notice the edge to his manner, an energy I can't quite place. "Lord Tennet? I can see from your face you have a concern. Please share it."

Though his request is phrased politely, no one can believe it was anything shy of an order. Still, Tennet braces one forearm on the table, his other hand drifting to his hip in an unmistakable manner of resting offense. "There's no matters we need to discuss beyond the one, Lord Fortiss, and you and I could do that on our own."

"Except *I* should be a part of that conversation, surely," my father puts in quickly.

Outrage bursts up through me so quick and hot, it's a miracle of the Light that I don't erupt into flame right in front of them. The flash is gone in just a second, but even though he doesn't look at me, I can tell by Tennet's smirk that he's marked it. The man is deliberately baiting me! For what reason? If it's to give me a hint of the pleasures I'll have in store as some Light-forsaken dutiful wife of the Twelfth House, he's doing a fine job of it. I'd sooner race across the plains of the Protectorate and join the band of Savasci at the western border than ride east with him.

"Humor me," Fortiss says, and if he's noticed Tennet's slight or if he even takes issue with the idea that three people who *are not me* could decide my fate in marriage or in any other role other than as a member of their fighting contingent, you can't tell it by his manner.

What's suddenly happened here? I don't expect Tennet to have the common decency to accord me the respect that I deserve. He's a man of the Protectorate, and the Protectorate isn't used to women in the fighting ranks. And don't even get me started on my father.

But Fortiss? He wouldn't even be in his exalted position if I hadn't dragged him all the way up to within inches of his precious, beautiful Divh, the glorious monster his uncle had trapped within the bowels of this pile of rocks. Without me, he'd still be thinking that his exalted uncle was the savior of the Protectorate, and the arbiter of all that was right and true between a warrior and his Divh. I haven't nearly died several times over on the battlefield to be cut to pieces with small slights and indignities at a formal banquet.

I stand, grateful for the short bench accorded to each guest at the main table, vs. The long low planks accorded to the rest of the hall. With this much gown weighing me down, I would have ordinarily been trapped, but as it is, I kick the bench back enough to step away from the table with something at least approaching grace.

"I'll see you in your chambers shortly, Lord Protector," I murmur, not sparing a glance toward Tennet or my father. Then I turn away from the table and stride away, my head held high, my fingers twitching for my sword.

Caleb is waiting for me in the hallway, and he takes one look at my face and turns around on his heel, hustling off with long strides until we reach an abandoned receiving room, intended for less formal meetups than the one I envision Fortiss planning.

He kicks the door closed as soon as I enter and hustles to the center of the room.

"Don't touch it, don't touch any of it," he barks at me as he throws his burden down. "You're about as impatient as a pregnant sandworm and twice as awkward."

He races around me as he talks, darting in to unhook my belt and detach the hooks running down the back of my dress, which goes a fair distance toward allowing me to breathe easier. Then he unlaces my sleeves at the shoulder, tossing them onto a nearby table, and returns to unhooking my dress.

"I can do the rest of the dress myself, but untie the laces at my back, if you would. I think Alis knotted them tight enough to bruise me."

"She didn't, she didn't, you're good, almost—there," he finishes triumphantly, and I expand my lungs in a mighty breath for the first time in hours. He turns away as I wrestle off the rest of the clothes, busying himself with folding everything up while I lunge for my breeches and heavy tunic. Now I look as comfortable as Fortiss and Tennet undoubtedly were all during dinner, minus the short capes they wear as a mark of their station. I have one of those too, and I throw it over my shoulders, straightening as Caleb returns to me to set the clasps at my neck.

"It's a good thing we're not in battle right now, given that it takes two people for me to dress," I grouse.

"You'd figure it out if we were in battle, and you wouldn't have a cape, besides. Who wants something like that to get caught on somebody's lance or a tree branch? Not me, that's for sure."

I snort, but as I think about the reality of what he's just said, I instantly sober. "We're trained to fight in tournaments, Caleb." I shake my head, reaching down to pull on my boots. "How in the world do you fight with Divhs on the open plain? You saw what happened in the melee. It was utter madness, and it's only by some miracle that more warriors and villagers on the ground didn't get trampled."

"Not a miracle." He holds up a hand. "They stamp, did you notice that? They stamped together in a rhythm. Pound, pound, pound. I'd show you here, but I don't know who's below me, and Nazar said that you were supposed to be in some sort of meeting, right? So we better get you to that."

"Right, right, but—what? They stamp?" I press as he hustles me out the door. He's left my gown behind, but as far as I'm concerned one of the servants can take it and sell it in the market-place. I hope I never have to wear it again.

"Look, you may not have been paying attention because you were bleeding out and all, but try and keep up," Caleb says with a grin as we head off down the corridor. "When the Divhs hit this plane, they did so with a boom. Anyone who wasn't on the battle-field for a reason, meaning they weren't a banded soldier or one of

Rihad's fighting men, they fell back. It was if the ground rose up and slapped them hard enough to send them sprawling out of the way. Granted, they were on the fringes to begin with, so if a battle broke out in the middle of Trilion, I'm not sure how successful the Divhs would be at clearing the ground of innocent bystanders. I'm telling you, though—this wasn't their first battle with a bunch of ordinary people running around. They've done this before."

"But they haven't done it in what, five hundred years? I've never heard of a tournament staging a melee like this. It's simply not done. For exactly the reason why it was such a bad idea this time. We lost so many warriors, Caleb. We lost Divhs too."

"And got some new ones," he points out. "I'm training them every night. They're solid, and with enough time, they'll be assets in battle."

I shake my head, grimacing as we stride quickly along the corridor. "But they're smaller, right? They're matched to their warriors. Much like Gent changed from the monster he was for the Tenth House when he was banded to Merritt to the goliath he became when he banded with me."

"First-blooded and firstborn," he agrees. "Those will always make a difference. And Gent is better for it, no? He's stronger, and your bond is tight."

"Yes, but he was going from a second son to a first born. Most of the men we lost...they were the best of the best. Where do you go from there if you're a Divh and not being handed on to the next generation? Are their monsters roaming around the plane of Divhs, lost? Do they mourn the soldiers who held their bond? Or are they just as happy to be rid of us? And why is it that nobody seems to know these *answers*? Not you, not you." I wave off his reaction as my mind churns through these thoughts. "I know you've been banded just about as long as I have. But I'm not getting the impression that anyone knows anything about our Divhs other than they come when they call, and they do what we say. What sort of arrangement is that? These creatures aren't a herd of barn-yard animals waiting at the gate to be fed. They think! They go into battle, they kill, and they die for us. How is it we don't know them *better*?"

"I..." Caleb exhales a long breath, slowing down as he considers the question, but not stopping entirely. "I don't know what to tell you. Nazar says they haven't had Divhs in the Imperium for going on a couple of generations. There might be more information there, but if there is and they still decided to get rid of them, to break apart the bonds and banish the warriors...I mean, maybe they know something we don't?"

"Or maybe they were too stupid to take the time to learn."

I use my foul mood as fuel to carry me all the way to the long hallway that leads to Fortiss's inner chambers, and Caleb salutes me with a reassuring grin as he remains on the stairs. He's not a warrior lord or the master of his own house—at least not yet. I sorely wish he was, so I could have him by my side in meetings such as these.

One day.

But for now, he has his own work—returning with Marsh to the coliseum to train the newly banded warriors of the Protectorate and their mighty—if not gargantuan—Divhs. Since these Divhs don't stand higher than the walls of the coliseum, and that structure is far enough away from the heart of Trilion that their training won't scare anyone, he's been able to make progress quickly without disturbing the peace. Caleb's strict no-roaring rule has also helped.

Almost reflexively, I glance up to see the huge glass doors that lead out onto the overlook of the First House. On this side of the castle, a wide deck sticks out over a sheer cliff, giving any who have the opportunity to stand there access to the open plains that stretch from the First House all the way to the coliseum. In the intervening weeks since the Tournament of Gold, the long grasses of that plain have rebounded, making the plain into a constantly moving ocean beneath the starlit sky. One night not too long ago I ran down this corridor out onto that deck and into those stars, praying with all my might that Gent would be there to catch me. I feel worlds apart from the girl I was that night. My problems haven't gone away, though. They've just gotten different.

Gritting my teeth, I turn into Lord Fortiss's inner chambers, nodding at the guards that stand respectfully to either side of the door. I remember this short hallway all too well, the alcove where I hid, terrified, as I first saw the creatures summoned by Rihad's dark magic. That night, Rihad was alone in his chambers by the time those creatures were summoned, and I knew he was the enemy. This time the councilors are assembled with Fortiss, as well as representatives of the Fifth, Second, and Ninth Houses. Warriors all, not house leaders. All of them are men save for Miriam, and all of them turn to look at me in my warrior's garb with reactions ranging from hostility to interest, with something far more dangerous in between.

My problems have definitely become different. Different...and decidedly worse.

"Lady Talia, good. We're all here," Fortiss says, giving me a hard, intent look that feels like a hand reaching out to me—as a warrior? A comrade? Or maybe something more? Questions that will have to wait as he glances around the room. "It appears we've run out of time."

CHAPTER 11

I feel Tennet's eyes on me, but I don't meet his gaze. I don't want him here, confusing my already hopelessly tangled emotions. If I had the choice, I'd send him off to the sand-worms of the south, never to be seen again.

That thought brings a sincere smile to my face as Fortiss jabs a hard finger at councilor Miriam.

"Today has been a day of unexpected truths, it seems. How long have you known that we've had leadership of the houses amassing in Trilion, staying at our inns with barely any indication of their rank and station? During our grand banquet tonight, I've had three separate runners tell me that the lords of half the Protectorate's households are within a mile of the First House, yet are they here? Have they approached? No. They're waiting to do so all at once. Not a bad strategy, if you needed a strategy to speak with the lord protector. Which you *don't*. How long have you known?"

Before giving the councilors a chance to reply, he turns to the warrior representatives. "And what of your houses? Are your lords coming as well? Can I trust you, or am I surrounded by liars?"

"Lord Fortiss," Miriam interrupts, but the warriors respond to this accusation with speed and force. To a man, they stand forward, crossing one hand over their chest, fists clenched at their heart. Not Tennet, of course, though he watches them with interest as the Fifth House warrior speaks. "Lord Protector Fortiss, be assured our houses know well the danger we face, and we have keenly felt the dagger of Lord Rihad's betrayal. Our houses stand with us. As to the rest of what you ask, I can't say. We've been here. Our men and horses have been here. We have no knowledge of what's going on in Trilion."

"Agreed." The Ninth House warrior's tone is more measured, the set of his jaw tense. He's a cautious one, I think, with good reason. There's been too much death at the First House not to be cautious. "But who is coming? If the lords of the houses are assembling, then warriors are not enough. We have no standing here."

"You don't, if the Fifth and the Ninth are in Trilion," Fortiss agrees. "That's yet to be determined. Apparently, some of these men have been traveling over a week to get here, some merely days, and I suspect that pace is only possible because they switched out horses in every major town along the way." He turns his gaze to my father. "Sort of like you and Lord Tennet, Lord Lemille. The timing is curious, no?"

He doesn't give my father a chance to reply but turns back to Miriam. "And that's only the houses that decided to come—or that we've seen so far. What of the ones who didn't? This doesn't feel like men rallying to support the Protectorate. This feels more like a coup."

"Strong words, and hasty ones," Miriam returns. "Especially since no one has come forward yet." She eyes him with more than a little curiosity. "If we didn't know the lords of these houses were assembling in Trilion, how did you?"

"While you have been holed up pondering the details of succession and proper transfer of power, I haven't been idle," Fortiss snaps. "Trilion fell under the purview of the lord protector, but its management has long fallen to me. You don't run a city for any length of time without understanding how to get the information you need about who is entering, who is leaving, and what they're doing while they're here. We're not talking about large delegations, we're talking about small companies of men—the lord, a few of his top warriors. With the first runner, I didn't put it together, because the houses were traveling under no banner or house colors, as if they were common merchants. But by the third alert, I knew. So many merchants wouldn't happen to be arriving all at once, not like this."

I can't help myself; I have to speak up. "But why waste their time with all this? If they had an issue with you, with your leadership or your proposed plans, why not just come to the First House and talk with you directly? Lord Rihad may have run the Protectorate as his own private fiefdom, but I suspect he didn't when he first took power. There'd have been collaboration, cohesion. There's no reason why the houses wouldn't expect the same of you."

"Except Lord Fortiss has already given them reason to doubt the viability of traditions." Tennet stands with his hands at his hips, his thumbs tucked into the heavy belt that's weighed down with precious metal and the empty scabbard where his personal weapon would normally hang. As a guest in the First House, he may not carry a knife or sword. But in all other ways, he looks exactly like what he purports to be—entitled, experienced, male. A warrior of the Protectorate, first-blooded and firstborn. He meets my gaze.

"Don't get angry with me because I say what everyone else is thinking. I wasn't here, Lady Talia. I didn't see your feats of prowess on the battlefield, I heard about them second- and even third-hand. None of the lords who are gathering in Trilion saw them either. Blood and stone, your own *father* has disavowed you, as well he should, according to the tradition of the Protectorate."

For him to mention my father with the man standing right there sends a wave of fury through me, quick and hot. I can barely keep from choking on my own outrage, but Tennet's still not done.

"No woman may claim a Divh, no woman may stand up in battle to defend her house. And yet before us we have a woman who does both."

"That's right!" I snap back, my voice ringing out across the room. "Not only stand up, not only claim, but I did those things and *won* the tournament. I have a right to be here as much as anyone else in the Protectorate. I would argue, *more* of a right. My family suffered a mortal blow when Rihad ordered my brother's death. I did what I had to do to protect my house."

My father utters some low, guttural noise, but I don't have time for him. My focus is only on Tennet, and he doesn't back down. If anything, he leans in. "And I would argue that there are a dozen old men and more than a few young ones who would contend that *none* of this was yours to do. What's more, they're the ones in power, by order of the Imperium. You're not."

"You've made your point," Fortiss says, but to my massive irritation, he doesn't refute Tennet's words. Instead, he turns to Miriam and Dolor. "You think this is a coup attempt? We don't have time for that if we have enemies converging on our western borders."

"I think it could become a coup attempt," Miriam says. "I think most likely they are discussing that possibility as one of the potential outcomes. You're very new to your position, Fortiss, and to Lord Tennet's point, your feats of bravery in ousting Rihad are acts that the lords can easily get behind, particularly those who chafed under his rule. Even those who benefited from the former lord protector's favor will likely welcome a change of power in the wake of their loss of men and Divhs. For despite their support of Rihad, those houses still suffered losses they didn't tacitly agree to. Rihad acted alone in that regard. So, you, as the new lord protector, would at worst, ordinarily, merely be considered a pawn in the larger political game they are more used to playing."

Fortiss's lips twist. "Your confidence in me is overwhelming," he says dryly, but he motions her to continue.

"But you've already demonstrated that you're not blindly cleaving to tradition. The idea of elevating anyone to the position of lord of a new house without calling the Protectorate leadership together to discuss the merits of that decision is bad enough. The fact that Talia is a woman, takes things to an entirely different level."

"Talia commands a legion of Divhs that's thirty strong by *herself*," Fortiss bites back, and I'm startled at the fervor in his voice. Startled and unreasonably pleased, if I'm being honest. "Even this morning she was out assisting one of those Divhs with the rite of passage of her young—a sandworm Divh, it should be noted. Sandworms aren't supposed to cleave to warriors from the mountains, and yet they did with her. Sandworms also don't involve warriors in the daily practice of raising their offspring, yet Talia woke up this morning and sent word to me that she needed to perform that assistance."

He turns to Dolor. "You tell me—have you found any record in Rihad's books about such a high level of interaction between warrior and Divh?"

Dolor shifts uneasily. "I've only had the day to look."

"Blighted path, don't play *games* with me," Fortiss snaps. "I know you've been looking for this past month for any evidence or unusual reference to female-Divh warrior pairings. You've gone back to the dawn of the Protectorate searching for that evidence. And there's none. None! There's not even a mention of the *possibility* other than as an aside, as if, of course, such a thing were impossible to conceive. Yet here this woman, not formally trained despite her noble birth, takes on the assignment as if she was born to it. Because she *was* born to it. Which takes me to my next point."

He turns and skewers another councilor with a glare. "When did it become practice for Protectorate House lords to slaughter their firstborn daughters?"

"It's not a question of slaughtering," the man stutters, his hands coming up as if to ward off an attack. I don't know this councilor's name. I made it a point to stay out of the way of all council members other than Miriam, and I can't seem to avoid her even though I long to. "By tradition, the anointed families of the Protectorate are blessed with firstborn sons to carry on the sacred duty of protection with their legacy Divh."

"Blessings and anointments," Fortiss repeats with disgust. "Yet here we have a firstborn daughter of a noble holding."

He rounds on Lord Lemille, skewering him with a glare. "A daughter who bears deep scars of abuse due to her birth order. So clearly, those births *do* happen and these Lords who are amassing on my doorstep may have committed such murders."

"Well, I obviously didn't murder my child," Lemille snarls. "And as to *abuse*—"

"I can't imagine why you think there might be a coup," Tennet drawls, cutting off Lemille as it's his turn to choke on his fury.

The Fifth House man steps forward. "Any warriors who fought in the Tournament of Gold will stand with you, Lord Fortiss," he says staunchly. "And any lord who trusts his men will trust their word on that."

Another of the councilors speaks up, a man perhaps double Fortiss's age. A contemporary of Rihad's then? He's as lumpy as a knob of garlic beneath his severe black robes. "I suspect you won't find those warriors among the retainers that they have brought to this assembly. They have come looking for answers from you, not from their own men."

"Then they should have come to me directly."

I speak up. "Maybe, but first, perhaps they wanted to get their stories straight." I'm surprised at the strength of my own voice, but the others merely look at me, expecting me to go on. I rock up on my toes and back again, considering. "They weren't here for the tournament, Fortiss. They sent their best men in good faith, some of whom died along the way, many others who fell on that battlefield, their Divhs sent back to their fertile plane. It's all well and good to get the official report, but these aren't men to sit idly by and protect their house while the Protectorate as a whole is at risk. You didn't summon them immediately."

"I've been a little busy." Fortiss rejects that tack with a dismissive wave. "These vaunted leaders that you speak of with such eloquence, how many of them have you met? How many of them traveled to the Tenth House to break bread with you, Lemille? Or to the Twelfth?" he asks, turning to Tennet. "Because I'm here to tell you, they didn't visit the First House, either. The only time we saw the house lords of the Protectorate was at the Tournament of Gold, and those were generally the local ones. The others came only once per year, right before the stormy season, or Rihad would go visit them. These past several years, it's been the latter."

"Really?" I ask. Steeling myself, I glance toward my father. "I don't think he's been to the Tenth House in all my years."

Lemille glowers at me but doesn't respond.

"The Twelfth, only once," Tennet puts in. "I was ten years old, and that's the first time that I learned of my father's duplicity regarding my birth. He needed me to stay hidden, but I was entranced with the idea of meeting the lord protector. I was having none of his attempts to shut me up in my room, especially with my baby brother being presented to Rihad like the prize of the east. I grudgingly accepted my lot once he explained I wasn't supposed to exist, but that's the only time that Rihad deigned to visit our holding. I honestly think he wanted to see our Divh. Father still held the band, and because we are so high up in the mountains, summoning the great beasts didn't cause the stampede it otherwise might other than at the tournament. So he gave a demonstration to Rihad, and he left."

He glances at the small group of warriors. "How do you practice, or even wage battle with the help of your Divhs out here on the open plains? Or are the villagers so used to seeing them that there's no issue?"

The Fifth House warrior snorts. "Not hardly. Truth be told, newly banded soldiers can train when they first get the band, but we don't call on our Divhs unless there's an exhibition or a tournament."

"It's why the tournament was created." Fortiss rubs a hand over his brow. "But that was when the Protectorate was a country more or less at peace, with no need to prepare for a greater battle that's even now on our doorstep."

"So I keep hearing." Tennet waves a negligent hand around the room. "But in this, I have to side with the assembling lords. I see no threat to the Protectorate other than Rihad, and you have effectively banished him to his own basement until the adjudicators of the Imperium come to decide his fate. Whatever stories he told himself about some threat from the West, how can you know it's true? How can any of us know it's true? You want to convince the houses to rally around you, you're going to have to give us more than whatever warnings you've found in musty old books."

Fortiss opens his mouth to speak, then thinks better of it. Apparently, now isn't the time to share that he has been indulging in magic from the blighted path. "We need a gathering of warriors, these lords and their Divhs, all of us together. It should happen at the coliseum, that's the only place that's big enough, but even then..." He grimaces. "Well perhaps not the Divhs together, not all at once. But a gathering, nonetheless. And it needs to be soon. It's been almost a full moon since the Tournament of Gold and Rihad's fall. Whoever he was working with from the Western Realms may already be on the move."

"You would have gotten word of that," Tennet counters. "The watchtowers would be lit from the borders all the way to the First House."

"They should be yes," Fortiss agrees. "But until I see that they're all intact with my own eyes, how are we to know that the line remains unbroken? Especially when there may be enemies in our midst even now?"

He huffs out a breath. "Lemille, you need to be banded anew as well. We need every Divh we can pair with a warrior, and your blood is the strongest."

"I'll serve," he grits out, but he appears to take no joy in that idea. But something else is turning over in my mind, a possibility barely taking shape.

"There's a way you might be able to learn the truth about the houses without having to trust anything but your own eyes," I begin, my voice hesitant. "But—"

"Understood, Lady Talia," he cuts me off, and when his gaze

meets mine, I barely recognize him behind his mask of fury. The speed with which anger overtakes him worries me. Is this truly Fortiss's nature? Or yet another effect of Rihad's dark magic? Whatever the reason, he can see nothing before him now but swords and flame. "First, we need to find the traitors in our midst."

CHAPTER 12

"We'll go," the lumpy councilor says, surprising me. He points to Dolor and Miriam. "The three of us are known enough to these men, and there are only a few inns suitable for a house lord. We'll go tonight—and be there when they wake tomorrow."

"Take a brace of guards—no, do it," Fortiss says, overriding Miriam's instant protest. "They don't have to loom over you, but they should be nearby if you need them. I'm not willing to assume goodwill when these men aren't showing themselves. And the warriors too—if your houses are here, you should know."

He shuts down the meeting quickly then, with assurances to the council that he won't do anything without consulting them first. Then Fortiss and my father argue some more about when Lemille will be able to see Rihad.

Even with all that, in less than a quarter hour, only the three of us remain in the hallway outside of Fortiss's chambers. There's something unspoken in the air between us—an energy of past, present, and possibility.

Fortiss holds my gaze for a quick, stolen moment, but Tennet doesn't waste any time. "What exactly is your plan to give Fortiss the sight, Talia?" he demands, the question clearly one he hasn't been able to let go. "Not the priest, I hope. You can't rely on visions and portents if you mean to truly defend the Protectorate."

"Let's get some air." Fortiss waves us to follow him, and we fall silent as we move down the hallway toward the wide overlook. When we step out on the decking, Tennet looks around, scowling. The torches are lit, brightening the space immediately around us, but the moon is full and bright, washing the entire plane in a blue-white glow that extends all the way to the coliseum.

And there...I smirk as Tennet jolts in surprise, then strides out to the farthest edge of the overlook, peering hard. "There's fire there," he says, squinting. "There—and again. Shooting up, you see that? Who's in there?"

"Caleb," I say succinctly, dropping my hands to my belt. It's a move I've watched warriors make so often, I assumed it was simply for comfort, but no. It's a subtle power stance, both grounding and preparatory at once. I grin as Tennet scowls at me. "He's training newly banded warriors there—soldiers all. Their Divhs are strong, but not as imposing. Suitable to guard a village or come together to serve several families in a conflict."

"That's not what Divhs are for," he retorts.

"Not up to now, no," Fortiss agrees. His gaze, too, is on the coliseum—fully a quarter hour's easy canter from the base of the mountain. "Up to now, there's been no need for Divhs to do much of anything but display their might and power—so strong that only marauders and fools try to take up arms against each other. It's been an effective form of deterrence to incidental battles these past five hundred years. Thievery and even murder happens, but not on any scale. That is the peace that the Divhs have provided us, a boon but also a curse. Now, with this threat that looms from the west, the playing field changes. We can't rely only on the mightiest of Divhs. We may need them all to come to our aid."

"And we're back to this nebulous threat." Disdain weighs heavily in Tennet's tone. "I have to say, I'd be inclined to side with the lords gathering in Trilion on this score. It's not that I don't believe that Rihad thought he was summoning creatures of true power and evil—I do. You don't kill that many warriors without a strong belief that you have some mighty force on your side. But he also could simply have been mad, duped into believing that legends and myths are true. He wouldn't be the first."

"I saw the creature he summoned, Lord Tennet," I counter quietly. Tennet turns to me, and in that easy motion I feel his warrior energy, both predator and protector. I recognize that same energy in myself. "You forget, I was willing to do anything to understand why my brother died and who killed him. My search took me to Lord Rihad's chambers. I hid myself away, waiting for a chance to search it when it was quiet. Before I got that chance, I heard him speak his incantations, and I saw who responded. A creature that could have been a man, but was covered in snakes, standing in the heart of Rihad's great fireplace, overtaken but not consumed by flames. It noticed me almost as soon as I laid eyes on it, and I fled. But it was real, Tennet—or as real as anything I've ever seen. It wasn't an illusion created to dupe me, but something that Rihad was actually interacting with."

"You ran," he echoes, focusing on what I consider to be the least important piece of the story. "Ran where? Is that when you were discovered by Rihad?"

"Oh—well, no." I smile a little as I remember that fateful night. "I ran like mad out here, then jumped off the edge."

Tennet glances over the railing to the wide expanse below. "You jumped. Meaning, your Divh caught you and carried you the rest of the way down."

He looks at Fortiss. "Do all the Divhs who participated in the Tournament of Gold perform such tricks on demand? I've never tried such a thing with mine. We bonded when my father finally gave up the band a year ago—an act I'm convinced sent him into his final decline, if I'm being honest—and I've never felt right summoning it just for my own needs. It's the guardian of our holding, and that's not a gift I take lightly."

I bristle at the implied insult, but Fortiss cuts across my ready response. "Talia's connection to her Divh—to all her Divhs—is unusual," he says, his tone placating. "There's no wrong way for a warrior knight to interact with your Divh."

"There's definitely not," I put in, irritated at being interrupted. "You simply ask for what you wish."

"If only it were that simple for all warriors, Lady Talia."

Tennet turns sharply at the new voice that floats to us across the open space of the overlook, which allows me to hide my grin. I pivot as well to see Nazar step out from the shadows. The priest of the Light is dressed in his heavy dark robes of deep blue, his lean face dominated by solemn eyes that study Tennet with an intensity I know all too well.

"Good evening, Lord Tennet," he murmurs. "May the Light shine upon you as you lead your house to glory. I would have come to assist you with the transition from father to son, had you need of me. I understand the Twelfth House doesn't have its own priest."

"Priest Nazar," Tennet says, surprising me by lifting his right fist to his heart, the same gesture that would normally be accorded to another lord, despite his uncertainty about the priest. "We could have used you, but we made it through. My father was a proud man and didn't want to admit the need. He particularly didn't want to admit it to Lord Lemille."

I grimace, understanding completely. Tennet wasn't supposed to exist, and nobody would believe that Orlof would give up the band to a boy of fourteen, especially when, a year ago he would only have been thirteen. But why had Orlof decided to give up the band at all—has he been ill for some time? I have so many questions, but once again I'm stymied.

"You haven't summoned your Divh since you were first banded?" Fortiss asks and Tennet nods, dropping his hands to his belt in a move I again appreciate.

"I wanted to, certainly, but no—save once," Tennet says. "My father, as I say, was a proud man, and he was doing what he needed to so that he would ensure the future of his house. He was also dying. I didn't know it at the time that he gave up the band, and neither of us expected his decline to be so precipitous after it. By the time he finalized the marriage contract with the Tenth House, he was visibly fading before my eyes. Upon his death, I summoned our Divh to send him to the Light in accordance with his wishes, but in the weeks that followed, I haven't sought its aid."

It? I send the question out into the starlit sky and hear Gent's huff of amusement in return.

Tennet gestures to the edge of the overlook. "I see now I've missed out on honing its skills for uses other than outright protection. I confess, it never occurred to me to ask."

"Lady Talia is correct in saying that you simply have to ask your Divh for the aid you need, but in your case—and yours, Lord Protector Fortiss—you were constrained by the beliefs and training handed down from your fathers," Nazar says. "So, in some ways Lady Talia had the benefit of not knowing what she could and couldn't ask. The rule of tradition has played long and heavily in the actions of our warriors. It has served us well for hundreds of years. It's also kept us in check."

Tennet narrows his eyes. "Us?" he repeats. "You mean the whole of the Protectorate, or all of the Imperium as well?"

"Both," Nazar says. "And I also mean us. The four of us, all for different reasons."

"But how..." His words fall away as Nazar shifts his robes back over his left shoulder, then peels back the sleeve from his wrist. There, the warrior band that is all that is left of Nazar's bond with his own Divh gleams from where it is buried deep in his wrist. The heavy scarring above it pays testament to the long ago attempts to unband him from his Divh. He stares from the band back into Nazar's face. "So, it's true. I assumed councilor Miriam was lying to put off Lemille."

I jolt at the harshness of his tone and at the rudeness of his words.

"Lord Tennet," Fortiss protests. "Remember yourself. In the

Protectorate, a man's story is his own to reveal in his own time. Nazar is both warrior and priest. He has served the Protectorate in both capacities well, and that's all we need to know."

"Lord Tennet's confusion is valid," Nazar says, lifting a hand. He smiles a little at Tennet's confusion. "I confess, I was grateful for the Protectorate practice of asking no questions when I came to this land. Lord Lemille cared only that I was a priest of the Light, able to help tutor his son Merritt in the ways of a warrior and give my blessing when the time came for the transfer of the band. He also enjoyed hearing the stories I could share about the capital city and the excess of the Imperator and his wives. But he didn't care about my own, personal history."

My brows shoot up. *Wives?* The history of the Imperium we were force-fed as children in the Tenth House never actually detailed the personal life of the current Imperator, and most definitely had never included the idea that the man had multiple wives. In fact, now that I thought about it, the amount of recent history that I knew about the Imperium could barely fill a thimble.

"We don't either." Fortiss tries again to preserve Nazar's privacy. "A man is as good as his sword and his service here, Priest Nazar. Miriam has already explained your story. It's enough."

"Wise counsel, but unnecessary in this case." He turns to Tennet, but he speaks to and for all of us, I think, bonding himself to our group as surely as he is bonded to his Divh. "I wasn't born a priest, Lord Tennet. But I was born into a family that once, long ago, protected the interests of the Imperium. Not all warriors who served in the Great War remained here. Those who sought to advance their interests closer to home accompanied the battle party back into the Hallowed Lands. There they were feted, given high positions in government and sizable allowances by the Imperium in exchange for their willingness to serve, should the need ever arise. Though the money petered out after the first Imperator passed to the Light, the honor remained. Some warriors let their connections lapse, choosing not to pass on their band—

and every generation, there were a few more of those. When a new Imperator was crowned, all remaining warriors were called to give an accounting in a great procession of battle Divhs, a three-week celebration to honor the past and pledge allegiance to the future. Eventually, though, the stories of the Protectorate faded, and the Imperator's councilors grew suspicious of warriors with so much power. Those families who wished to preserve their connection to their Divhs moved farther and farther away from the capital city, coming back only for the grand procession. Some fled into the Protectorate itself, and others, again, let their connection fade away. Eventually, there were only a dozen of us. And then a new successor was born fifty years ago, and to honor his arrival, the current Imperator decreed the forced unbanding of its remaining warriors. They made a great display of another allowance of wealth settled upon each of the warriors and their families, but that was cold comfort as you may imagine."

"What a waste," Tennet mutters, but he looks queasy as he stares at Nazar's scarred forearm. "I can't see how you could survive that...or why you'd want to."

"Many didn't," Nazar agrees. "It was a brutal ceremony. The warriors who survived either joined the priesthood or secluded themselves with their families. Many of them migrated to the edges of the hallowed lands, hoping that they would be reunited with their Divh when they returned to the Light. None of us thought anything but death would allow that reconnection."

"But clearly, you did reconnect. How did it happen? This was during the Tournament of Gold?"

"It doesn't matter how it happened," Fortiss interjects, and there's an edge to his voice I don't quite understand. "What matters is we have another Divh to aid us. We'll need every one we can get."

With a flourish, he throws his own cape over his shoulder, baring his left sleeve. His band clearly lies beneath the silky fabric of his tunic. When he speaks again, there's an odd timbre to his voice, and a curious compulsion comes over me, making my own band tighten on my arm, and my blood hum with urgency. "We should introduce you, Lord Tennet. And be introduced as well."

He drops his hand, and the wide plain before us is suddenly... not so empty.

Three enormous Divhs stare back at us.

CHAPTER 13

ent! As genuinely happy as I am to see the other Divhs, my heart and soul leap in unison to see my great green-and-silver goliath standing fully upright, looking around with what I now understand to be a nearsightedness that renders all men and women into a blur—except for me. Because of our bond, Gent could find me anywhere. And he would, too. That kind of complete loyalty shakes me. I wonder if any man has ever seen me so clearly, or would fight through worlds to find me.

I pray to the Light that Gent always will.

He's almost at eye level, the size of three First Houses stacked on top of each other, fully five times the size of my own manor house back in the mountains. Horns sprout from his head and shoulders, and his enormous forearms are slightly too long for the rest of his body, serving to tilt him forward whether he is sitting or standing. His hide is covered in thick green scales now shot with silver, and fingers and toes are tipped with enormous ebony claws.

He sees me, and his delighted howl cry echoes in my brain, though he makes no move toward me. Instead, he looks back, squinting at the two other monsters alongside him, and then up to the sky.

Fortiss's and Nazar's Divhs are doing the same, but I take the moment to admire them before trying to see what they're looking for. Nazar's Divh is a glorious creature that's almost as large as Gent. With the white plumed head of an eagle, his body transforms into the powerful figure of a midnight blue winged lion, complete with gold beak and gold-tipped paws. Beside him, the deep blue Szonja levitates easily above the earth, her newly healed wing fluttering in a slow, steady cadence as she snakes her head around, searching the heavens. She's perhaps two thirds the size of Gent, small for the Divh of a first-blooded and firstborn warrior, but her size is also her strength. She's incredibly fast, and one of the few full dragons that fought in the Tournament of Gold. There were several winged lizards, and a number of winged snakes, but the sinuous long-limbed, long-tailed beauty in front of me is unlike anything I've ever seen before.

Tennet is clearly surprised by it too. He takes a quick step forward, his mouth agape, and then a rush of wind blows into us, so strong we stumble back. A new monster has joined the conclave of Divhs.

"*Light*," whispers Fortiss, and I can't help but share his surprise. His voice is barely a breath, but it strikes something deep inside me. We're all staring at the same miracle, but I know, somehow, that Fortiss sees it the way I do—not just as a threat or advantage, but as something sacred. And this Divh is truly sacred.

A second dragon, this one almost the exact replica of Szonja, levitates behind the group, burnished gold even in the half-light of the moon. He's bigger than Szonja but not by much, still well smaller than Gent and Wrath, Nazar's beautiful Divh. This new dragon twists and turns on himself with sinuous precision, sliding forward, then beating his powerful wings to keep him apart from the others. Szonja for her part hisses at him, blinks out, then appears again on the other side of Gent, placing the two more familiar Divhs between her and the interloper.

The dragons posture like kings, and I feel the same tension humming between Fortiss and Tennet. They aren't enemies—at least not yet—but there's something primal rising here, visceral and real, a storm spinning up all around us.

For the moment, I'm in the center of that storm...but I'm not at its mercy.

At least not yet.

Nazar speaks first. "There's nothing in the annals of the houses that indicates the Twelfth House Divh is a golden dragon. When did the shift occur?"

Tennet grimaces. "When I was banded a year ago. Before, our Divh was a falcon, still golden, but not scaled and tailed. My father took it as a sign that our fortunes were improving, but also as a warning that our fortunes needed to improve. Another reason why we weren't in any hurry to introduce our Divh to anyone."

He swings around to glare at Fortiss. "And I wasn't planning on doing so tonight, for the record. How is it you summoned all our Divhs so easily?"

"I didn't," Fortiss says, but too quickly, I think. I think again about his deep study of Rihad's books and wonder just how far down that path he has gone. "I asked for the introduction, and either you or your Divh was willing to go through with it. Though mine is somewhat less sure, as it turns out."

"You've always had a dragon?" Tennet asks, turning his attention back to where Szonja is soaring high against the stars. "I was expecting a scorpion."

Fortiss's lips twist. "Well, I'm not Rihad's son, so he retains his scorpion...or at least he did. I don't know enough about the Divhs' plane to understand the images they show me."

"Wait—what images?"

Tennet's newest question barely registers in my mind as I'm distracted by the brief bursts of fire that still arc up from the coliseum well behind our mighty Divhs. I can almost hear the sound of cheers and imagine Caleb's successful training lifting the spirits and the confidence of the newly banded soldiers. Then my gaze lifts to the moonlit plain that stretches far to the west, and something catches my eye. A cloud almost, a stain across the moon-brightened sky. Like a low-moving cape or cluster of birds. But it's too thick, too dark to be birds. Almost like a swarm, really. Almost like—

"What's that?" Tennet asks sharply, and I know he sees it too. Fortiss glances up, then jerks back. "Szonja!"

In my mind's eye I feel Gent turn, sense him peering hard, but he can't pierce the darkness with his limited eyesight. I reach out to the other Divhs and realize that while their sight is solid in the daytime, they too are having a hard time tracking the thick wave of *something* that's spinning across the sky.

"They can't see!" I blurt. "They can't see. *Gent!*"

My beautiful Divh rotates back towards us, his arms sweeping out, and he lurches toward the First House as I take off across the platform.

"Talia! What are you *doing*?" Tennet's cry sounds genuinely terrified.

"They can't see well on this plane! You have to help them!" I repeat, then I have no more time for words. Instead, I leap into the sky, barely clearing the edge of the overlook before Gent snatches me out of the air. Our minds touch, and he understands what must be done. Because of course he understands. He holds me up, clutched in his paw like a torch, and I lean forward and urge him to run.

Something is coming out of the west, ready to attack.

"Wrath!"

Nazar calls out the name of his Divh, and I hear Fortiss and Tennet cry out as well. I urge Gent forward, but this creature is coming from the sky—the sky! Gent may be immense, but he can only defend the coliseum from this attack, he can't go on the offensive.

Fortunately, I know three other Divhs who can.

Szonja. Fortiss's beautiful dragon is the only Divh I've deeply connected with before, and her mind is open to me and to the dark sky. I open my eyes wide and will her to see what I see and understand it more than I can, but instead she's focusing on the First

House—and Fortiss, who is standing with his arms outstretched, as if he can somehow guide his Divh from the sidelines.

Szonja! I plead, urging her down, but another creature erupts in front of me, racing at Gent so quickly my mighty goliath wheels around, flinging me into the air. A streak of gold flashes past, then back again, and suddenly I'm hauled up so hard I think my neck may break. My arms and legs flail wildly and Gent howls in... laughter?

My Divh is *laughing* at me?

"Blood and stone!" I screech, spinning around and craning my head up, up—and I realize I'm pinned up against the muzzle of Tennet's golden beast, his teeth clamped tightly through my cape. His name shimmers through my mind as fast as a shooting star—*Ayne*—and then he rockets toward the overlook where Tennet stands, still looking stupefied.

Only then do I know what to do. "Jump on!" I scream as we make a passing run, but Tennet scrambles back and out of our way. "Come on—we don't have *time*!"

The second pass he's almost able to connect, and then with the third, he flings himself off the overlook and crashes into me. The two of us wrap around each other tight as Ayne wings off across the open plain.

"He needs you to see with any detail! To *see*—"

The wind rips the words from my mouth and as I twist around, I see Gent pounding across the grassy plains, his hand stretched out. Too late I realize what he and Ayne have planned, and I scream as Ayne opens his powerful jaws and both Tennet and I plummet down, down—abruptly landing in Gent's meaty paw. He dumps us both in his left then plucks up Tennet like he's a fig dangling from a low-hanging branch, then turns back to where Ayne is beating his wings in place. I catch only a glimpse of Tennet's starkly terrified face as Gent lays him atop Ayne's ridged neck—and then the golden dragon is streaking off again.

Fortiss's voice sounds in my mind as Gent turns back toward the coliseum.

"I can see more from down here—show me what you see."

I squint against the whipping wind and struggle to understand what I'm looking at as Gent reaches the coliseum and spins me toward the incoming storm. *Storm* is about right, but it's not a mere cloud that is hurtling toward us, but a writhing mass of winged snakes, glistening wet with a viscous ooze that can only be poison. It's as if the creature that I saw in Rihad's fireplace has transformed into an entirely new monster, this one the size of a mountain. The whole of it can stretch over top the coliseum, and if those creatures are dripping poison, they'll become a rain of death on the untrained warriors and Divhs just now getting their feet underneath them. And Caleb is down there too!

Then the snakes are upon us. Gent punches through the first wave of the creatures as I crouch into his carefully closed fist, and a high-pitched screeching noise is all I can register for a moment. Then they are past us and Gent shifts to the side as Wrath swoops by. The powerful draft of the griffin's wings sends the snakes hurtling beyond the edge of the coliseum, and the few that clear the surface are incinerated by Szonja as she emerges from the center of the coliseum, breathing fire.

But the many-headed monster isn't finished. The snakes that weren't destroyed zip up into the sky and regroup, creating a new irregularly shaped blob, this one thick and bulbous. It darts past Gent's swinging paw, and instead of attacking the coliseum, it lurches toward Wrath; the mighty lion immediately darts away, so fast it takes my breath away, and whether its mesmerized by Wrath's eagle-scream or its flashing claws of its scrambling lion's body, the stream of snakes screams after it, thinning out like a deadly arrow—

Then I hear a twin howl of rage over my shoulder. Gent half turns, then hauls me back into his chest as a streak of gold blurs by me, and I catch only the swiftest glimpse of Tennet crouching alongside Ayne's sinuous head, the two of them riveted on the stream of snakes shooting through the sky. Ayne breaks off from his scream and the sound is replaced by a fiery woosh as flames race along the surface of the snakes' oily bodies until it reaches the thick center mass and explodes outward.

A shower of fried carcasses rains down on the coliseum. When I conjure up a clear image of Marsh and Caleb, coupled with a surge of worry, Gent bounds back to the outer walls of the coliseum—and slings me into the center of the field...directly at Marsh.

I collide into the mighty Divh, and he grabs at me, then falls backward, the ungainly Divh rolling to the side to let me slide off him and hit the snake-strewn tournament field. I don't fall the final few feet to the ground nearly as gracefully as I probably should, and I lay there, dazed, as the sounds crackle and chatter around me, my sight completely blacked for...far too long. Gradually, a familiar voice breaks through the thudding chaos in my ears.

"Talia!"

I squint up to see Caleb bounding over to me, then haul myself to my feet. I sway on wobbly legs as the warriors emerge back out onto the field from beneath the stands. Their Divhs, at least, had the sense to vacate this plane during the firefight above, and to my intense relief, it doesn't appear that any of the warriors have been injured. "What were you thinking? Gent can't just toss you into the air like that and expect Marsh to be able to catch you. He's not that great with his hands, even if he has two of them—and what in the blighted *path*—!"

Caleb's words are drowned out as a cheer goes up, and I strain up to see the mighty dragon soar into the coliseum. Tennet is still astride his Divh, who banks sharply, then arrows down to the field, skimming the carcass-strewn dirt for half a breath before angling up again, then finally landing on the dirt, settling into a seated position on his haunches.

Tennet, appearing like a man frozen into a block of ice, topples off to the side. His Divh disappears.

"Lord Tennet!" Caleb and I surge forward at once, reaching Tennet as another commotion erupts overhead and two more Divhs take the field briefly—Szonja and Wrath, who do little more than release their own riders before taking their leave as well. By this time, Tennet is convulsing on the ground, his skin as pale as marble and covered with a sheen of sweat. Nazar and Fortiss reach us moments later, and Fortiss drops to his knees as well.

"Were you connected to his mind while he did that?"

"I..." I blink, scowling down at Tennet. "Not after we got him on Ayne. I wasn't connected to anyone." I jerk my gaze back to Fortiss. "Was it hard? To ride like that?"

He shrugs. "Szonja's neck scales are smaller than the scales on the rest of her body, almost like flaps of skin that adhere to themselves until she doesn't want them to. When she settled on the side of the First House, she sort of fluffed those scales. It wasn't difficult to climb up and then tuck my legs under completely and just hold on. But—I wasn't transferred to my Divh midflight, and I wasn't trying to hold on during battle." He stares down at Tennet. "He did well."

"More than well," Nazar agrees. He stands with his feet slightly too wide, his hands out at his side, as if he's afraid he'll topple. "I had maybe a dozen years with Wrath before I was unbanded. Never once did I attempt to fly on his shoulders. It never occurred to me to ask."

"Yeah?" I grin at him. "So how did that go?"

He grimaces. "Not all of Wrath's screaming was due to battle rage. The villagers of Trilion will be finding far too many fluffy under feathers strewn between here and the town."

"He's coming around," Caleb announces, and though there's no discernible change in Tennet's waxy face that I can see, a moment later he groans and shakes again, but this time with greater force. His eyes flicker open, and he stares up at the four of us looking down.

"Blood and...*stone*," he mutters, his words as reedy as the wind. "Where did the second mess of those skrill go? You saw it, right? The knot of them that shot off to the east?"

I jolt and Fortiss leaps up, his feet hardly seeming to hit the ground before he turns toward the entryway. "Szonja!" he roars as we start running. Our ringing ears are useless until we clear the doors of the coliseum, until the world snaps tight again and our Divhs return.

For just a moment, before the roars of our Divhs shake the sky, we can hear another sound all too clearly—the far-off sounds of screaming.

CHAPTER 14

Even with our Divhs speeding us to Trilion, the shock attack of the skrill on the town is over before we get there. Our task consists mostly of plowing through fried snake guts, reassuring terrified townspeople, and putting out the last of the fires.

It's another four hours before we finally make it to the First House, but despite the fact that it's the middle of the night by now, none of us are destined for bed anytime soon. Instead, Miriam and Dolor, and the lumpy councilor—whose name I've finally learned is Balric—stand in the center of the formal receiving chambers of Lord Protector Fortiss, their faces streaked with soot and sweat, their shoulders drooping.

Filling in the space behind them are representatives of eight of the biggest houses—those who can stand, anyway. The rest of the lords and their soldiers remain under heavy guard in Trilion, too sick to be moved even to the privacy of the First House. Between the newly arrived houses and Tennet, Fortiss, and Lemille, only the Eleventh and Eighth Houses aren't represented.

"The house lords were targeted," Fortiss says, more to himself than to the group as he continues to process the newest intelligence Miriam has shared. "They didn't come here to mutiny...they came because they were summoned. Because they thought I summoned them. And then..."

"And then we were attacked." The Fourth House lord stands with his thumbs tucked into his belt, but only because he's apparently grown weary of standing with his arms crossed heavily over his barrel chest. "No matter how many times you ask for this accounting, Lord Protector Fortiss, it's not going to change. That abomination of snakes blasted into Trilion with a sole focus—the Inn of Levengers. It's where most of the lords were housed, where I should've been as well, but I have friends in Trilion, and never enough time to break bread with them. I was in an ale house that should've closed down long since—but stayed open out of deference to the friendship I proclaimed—not a hundred paces away from Levengers when the swarm hit. We gaped like village idiots as the snakes rolled up the street, ignoring us completely though there were plenty of souls within. Instead, the lot of them hit the inn. There had to have been a thousand of them, all told. From as short as your thumb to as long as your leg. All of them with wings and pointy teeth and dripping with corrosive oil. Your councilors had the right of it to set them on fire. If those things had kept going..."

I glance at Fortiss. He meets my gaze, and for a breath, we're just two warriors on the edge of understanding. The world is shifting under our feet, but in this moment...we're shifting together.

I blow out a steadying breath. By the time we arrived in Trilion, the Levengers Inn had flames leaping from every window, and smoke pouring out the front door. Villagers had swarmed out to drench the buildings and grounds surrounding the inn with water and sand, but the fire that had so appeared to consume the property didn't burn like any ordinary flame. It seemed constrained to the snakes themselves, a spectral blaze that left little more than a streaky, oily stain on the walls and fixtures of the inn.

It'd be a blighted struggle to clean that mess, but at least the inn itself still stood. The burnt snake carcasses were being hauled to huge piles outside the town, and very few people had been directly attacked—only the lords and their warrior knights who hadn't managed to barricade themselves safely away. Those unfortunates, however, were still lost in a thrall of pain and horror.

"You knew what they were," Fortiss says, turning from me to eye the councilors directly. "You knew what they were, and you knew how to kill them. You didn't think to *warn* me of this threat?"

"The threats from the Western Realms are a matter of ancient history, embroidered several times over," Miriam protests, her voice as gray as her skin. "We had no way of knowing that those threats would be summoned up again, and we had no reason to fear that they might come at us unprovoked, especially with Rihad safely imprisoned. To most of the current residents of Trilion, the idea of a monster made of snakes is nothing more than a bedtime story meant to scare children into staying in their rooms at night."

"The skrill," humphs a man dressed in Third house blue, Lord Alaric. "We know those stories well, but anywhere east of the Eighth, they're just stories."

Miriam nods. "No one would have taken it as a credible threat. Besides that, though we knew what the creatures were that bore down on the inn, we didn't at first know their target, and we still don't know why they came. Or how they knew to split apart and distract you and your Divhs from coming to the town's rescue right away."

"Not that Divhs could have stopped that horde anyhow," the Sixth House lord huffs, a tall, hard man as pale as ash. He'd managed to bar himself into his room, shuttering the windows and fending off the few thin snakes that had breached his stronghold with both shield and sword. "These things are too small for Divhs to fight. Too small and too fast. We have no defense against enemies like this."

I consider raising the idea of the weevishes I'd helped train... was that just this morning? But before I can speak, Fortiss interjects. "You say that, and to be sure—we have several good men down. But once our councilors understood what they were, they were able to neutralize them."

Fortiss swings to face them again. "Why did you choose fire to attack them? I mean, that's such a specific weapon, and to unleash it inside a holding, inside a village, you had to know it would work."

I don't miss his rapid repositioning of his original question. Nobody in Trilion, certainly not the lords in the midst of being attacked, would have raised their eyes toward the coliseum to see the attack going on there, the bursts of fire from Ayne's jaws. The few lords who are still standing, the Fourth, the Sixth, and the Ninth, aren't paying any attention to Tennet. He isn't encouraging their notice, either, and his skin is still far too waxy, his eyes dull.

I frown. His eyes are far *too* dull. There's more than exhaustion at work here.

"What is the poison that these things drip from their bodies?" I ask sharply, drawing the attention of the councilors. "We've got four lords laid out on their beds, tended by our best healers, but what have they been poisoned with? How deadly is this toxin?"

Miriam sighs. "It's closest to solana weed poisoning. As to its danger, five hundred years ago, my answer would have been different. When the Imperium first claimed the Protectorate for its own, the toxin was unknown to us. Our warriors who fell to it weren't poisoned intentionally but came upon the plant in their foraging. Back then, the smallest taste could be deadly, but those who survived that first exposure proved to be hardiest in the fight against the skrill. The connection wasn't lost on the founders of the Protectorate."

Caleb huffs from his spot in the corner. "They made it into a medicine?"

"After a fashion. The earliest leaders of the Protectorate weren't willing to let such a common plant destroy us—and the threat of the skrill was ever-present in those early days. Children were given the herb in small doses, and over the generations, we developed a tolerance to its poison. But that's only effective in the case of chance exposure—and the toxin isn't an exact match, especially after so many centuries. With what these men were subjected to, the snakes wrapped around exposed skin, hissing and spitting, there's no way of knowing. Worse, there's no way to counteract the poison once it takes hold. The men who have been exposed will follow a similar pattern, if they mimic the victims from the early days of the Protectorate. They will rave, then they will sleep, and then, after a period of hours or days, they will wake up again...or maybe they will not. If they do wake, they'll never fall victim to solana again. It's a poison with limited efficacy except for as a surprise."

"And the villagers?" Nazar asks as I swivel away from my position and move through the group, heading for Tennet. He's been nothing but a thorn in my side since he first opened his mouth, but he fought fiercely and well. And there's something about the way he's swaying slightly on his feet that sets my teeth on edge. *What's wrong with him?* "There were enough still awake and milling around when the attack happened, even if they weren't targeted. It only takes a few voices to build to a roar of fear and outrage."

"Yes, what of the villagers, Miriam?" Fortiss's tone is sharp enough that it distracts me from my quarry, but only momentarily. Still, I glance over to see a surprising flush skate across the cheeks of the normally stoic councilor. "You seem to be particularly skilled at managing their concern."

"Lord Protector," she begins with a placating tone that Fortiss quickly shuts down.

"No. I know what you're going to say, and I know the intention behind the words. We are in crisis, councilor Miriam. The men in this room are now a part of an ever-smaller cohort of warriors who can command Divhs of great stature. How many do we have in the Protectorate now? Twenty? Thirty? Losing five as we have tonight makes a difference. Even if they recover swiftly, I can't use them in battle. When you have such a small army to level against an unknown threat, we don't have the luxury of secrets. From this point forward, the rules that you followed under Lord Protector Rihad are no longer merely dangerous, they're treasonous."

A startled gasp rises up from the councilors and maybe one or two soldiers, but none of the lords flinch. "And no, I know that's not your intention," Fortiss continues, "but I need you to understand what *my* intention is. And that is to save the Protectorate from the enemy that Lord Rihad has invited onto our doorstep. He's made the call and it, whatever in the blighted path *it* is, has answered. I thank the Light that you were there to stop today's attack and keep as many warriors in the fight...but who else will be targeted, and where? And if we bring them together here to take up arms in Trilion, will their houses be at risk?"

No matter how much I want to just watch him command the room, Fortiss's words fade into the background as I reach Tennet. I sidle up beside him to the left, my hand slipping under his elbow as he sways again.

"This isn't just sickness from your flight on Ayne, is it?" I whisper as he swings his head toward me, his gaze not quite fixing on me as his jaw tenses.

"I'm *not* injured," he mutters between clenched teeth. "And don't think I don't see what Fortiss is trying to do up there. He's attempting to talk himself into not using the lords of the houses in this fight. *Protecting* them, in some way. That's not acceptable. The Protectorate is ours to defend as much as it's his—lest he forget, he's a house lord, too."

"Sure he is—there you go. That's good, stay upright." I shift my stance wider so I can take more of his weight. I'm not surprised when Caleb steps up to the other side of Tennet. The two of us lock eyes as Tennet lists again, and Caleb wraps his right arm around Tennet's waist as I grip Tennet's right forearm, forcing him to look at me. "Tennet, where are your rooms? Where did they put you and your men?"

"He can't—he can't keep us from defending our land. Our people. He..."

"There you go." With Caleb's help, I muscle Tennet out of the chamber and into the hallway. Caleb grunts as Tennet swoons, and one of the two guards at the door steps up smartly, looking briefly to me. At my nod of assent, he bends down and tucks his shoulder into Tennet's gut, lifting him over one shoulder. The guard staggers a little, then he stands tall.

"He's out," Caleb says, also bent nearly double to get a look at Tennet's face. "I have no idea where Fortiss stashed him and his men, but—"

"We'll take him to Nazar's chambers." I direct the guards, and Caleb and I follow close behind. Nazar's still back in the great hall with Fortiss, but there won't be much he can do with Tennet anyway until he wakes up.

Once we reach Nazar's rooms, the guard deposits Tennet on a low couch near a window, the view looking out over the vast plain. Caleb busies himself at the hearth, stoking the fire there to a cheerier glow. The moon has tucked itself behind clouds now, and with the fire leaping again, there's nothing much to see outside.

"He *can't*..." Tennet's low moan jerks my attention back down, and I drop to a crouch beside the bed, physically pushing him down as he tries to rise. Worse, his pallor has given way to a low, rosy flush, and when I move my hand to his cheek, I grimace.

"He's too hot. Get water or something."

"On it." Caleb darts away but doesn't leave the room—instead, he moves deeper into Nazar's personal sleeping room, where the man doubtless has some provisions stashed. I certainly do in my own chambers.

Meanwhile, I loosen the collar of Tennet's tunic, setting my jaw as I see his skin is an even darker red beneath his clothes, as if there's a fire burning away at him from within. I move to his belt and unsling it, but the tunic is all in one piece, and Tennet's as heavy as an ox. "Caleb, come on!"

"Coming!" Caleb rushes out of Nazar's room again and skids to a stop beside me, stowing the large flagon of—something—next to where Tennet's lying on the couch. "What in the blighted path happened to him? The others didn't look like this, did they?"

"Who knows what they look like now? Help me get this thing off him." Given that Caleb has only one arm, we both tug Tennet into a seated position again, then throw his weight on Caleb while I yank at the man's tunic, peeling it up his back and over his head and shoulders. "If he was truly injured, we would've had to cut it off," I grunt as I finally pull the garment free. I scowl down at it. "Not great for a towel, either. And I don't know how much poison got on this."

"Blood and *stone*." Caleb pushes Tennet back onto the cushions then turns to me all in one motion, ripping the tunic out of my hands and tossing it halfway across the room. "I didn't think about poison. Don't move." He races back into Nazar's bedchamber and emerges moments later with an armful of towels. Throwing the pile down next to the flagon, he grabs the topmost one and dunks it in the water, then thrusts it at me. "Clean off. I don't want to have to deal with two fainting warriors if I don't have to."

I dutifully wipe down my hands and, for good measure, the front of my tunic while Caleb ministers to Tennet, who's at least done us the favor of passing out again. But as Caleb shifts back for more water, I sweep a hard glance over Tennet's bared chest. The skin is as pristine as Fortiss's—smooth and unscarred, but that angry red blotch at his neck...

In my mind's eye, I see him crouched over the neck of his Divh, streaking through the sky toward the roiling mass of snakes. "His back," I blurt. "They got to his back."

Not wasting anymore time, I thrust my hands under Tennet's armpits and haul him toward me. Once again, I'm reminded at how unreasonably heavy the man is, and before I can stabilize myself, the crushing weight of him comes down on me, and we both crash to the floor.

"Blighted *Dark*," Caleb curses. "Don't move!"

To my shock, I hear the slide of steel on level as Caleb rips his knife free from his belt, and Tennet jerks above me a moment later. I clasp the man to me hard as Caleb slashes down, my stomach roiling as a high-pitched, unearthly chitter fills the room. Caleb continues his cursing as he half stumbles, half throws himself across the chamber toward the fire, and the leap of the flame in the grate puts out the nattering squeak for good. "Stone and blood, blood and stone, blight and blast..." He sucks in a deep breath and thuds back, picking up another towel, dunking it, and pressing it into Tennet's back—nearly crushing me in the process.

"Did you see that, Talia? How did you *know*? Blighted stone and bloody dark..." Caleb throws down the first towel beside my head and grabs a second one, and I twist my neck enough to see the heavy crimson stain and char marring the cloth.

"Mmf," I manage. "Get me...mmf."

"*Light*," Caleb blurts, suddenly refocusing on me. "Talia, sorry —let me—"

But even as he drops his towel and lurches for us, the pressure on my chest eases, Tennet lifting up just enough to stare down at me with wild blue eyes.

"You!" he blurts, the heat of his body increasing a hundred-fold with that one word. His mouth twists grotesquely, and words spew out of him like fire. "The Light burns to and through you, lighting the paths between the worlds from talonstone to grounding stone. What is dead is now awakened. You who wear the winged crown, fire and ash will be your legacy, and shadow yours to command. For you are warrior and you are death—"

"*Tennet!*" I scream, loud enough that my own ears ring. He shakes himself, hard, and his eyes slowly clear. He blinks as he stares down at me, and I see that for the moment, at least, he's back among the living.

He grins at me, his body still an immovable weight pinning me down. "Well, it didn't take long for me to get you on your back, I see."

Clearly, what's left of that life will be short and painful.

CHAPTER 15

"Get *off* me, you ox." I shove at him, and he moves willingly enough, though his face drains of color just enough for me to realize he's still hurt. I grimace and force myself not to grab him close to me again. Not because I want him—definitely not that—but in that fevered moment, he isn't just a warrior undone...he's something softer, something real.

He's a fellow warrior in a fight we barely understand.

"Here you go. I've got you." Caleb is there, of course, because Caleb is always there. He flattens his right arm against Tennet's back, bracing him as Tennet struggles to a standing position then collapses down onto the low couch. I scramble up as well, circling Tennet until I get a decent view of his back.

"What in—how did this happen? When? You had one of those things *attached* to you?"

Tennet leans his elbows heavily on his knees, his head still down. I can't tell whether he's about to pass out or throw up, but I almost miss the short-lived energy that fueled his smirk a few moments ago. "It caught on my clothes and burrowed beneath my tunic. I thought I'd pulled it out, but apparently there was more than one. There was enough going on that I didn't notice it, and then I just—I didn't feel it anymore."

I grimace as I survey the long, ugly slash of skin, the edges still puckered and charred. It strikes me that for all his arrogance, Tennet never thought to stop to check for wounds. I suspect he pushes forward, always. Maybe it's pride. Maybe it's something lonelier—like he's not used to anyone caring enough to stop.

Shaking myself back to the moment, I glance at Caleb. "It was under his skin?"

"It wasn't moving much, but it was trying to, still." Caleb nods, and I note that his eyes have gone a little glassy too. "Fortunately, it wasn't dug in deep. Once I sliced into his back, I could pull the whole thing out by the middle."

"Blighted Dark," mutters Tennet. He tries to straighten, but the result is a little more than a shrug. "Is this what's happened to the others?"

"No."

I turn sharply as Nazar strides into the room, Miriam and the other two councilors hard on his heels. Miriam mutters a curse as soon as she sees Tennet doubled over. She stalks across the room, then exhales in a small gasp when she sees the wreckage of his back.

"I tossed it in the fire," Caleb says before she can say anything. "If I was supposed to keep ahold of the thing, I'm sorry. I didn't know."

"No—no," Miriam says. She rubs a hand over her face, seeming genuinely stunned. "Has he said anything out of the ordinary? Anything at all?"

"He's not real talkative right now." I wave at her impatiently, in no mood to relive Tennet's ravings right this moment. "Are the rest of the house lords this injured?"

"None of the other lords endured one of the creatures for this long. The skrill were weak, depleted from their journey, I expect, and died quickly. Had they encountered us at the border, they would have been far more deadly, but they traveled a great distance to get here, so—"

No, they didn't. I jolt with the realization, but I know I'm right.

And because I'm right, the entire Protectorate is in so much more danger than we realized, and the battle we're about to face is coming far more quickly than we had any idea.

Rihad had planned his betrayal of the Protectorate far better than any of us had given him credit for.

"Caleb—get Fortiss," I say quietly. "Bring him here, alone. He needs to be in this conversation."

He nods. "What of the other house lords, if there are any with him?"

"Not them, not yet." The plan that's forming in my mind is the attack of a warrior against a many-headed serpent, particularly apt in this case. But I need Fortiss to advance it, not me. And only a few warriors will be right for this task. Other than Fortiss, they're all in this room already. "Have him put my father in charge of them, to give him something to do too. I don't want him here."

Caleb grins at me, makes a fist to tap at his heart, then heads out.

I meet Nazar's gaze next, then turn to Miriam. "What are Lord Tennet's prospects?" I ask as I gesture to his hunched-over form. I can practically feel the tension radiating off him—not pain, I don't think, but a profound feeling of wrongness that he's doing all he can to stamp down. "Is he going to just stay curled up and moaning for the rest of time or is he going to recover anytime soon?"

"I'm right here, you know," Tennet grits out, managing to twist his head enough to glare up at me. The pallor of his face has definitely lessened, but I can barely keep from skipping my gaze away from his to focus on the angry rupture along his back, still seeping blood and gore.

I gesture Miriam toward him, and she steps forward, dipping into her satchel for a pouch of herbs. "I'll need two bowls and more towels," she announces. Nazar nods and turns toward his inner chambers while Miriam scowls down at Tennet. "He should be isolated and given time to rest."

"No," I interrupt her before Tennet can protest. "He's not

leaving this room until he can travel without swooning. You'll clean him up in this room and seal that wound, and then you'll tell us what we need to do to keep it from re-opening. You'll also explain whatever you know about those creatures that tried to burrow inside him."

She doesn't miss the edge in my voice, and she peers up at me as Nazar places two shallow bowls beside her.

"He did say something to you," she says quietly as she pours some of her herbal concoction into the water, then soaks a towel in the water before turning to Tennet, her quiet, even voice continuing over Tennet's hiss as she peels away the bloodied cloth from his back and sets it aside. The edges of Tennet's wound are charred, but there are no telltale angry, red claws that spike out from it, indicating a body at war with itself. That's at least a blessing. "Did you understand it? Did anyone else hear it?"

"I don't—remember speaking at all until Talia shouted at me," Tennet says through gritted teeth. "I didn't realize she was even trapped beneath me until then."

"Caleb was here, but I don't think he heard anything clearly. His words were gibberish to me," I lie. For whatever reason, I don't want to share what Tennet said. Not with Miriam...not with anyone. Not yet. "Foreign words I couldn't understand. I thought he was overcome with pain. He's earned that, certainly."

"Yes." Without warning him, she lifts the sodden towels from the bowl and presses it into Tennet's back. He lurches forward with a shout of shock and rage, and I drop to my knees and attempt to keep him from crashing to the floor again. My swipe for his forearms miss, but his large hands clamp over my shoulders, the fingers digging into my muscles. His face, contorted with pain, is only inches away from mine, his lips peeled back from his teeth and his eyes once again wild with this now-familiar frenzy.

"The path of shadows lights for you, the dead await the unwary," he seethes. "The crown of wings—"

"I've got you, Tennet," I soothe over his moans, but his eyes don't shift away from me. He clutches me like a man hanging from the edge of a cliff, and I'm grateful for the reinforced shoulders of my tunic. The design may have been intended to give me a bulkier, sturdier silhouette, but it's the only thing keeping me from being bruised for a week from Tennet's punishing grip.

"Keep him talking." Miriam speaks to me as if she's talking from a great distance, her words a slurry breeze on the edge of a lightning storm. "His words may eventually make sense to you, and you can speak them to us. It's important, Lady Talia. The sight he has is only temporary, a shared memory with the creatures who attacked him. There are stories about this, conjectures, but they're all consistent on this point. It won't last."

I offer the crazed Tennet a reassuring smile as I realize Miriam is preparing a second wet heap of towels, pouring even more of the concoction into the bowl and soaking the thick cloth. My nimble mind leaps ahead to what surely must come, and I manage not to shriek when she rips away the first application of toweling and what sounds like a layer of Tennet's skin as well, and then, almost in one motion, plasters a new poultice over his back.

"The promise has been fulfilled! The covenant made!" Tennet roars in new pain at this attack, yanking me toward him so that our faces are but an inch apart. "Grounding stones will guide us through the lighted horror of this plane, the barriers at the eastern mountains the only door we face. But first we feast, building an army of shadows to do the Sahktar's bidding." He leans into me, fairly keening in pain, his eyes like pinwheels. I have a vague sense of Miriam turning to Nazar, who now stands beside the fire, drawing out—something. Not a poker, but—

Tennet's choked voice drops into a guttural purr, so vile I can't help but focus on him again. "The promise has been fulfilled, the blood price paid. It is complete. The covenant has been made, and you cannot unmake it."

"I can absolutely unmake it," I respond almost cheerfully. "I'll follow your trail, to and through the shadows, and drive a stake through the Sahktar's heart." Whatever the Light Sahktar is.

"You cannot!" he insists, and his breath is hot and desperate on my face. His brow is wet with sweat again, dark-brown hair hanging over his eyes in soaked curls. It's as if a bonfire has been lit within him, boiling his blood. "Sword and shield, mud and magic, blighted Light and beloved darkness. Blood rules all, though. Blood has always ruled. Blood and blessed dark shall spread across the land and flow all the way to the heart of the infidels. Blood will rule. Blood must—aigh!"

Moving all in one action, Miriam peels off the towels and comes back not with another round of soaked cloth, but a long flat blade fresh from the fire that she presses against Tennet's back. He goes rigid with shock, and I brace myself for another torrent of babbling nonsense. But though he opens his mouth to speak, he only manages a ragged breath.

"Lord Tennet!" Fortiss's voice explodes in a horrified shout from across the room, and Tennet swings his gaze that way. I don't know if he recognizes the lord protector, or if he even understands where he is or what's going on at this point. Tennet is a man who's been pushed far past his limits, limits he likely never expected to be tested so thoroughly in such a short period of time. And he also has the poison of the Western Realms snaking through him.

I shift beneath his brutal grip, then flinch as he swings his head back toward me. I'm ready for a new round of vitriol, praying I'll remember all of it. If it actually turned out to mean something, I'd listen to Tennet ramble for the next week straight.

But Tennet only exhales sharply when our gazes connect again, and I realize his eyes are no longer spinning pinwheels of chaos. Instead, they've flashed back to stormy blue depths that stare at me with perfect clarity.

Well, not entirely perfect. In barely a blink, his whole face seems to soften, his lips part, his eyes bore into mine as if I am the answer to every prayer he ever longed for in the depths of his heart and soul.

"Lady Talia," he half-moans, the words caught somewhere between a caress and a benediction. His voice shouldn't affect me, but it does. There's something in it—reverent, searching—that makes my breath hitch before I can catch it. He says my name like it matters. Like I matter.

Then he tips forward in a tumbling collapse. For the second time tonight, I face the prospect of being flattened by this infuriatingly half-naked man.

Only this time, Tennet pauses at the last moment, stopping his forward motion as our faces barely touch—

And his lips come down on mine.

CHAPTER 16

This time, I'm faster.

No sooner do I taste the barest hint of Tennet's coppery-salt kiss than I pivot away, which *should* result in him pitching forward to the floor.

It doesn't, which proves my instant suspicion that Miriam's brutal healing practices did exactly what they were supposed to do, and Tennet is back to his usual, irritating self. I smirk in satisfaction—but keep the expression buried, since I regain my feet under Fortiss's stormy gaze. Tennet also hauls himself upright, taking the tunic Nazar hands him but making no move to put it on.

"I have never looked so forward to a report," Fortiss says dryly, but Miriam is already on her feet, saving me from having to speak. I blow out a tight breath as I focus on her. Even as she begins to speak, the taste of Tennet's lips lingers—copper and something darker—and though I pull away, something inside me flickers like struck flint. I shouldn't want the taste of him, by the Light. I don't want it.

I don't.

"I think you'll find this report very instructive, Lord Protector Fortiss," Miriam announces crisply. "Lord Tennet, perhaps without fully realizing it, sustained a personal attack from the skrill, much

131

like Balthazar of the Second House and Grennel of the Seventh. Unlike them, he didn't receive attention for his wounds right away. Whether sustained by his racing heart or his close connection with his Divh, he didn't begin to feel the effects until this past quarter hour. Lady Talia removed him from your receiving room when she noticed he was failing, but she and warrior Caleb were startled to see he was still carrying one of the skrill on his person."

"Carrying it?" Fortiss's grimace betrays his horror. "Carrying it how?"

"In my back," Tennet supplies. He turns and presents his newly seared skin to Fortiss, and I have to admit, it's an impressive sight. Caleb's long downward slash hooks to the left, but the skin is fully sealed now, the imprint of a flat blade coming to a tip just below Tennet's neck, between his shoulder blades.

It's not just the scar that grabs me. It's the curve of muscle, the way the torchlight glances off Tennet's skin. And for one reckless moment, I remember the heat of his body pinning mine to the floor—and the weight of that kiss I didn't see coming.

Focus, I implore myself, all too aware of Fortiss's keen attention on me.

"When I first encountered the creatures, they were clustered together in a tight ball," Tennet says. "Ayne burst through them, and several tried to attack me directly. Most of them I flung off, but a few apparently took refuge beneath the collar of my tunic. I thought there was only one and when I wrenched it free, and felt nothing else, I turned my attention outward again. I honestly didn't think of it again until Lady Talia and Caleb discovered it. It didn't cause me any pain, not after the first shock. I didn't know it was there."

He says these last words to Miriam, and she nods. "That part at least is consistent with the attacks on the House lords. Once the initial puncture is made, the poison serves as a sedative, calming the victim and limiting any inflammation at the point of the wound. You saw this as well, Lord Protector."

"I saw bite wounds that weren't inflamed, not an entire creature buried in someone's *back*," Fortiss corrected. "Are you saying that if we hadn't gotten to the House lords in time, if you and the others were not already there, this would have happened to them? Some of those skrill were small. No bigger than the size of a hand. Would they even have noticed?"

Tennet grimaces. "I noticed that I didn't feel well, I just didn't know why. And I had no memory or even reason to think that it might be one of these what did you call them? Skrill? Attaching to me."

"And now?"

He crosses his arms more tightly across his body, then spreads his arms wide. "I feel like I have an old wound down my back. It hurts, but it doesn't hurt as much as I think it should, considering the fact that councilor Miriam branded me with a flat blade."

He glances at her. "Is this more of that sedative effect from the poison? If so, this skrill poison could be useful—assuming it doesn't eventually kill me."

"We haven't had a live specimen of skrill to study, and we still don't," she says pointedly.

"That's not my fault," Caleb protests, gesturing wildly with his right hand. "That thing was buried inside Lord Tennet's back. It was still alive when we pulled it out and writhing around like mad. I didn't think we were going to want to keep it as a pet."

"No, you were quite right in killing it," she agrees, waving off his dismay. "These things are too dangerous to cultivate, especially when we don't yet have an understanding of how we may trap them alive without exposing ourselves to danger. Nevertheless, if we do manage to keep one of them alive for long enough to harvest their poison—"

"You think there's going to be more of them, more attacks? Is that what we're looking at now?" Fortiss asks.

The words pound in my head so violently, there's no way I can't say them aloud. "Grounding stones," I blurt out, and everyone in the room turns to me. I lift my hands as if to ward them off. "Did none of the rest of you hear what he was saying? He was loud, and he wouldn't shut up. He also mentioned a formal name—Sahktar, I think."

"I couldn't make out a word of it," Caleb says. "I mean yes, I could hear him muttering at you, but it sounded like gibberish. You were closer, councilor Miriam. Could you make any of it out?"

"To me, I didn't even hear words, just harsh and guttural breathing, the sound of a man trying to overcome his pain. But I don't possess a band, I am not connected to the Divhs. I don't know their language."

I make a face. "You can't tell me that those snakes were Divhs. Divhs don't ravage the Protectorate without a warrior to guide them. They don't simply drop into our land unasked."

"Who says they weren't summoned?" she counters. "Lord Rihad hasn't regained consciousness since he fell on the battlefield fully a month ago, but his body isn't deteriorating. He doesn't eat, doesn't drink, and he makes no waste, and yet his skin is warm and dry to the touch his breathing is easy. Something is sustaining him, and if he could be sustained, he arguably could summon a Divh to do his bidding."

"Then you should kill him," Tennet says flatly. "There's no other possibility. That thing that he summoned, if he summoned it, attacked the lords of the Protectorate, incapacitated them."

"And they tried to eat your spine," Caleb points out.

"And that," Tennet agrees with a grimace. "And apparently had me speaking in tongues, with only Lady Talia able to interpret. I certainly didn't know what I was saying, I was simply reacting to councilor Miriam here attempting to heal me."

"Not just attempting," she comments drily, but her gaze is on me. "Can you remember anything else he said?"

"I can't," I say with what I think is a credible grimace. "Just pieces of it, but one of them was grounding stones. As I received that information, I received the image of small, colorful curved stones buried in a cornerstone of some enormous structure, which I took to mean one of the great houses of the Protectorate. It's a beacon, I think. A beacon that any skrill can use to light its way. If those grounding stones have been placed at the great houses throughout the Protectorate every time Rihad ventured out—or if they were always there, somehow—and if the skrill are now on the loose and can use them as guides, it's just a matter of time before they attack the lords and their houses. They have to be ready for it."

"We handled it here, and with very short notice. They burned and self-consumed in that fire, and it was ordinary flame, right?"

"It did the trick here," Caleb agrees. "Unless Nazar has put something in his fireplace that he hasn't told us."

Nazar doesn't answer, but Miriam shakes her head. "No. Simple fire destroys them, and a poultice of sage and oleander draws out the poison from the skin, allowing it to heal." She cocks an interested glance at Tennet. "I'll be curious to see when the pain returns to your back, or if you experience any other reactions given how long you carried the creature with you."

"I'll be fine," he says gruffly. "If the pain that comes is strictly that of healing skin, that won't be anything new."

"But which houses have these stones?" Caleb asks, though no one has an answer to that, of course. "And was it only Lord Rihad who carried these things? He had bards in his employ, and no one would notice if one of them dropped a pretty rock out of his bag and snugged it up against a cornerstone. The bards all fled the First House after Rihad's fall, supposedly to take the story far and wide. We'll never be able to warn them in time—and what are we supposed to warn them about? A random curved rock that looks out of place?"

My lips twist in dismay. "That's only part of the problem. Something is sending these creatures out, something tied to the threat that lies beyond the western borders. These skrill, I assume, are part of that history?"

Miriam nods. "There's very little left in the libraries about the history of the Western Realms, but Rihad could only control the information in the First House. We will need to travel to the Western Realms in order to understand this history fully. They will have records, I suspect. Records they preserved regardless of Rihad's demands. Any attempt he would have made to destroy a given book, they simply would have complied with after making additional copies—and they never would have revealed everything to him, even if they trusted him. Which, knowing Lord Daggar... they probably didn't."

"So, we need to go there," Tennet says.

"We need to go there regardless," Fortiss agrees. "That's where the threat is coming from."

"Maybe it is, maybe it isn't," I counter, and everyone's attention flows to me. "If these things *are* Divhs, how did they get here without a summons? Which then begs the question, how did we meet the Divhs in the first place? What specifically happened to incite that first contract between man and monster?"

"I mean, everyone knows that," Caleb protests, going on to recite the history lesson at rapid speed. "The Imperial army entered these lands and conquered everyone in their wake, all the way to the far western range of the Meridians. There they encountered an enemy so vile, they knew they must not only block it from entering these lands, but that it was necessary to protect all the Imperium from it as well. But they couldn't fight it alone. They exhorted the Light, and the Light delivered the Divhs. A great battle was fought and we won."

He executes a short bow. "Literally, they teach that story to babies less than a week out of the womb."

I turn to Nazar. "Is that the way they teach it in the capital city?"

He inclines his head to me, the master who at last can acknowledge that his student has learned the lessons he came to teach. "It is what I was taught when I was a child. What I knew to be the truth up until the unbanding of the Divhs and their warriors. From that point forward, the story shifted. In the new version, the might of the Imperium was all that was required to keep our lands safe. The army read from ancient texts to conjure up great beasts of power, but those beasts were little more than distracting illusions. It was the army that fought back the enemy. The army that kept us safe and whole."

"That's what they're saying now?" Caleb asks, aghast. "But the Divhs are *real*. We have a tournament every year. They can come and see them for themselves!"

"They could, yet how many of them do?" Nazar turns to Tennet. "While I was priest of the Tenth House, I can say with certainty that the souls who crossed into the Protectorate were mostly marauders and villains, men who were too busy running from the justice of the Imperium to pay much mind to old stories about protector monsters. Those that managed to survive long enough to make a home in the Protectorate weren't likely to carry tales back to the Imperium. What was your experience in the Twelfth House?"

"The same, though we drew even fewer marauders. The terrain surrounding our mountain holding is difficult and not favored with the same pass that the Tenth House guards. Our holding was placed there more as an afterthought, I suspect, an auxiliary outpost to lend aid when needed to the Tenth, or to serve as a contact point for the Imperium should the primary pass be compromised. Or that's how it has always been explained to me. But I understand your meaning, Priest Nazar. If there's no flow of idle travelers into the Protectorate, and certainly no flow out other than the delegations sent by Rihad himself, there would be no passage of information. And any delegations that he sent would have been carefully managed to ensure their message was consistent with what he wanted the Imperium to know."

I frown. "How frequently did Rihad send ambassadors back to the capital city?"

"Yearly," Fortiss says, and Miriam nods.

I glance over to Nazar, and he shrugs. "We received no guests of the lord protector in all the years that I have served as priest of the Tenth House. While he may have sent ambassadors to the Imperium prior to that time, and while of course these souls may have chosen not to divert to the Tenth House while going through the pass to the east, it seems far more likely that he sent out envoys who had no intention of completing their mission. They simply returned months later and shared no tales."

"So, we've effectively been cut off from the Imperium for decades?" Caleb protests. "Do we not provide tithing and reports to the Imperator, or...something? Do they have any idea what's happening within the Protectorate?"

"They do now," Fortiss says. "I sent out riders the day after the tournament melee. According to our maps, they would only just now be reaching Hakkir. It'll be another month and more before they return."

Caleb scoffs. "We could all be dead by then."

"Or we could be in possession of a power so strong that we could challenge the Imperium outright, commanding our battalions of Divhs and operating with an ally that could topple the Imperator from his throne," Fortiss says quietly. "That's what Rihad has set in motion, and that's what we have to stop—if it's not already too late."

"We can leave at daybreak," Tennet says. "I pledge my men and my horses. They are both made of sturdy stock."

"When we leave, it should be in the dark," I agree. "But not without another full day to prepare and to make sure you don't turn into a baby skrill, Lord Tennet. Besides all that, we'll be leaving both your men and the horses behind."

I wait until they're all looking at me, the drop my hands to my belt, tucking in my thumbs. "Where we're going...we won't need them."

CHAPTER 17

It's another two hours before we break up, and it takes Tennet nearly toppling over with fatigue before Fortiss is willing to let everyone go. He orders Nazar and Caleb to get as much sleep as possible before noon when the councilors will be returning in force with all of the information they've been able to scrape together on the Western Realms after Rihad's purge of the library.

But I can tell from how keyed up Fortiss is that he won't be sleeping any time soon.

"Walk with me?" he murmurs, and we fall into step together, threading our way back through the First House and to the great banquet chamber. I smile wearily to see it. While he entertained Tennet and his men in one of the smaller, more intimate dining halls, this great space was filled to bursting just a short while ago during the Tournament of Gold. Men and women—mostly men—chanting and cheering with genuine camaraderie and excitement for the battles to come.

My smile fades. How many of those men were now dead? Husbands, fathers, sons...brothers.

Fortiss is clearly thinking the same thing as he stalks through the shadowed room, past the empty tables and tidily tucked benches, heading for the far wall and its door into the caverns of the keep. Up until a short while ago, a dragon had been trapped in the bowels of this great fortress. Now, that dragon has been freed and the current prisoner residing beneath the First House is arguably far more dangerous.

"Should you be coming down here?" I ask Fortiss. "Can he sense your energy, even if he doesn't wake?"

"I don't care if he does. At every turn—especially after I think we can sink no further into the abyss of his betrayal—he surprises me still. Destroying the history of the Western Realms, the history of the Protectorate? Dropping homing beacons at the houses so that our enemies can find the location of our strongholds without even having to look? Lying to us about the dictates of the Imperium when year after year, he sent envoys that he never intended to breach our own borders, let alone journey all the way to the capital city? Is there no end to it? Are there yet more lies we have yet to uncover? Is he even near death like he appears, or is this shell, this husk of a man just an illusion meant to deceive us while he is off plotting our destruction?"

I shake my head. "I don't think he's off doing anything in a manner that he wants. Lord Rihad was nothing if not a proud man. Now he's a prisoner completely at our mercy. He wouldn't want that; I don't care how much he's plotting."

Fortiss grunts, then moves ahead of me in the narrow corridor, bypassing the stairs that lead down to where I'd first met his beautiful Divh. These stairs go to the holding cells, and barely a quarter of an hour later, we step out into the final passageway.

This corridor is lit up like full day. Two guards stand at the top of the corridor and two at the base next to Rihad's open door.

"Any movement?" Fortiss asks, and the guard shakes his head.

"He's resting comfortably, and he doesn't wake or speak in his sleep. The guards at the door continue to wear their ear protectors, but we've heard nothing this far up. The councilors who have come down to sit with him appear unaffected by him as well; their questions go unanswered, and he doesn't volunteer any direction or orders. They don't touch him, though." The guard gives a little smile. "That at least was an order that they had no problem following."

"Keep the watch," Fortiss says, lifting his fist to his heart, then extending his hand to clap the other man on his shoulder.

"Always," the guard agrees.

He repeats a similar greeting and brief touch with the guards at Rihad's door, and with this second display, I watch the connection more closely. The guard isn't surprised or awkward—he's used to the move, expects it. Welcomes it, even. In all the times I saw Rihad interact with his guards, had he ever so much as looked at them, let alone touched them?

We move into Rihad's room.

As prisons go, this one is more comfortable than most—certainly more comfortable than the cell where they had held me overnight, with my father seething in outrage and Rihad calculating how he could turn the situation of a woman combatant in the Tournament of Gold to his advantage. That night, Fortiss had realized who I truly was, and how I'd been deceiving him for weeks. I push those thoughts away as I focus on the man stretched out before us on a pallet heaped with blankets.

For a man who should be dead, Rihad doesn't stink. He doesn't even appear to be sleeping. Just...shrunken. Which is somehow worse.

The former lord protector is a tall man, lean and hard, his face dominated by harsh cheekbones and a knife blade of a nose. His eyes, sunken on the best of days, now are closed beneath their hooded lids, his mouth drawn into an expression of peace that I never saw on his face while he was among the living. There's no sound at all in the room save the rhythmic rise and fall of his chest, our only indication that he's still alive.

"He doesn't dream, I don't think," Fortiss says quietly. "I've never seen his eyes move or his lids flicker as if struggling to open. We've changed these bedclothes every other day, looking for any hint of blood or even sweat to indicate a fever, and there's nothing."

"And you found nothing in his books of magic to indicate how he might have done this? Because it's certainly not of the Light."

He snorts. "It's definitely not of the Light. Very little that Rihad did was. And yes, there are incantations to preserve life, to thrust a body into a sleep so deep that none may wake them so that they may heal. But nothing lasting this long. And nothing to indicate that the body would be so perfectly preserved the way it is here. For our purposes it serves, though. When the agents of the Imperium come, they can take him away as they see fit, order his execution, or demand that he remain our prisoner until his eventual death, natural or otherwise. It's a waste of time to guess what they may choose. So, until they arrive, we wait. But we don't wait idly."

"Mm." I don't sense that these words are for me alone, and who's to say if Rihad can actually hear us in his self-imposed stupor? But I blinked with surprise as Fortiss takes another step closer, then reaches into one of the pouches hanging at his belt. He extracts a slender set of shears and a square of white cloth. Quick as a handmaiden, he snips off a lock of Rihad's hair, and folds it into the cloth, then tucks it back into the pouch, dropping in the scissors. While he does this, I stare hard at Rihad. I don't understand what Fortiss is doing, but the dark wizard should.

Rihad makes no move, his breathing remaining steady and unconcerned.

Fortiss however isn't done. He leans forward, his face only a hand's breadth from Rihad's, and his expression changes. His jaw locks, his eyes flash, and a cold certainty seems to turn his skin to stone. "*Sahktar,*" he murmurs—

Rihad's breath stills in his throat.

I stare from him to Fortiss, but after another breath, a third, a fourth, Fortiss speaks again, only this word I cannot even attempt to make out. It serves what I suspect to be its intended purpose, however, as Rihad's body arches, his mouth falling open to draw in a harsh, full breath of air. After a shuddering exhale, the man returns to the steady rhythm of airflow once again.

Fortiss straightens, and when he turns to me, I'm struck by the difference in his expression. He grins at me, his eyes alight with purpose and intensity. "Got him."

He gestures me out the door, and we don't speak, not to each other anyway. He shares a few murmured words of thanks with the first set of guards, then the second, then we're out and on to the stairs again climbing swiftly. Within a few moments we've cleared the caverns and are back in the empty banquet hall, but when I expect him to lead us on, he stops and gestures me to a table.

"It's been a long day and when we finally rest, tomorrow will come too quickly. Have a drink with me?"

He moves off before I can respond to this, striding towards the kitchen where the great feasts were prepared for the warriors of the Tournament of Gold. I hear the scrape of stone, the rattling of dishes, and I smile to think of my own time in those kitchens, grabbing flagons of wine and ale while I was dressed as a servant girl, desperate to find the truth behind my brother's murder.

As I always do, I imagine the joy he would have had in seeing all the warriors gathered together, cheering and laughing and eating Rihad out of house and home. Merritt should have competed in the tournament, the feted son of the Tenth House. Instead, he died in a lonely vale outside the Shattered City, pierced through by an arrow shot from the bow of Rihad's assassin.

Why? What power could the creatures of the Western Realms have promised the lord protector such that he was willing to betray his house, his land, the Imperium itself? What promises had been made? What covenants?

"You're thinking about your brother."

I look up with a jolt, then blink as Fortiss lays down his impromptu meal. A flagon of wine, a loaf of crusty bread, a part of stewed fruit so aromatic it sets my stomach growling. I reached for the wine to cover the sound as Fortiss drops down next to me on the bench.

"Not just Merritt. All of them. So many warriors here, and more sons upon the road to Trilion—killed without a second thought for their families, their Divhs. More still tonight, where the darkness he summoned was targeting the fathers of those fallen warriors."

"None of them died," Fortiss points out. "From that perspective, the attack was a failure."

"It depends on the goal." I reached for the bread, the fruit, anything to keep my idle hands busy. "If Rihad had simply wanted to sow fear, or renew it, in the hearts of men who had not seen the worst he was capable of, he certainly succeeded there."

I glance at him. "What did you say back there, to Rihad? Do you know what that name meant? Sahk-whatever?"

"Sahktar," he says, munching around his own chunk of bread. "And—not at all. But when I said that name, Rihad definitely retreated into himself, blocked himself in. It took a spell of vitality to rouse him back to his normal state. If that's what normal passes as these days."

"If he could rouse himself completely, he would," I tell him again. "He's still damaged. There's no other explanation."

"Maybe," he agrees, taking a long drink of wine. I press my hands into the steady reassuring wood of the tabletop, willing my fingers to stop trembling

It's not just the troubling topic that accounts for my nerves, but sitting here alone with Fortiss, quiet in the night. In all the weeks since the Tournament of Gold, this hasn't happened. Whenever we've worked together, there's always been a councilor present, stacks of books and guards. Villagers with petitions or information to share, runners from the nearest houses with reports of support or fresh waves of criticism and concern. In all that time, we could have easily stepped away to have a quiet conversation, to share the simple connection that he so easily expresses with his guards and staff. But he didn't offer, and I didn't ask, and the days slipped into weeks. I focused on my training with Nazar, and he focused on stitching the Protectorate back together.

"What did Tennet say to you?" Fortiss finally asks.

I sigh, grateful for the question that had to come at some point. "They were warnings mostly. First that we would be attacked, secondly that I would be an agent of betrayal, but whether I was betraying the Protectorate, our Divhs, or the interests of whatever dark force sent the message, I don't know. It all ran together, almost like poetry, but with an edge that threw it all out of balance."

"I saw that Miriam brought you quill and paper after I summoned the other councilors. You wrote it down for her?"

"I wrote down two versions," I tell him honestly. I reach into my tunic and pull out a folded page. I offer it to him, but he gestures to the table, still eyeing me closely.

"You don't trust her."

"I don't trust anyone who was that tied up with Rihad, not yet. Do you?"

He sighs and shakes his head. "I don't even know if we can trust Tennet now that this thing's poison has mixed with his blood. It's bad enough that I've started sampling the magic from the Western Realms. I did so with protections in place. Tennet had no time to protect himself before that attack."

I frown, poking at the folded-up sheet as I try not to think about Tennet's eyes as he spoke those strange words to me. "I don't know that he was anything more than a channel. I don't think he knew what he was saying. It certainly wasn't in any cadence I'd ever heard him use up to that point, for all that I'd just met him hours before. He doesn't seem to recall anything that he said, let alone understand it. Right now, he's mostly concerned with not feeling like he's been flattened by a sandworm."

"I wonder how many other secrets the other houses are hiding. Surely the Tenth and Twelfth Houses are not the only ones who have hit on the idea of lying to save their sacred sons."

I snort. "Well, to be fair, we're more cut off than most of the houses. Most everyone else has reason to come to Trilion, to barter and buy, to share their stories and deepen their connections with the First House. Up in the mountains though, visitors are few and far between, and it's easier to sow the seeds of lies and nurture them into a protective hedge."

"He seems quite committed to the idea of honoring the contract struck between his father and yours."

The words are quiet, uninflected, but the tension sparks between us, coiling and dangerous. "A contract that I had no interest in or awareness of, other than to save the honor of my house," I retort. "I've found a different way to do that. So he can find another wife."

"He could find no one better."

I blink up at him, startled, and somehow, he's leaned even closer to me, his eyes flashing dark in the shadowed room, his lips soft as his mouth quirks into a smile. "He kissed you," he murmurs.

I make a face. "That was no kiss. He knew you were watching him. He just wanted to see your reaction."

"I think mine wasn't the only reaction he was interested in."

"Well, if you were paying any attention, I didn't kiss him back."

"I noticed that too." He's leaned even closer now, and there's no mistaking his intent. My heart surges in my throat, my fingers are pressing so hard into the tabletop there's no doubt they're gouging the wood, but I don't know what to do. I don't know how to be. "Why are you trembling, Talia?"

"I'm a liar. And once a liar—always one," I blurt out the childish maxim, and no one is more surprised than me at these words tumbling out of my mouth. "You need to know that. I thought you may have killed my brother, and I couldn't rest until I found who did. So, I lied to you. And I'll do it again, Fortiss." I swallow. "I'll lie if I feel I must. "

His gaze captures mine, and where Tennet's eyes had been hazed and wild, his are piercing and sure as they hold me fast. "You're not a liar, Talia. You were fighting a battle as one warrior against a legion of enemies. You are mighty and fierce."

He leans closer, his lips brushing against mine in a soft sweep with each new word. "Beautiful," he murmurs. "Strong."

Warmth spreads through me as he settles back again, and now his eyes take on a heat, an intensity that sends my heart into a nervous jitter. "You've become the person I trust more than anyone in my house who hasn't pledged his sword to me. You have stood by me, you brought me my Divh, and you helped me fight Rihad when I was still too blind to see the destruction he had set into motion. I owe you everything, Talia."

His lips twist into a self-deprecating grimace. "But all I want to do is this."

He leans toward me slowly—deliberately—but my heart is already galloping. I know what this is. I know what I want. But I also know what this costs.

Fortiss seems not to care. He lifts his hands to either side of my face and pulls me to him. I go willingly, bending my body to his, surrounding myself with his warmth, his steadiness, his strength. In his embrace I feel stronger, truer, and the fire that ignites deep in my belly is all the fiercer for having flared once, so briefly, only to be relegated to embers after that period now it threatens to roar between us—consuming me, consuming him—and I revel in the feeling. This is what I want, I think. What I need. This connection, this truth. This beating heart pounding so loudly against me that it is the only thing I can hear, even above my own rushing blood and rabbiting pulse.

Fortiss sighs, leaning into me. "Blighted Light and beloved darkness..."

The muttered words rip through my delirium, and I pull back with a sudden gasp, my eyes flaring wide. I've heard that line, of course. Once from a man half-dead and fevered, now from one who holds me like I'm everything. Why are they both saying this? Why now?

"What did you say?" I demand. "What was that?"

"What?" Fortiss blinks, his eyes unfocused. Then his gaze

suddenly narrows on mine. "What did I say? I didn't mean to speak."

"But you did." With a shaking hand, I snag the parchment page and push it toward him. He unfolds it now and smooths it out, and I stab the page with my finger. "That's the second time tonight I've heard those words, from two different people. Maybe the problem wasn't Tennet, Fortiss. Maybe it's me."

"No, Talia..." Fortiss shifts back to me, lifting his hands, and when I would pivot away much like I did with Tennet, he grabs me and pulls me to him again. He kisses me soundly, deeply. He kisses me like a drowning man clinging to breath, like he's afraid I'll vanish in his arms. That fear isn't just mine, I realize—it's his, too.

But when he pulls his head away, his eyes are swirling again, his breathing rushed. He looks like Tennet did, I realize with a jolt —his eyes, his expression.

"You will *never* be the problem, Talia," he murmurs. "Only the solution."

But as he draws me into a firm embrace, and I hear the frantic pounding of his heart once more, I'm not so sure he's right.

CHAPTER 18

"Y ou're out early."

The brusque voice startles me, and I look up to see Tennet leaning over the banister of the balcony as I trudge across the courtyard. The weevishes had demanded more training practice this morning, but at least I'd managed to usher them all into adolescence without getting covered in muck. Still, my back and shoulders are aching from wielding the heavy sword, and my lungs feel like they're filled with sand.

"It's easier to fight when no one's around." I squint up at him. There's something ridiculously galling—and faintly thrilling—about the way he lounges up there like he owns the view and everything beneath it. Including me. Which he absolutely does not. Obviously. "What's your excuse? You certainly don't need to train in hiding."

"That I don't. Join me. I'm all but recovered and officially bored."

He moves back from the banister, and I look from him to the stairs. Then his voice floats over the edge of the railing. "Oh, so now you're going to show fear?"

I roll my eyes, but I'm not so tired that I'm willing to cede this oaf even a false sense of superiority. I trudge up the stairs and down the side flank to the balcony, glad I don't have to try and shimmy up it a second time. I don't think I'd be able to accomplish it today.

By the time I cross the balcony to him, Tennet is sprawled in one of the carved chairs, his legs stretched out as if he's about to collapse into a nap. But there's nothing about him that's relaxed. He watches me through slitted eyes, his smile almost predatory. It's not the smile of a man in love, or even a man hoping to be liked. It's a challenge—feral and assessing. But my breath still catches in my throat for the barest second, and I smooth my expression so he won't see even that slight weakness.

He better not see it.

"You have to know your father offered you up to me again this morning."

I grunt as I drop into a chair across from him. "He doesn't have that right anymore. All that went away when I banded to Gent."

"Which he still considers illegal. And Rihad would've backed him up."

"Against tradition and illegal are two different things, especially when the laws that we're talking about were never codified. No—not once." I lift my hand when he would argue. "You think the councilors didn't look after it the moment they figured out what I truly was? First, they were angry because it shouldn't have been possible for a woman to band to a Divh, then they were angry because these so-called laws governing women's lack of rights in this matter don't exist. And believe me, I expected them to exist. Everyone did."

He leans forward and drops one elbow on a knee. "Even Fortiss?" he asks, the edge back in his voice.

"Especially Fortiss. He wasn't looking forward to his first act as lord protector to be an open rebellion against his leadership because he flaunted ancient law. But there was no law."

He stares at me like he's trying to unearth the truth straight from my bones, not just my words. And for a moment, I feel it again—that unbearable weight of fate between us. Of paths not chosen, of promises neither of us made but somehow are still expected to keep.

"I don't believe it." Tennet pushes himself to his feet and stalks across the balcony. The morning sun glints off the metal fastenings of his belt and his hilt as he turns back to me and gestures out over the courtyard, already abuzz with activity as the locals set up for market day. "It's too important and too well ingrained in our society for it not to exist—somewhere. Which means those laws *are* written down somewhere. Even if they've been altered beyond recognition, something must have existed originally. And don't think I care about you and your claim to the Divh. I've heard enough stories in the last day since I found you to believe your connection to your Divh is real and powerful. If I didn't want to believe it, I would have been convinced by your work with those sandworm weevishes."

My brows drift up as he paces. "So, you did see me fight?"

"I saw everything from the moment their mother arrived and blacked out the sun, scaring my men half to death," Tennet says grimly. "You can fight, Talia. And you clearly can connect to the Divhs."

"I sense there's a 'but' coming here," I put in, and he huffs out a hard laugh.

"There is. There's more to being a warrior than footwork and connecting. There's a society, a code of conduct—and there's men. Hundreds of them, maybe thousands if you count every foot soldier out there. It only takes one...maybe five in your case, but still, only five to attack you unawares. You're not safe on this course without protection, and you know it."

Equal parts rage and shame flow over me at his words, rage because he isn't completely wrong...and shame because I know he's not completely wrong. "I'm not going to marry you, Tennet, for my own *protection*," I inform him. "That contract no longer applies."

"The contract isn't the point," he snaps back. "You're putting yourself in unnecessary danger, Talia. You want to fight for the

Protectorate—for and with your Divh? You want to stand up and be a role model to other women? You can do all that and more. What you can't do is assume you can stand toe-to-toe with a group of men who've never been taught that a woman can be valued for anything more than coupling and motherhood—and maybe, if you're lucky—a helpmate in times of need. That's it. Until all these generations of beliefs are undone, they'll never let you stand as their equal, Talia. They may respect you, but they won't accept you."

"I don't need their acceptance—or yours," I inform him stiffly. I squint at the courtyard, the First House gates, the sun. Anything to keep from looking at him. "I just need them to stay out of my way."

"And I would clear that path for you." Tennet's words are unusually quiet, but they strike me with the force of a blow. I look back to see him regarding me with unnerving intensity.

"You don't even know me," I point out, but he shakes his head.

"I think I do. I think you're as hotheaded as your father and just as shortsighted. You want to make a difference, Talia? Then stop thinking so much about yourself. Think about those who'll come after you. What will be waiting for them if the one woman who was able to stand head and shoulders above the rest, who was able to bend a Divh to her will, win the Tournament of Gold and earn the right to wear the winged crown—what happens if she's killed by the first stupid, jealous idiot who sneaks up on her in the middle of the night? What will they have left to fight for if the first woman who could raise the standard for them squandered her chance?"

Twin snakes of anger and shame coil around my windpipe, threatening to cut off air. I haul myself out of my chair, muscles screaming with the effort, which only adds to my irritation. "Why is it everyone is so eager to tell me what I should be doing for the future, when none of you were willing to stand up for anyone but yourselves?"

"We're not the one challenging the system, Talia."

I dismiss that with a furious, cutting wave of my hand. "Well, maybe you should be. Maybe if more of you challenged the system, the rest of us wouldn't have to work so hard to be accepted just for *existing*."

Furious, I turn on my heel and stalk off, ignoring Tennet's sharp curse. First Nazar and Caleb want to tell me how to model right action for every woman in the Protectorate—now so does this stranger, whose only claim on me is a piece of paper drawn up by two men without a thought for my needs or concerns. I may as well be cattle.

A low, hooting yodel of concern echoes across the back of my mind, and I grimace, struggling to put my thoughts back into order, so as not to disturb my beautiful Divh. Gent, at least, has never strived to put me in my place. If anything, he's done nothing but encourage me to jump. More than that, I know he'll always be there to catch me if I fall.

It's good to know somebody will.

I stamp my way into the First House and down the long, cool corridors, not much caring where I go as long as it's somewhere no one else is. I slow as I realize I'm in the same hallway I was yesterday when Fortiss collared me...

Fortiss.

Why exactly was he on this level yesterday, so soon after he sent Tennet and my father to their rooms? He did a good job of distracting me then...that isn't going to work now.

I slow my steps and exhale a long breath, trying to retrace my path from yesterday. It was the third—no, the fourth door from the center line, I'm almost certain, not quite to the end...

I move along the corridor now with catlike steps, drifting my fingers along the wall until I reach a door that makes my skin prickle. Slowly, I drop my hand to the handle, pushing it down as quietly as possible.

The door swings open silently.

"I was wondering if you'd come looking for me. Lock the door, would you?"

Fortiss sits at the table at the far end of the room, the surface covered over with books and stacks of parchment pages, with open boxes all around him.

"Wait. Were all those books here yesterday?" I close the door behind me and turn the key in the lock. It clicks with a force that makes my hand jerk a little, and I yank my fingers away, turning back to Fortiss.

"It was, but I hadn't had the chance to crack into it." He smiles a little sheepishly. "I was too interested in intercepting you once I heard you in the hallway."

"But..." I glanced around the room, obviously confused, and he smiles and gestures to a far bookcase.

"One of the benefits of becoming lord protector is you learn all of the secret passageways in the First House," he says. "Amusingly enough, it wasn't Rihad who showed them to me, but a mix of servants, councilors, and even some stewards. I have no doubt that there are other passages that I have yet to figure out, but, Light willing, I'll have the chance to walk the length and breadth of the First House a thousand times over once this crisis has passed. I just wish I could understand why Rihad wanted to awaken the dark powers in the Western Realms. There's so little in our archives about the early days of the Protectorate—those first years after the attack they survived at the western border, or even much about how the ruling houses were established."

"Really?" I frown, annoyed that his words are almost a direct echo of Tennet's concerns. "But how is that possible? This is our system of government you're talking about, the rules and codes of conduct that have been handed down since the dawn of the Protectorate. If that's not accessible here, what are we basing our decisions on? That makes no sense."

"Oh, there are plenty of later works to provide that guidance, you can be sure." Fortiss taps a large stack of thick, dusty tomes, then gestures to a far-shorter pile of books with bright leather covers. "But I'm looking for books that were written at the dawn of the Protectorate or shortly thereafter, any sort of indication about how those initial houses were set up and why the decisions were made as to who ruled where. And I know what you're going to ask, Talia. I've been looking for that too. But there's no historical account that mentions women in the leadership of houses as far back as these go. Granted, they only go back about three hundred years. That leaves two hundred years of unaccounted-for history that surely exists, as you say, somewhere. Miriam contends that those old books were originally stored at the Eighth House, but if they were, why wouldn't Rihad have already brought them here? Even if the Eighth kept back some copies, why would Rihad leave anything behind?"

I make my way over to him as he talks, then lean over a table and open a book at random, frowning to see it was only written a hundred years earlier. Still ancient, by any accounting, but far too recent to matter. "Maybe he did bring them and just simply destroyed them because they didn't say what he wanted them to say? If no history exists to counter the lies that you're pedaling, are they truly lies? Or have you simply created a more palatable truth?"

Fortiss rubs his hands through his hair, making it stand out at odd angles. For the first time, I notice how tired he looks. I frown, worry skiffing through me, but he merely continues.

"The other thing that I've been looking for is the crown of wings," he says. "The more I read in these old books, the more I'm convinced it exists as an actual artifact—something that pre-dates the Protectorate. It's not just some myth or bit of pageantry that was created to give the tournament meaning. Even Tennet mentioned it in his delirious speech to you. But if it existed once, where did it go?"

I blink at him. "What are you talking about?"

"It's right here." He reaches for a heavy volume set carefully to the corner of his desk and pulls it into the light to read from it. "When the delegation of the Imperium made their way across the wild lands that would eventually become the Protectorate, they found great treasures and took them for their own. Among them was a golden, winged crown of great power. Their leader, Mirador, claimed the crown for his own, as was his right."

He glances up to me. "According to this account, however, he didn't put the crown on his head until they were attacked by the creatures from the Western Realms—and at first he did it simply to draw the attention of the enemy, to give them something to focus on in order to keep the other members of their party safe for as long as possible."

I make a face. "I have a hard time believing any man wouldn't at least try the thing on to see how he looked as a king."

Fortiss laughs, and the tension eases between us. "Fair point, but that's not what I'm focusing on here. He put it on to distract the Divhs—to set himself up as a decoy. But the account goes on to say that the crown connected him to the blighted army and the creatures of shadow who ruled it. And through the connection, he could rule the army as well."

I blink. "That's the purpose of the winged crown?" I ask him, stunned, Tennet's crazed words sounding in my mind. "To rule the darkness?"

"It gets worse. After this mention of Mirador's crown, there's at least one other crown mentioned—and a possible third reference, though I can't—"

"*Three*?" I demand. "Three crowns that rule those flying snake things?"

"The skrill, yes—and *maybe* three. Maybe two, maybe more. We just don't know."

I make a face. "And Rihad has one of them? That's how he was able to summon these things?"

"That I also don't know," Fortiss gestures helplessly. "Obviously, he's not wearing it now, but the skrill came all the same. But did it simply take that long for them to show up because he collapsed on the battlefield? Is this some long-gestating magic that's finally coming to life? Or is there someone else with a crown out there—"

"Light, Fortiss," I breathe. "Don't even think such a thing."

"We have to think it—and, what's more, we have to see for ourselves. We've got to get to the Western Realms as quickly as we can...and return before the agents of the Imperium arrive. Last night you thought you might have a way to do that. Do you still?"

I grin at him. "I might," I tell him, leaning forward to brace myself on the desk as I offer him a grin. Our eyes meet, and something thrilling and fierce stirs between us, whispering of what might be. He grins back at me and my heart skips a beat, but for once, I keep my focus...only because I must. "Tell me again how much you trust me."

CHAPTER 19

"You're the *lord protector*, Fortiss. You can't just leave the First House without its leader."

"I run the Protectorate, not this house. So, I can leave and I will."

I exit Fortiss's private chambers where he's well into the third round of arguing this point with the patently panic-stricken councilors. Following the faint whiff of smoke down the corridor towards the overlook, I finally step out into the cool night air, expecting to find Nazar comfortably enjoying his pipe, possibly with Caleb bouncing on his toes, eager for the adventure to begin. Instead, Tennet's bulky form blocks my view of the wide, moon-washed plain below.

We've barely got an hour before the sun will start its swift ascent toward daybreak, and tension rolls from his shoulders like an uneasy tide.

"Lady Talia," he murmurs as I step out on the deck. He turns and leans on the counter, watching me as I approach. "I've spent the better part of the last day, when I wasn't dealing with the councilors fussing over me, wondering how it is that you could suggest such a remarkable course of action with no true understanding of what it is we are going to encounter in the land of the

Divhs. I assume you've been there multiple times, and undoubtedly more than I have. But have you really explored it beyond performing training exercises with your Divh?"

I smile. Leave it to Tennet to get to the heart of the matter that no one else has dared ask me, even Nazar.

"I haven't," I admit. "Truth to tell, it never would have occurred to me to have any reason to travel into their plane without their invitation. Or even with their invitation, it never occurred to me that they would want us or have any need for us there. Then Dele asked me to help with her babies and—"

"Dele?" He blinks at me, but his tension has already eased. That pleases me more than it should.

"The sandworm you saw up in the canyon. A very pregnant sandworm up until a short while ago. She was one of the Divhs who pledged herself to me and to my house, for all that it doesn't yet exist. She recently gave birth to an entire kit of weevishes, and I didn't realize how quickly those children would grow up. There are ample spaces for them to enter our plane near the Third House, where the world is filled with sand and there are many natural predators that they can use to help them transition to their next stage. But here, there are fewer."

"Which is why she wanted you to do battle with her own offspring?"

"To them it's a game, a very healthy, practical game. Unbanded Divhs can't be killed in our plane, so if they come across a predator that stamps them out, they just return home. But if they endure a challenge and battle long enough to molt, they move to their second stage of development. It's the perfect example of the natural balance between their plane and ours. It's just never one that I actually considered before this past month. Then again, there's a lot of things I didn't consider before this past month."

"There's no balance between our plane and the Divhs'." Tennet humphs. "There doesn't need to be."

I blink up at him, struck by the difference in manner between him and Fortiss. With Fortiss, every interaction is an opportunity to explore, to balance, to learn from each other. With this warrior—

"Is everything a fight with you?" I don't mean to snap so harshly, but now that my rebuke lingers between us, I can't take it back. For his part, Tennet grins at me and settles one heavy arm on the railing of the overlook. He's not anywhere remotely close to angry, but that doesn't make him any less dangerous.

"It seems like every conversation you and I have becomes a fight. But then it would almost have to, wouldn't it? I want something that you don't want, for all that it was arranged for both of us. Never mind that you were originally willing to honor the contract made up by your father and mine. Your priest here shared with me the details of your bridal attire when you set out for the Twelfth House, so clearly your intention started out as honorable."

I know he's deliberately trying to bait me, and I'm not pleased that he's so successful at it, but I can't help myself. "You mean the day that my brother died? Then, yes. Yes, I'll admit that on that day, that morning, I had no other options, no other purpose than to ensure the safety of my house. And in the hours and days after Merritt died in my arms, I still had no other purpose other than to ensure that safety. But at that moment, my path changed, and it's never going to change back, Lord Tennet. I don't care if your house wages war against mine, I don't care if you go all the way to the Imperator, I'm never going to honor that contract. I'm never going to be your wife."

His grin never wavers, but his brows drift up. "I would say those two don't need to be mutually connected sentences," he counters. "I knew the moment I realized who you actually were—especially given that you were covered in the gore and saliva of sandworm offspring—that your situation had markedly changed. I would never expect you to honor that original contract. You're no longer that original woman. But as to whether or not you'll ever be my wife, well, it seems reasonable that you might reconsider that possibility. Two houses joined together in the Protectorate isn't a bad decision for the strength of all."

I bare my teeth at him. "You forget, I'm no longer tied to the Tenth House."

"And you mistake me for giving a damn about the Tenth House. I speak of the Thirteenth, for all that you haven't broken ground on it. The Twelfth and the Thirteenth bound together as one would present a mighty front against any foe. And it would serve you as well."

"I don't need your protection, Lord Tennet," I remind him, but he shakes his head, cutting me off with a dismissive wave.

"I'm not one of these fools who think you cannot successfully run your own house alone, Lady Talia. I simply think—*know*—that you're not going to want to."

Once again, he's taken me by surprise. I blink at him, my pulse pounding so hard it bangs around my skull, but he turns back forward, peering out over the moon-swept plain. "No matter where a castle is built, the stones that serve as its foundation are part of the earth of that space, the power and the history and the personality. You and I are products of the mountains where we were born, just as Lord Protector Fortiss is a product of these wide plains. He is farseeing and expansive in his beliefs. He can gather in many opinions and perspectives and land on what is right. He can sacrifice the individual for the need of the whole."

I shift uneasily beside him. He's only known Fortiss for a few hours, yet his understanding of the man is keen. Worse than that, in his words I sense a warning that has nothing to do with battle plans and the management of houses.

But Tennet isn't finished. "You and I are different. We are inheritors of the mountains, warriors who know that rocky paths can lead just as easily to open vistas as they can to deadly falls. We know the canyons can hide sparkling treasure or deadly predators that you'll never see until they're upon you. We can't see far, but we can see what's right in front of us with perfect clarity and understand it for what it is. And we know, sure as the Light, that we'll never be able to waste time with ponderings about the wide world, if we don't survive this moment."

"Uh huh." I cross my arms over my chest. "Why do I get the feeling we wouldn't even be having this conversation if I'd made it to the Twelfth House that first day, my hair coiled in a grand mass around my head and laden with trinkets and jewels?"

He shrugs and offers me a grin. "I guess we'll never know. Because that's not where that particular mountain path took you. It didn't lead you deeper into the mountains but out onto these wide plains. That said, such paths have a way of circling back on themselves. So, like any good child of the mountains, you should keep a sharp eye out and assess both dangers and opportunities when they present themselves for what they are, and for nothing else."

I study him, well aware of Nazar still smoking his pipe deep in the shadows. Tennet knows it too. Does he simply not care? Or is he trying to convince both of us...and of what exactly?

"That's fair advice," I finally say, settling on the least offensive reply I can come up with. And then I ruin it, because, of course I do. "From what I've heard of your father, I'm surprised he spent so much time training you in the art of discourse."

Tennet only chuckles. "Lord Orlof was never one to use words when his fists would do. But he also had a taste for the absolute best the world had to offer, even high up in his mountain stronghold. My mother was Imperium born."

Because I know the man so well, I can hear the slight shift in Nazar's body, the movement probably no more than the tilting of his chin and the narrowing of his eyes on Tennet. This revelation is important to him. Why? Does he regret now not carrying on to the Twelfth House to meet an Imperium comrade? I remember the young Imperium woman in Lord Rihad's court whose ways he knew so well. Nazar has spent the last ten years and more in the Protectorate...does he miss his homeland?

Fortunately, Tennet doesn't notice the warrior-priest's sharper focus but continues along with his tale. "Given how close we are to the border, it wasn't as much of a leap for my father to find her as you might think, especially given the quality of our wine. But she came from a wealthy house, and she'd been taught by tutors trained in the capital city. To save herself from a life of boredom, she taught me to carry a conversation from the moment I could credibly talk."

"How long ago did she die?" I asked quietly. Because this much I knew about the woman.

"Eight years ago," he says, nodding at the stars. "She slipped away on a night even brighter than this, her eyes already turned to the adventure that awaited her over the horizon." He flashes me another glance. "So, I guess I amend my earlier statement. There is a time to take a wider view. But may it be many long years before you feel you must."

We stand there staring at the stars another few moments, and I feel pushed to say more, to learn more from Tennet—but also to hold back.

I don't know this man; I don't want to know this man. I have my own path before me—to serve the Protectorate and build my house; a house that can offer paths to any who would follow me to do more with the Divhs. And now this is my chance, assuming we can vanquish the threat of the Western Realms and return to peace in the Protectorate.

Lofty dreams, all, and none of them possible if I don't keep my focus. A warrior sees the whole of his opponent and uses all of it—I need to understand more of Tennet, yes. But not the pieces of him that call to my heart, but to my mind.

"Your mother came from the Imperium, lived in Hakkir, and she taught you," I say instead. "What information do they have about the Protectorate, the way we live, our history? How much does it differ from the way that history is taught here?"

"That last is a very good question, and one that I never thought to ask until these last few days, traveling out toward Trilion, sharing idle chatter with warriors and townsfolk alike. The perceptions we have of our own past are fluid. They change with each generation, gradually shifting as politics and society changes. The information provided in the Imperium about the Protectorate's past never changes, I suspect. It's history from five hundred years ago, great events that secured the glory of the Imperium and its protection. It's also caught in time, a perfect fully rendered painting that might as well be depicting mythology, not people, not even Divhs in terms of breathing, living creatures with their own purpose."

He smiles a little grimly, shaking his head. "I never thought of it that way, of course, when my mother taught me the history of a country she wasn't born in. I simply accepted her depiction of the past as the truth. It never occurred to me that it could be anything other than what she said. But now, I wonder how little I truly know, and how much the frame of my perception was bolted together with the ideas of people who have never lived our experience. It certainly was never an issue before I took the band. But once I became linked with Ayne, I realized how small I was, how insignificant, when I should arguably be so much more. We were meant to be warriors, and we've become entertainers."

"Not anymore," I point out. "You took on the creature from the Western Realms as a warrior. And unless I miss my guess, there's more where that comes from."

The sound of voices raised in argument pulls us from our conversation, and we turn to see Fortiss and Miriam stomp out onto the overlook, Caleb following several steps behind, as if wanting to stay out of range of their anger.

Fortiss stabs a finger at the councilor.

"Miriam, you've already lost this battle. You're not going to win it here just because we're outside."

"I don't plan on trying to win it anymore, but your plan is still flawed. However at least this flaw I can fix." She draws herself up tall, smoothing her long gray robes. "I'm coming with you."

"No." Fortiss rejects that idea flat. "You're not a warrior; you're not banded to a Divh. You have no business traveling with us."

"I have every business," she retorts. "If this were a normal traveling party to the border, you would take a councilor to show that the ways of the Protectorate are being honored. It's not an ordinary traveling party, but the need still remains. You think the lord of the Eighth House will respond favorably to four people he's never met and the lord protector who has but recently ascended to the role, nephew of the lord protector who massacred warrior and Divh alike? I have met these people, Fortiss. Beyond that, I was born in the Eighth House. They know me. Arguably, they trust me. Certainly more than they trust you. They don't know you or the rest of your party whom they have not met. More so than that, here you are trying to guide your Divhs across the distant planes, from your home to a space that your Divhs may not have traveled to. Certainly not anytime recently. How can you do that when you have never seen the great Meridian mountains, when you have never watched the sunrise over the granite and red-stone ramparts of the Eighth House? If you connect to me in the manner I know you now have the ability to do, Fortiss, I can give you those visions, I can help you see what I see. Failing that, I can at least recognize it when we get there. You have to take me."

"There's no possible way—"

"Lord Protector Fortiss, the decision is yours, but I will say that councilor Miriam's advice is well made, her position a sound one." Nazar's quiet words draw all our attention, but the old priest isn't looking at us. He's risen to his feet, and now he's looking up to the stars. "But unfortunately, we can no longer debate the issue, only decide. It's time."

CHAPTER 20

I step forward to the edge of the overlook, and beckon Nazar forward. Together, we face Fortiss, Tennet, Caleb, and Miriam.

"The first time I ever entered the plane of the Divhs was under Nazar's tutelage," I begin. "I went farther, experienced more than I should have. But I didn't think anything of it because I didn't know what I was doing. He knew better, of course, but he didn't tell me to stop. After that, I ventured out more in training with Gent, racing over the hillsides of his home, trying to understand what it was and where it was, but mostly just trying to bond with him so that I could hold my own in battle after very little practice."

Tennet rubs his jaw. "I never went anywhere outside of the initial training grounds, the field where I first banded to Ayne,"

"At least you did that," Caleb scoffs, waving the comment away. "Until Nazar told me how things were supposed to go, I'd barely even thought about *trying* to see these training grounds. Marsh banded with me on the ground outside the coliseum during the Tournament of Gold. I haven't had to go anywhere else but here, given that I've been training the new banded soldiers. Marsh has always come to me." He offers a lopsided grin. "I think he likes it here."

Nazar exhales a long stream of sweet-smelling smoke. Clearly, he already understands that we won't be in a place for long where the luxury of pipes will be possible. "In the early days of my connection with Wrath, we followed the traditional path. Warrior and Divh met on the claiming fields of the Blessed Plane to bond together, to forge that first connection or to strengthen it if the bond itself was first made in this world. But there was no need for most warriors to interact with their Divhs outside of this plane. And, to be sure, the expectation was always that the Divh served the warrior, not the other way around. Those of us who have done battle with our Divhs—actual battle, not simply performing in exhibitions—know the truth is somewhat different than that."

"The truth about a lot of things is different than that," I agree. "And where one dispute occurs, more are possible. Why travel by horse across our great Protectorate when we could reach any destination in a quarter hour traveling through the plane of the Divhs? When my sandworm brought me her children, they still smelled of heat and sand. They'd been unsuccessful in their transition, and she was tired of waiting for them to figure it out. She plucked them from her plane to bring them here for training. That journey would have taken days on horseback."

Tennet squints at me. "And you believe that because you have survived your brief encounters with the Divhs in their plane, you'll be able to travel *anywhere* in their plane?"

I shrug. "Maybe not alone, but with their presence, yes. They survive here. Not for very long, because we can't sustain creatures their size."

"And even that we know not to be entirely true," Fortiss says, his voice turning bitter. "Rihad trapped Szonja for more than a decade in the caverns of the First House. He needed magic to do it, but he did it. She ate, she breathed, she survived. There's no reason why we can't do the same, especially if we'll only be there a short time."

I turn to the female councilor. "We should be fine, because we're bonded to our Divhs. Miriam, there's no guarantee you'll be comfortable there. But Gent will know, and he'll return you immediately if you don't thrive. Worst case, you'll end up somewhere in the midst of these plains—he'll get you as close to the First House as possible."

"I have horsemen already patrolling the area, searching for any remnants of the skrill," Fortiss says. "You'll be found."

He issues that statement with an unshakeable confidence that feels right and true. He's a commander, through and through—our commander. Mine. At least when it comes to the battlefield, if not anywhere else.

My lips twist in self-derision. *Right. Keep telling yourself that.*

"I'll be fine." Miriam waves off our concern with a dismissive, cutting gesture. "I haven't endured this long as the only female on Rihad's council to die a quarter mile from the First House with my face in the dirt."

"Good enough." I turn toward the wide plain, squinting into the darkness. "You, Gent, and I will go first. If we don't reappear immediately, the rest of you follow. Once we all arrive in the Blessed Plane, we'll reconvene, make sure we're all stable, and decide how to proceed from there."

Before anyone can gainsay me, I lift up my left arm, extending it to the heavens, and curl my right hand into a fist to lay on my heart. "Gent," I whisper, the words soft and full in my mind.

From a seemingly far distance, I hear his distinctive ululating howl, a cry of sheer jubilance. A moment later, the sky seems to snap tight, and Miriam emits the tiniest whimper of surprise as Gent's gigantic form appears on the far horizon. He gallops across the wide plain toward us, covering massive distance with each mighty stride. I picture him gathering us both up, one in each hand, then remember almost too late how poor his vision is, how easily he can see me and no one else.

"Miriam!" I shout and lunge for her, wrapping her up tight. To her credit, she doesn't struggle but grips me back. A moment later, the two of us are swept from the overlook and plastered against the back of Gent's mighty palm. He pauses, lifting us up so that we are even with his enormous black eye, and I turn, one arm still firmly around Miriam. "Your home—the Blessed Plane," I tell him, using Nazar's term for it both in words and thought, while in my mind's eye I imagine the beautiful blue sky and the endless hillside terrain covered in white and blue tipped flowers.

Gent could have no idea what my ultimate goal is, but he clearly doesn't care. He turns around, his arms swinging in a wide arc as Miriam tries unsuccessfully to stifle a scream, and then he's off and running again, two steps, three, five, and he leaps—

My sight winks out, blackness surrounding me as he grips his fist tight around us—but only for a second. When my vision clears, I can see the world has utterly changed. The dry, almost harsh air of the First House plains has been replaced with a heavy, humid mist that instantly covers my skin with fine droplets. It's dark here, but not completely black, the light of a distant rising sun somehow mimicking our own experience of day.

"By the Light." I turn and see Miriam bracing herself against the knuckles of Gent's mighty paw, her eyes peeled wide as she stares around, and her gaze eventually coming back to rest on me. "I can breathe," she assures me hurriedly. "I can see, I can breathe."

Gent howls in joy.

I imagine the other men and their Divhs, all of them coming at once, and Gent doesn't hesitate. Pulling his arm in close to his chest and covering the hand that is holding us with his other, he turns and moves swiftly up the embankment. And it is an embankment, I realize, though I'm unable to pick out more than lush grass dotted with white and blue flowers as he climbs higher and higher, finally cresting a ridge before turning back. With a mighty whoop, he topples backwards and crashes to a seated position, as if ready to enjoy a show. A moment later, he peels away his fingers and shakes us out onto his palms—me sprawling into his left hand and Miriam his right, like two-fisted dice about to be thrown.

I look over at the councilor, who looks like she desperately wants to throw up. Instead, she manages to stagger to an almost-upright position, clutching Gent's little finger as if she's hugging the base of a mighty tree. Still, she's awake and she's watching, and a moment later so am I as the sky rips open with the arrival of more Divhs.

Talia! Fortiss's voice pounds first through my mind, as he bursts into view out of nowhere, perched high atop Szonja's neck. The beautiful blue dragon has her wings spread wide. In this heavy air, they look whole and complete, without even the hint of the debilitating injury she endured for so many years trapped in Rihad's caverns. She swirls and turns, soars and darts through the air, her joy at showing off her agility practically radiating out toward me.

Fortiss, for his part, holds on with all his might, laughing with such unbridled happiness that it draws me up short. Have I ever heard him laugh like this? In all the weeks I've known him, he's been so burdened by his role first as the lord protector's nephew, and then as the lord protector himself, that it's hard for me to even imagine him as a man. We shared one evening in the market day-style atmosphere of the tournament celebrations, when he had thought me a woman—never suspecting I was also playing the role of my brother. That day may as well have been a century ago. But now, in this moment, I can feel his joy, his excitement, his thirst for adventure.

I can also hear his words clearly. *Talia, are you seeing this, can you feel? I feel more connected to you, to Szonja, to everything!*

To Miriam? I think back to him hard, turning to the councilor.

"Try to reach out, imagine Fortiss in your mind, think to him as if you wish to connect to him."

"I..." Her eyes are a little glassy as she watches Szonja's acro-batics, but a moment later there are two voices in my mind, not just one. My mind fills with the image of a drab, brown-colored fortress carved out of what looks like sandstone cement, with red mountains all around. Deep pockets of unexpected green and blue shimmer like misplaced jewels tucked into the embrace of the red mountains, that gradually fade to a slate gray in the higher reaches.

I see it! Fortiss's thoughts are limned with excitement, and Miriam bursts out with laughter as well, the sound equally foreign coming from her mouth. I watch her, my own smile teasing at the corners of my mouth. What a somber place the First House must have been.

Those thoughts are chased out of my mind a moment later as Wrath streaks into view, his golden beak and the bright white plumage of his head and wings catching the sunlight as it suddenly flares over my shoulder. Instinctively, I crane my neck to see the source of that light, but it's blocked by Gent's mighty form. I turn back to peer at Nazar and his Divh, unwilling to miss even a moment of their splendor.

For all that Nazar claims that he never rode his Divh prior to last night, he holds his seat with far more skill than Fortiss does. His knees lock tight under the feathers of Wrath's neck, his body tilts forward, but not to clutch for balance, merely to see. His gentle salute of hello flows through my mind and to Fortiss as well, but Miriam betrays no reaction to it.

I begin to ask her if she can hear, only to be distracted by a mighty chortling howl. Far below us on the ridge, Marsh appears with Caleb grasped in his hands. The impossibly ungainly Divh, with his falcon head, torso and arms of a man, and legs as thick and hairy as an ape's is nowhere near as big as Gent...but he's still a giant, and Caleb is barely visible huddled against his body as Marsh rolls head over heels down the grassy slope for no apparent reason other than because he can. The two eventually tumble to a stop, then burst apart, Caleb flinging his arm out wide in the dewy grass as he stares up at the brightening sky.

"I never want to go back!" he howls, his words both reverberating through the open air and in my mind.

Then the final member of our party arrives.

The shining sun catches Ayne in his full glory as he streaks into existence in this plane, his wings outstretched, his neck lengthened, his sinuous body slicing through the air with his long tail lashing out behind. He shoots across the horizon, then spins back toward us like a streaking star. Tennet is hunched over his neck with the same gritty resolve that Fortiss expressed, clearly holding on for dear life, but determined not to fall.

I won't fall, he informs me stiffly, but it's Fortiss who responds to him, appreciation and shared experience vibrating in his voice.

I'm with you, brother, he tells Tennet, and even from a distance, I can see Tennet whip around with surprise, finding Fortiss atop Szonja swooping toward him. Fortiss attempts a shaky wave for just a moment before dropping his hand to clutch his Divh's neck again.

But we are together, I realize. We are here; we are in the Blessed Plane of the Divhs...

And I can see it more clearly than I ever have before.

With the sun rising fully, I gaze out over the long grassy slope and realize that it's leading down to a wide body of water too placid for an ocean but too enormous to be any lake I have ever seen. A rocky peak covered in trees stretches up in its center, and near it an eruption of stone forms an odd butte sticking up out of the water. The peak and the rocky outcropping are so far away, it's tough to pick out details, but it feels oddly comforting looking at them, like a painting I once saw long ago.

How broad is this lake? I ask in my mind, amused to see all three of the airborne Divhs dart off in separate directions, as if they plan to personally show their riders the scope of their world. To my surprise, though, the answer doesn't come from Fortiss's excited shouting or Tennet's gasping descriptions.

For you it would take several days to cross. For the winged ones, a day of heavy flight, and there are many places to stop and rest. But that's if we needed exercise. I prefer to run, to leap and be done.

Slowly, as if I am in a dream that I do not want to wake from, I curl around and stare up at Gent, his mighty snout sniffing the air, his bright eyes fixed on the far horizon, and his fanged mouth curved into a fearsome, devastating smile. His horns gleam in shiny onyx curves in the sunlight, his green scales practically glowing in the heat of the morning sun.

"Jump?" I ask him, and from Miriam's jolt beside me, I realize I've asked the word aloud. She turns to stare at me with wide eyes then up at Gent, flinching back into his palm at the sight of his face in the full sunlight. I realized she's never seen a Divh up close. Certainly not this close.

An image bursts through my mind of Gent galloping along a ridge that rises toward the open water. He's running-running-running, his pounding back legs churning, his hands and arms serving as forelegs. Step-step-step leap—and then he's soaring through the air. Water flashes beneath him, then darkness, then water again and a shoreline, a distant shoreline, this one rockier. He drops into the water like a stone, reveling with joy at its embrace, then eventually striking bottom and bounding out to stagger onto the shore.

"You can jump the entire *lake*?" I ask aloud in disbelief, but no that's not it, not exactly, as he goes through the process again in my mind. He begins the jump and then winks out, I think. Then he winks back into view, much like he enters our plane.

And here I thought their world was no more than a small island...when it's easily fifty times larger than the Protectorate, sized to match the Divhs' giant forms.

Larger, but...

"Wait...that can't be possible, can it?" Miriam's voice sounds strangled, and I glance back toward her, but she's not looking at me anymore. Instead, her gaze is fixed on the tiny islands far out into the center of the lake.

She breathes out an unsteady breath. "Is that...is that the coliseum?"

Above us, Gent howls with delight

CHAPTER 21

The others start returning within an hour, their Divhs dropping them to the earth according to their nature. Wrath gently lands on four paws, bending down to let Nazar slide off his shoulder and down his leg with dignity. The priest of the Light looks as if he has enjoyed an easy ride on his favorite stallion across the open plains. He pauses to lay a hand on the mighty foreleg of his Divh, then turns to where Miriam and I are standing. Gent has long since abandoned us for the lake and is currently floating on his back in the sun. I get the feeling he does that a lot.

Marsh returns at a full gallop, Caleb now standing braced against his chest, holding on to what looks like a strap of braided leather and jewels that's as wide as a man. Neither one of us can quite figure out where Marsh got the contraption, other than Caleb simply wanted a harness to work with, and suddenly it was there.

Now he's shoved his right arm through the weave, and he leans forward, both rider and guide for his mighty Divh. The two of them have been exploring the shoreline, trying to find more landmarks to confirm Miriam's belief that this land is a much larger, slightly warped mirror of our own. So far, we've seen nothing definitive, but with so much of what we can see covered in water, it's tough to tell. Still, it's possible that these gentle slopes covered with grass and flowers mimic the foothills that lead up to the eastern mountain range. I can't quite see it, but it's possible.

Then Szonja and Ayne return, streaking over the grassy slope and out over the lake to where Gent floats. As if in some unspoken agreement, they turn in corkscrews at the same time, both of them dislodging their riders. Fortiss and Tennet howl as they streak through the air, their screams abruptly cut off when they hit the water. Gent is there of course and scoops them up, shaking them like kittens before hauling them to the shore. They're both soaked, rumpled, and exhausted—and for the first time in a long while, human. Not warriors. Not rivals. Just two men who've stood beside me in battle. And somehow, that makes it harder to look away.

They stink, Gent informs me happily, as if that is reason enough to give a warrior a dunking.

It seems like the others cannot hear the conversation I privately have with my Divh, though I can hear the subtle echoes of their conversations. I turn my mind from them, though, giving them privacy. It's breathtaking be able to connect so easily to so many Divhs, but it's not a skill I want to hone. Conversations such as these should be private until they cannot be for the purposes of war. A warrior uses her gifts in right timing.

Fortiss and Tennet stagger halfway up the slope toward us, then collapse to the ground, clearly exhausted. But Miriam and I haven't been entirely idle.

"There's water here, a fresh spring, just over this ridge," I call out. "For food, Gent showed us berry bushes. They're enormous, not surprisingly. I'm not sure how we'll eat them, other than messily."

"We won't be here long enough to need to eat," Fortiss points out, but Tennet looks curious.

"Maybe not this time, but seriously, there's no way we're not returning, right?" Caleb demands. "Like when all this is done and the Protectorate is restored and the creepy snake monsters are sent back to wherever in the blighted path they came from?"

He pushes himself up on his arm and looks around. "I never realized how much I'm missing out, not being near this kind of water. I mean, *look* at it."

We all do, turning our attention to the enormous glittering lake. Tennet and I had access to water up in the mountains, of course, but nothing on this scale and certainly nothing so wide open. Fortiss and Caleb have spent their lives in the wide, grassy plains of the center of the Protectorate. Nazar, coming from the Imperium, knows forest, plains, and mountains. But does he know great water like this?

I turn to him. "Is there anything like this in the Imperium, any similar body of water that you've ever seen?"

He looks out over the vast lake. "There is an ocean, but not like this. It's stirred up by angry currents and battered around by a cold wind. Only the heartiest of seafaring men attempt it. Its bounty is vast, though, offering enough fish to feed half the Imperium. But it gives up its fruits only at great cost, and it's rimmed with rocks and cliffs. No. I'm inclined to agree with Miriam that this land, the home of the Divhs, mirrors the Protectorate, just at a much more massive scale and in a primal state before the hand of man or the turn of ages dried up its lake and built its towns."

"With that reasoning then, the Western Realms is just on the other side of the lake before we hit this plane's version of the Meridian mountains," Miriam says. "But if it mimics the Protectorate..."

"I thought about that," Fortiss says, finishing her thought. "If it mimics the Protectorate, would it not also mimic the danger that exists beyond the western boarder? I've asked Szonja, and Tennet has asked Ayne. But all the Divhs really know is this side of the water. They've been to the far side of the lake to acknowledge it exists, but they haven't stayed there. Much like the Divhs of the sandy southern reaches know their place, so, too, do the Divhs to the west."

I shake my head, trying to imagine what the Meridians might

look like, blown up to the scale of the Blessed Plane. "Then, in other words, we'll have to go and see for ourselves."

He smiles at me, his easy expression catching me off guard. "As adventures go, I've had worse."

Miriam pulls out her satchel. "Eat, rest, and dry off. This path will save us several days of travel and allow us to move unnoticed, but if we can travel with this much ease, so too can the creatures who attacked yesterday. We can't take the time to truly enjoy this land. Though I must say, even being here is a gift I'll never forget."

I consider her words as she breaks out provisions and passes them around. When I take one of the small, dense loaves of bread, I wave it at Fortiss, then out to where Gent is floating in the lake again. This far away, he looks like his own miniature island, and I don't try to project my thoughts to him. I'm not sure if he, too, needs to rest up to bound across the great expanse of water and sky to reach the western shores of the Blessed Plane, but it has to take some effort, surely.

"Gent didn't seem to have a reaction one way or another to the skrill when we were fighting them. He simply took me at my word that they needed to be destroyed, and he set to it, much like he set to fighting any monster that came at him during the tournament. But there was a difference this time. The creatures that you and Tennet roasted didn't disappear. They rained down on the coliseum, little more than charred carcasses. And one of them actually attacked Tennet—that's not normal either."

Fortiss leans forward. "It isn't normal, because they're not Divhs. Not the way we understand them, anyway. I've thought about this too. Whatever it is that lurks on the other side of the western border it's powerful, but it's not a Divh—different rules, different weaknesses and strengths. So no, Miriam, I don't think they can traverse through this land. But..."

"But they had to come from somewhere," I finish his thought for him. "My entire idea of using the Blessed Plane to transport us across the Protectorate was partially based on the idea that, well, maybe that's how the skrill did it. Because there's no way that a swarm of those things traveled all the way from the Western Realms without anyone noticing it. Alerts would have been made, the fires would have been lit. They had to have gone through some other passageway, some plane like this. They're actual creatures, not just illusions."

"There's no chance that they could have snuck through here without the Divhs noticing it?" Caleb asks. "I mean this is a big place, and it's not a natural place. We don't know what its rules are."

Fortiss turns to him. "What do you mean, it's not natural?"

"Well, look around you." Caleb uses his own loaf of bread to gesture at the rolling hillside, the great lake. "We've got sun and sky, water and grass, and flowers as far as the eye can see, but you know what we don't have? Bugs. Birds. Any sign of death or decay. The only living creatures that I've seen or heard since we got here are the Divhs. And that grove of trees and vines over there may be producing berries the size of ponies, but where are the actual ponies? Or bees, rabbits, or snakes, even? Where's any animal at all, other than the Divhs—and only *our* Divhs?"

"Grapevines don't need bees," Tennet the secret winemaker points out, but his voice is oddly modulated, as if he's rolling around the idea in his head and not liking the answers. "But can these creatures actually survive just on berries and water? I confess I've never seen Ayne eat anything, but it was always assumed that we couldn't sustain the creatures in our plane because of the resource demand. And yet you say that Rihad kept the great dragon Szonja in his cavern for, what, more than ten years? What did she eat?"

He asks the question of Fortiss, but Fortiss only shakes his head. "She won't speak of that time, and I haven't pressed her on it. The servants I've queried mostly were in charge of dumping vats of healing salve over the side of the wall to help her injured wing. They assumed she hunted at night, when no one could see her, but they couldn't tell me how." He sighs. "Szonja and I still don't know each other that well, barely longer than you and Marsh, Caleb. Do you know what he eats?"

Caleb makes a face. "I don't, and it never occurred to me to ask. What about you and Wrath, Nazar? Did they have different protocols in the Imperium for interacting with your Divhs? Did you know him better?"

"I didn't," Nazar says, and from the heaviness in his tone, his regret is plain. He looks around at us. "We're all thinking the same thing except perhaps, you, Talia. You had no preconceived notions of what it was to have a Divh, because you were never trained on what it is to have a Divh. When Gent drew you into this world, then brought the flowers of this world to ours during the tournament, you took it as a wonder and a definite nuisance since you had to hide it from Rihad's notice. But you didn't see it as a violation of some ancient protocol. You didn't know the protocol. You alone had the idea to travel through this plane, and here we are. It took no more effort than simply to ask, and we never asked."

"It's against Protectorate rule to ask," Fortiss says. "The Divhs are our sacred warriors, meant only to do battle in times of great need, other than during the exhibition of the tournament and the incidental training when the band moved from father to son. That's always been the way."

"Except for the fact that Talia commands thirty of the things, and she's not anyone's son," Caleb points out cheerfully. "So, we already know that the way has twisted a bit over time. What else did they used to do at the dawn of the Protectorate that they no longer do? And why don't we have this history? I can't tell you how many hours I spent poring over the books we had in the Second House libraries. It all was the same, as if the ways our Divhs work with us today is exactly the same way they served and worked with us when the Protectorate was formed. It never occurred to me to suspect otherwise. I'm an idiot."

"Even the books that we managed to keep from Rihad's purge of historical records told the same story," Miriam says. "Which means that Rihad wasn't the first lord protector to cleanse our histories. Any books or scrolls that came to us from other houses were undoubtedly recopied by each generation of leader. The pieces that fit the story they preferred were preserved, and those that didn't serve doubtless got scraped away."

"But it's been *here*. Right here, all along." Fortiss shakes his head. "Surely somebody made the attempt."

"If they did, it wasn't the Twelfth House. Not ever," Tennet says. "Our respect for the Divhs was too great. We were kept safe because marauders knew what we had—or believed they knew what we had. My father once told me that he'd summon Ayne whenever there seemed to be an uptick in marauder runs, which happened, in his telling, once every few years. Ayne would tour the area, set a few fires, return to my father, and then return to its—his —plane. At the time, I never knew when Ayne had been here, only that there'd been a fire in the mountains."

I make a face. "Merritt wanted to practice with Gent more, and Father certainly welcomed that. Gent wasn't large but he was big enough, and we were lucky for the box canyons near our manor house that allowed them to practice unobserved. I watched when I could, being careful not to be seen. But it never occurred to me that there might be an ulterior motive to those practices, that my father also wanted the marauders or any travelers through the mountains to hear Gent, to imagine the destruction he caused, and to be afraid. It worked, I think. And we were as guilty of such assumptions as anyone. That day in the forest near the Shattered City, Merritt was convinced that a Divh had been in the area practicing for the Tournament of Gold, mostly because of all the trees that were knocked down. I agreed with him, but whose Divh would that have been?"

I gesture to Tennet, who's watching me now with somber eyes that betray nothing. "Merritt thought it was someone from the Fifth House who snuck into the mountains to practice in hiding, and I simply accepted that. It never occurred to me to ask when I had the chance."

"Don't judge yourself too harshly," Miriam says. "It's been five hundred years since the Divhs helped forge the Protectorate, and other than, I'm sure, some early interhouse warfare at the power of this nation's birth, we've had peace. Part of that peace was assured by a population that didn't ask too many questions. We've had wealth, we've had prosperity, and we've had precious little inter-action with the Imperium. Its wars have never been our wars, and other than for tithes in the past hundred years, delegations have been few and far between."

"It's an arduous journey to travel from the heart of the Imperium to the Protectorate," Nazar puts in. "And the land itself was considered a savage wilderness. No one willingly wanted to travel here, unless they were part of a delegation of the Imperator, or they were driven to strike out on their own and trust the Light that they would survive the journey. There were no tales of wealth or prosperity, only wild-open spaces and hardship. To hear the opinions every household I passed on my journey to the Tenth House, that tale served both sides."

"So, lies, you mean," Caleb says, and Tennet grunts.

"And if these are the lies that we've accepted when we could have gone out and challenged them for ourselves...?" he asks. "What lies await us in our own history with the battle of the Western Realms?"

I grimace and join them in looking out across the wide lake, where Szonja and Ayne are circling the mirror coliseum—then further west, to the hazy blue horizon of the western borders of the plane of the Divhs. It's only a trick of the light, but the blue seems deeper now, darker.

It's time for us to go.

The Divhs respond immediately, and within a quarter hour, we're lined up at the high promontory. Caleb, Miriam, and I remain on the ground, while Nazar, Fortiss and Tennet are mounted. Marsh is balancing on his toes, eager to roll, and even Gent is swaying slightly, his lips peeled back in a bright, eager grin.

Caleb grimaces. "I don't know about this," he mutters. "Marsh is nowhere near as big as Gent, and his wings are pretty much for show. I don't know if he'll make it in one giant jump."

Gent huffs, an unconcerned rush of air, and Caleb chuckles. "Well, I appreciate the vote of confidence, but you're just going to jump and what, we follow you?"

As he speaks, an image flashes in my mind, so wrong-feeling I take a step back. "No," I say aloud, and Caleb and Miriam turn to me. Gent pushes the image again, and Caleb frowns at me.

"What do you mean, no? How do we do this then?"

I grimace, but if Gent thinks we can do it his way..."Do you trust me?"

"Not even remotely, but sure—"

"Then hook into your Divh." I turned away from him as Marsh kneels down, boosting Caleb to his chest and sliding him into his harness. When I turn back, Caleb is squinting into the sky.

"Um...is that a storm brewing out there?"

"I don't know—but it doesn't look good."

I'm swamped again with the unmistakable certainty that our time is running out. I nod to Gent, who throws his head back with a mighty roar, his arms stretching wide as he draws in a huge, gusting breath. He whirls in one motion, clamping his enormous hands on either side of Marsh's torso. He picks up the Divh as if he isn't nearly half his size but no bigger than a bucket of water, and with a second roar, he flings him out over the great lake.

"Go!" I shout in my mind, and the winged Divhs take flight. A moment later the wind is completely knocked out of me as Gent snatches both me and Miriam up in a single great paw, somehow managing to clamp his fingers around us without crushing us. As it is, Miriam is curled into a tight ball beneath me, cradled in the base of Gent's palm, while I am hanging on for dear life to his topmost finger, my head barely clearing the ridge of his leathery finger, the tip of one claw curled around to rest too close to my head for comfort.

But at least I can see, which is both a blessing and a curse as Gent turns and jogs five great strides deeper down the slope, then turns around with another huff of excitement. He doesn't roar but instead draws in a deep breath...then takes off running.

After a few short hops, he settles into massive ground-eating strides. Everything is a blur at that point as he wrenches his fist away from his chest and recruits his own arms to help him amass speed, Miriam and I trapped in his palm as he pumps his great arms with vicious force. My only sense of what's happening is the pounding of his massive feet against the grassy incline. I count one-two-three-four, and then I'm thrown back with a sickening lurch as we catapult out over the lake. Gent's fingers have loosened their hold enough that I can see a shock of open water beneath us, then sky, then water, then sky—

Then blackness surrounds us, and all breath is ripped from my lungs.

CHAPTER 22

I awake to a fierce pressure in my chest, like I'm buried under a mound of rocks, and I've been set on fire. It takes me a moment to process that pain, because I can't think. I can't hear.

Or rather, I'm hearing too much. As terror and pain split and meld together and split again, I gradually understand that I'm surrounded by a howl so horrifying, my bones and guts practically melt.

We're not soaring through the sky anymore, we're plunging without ceasing, and not over the placid waters of some serene, otherworldly lake, but into the teeth of a storm.

Gent's claws remain wrapped around Miriam and me, but I can't tell if that's out of a sense of preserving us or merely because my giant Divh has frozen to death. *Cold*, we're so cold, and Gent's thoughts are shut off from me. When I try to reach out to him, I see only an endless vista of stars and sparking lights, as if his very mind has broken away from his body and is soaring up while we are soaring down.

A squawk to my right barely penetrates my pounding fear, and then we slam into something hard that I somehow realize is not the ground, mainly because it strikes us from the right, sending

Gent cartwheeling through the air and destroying any sense of equilibrium I thought I had. My stomach churns, my heart pounds, and I'm smashed back against the wall of his hand, shoving into another huddled form there, who doesn't move. *Miriam*!

Then even that thought is ripped away from me, as another collision strikes Gent, this time from the other side. We tumble into another direction, and my mighty protector's hand loosens its grip. I fall into open sky, Miriam's huddled mass of robes seeming to spread out and catch the wind before she's carried away from me on another gust. I spin, flailing helplessly, and see Gent below me, already impossibly far away, the ground rushing up to us both. For a second, I want to call for someone—anyone. Fortiss, with his impossible calm. Tennet, with his recklessness.

But no one can help me here. I'm alone, and I'm falling.

For one choked breath then another, I see the wild world beneath me, the wonder of the western border of the Blessed Plane.

It's a nightmare come to life.

Where Gent's home was nothing but rolling hillsides, flowers, and the wide, wide lake, this section of the Divhs' territory is harsh and unforgiving. Jagged peaks descend into rocky shale, fire leaps from great open maws in the earth, and the once-serene waters of the lake now churn up from unseen forces—as if a gale erupted in the middle of the water and rushed inward toward the shore, only to crash back out again.

This is the last thing I'll see before I die.

My short cloak flares behind me, but it does nothing to break my fall, and I search the horizon with streaming eyes, seeing nothing but Gent's descending body, then open sky, then a mass of tears.

I reach out to Gent, but there's nothing there, and though I want to close my eyes, they're peeled open by the force of the wind that rips my breath from my throat and sends me spinning, spinning—*Wham!*

I'm yanked up so violently, I feel like my head may be ripped clean off. The pressure at my neck is excruciating, and I clap my hands to my collar, my fingers struggling to release my cloak as my legs kick violently out and back. The world spins away in another direction, but I'm too crazed to think, too desperate to do anything by claw at my collar. I drag it away and manage a breath then strain to wrench it free—

Talia! I hear the shout inside my mind but also mixed into the wind, and my hysteria clears just enough for me to realize I'm dangling—dangling! From something enormous above me and I'm no longer spinning, flailing, dropping through the air.

I can't breathe!

My sight narrows down to a pinpoint and is on the verge of winking out when the pressure abruptly cuts away from my throat. Crazed with the need to survive, I hook my hands into the neckline of my cloak only to sustain a violent jerk to my shoulder, harsh enough my right arm almost has to be dislocated—

Then that pressure switches as well, and my cape is once more snagged. My hands are shoved beneath the neckline now, scraping it away, and I'm deliriously struggling to draw breath as I'm dropped again—

Landing easily in the outstretched palm of my Divh.

Gent.

I'm so disoriented, I can do nothing more than flop into the base of his palm to where his pulse thunders in jack-rabbiting rhythm, my own mind slurring around in confusion as he convulses. He's alive, but I can't connect to his thoughts. I can't seem to do much of anything other than push air in and out of my own lungs and stem the surge of nausea that—

"Oof," I manage, and with an effort of shoving a mountain uphill, I struggle over to the side of Gent's palm and crane my head as far as I can before another brutal wave of nausea overtakes me. Now it's my turn to convulse, and I empty my stomach violently over the edge of Gent's palm...most of it spewing out onto the rocky ground. Then I sag against the warm, reassuring heat of Gent's leathery hide, mindless and numb.

Fortiss's amused voice pierces through my fog. "Are you done? Or should I stand clear?"

Without lifting my head, I make a sharp, cutting motion with my outstretched hand, the rudest of all the gestures I learned during my time at the Tournament of Gold. His laugh does little to improve my mood, but when I don't immediately answer his question, his next question is more urgent.

"Seriously, Talia—are you all right?" Fortiss's quick steps skirt the sprawl of Gent's outstretched claws, and a second later he's vaulted himself into the monster's palm and moves to my side, braving the possibility of another surge of bile to roll me up to my side. Despite my best efforts, I can do little more than curl up in a half ball.

"Miriam?" I croak. "The others?"

"The others are fine," he says quickly. There's a sound of material sliding over skin, then he's wiping my hair away from my brow, mopping off my face. It must have rained at some point, I realize, because I'm sopping wet. Though Fortiss's cloth is dry—or was, anyway. "Ayne caught Miriam a little easier than Szonja was able to catch you. Miriam had heavier robes and wasn't wearing a cloak tied around her neck."

"Smart." I cough, willing my right hand to lift itself to test the bruising at my throat. My right hand is having none of it, and remains flopped down beside my body, supposedly still connected to my body via the arm I can't feel. "Cloaks are a menace."

"Well, if you hadn't been wearing one, you'd be in even worse shape..." Fortiss breaks off, and I can feel him shift beside me. "Talia, what's wrong with..." Again his words peter out, and he says nothing as my mind shifts and eddies in a shallow pool of detachment. Idly, I wonder if Gent minds serving as a bed...or maybe he's more of a couch—

A white-hot rip of agony knifes up from my right shoulder as Fortiss drives all his weight into it in a merciless shove. "*No!*" I scream, my sight going dark as nausea swamps me again, and my world spins as we're both wrenched skyward. Fortiss pinions me to Gent's palm, his body spread eagled over my torso and legs, but Gent yanks his hand close. A moment later, still weeping with pain, I blink up into my beautiful Divh's dark, furious eye, his breath blowing hard beneath his palm. I realize my left arm—my good arm—is wrapped around Fortiss...probably the only thing that's saving his life.

Hurt.

Gent's voice blasts through my mind in a jumble of babbling words, anxious and fast. In my mind's eye, I retrace the trip from his perspective. The joy and anticipation, the leap of pure and utter possibility, transition into the space between plains. This last part is awash in stars, and I vaguely remember seeing it the way he is seeing it, though there is no way in my eyes could have processed so many points of light. Then comes a scene I don't recognize, being whipped into a violent storm with lightning crackling all around wind and rain buffeting us. Gent rumbles in confusion and annoyance as he realizes the truth of what happened, watching how he became momentarily paralyzed as we re-entered his plane and he fell, fell, fell...

And then Marsh appears out of nowhere and bangs into him, his small wings churning violently, his fists like battering poles. He breaks Gent's fall once, twice, and Gent loses his hold of his tiny cargo. The huge eye glistens, suddenly too bright, and I clutch Fortiss tighter because there's nothing else to hold.

"It's all right, Gent," I say aloud, and also in my mind. Feeling has returned to my right hand, and I spread my fingers wide on his thick palm. "Szonja caught me."

Fortiss has levered himself off my body by now and stares from my shoulder to Gent's anguished face. "Tell him you hurt your shoulder, and the pain you felt was me putting it back in place."

Gent huffs, clearly able to understand Fortiss all on his own, or interpreting his words through my mind, but I keep my arm around Fortiss to make sure my angry Divh doesn't flick him off like a fly. "You still caught me, Gent," I whisper to him.

Fortiss moves off me completely, then helps me to a seated

position. I lift my left arm high, and Gent pulls his hand close enough that I can lay my palm against his cheek, my hand so tiny against the vast plane of his face that it might as well be a speck of dust. "You caught me. You'll always catch me."

Gent stares at me another long moment, and I reach up a little further to brush the drop of wetness that has seeped over his lower lid. Then he swings his hand away, and a moment later, he lays it on the ground again.

Fortiss helps me off, supporting me when my legs are too wobbly.

"Miriam is still out cold," he reports. "But she's breathing, and nothing appears to be injured. Tennet is watching her. Marsh is exhausted, too—he's also in a dead faint."

He gestures and I can see the giant heap of a Divh through the gathering night. And that finally strikes me as a detail too.

"It's night?" I say stupidly, staring up the sky. "I know there was a storm, but it was daylight when we reached the plane of the Divhs and barely dawn at the First House. How is it already so late?"

"Szonja said that time moves differently here—and has no meaning in the way that we mark it. After all—she's served my family for as long as we've been keeping records in the First House. That's not possible if she actually ages."

"Yes, but..." my head is swimming again, and I lift my hands to steady it, wincing as my right shoulder protests. "The sandworm had babies. How does that...I mean..."

He laughs as I shake my head. "Light willing, we'll have plenty of time to answer all the questions we have about the Divhs and all the ones we don't even know enough to ask. Right now, we need to get back to our own plane and pray that Szonja is correct about the passage of time there. Caleb and Nazar are scouting the outer perimeter of the Divhs' plane, which seems to end at that western range." He points to a track of mountains jutting up from the horizon, enormous even at this far distance. "The closer they get to it, the more the winds churn."

"That range is congruent with the Unlit Pass—the only known pass through the mountains to reach the Western Realms." Miriam's voice floats toward us, and I turn to see Tennet with his arm wrapped around the woman, helping her move forward. Miriam's skin is as white as bleached parchment, and she appears about thirty years older than she did when we left the First House this morning. I jolt as a spurt of fear zips through me. Miriam isn't banded. Does time work differently for her in this plane?

There's nothing wrong with her mind, though. "We need to look for a collection of mountains all bunched together, as if they were pulled together by a child. In the domain of the Eighth House, those mountains formed a natural protection for the house despite its location so close to the pass, and between that and the protection of the Divhs, it's survived unscathed these many generations."

"Unscathed?" asks Tennet, stepping away as she straightens and smooths down her robes. "How much contact does the Eighth House have with the First? Were they party to Rihad's plans to overthrow the other houses?"

"They were not," Miriam says sharply, turning to him. Her voice comes out a little raspily, and she blinks, then lifts a hand to her throat. She clears it and tries again. "You forget, not only was I born there, but I've traveled many times to the Eighth, though it's been years since I saw it last. No amount of Rihad's machinations could have pierced the heart that beats in that house. It is Protectorate born and Protectorate bred. They would never do anything that would lead to the end of our state. I wager they'd rise up against the Imperium itself if it sought to impose its will against the will of those born here."

She blinks, as if startled by the severity of her own words, but they have my thoughts racing in a new direction.

"The Savasci," I blurt. Fortiss and Tennet turn to me, but my eyes are on Miriam. "You were aware of them, that they'd come to the Tournament of Gold. You may have even known where they were hiding out."

I glance at Tennet, seeing the obvious question in his eyes.

"The Tournament of Gold was harried by marauders of a unique sort, thieves of stealth and cunning who didn't kill their victims, and who moved like the night. They were a band of women, and they hailed from the mountains of the western border. Not exactly the Eighth, but close."

I turn back to Miriam. "How well do you know them?"

"Well enough to protect them when I can—and ignore them when my attention would only cause them harm. Lord Daggar of the Eighth was aware of them too, of course. His father's father tried to root them out when they first formed their commune in the mountains between the Eighth House and Merrivale. But theirs was a movement that wouldn't die. Eventually, they came to an agreement—the Savasci could serve as hunters for the Eighth, and in return, they were not hunted."

"Hunters," Tennet scoffs.

"Some of the fiercest you'll ever meet, Lord Tennet," Miriam says coolly, offering him a dismissive a wave of her hand. She completes the movement, but her glance alights on her fingers, and she goes still.

"Well, if they're hunters, maybe they know a way up to the pass into the Western Realms." Fortiss grimaces. "I confess I thought simply that I would give Szonja the instruction to enter back into our plane and it would be done, but she seemed... confused by that."

"Confused?" Tennet looks back to where Ayne is soaring low over the churning lake, barely visible, but my eyes are on Miriam as she stares, dumbstruck, at her hands.

"What—what is happening?" she whispers, as if they are crumbling to dust before her eyes. And maybe they are.

I reach out to Gent, my mind racing furiously, and am rewarded with his short, delighted huff. The rest of us barely remain standing as he leaps to his feet, coming down with a mighty chomp. And then he disappears.

"What is that?" Tennet demands, rounding on me. "Where did you send him?"

Fortiss gapes at me too. "You didn't just send him back to our plane, did you? It can't be that easy."

"I didn't, and it's not. Think about it, Fortiss. We've been moving so fast, we're not remembering how Divhs interact with us. They interact with *us*. They're connected to *us*. That's the only way this works—the only reason why we can thrive here. But Miriam's not connected."

"But I was fine..." Miriam stutters, but the words are strangled.

"Time passes differently here," I say—it's my only guess, but I think I'm right. I hold up my left arm, glad it's not my right. "Fortiss?"

He moves to me and unlaces my sleeve, stripping it away while Miriam goggles at us. My primary band is barely an inch wide, with two-dozen whisper-thin strands still stacked beneath it, each of them shimmering bright with their own, distinct movement.

"No," she says, taking a step back. "I'm not a warrior, Lady Talia."

"Not yet," I agree, and flash her a grim smile. "But if you're going to survive this place, you have to be."

Gent's howl fills my mind, and I step back abruptly.

"Give them room," I order, squinting up into the stormy sky.

"*Them?*" Tennet demands. "Who's *them?*"

The air snaps tight around us.

CHAPTER 23

The Divh that Gent has brought back with him is like nothing I've ever seen. A brilliantly feathered, multi-colored, long-necked bird of prey spreads her wings and screams at us, her accusation filling my mind with fury. This Divh was supposed to be at the Tournament of Gold, I realize. She pledged herself to me as a rightful warrior, but she couldn't just leave because the warriors on the Fated Plane had decided to ruin themselves. She had responsibilities! She was a collective!

Her outrage takes on new meaning as she spreads her wings in a sharp, cutting flap, and a half dozen miniature versions of her spin into the sky, darting and whirling, snapping and churning, furious with activity. This is the *them* that Gent meant, I think. These miniature Divhs are feathered with every color of the rain-bow, their wings spreading wide to reveal two sets of claws on squat little legs with long, grasping talons. Each of them are the size of a pig, and their inquisitive, slender faces cock and roll to take in every detail of us as their wings whir in furious, nonstop motion.

"You're a hummerbill." Miriam's shocked voice rolls over us, and I turned to see her staring with unabashed adoration at the primary bird-like Divh. It's not a large one, maybe only two-thirds the size of Marsh, the height of two sturdy barns stacked on top of each other. But with its six auxiliary miniature Divhs, it's an impressive, swirling menace. It cocks a glance at her and then at me.

I was going to be there at the battlefield. I can serve, but I'm not meant for stupid warriors who cannot stop killing long enough to think. I cannot—

"I present you a warrior of the mind," I say quickly, if only to get the creature to stop howling in my mind. Miriam's hands go up, but Tennet and Fortiss are at her sides, each of them moving forward. The hummerbill looks at the councilor, leans forward, and spreads its wings again, sending its whirling dervish miniatures into renewed frenzy. It stretches up its head and cries out with a call that sounds like it emerges from the dawn of the Light itself.

With that otherworldly shriek, it launches itself at Miriam, and I realize that it too has two sets of powerful claws on long, tucked-in legs at the base of its belly. It plucks Miriam up as if she weighs nothing and soars into the sky. I hear Miriam scream, and I wince as flame erupts around my left bicep. The band!

Sure enough, the lowest thread of band has loosened itself from my collection and scrapes a bloody trail down my hand. It spins off just as the hummerbill returns with Miriam and practically dumps the woman on me. Not bothering to wait a moment longer, the band connects with Miriam's outstretched hand and races up her arm, burning a line through her pale skin.

But she doesn't shriek, she doesn't shake, instead, Miriam staggers back from me, wide-eyed and open mouthed. When her gaze meets mine, her eyes open wide with wonder.

"What have you done?" she gasps.

And *then* she collapses.

Her hummerbill Divh squawks and instantly disappears, poofing back into sight on a distant ridge, all six small hummerlets spinning around her in agitation.

Fortiss drops to his knees, shouting to Miriam to breathe, to work through it as her body processes the change. I crouch down on her other side, keeping her head from banging against the rock-strewn ground. Tennet stands and stares at the hummerbill, who eventually, little by little, starts to stalk closer.

"Are those her offspring?" he asks, then checks himself. "I mean, is it a she?"

"Kreya," croaks Miriam, as she struggles to a seating position, then uses Fortiss as a brace in order to stand. Her color already looks better, as far as I'm concerned. She may be still reeling from banding—and I'm pretty sure there will be several bouts of nausea to come—but she's no longer actively dying in front of me. Progress.

"Her name is Kreya, and those aren't her offspring, not in the way that we think of them," Miriam continues. "They're extensions of her, duplicates that she can direct separately. There are mentions of hummerbills in some of the earliest annals of the Protectorate, but nothing recent, they certainly have never been entered into the Tournament of Gold. There was some question as to whether they were suitable for battle." She shakes her head and gazes at the hummerbill with pure adoration in her eyes. "As if that should ever be the only reason for a Divh to bond with us."

I blink and share a startled look with Fortiss. Miriam is a councilor of the Protectorate, one of eight learned souls who are charged with guiding the lord protector in all things related to the safety and stability of our border nation. What she's just said amounts to sacrilege and treason wrapped up in one breathless observation.

Probably not a good time to point that out to her, though.

Incoming! Caleb's shout reverberates through my mind as well as in my ears, and the hummerbill disappears with a squawk—all of her—as Wrath swoops into view, Ayne and Szonja directly behind. It's a testament to the scale of the wide, rocky beach that it seems like there's plenty of room for three enormous Divhs to congregate, especially when Gent howls from somewhere over a distant mountain. Within moments, though, Wrath has galloped, then trotted, then slowed to a walk, finally extending one leg for Nazar to gracefully slide down...with Caleb sprawling after him.

"This entire side of the lake looks like the entryway to the blighted path," Caleb says, coming up onto his toes easily and swinging his right arm wide. "There's nothing here. No Divhs that we could find, no grass, definitely no giant berries. There's maybe a pocket in the mountains that could correlate with the geographic setting of the Eighth House, but..." he pauses to peer at Miriam more closely. "Are you okay?"

"Councilor Miriam has been banded," Fortiss announces, and Caleb visibly jolts while Nazar turns sharply as well, taking in first Miriam, then Fortiss in his shocked gaze. "Not as a warrior—or at least, not intentionally—but she was failing in this plane. Talia guessed, and I agreed, that the problem was that she wasn't banded to a Divh. This is their world, after all."

"Their world..." Nazar draws the thought out, then grimaces. "That would explain why we can't leave it as easily as we entered. Caleb and I tried multiple times to get Wrath to return us to our plane—anywhere except the First House. But our options were limited to our homes—the Twelfth, Tenth, Second, or First." He grimaced. "Wrath told me he could return me to Hakkir, if I wished. He remembers the way. Otherwise, we're stymied. As Wrath put it, Divhs are summoned to the Fated Plane; they are linked to where we are linked. They are bound to carry us home."

"Home." Tennet repeats. "That's of no use at all. We would have been better served with fast horses—or traveling with the Divhs in dark of night, never mind the noise."

Caleb snorts. "Or the villages trampled beneath their stampede."

"At least they'd hear us coming," Tennet shoots back.

"It's a question of strategy, then, and strategy is in our favor here." I draw in an unsteady breath, not at all sure that the logic that seems to flow together so seamlessly in my mind will hold up under scrutiny. "The First House has been councilor Miriam's home for the past twenty years and more, but she wasn't born there. She was born in the Eighth House. There's at least a possibility that Kreya can take us there."

Tennet scowls. "But Kreya has never been to the Eighth House —or anywhere in the Fated Plane. How would she know where she's going? How will Miriam, after all this time?"

"I'm not so feeble as that, Lord Tennet," Miriam informs him wryly. "I can remember my home."

I hear the querulous murmur of Gent the second before Wrath spreads his wings, and the screams of far-off dragons echo off the mountains. The enormous mound of Divh that's Marsh lurches upright, clamping his hands over his ears, staggering back and forth as his head swings around, his eyes widening as he locates Caleb.

"What's this?" Fortiss demands, but we're all getting the same images from our Divhs—images that have already been so deeply burned into our minds we'll never forget them— a thick, writhing throng of snakes pouring toward us through the night sky, an avalanche so thick, it blots out the stars.

Caleb staggers back, staring upward, though nothing is visible yet. But there's no denying the agitation and confusion of the Divhs. I know how they feel.

"I thought you said they weren't of this plane!" Caleb demands. "How can they travel through it?"

"It's full dark," Tennet offers, also staring hard into the sky, as if by his sheer fury he can materialize the threat so we can handle it. "Maybe they can only see in the dark, and that's why the fire confused them so easily."

Caleb flaps his right arm dismissively. "Well that's *great*, but we can't just—"

"Drop flat!" Fortiss shouts over them, and his next words both reverberate in my ears and within my mind. *Cover your bodies with your cloaks. Talia, get the Divhs out of here. Only Szonja and Ayne should return on our call.*

Without thinking, only responding to the urgency in Fortiss's voice, I will Gent away, ordering him to vanish from this spot as efficiently as the hummerbill had. Marsh vanishes a moment later as Caleb crashes into me. The force of his push sends me sprawling toward Tennet as Fortiss dives for councilor Miriam. Nazar bounds up to us, and the five of us hit the hard unforgiving ground as one, scrabbling together, wrapping our cloaks tight.

Within moments, the unearthly chittering noise I'd hoped to never hear again fills the air. At first, it's a bare murmur beneath the crashing waves of the lake, but it quickly becomes a screeching, hurtling tide. The crescendo builds and builds, and when I don't think I can take it anymore, I hear Fortiss ground out his next order. As one he and Tennet howl, "*Now!*"

This time I can't tell if the sky snaps tight, but the arrival of the dragon Divhs is obvious for another reason. Fire lights up the night, catching the trailing edge of the skrill aflame. Now that I can get a closer look, I realize this is a far smaller horde than we fought at the coliseum, never mind how loud they are.

But their lesser size only makes Fortiss's battle strategy more effective, as Ayne and Szonja attack them again and again with gouts of fire. The poison coating the skrill's skin acts as an accelerant, and flames lick through the entire horde, blasting it apart and sending fried carcasses skittering through the sky to land against the rocks and into the water with angry hisses. Several of the dying skin rain down over us, and we hunch together tight until the blighted assault peters out. With twin screams of pure dragon satisfaction, Ayne and Szonja wink out again, and the five of us roll apart, shucking the last few roasted snake skins caught in our cloaks. The skies are empty, but the rocky beach and water are littered with skrill carcasses.

"Can any of them survive the water?" Caleb asks, turning to Tennet.

Tennet scowls back at him. "Do I look like an expert in skrill? I've never even seen the things before the other night."

"There will be more," Fortiss says. "That first group may not have been expecting us, but we won't be so lucky the second time. To the Eighth House!"

Without another word, he thrusts his left fist into the sky. Szonja appears again, Wrath and Ayne right behind her. Gent howls from the rocky foothills and Marsh pounds up, his wild eyes searching once more for Caleb.

I turn to Miriam and shake her, realizing too late that she is once more covered in sweat, her eyes unfocused, her skin clammy. Now, finally, she's going through the shock of being banded to a Divh.

"Summon Kreya," I order her. "You've seen it done a thousand times, at tournament after tournament, you know what to do. *Summon* her."

Miriam stares at me, then wheels away. Shakily, she lifts her left hand high, forming a trembling fist. Then she closes her eyes, sucks in a deep breath—

Almost before she is able to get her Divh's name out, Kreya appears in a flurry of whirling wings and attendant hummerlets, bursting into our small group. A moment later, she's surging upward again, only this time with Miriam in her clutches.

"Gent!" I shout reflexively, not sure at all that Kreya will have sufficient upward motion to carry Miriam anywhere, let alone to the Eighth House.

My Divh seems to agree with me. He roars and rips his paw toward me, sweeping me into his grasp. I try to breathe out my fear and fail as he pumps his arms once, twice—then he leaps up, wrapping a mighty arm around the squawking hummerbill midair. He pulls her close to his body as if he's plucked flowers for the journey back to the Fated Plane. Then he touches down lightly on one of the craggy mountaintops he's spent the day exploring and uses that as a springboard to leap again—this time far, far higher.

As the original bonded warrior to Kreya, for all that she wasn't able to appear on the battlefield at the Tournament of Gold, I can hear the Divh's thoughts alongside Gent's. I expect her to be furious, but instead she coos and chirrups words of encouragement to her half-dozen hummerlets and a traumatized Miriam, wrapping her wings around them and cuddling close in Gent's grasp as we rip through the storm clouds.

We break through a thick cloud of heavy mist. Around me, stars explode in a kaleidoscope, zipping currents of energy and pinpoints of brilliant light that I can barely see through Gent's loosely clenched fist. No sooner do we arrive at this staggering space, than the stars seem to jitter and change direction—or maybe we do. The dizzying blur of them blanks my mind and everything goes black—

And then all I hear is screaming.

I jerk more fully awake, my skull nearly splitting with the cacophony of voices jumbling in my head. I hear Szonja's and Ayne's roars, Marsh's squawk, Wrath's imperious scream—but their actual words are lost beneath the roar of Divhs of all types and sizes. Sandworms and flying lizards, four-legged and six-legged beasts covered in fur or leathery hides, chitin-covered winged insects—we all burst out of the sky over a vast, sundrenched landscape of high plains, grasslands, and mountains that stretch up-up—then sheer off at the top, looking more like manmade walls than any purely natural barrier. But I can only peer at them for an instant as the entire lot of us—nearly forty Divhs strong—land in the great open bowl of grasslands an hour's slow ride from an imposing fortress of red-and-gray stone tucked into the base of the mountains.

For a moment, everything is silent. Then I hear Caleb's shaky groan. "Let me down, Marsh. I'm so gonna be sick again."

"Same," I gasp, and pound on Gent's palm.

My Divh opens his hand and drops me onto the thick, waving grass, while Kreya nudges Miriam out beside me. I stagger over to the councilor, trying desperately to regain my equilibrium as the hummerlets soar skyward in squawking joy. Miriam's fully passed out, but she's breathing, and I lift a shaky hand to shade my eyes as I peer at the Eighth House.

"Where did all these Divhs come from?" Tennet's exasperated

voice explodes in my head, as loud as if he's standing right next to me.

Then I realize he *is* standing next to me. Of course he is. He doesn't speak in my mind, only Divhs speak in my mind. That's the way that works—the only way.

I turn to explain everything to him, and he glares down at me for half a moment before his eyes go wide with shock. "Talia!"

I collapse into his arms.

CHAPTER 24

"I've got her. You deal with *them*."

I feel oddly disjointed, like I'm no longer rooted in the earth, and yet definitely not caught up in my Divh's mighty grasp. In fact, I don't sense Gent anywhere near me at all, and yet I'm definitely not standing, not lying down, I'm—

I blink my eyes open and stare up into Tennet's laughing eyes. "Well, hello, Lady Talia. Glad you decided to rejoin us."

"Put me down."

"Not yet." To my surprise, it's Fortiss who issues this order, and I realize he stands next to Mirriam's still-collapsed body, while Caleb kneels beside the councilor, dabbing a folded sash at her brow as if she's bleeding.

"The warrior distracts and lulls his opponent into false thinking," Nazar says, drawing my sharp focus. I crane my neck to see him better, and Tennet obligingly shifts me toward Nazar. The priest's eyes are on the far distance—where I'd seen the Eighth House. "We arrived like a battle party, forty Divhs strong. Before the Eighth House could even open the gates, we'd sent our Divhs home and looked more like a troupe of bards in need of a rescue. Both presentations were useful, but the second will ensure our safe passage into the house more quickly and easily than the first."

"Miriam's already down," I argue. "There's no need for—"

"Nazar's right." The surprisingly strong voice of the councilor floats up from her huddle of robes. "Lord Daggar is the newest in a long line of leaders who don't know what to do with capable women, and he's trained his house to be the same."

"Lord Daggar," Tennet echoes, as if he's rolling the name around in his mouth and finding it suitable. "I like him already."

He clamps his arms around me tighter as I elbow him in the gut. "The Eighth House lost good men in the Tournament," I grouse. "Those who survived would have told him who I am. I'm not weak or needing to be carried by an oaf."

"Just a little longer," Fortiss says, and his voice also sounds odd —everyone's voices do—fuller and richer, more nuanced. Did the fall from the Divh's plane damage my hearing or augment it in some way? "Curious warriors are easier to defeat than wary ones."

"But why do we need—"

"Hush, Lady Talia," Tennet says, then—infuriatingly—he lifts me up higher in his arms, just far enough that he can lean down to brush a kiss over my ear. The move is so unexpected I barely avoid bleating in surprise as a shimmery shiver of energy rips through my blood, awakening every inch of me.

"Fortiss is injured," he hisses urgently to me. "You're the distraction from that. Go with it."

My eyes lock on his as he edges back, but there's no deception or teasing in them. "How?" I murmur, but Tennet's back to staring at the company of armed horsemen streaking out toward us. "Just —put me down already. I can look pitiful from the ground."

"Maybe I like carrying you."

I snort. "Maybe you can go hang your—"

"Lord Protector Fortiss!"

I flinch as Tennet's grip tightens convulsively on me, as if the loud, booming-voiced man riding toward us is somehow a threat. After what I've survived these past several weeks, it would take more than shouting to unnerve me, but I find Tennet's instinctive reaction both strange and...oddly appealing.

Clearly my transition back to the Fated Plane has crippled me harder than I thought.

The head of the Eighth House delegation gallops up, leading his brace of fighting men. He's older than I expect him to be, older even than my father and Rihad. Given the fiery orange of his cloak and tunic, this has to be Lord Daggar.

I view him through my lashes while I pretend to still be in a dead faint. If not for Nazar's approval of this farce, I would've already punched my way to a standing position. Still, it allows me to judge Lord Daggar without feeling awkward about staring.

Gray-haired, wiry, and stern-faced, he carries himself with both authority and resolve, a steadiness in his bearing that I didn't expect given Miriam's judgment of him. He sweeps our small group with a quick, assessing glance, and I can feel his gaze hard on me and then his scowl at Miriam. Does he know who we are, specifically? Has he heard what I did? Beyond what his men have told him, seeing an entire battalion of Divhs on his doorstep had to be unsettling.

Fortiss strides forward, and to his credit, Lord Daggar dismounts. He cuts the distance between them another few strides, then lifts his right hand to his chest, forms a fist and places it against his heart. He bows formally to Fortiss.

"We were not expecting you or your company, Lord Protector Fortiss," he says as he rises, his oddly timbred voice carrying to us on the wind. "We certainly weren't expecting a brace of Divhs. And for you to arrive on their shoulders or clasped in their grip...such a thing hasn't happened since the Great Conflict. We are honored with this sign of solidarity."

"There's much that has changed in the past month." Fortiss turns to gesture back to us. "We've suffered in our travels, and two of our company are injured. If we can trouble you for horses...we can speak more easily inside."

"Yes." Daggar lifts a hand and a half-dozen riders move forward out of the center of the group, each with a second horse. "Can your injured soldiers ride?"

"They can," Fortiss assures him, and I watch Daggar stiffen as Caleb helps Miriam to her feet. Tennet finally takes that as a signal to drop me to mine. He still holds me as if I'm going to crumple, and it's all I can do not to stomp on his instep. Beneath my feet, the ground is strangely sandy, tall grass twisting up out of the loose soil. I broaden my stance to keep my balance.

Daggar scowls from Miriam to me. "Why are you traveling with a...*you*." He practically snarls the last word, and he takes a long stride toward me, then checks himself and turns back to Fortiss. Tennet's arm around me has turned to a solid band of iron, but he makes no other move.

"My warriors sent riders ahead with orders to switch out horses wherever they could to help speed them along," Daggar continues, his words now harsh and clipped. "The catastrophe of the Tournament of Gold cannot be understated, but that a *woman* was involved..." His lips twist in an ugly grimace as he glares back at Fortiss. "Do you know what you've unleashed, Lord *Protector* Fortiss?"

"I know that the former lord protector put our entire nation at risk to further his own aims," Fortiss says stiffly. "I've yet to understand exactly why. I further know that there's a threat emerging from the Western Realms which has already breached our defenses. I wouldn't come here in such haste otherwise, Lord Daggar. But let me be clear. Lady Talia is a critical reason why we're even standing here at all, and why you had any soldiers able to return from the tournament. If they told you the story, you know I speak the truth."

"I know you speak the truth as you understand it, but there's far more that you do not understand, Lord Protector. That needs to end now. Because you're right, there is a new threat emerging, or better stated, an old threat returned." He jabs an accusatory finger at me. "And she's the reason why."

For just that moment, I'm grateful for Tennet's stalwart presence beside me, because the key emotion rolling from Lord Daggar isn't disgust or rejection, both of which I expect. It's fear.

Daggar turns back to his riders. "Escort the others," he orders as they bring the horses forward. They all step back to allow us to mount on our own. Tennet practically throws me up on my steed like a sack of flour, securing my feet in the stirrups with quick, fierce movements. He's furious, I realize with some surprise. It seems an odd reaction, but if he's angry at me, he'll have to get in line.

Still, I can't help but contrast the very different reactions of the men who surround me. Daggar might hate women like me, but Fortiss wields me like a weapon. And Tennet... Tennet acts like I'm a storm he's already survived once. And maybe wouldn't mind being struck by again.

"Lord Protector Fortiss, we'll start our discussions in private," Daggar says, interrupting my rabbiting thoughts. "Your company can join us—*Miriam*?"

He breaks off as he glances back to our small group and sees the councilor for the first time with her hood thrown back, mounted on a horse. Because I'm staring at him with such focus, I can track not only the change in his voice but the flash of recognition in his face. I glance back to Miriam, and she's staring at him with an expression of such studied neutrality that I would laugh if the moment wasn't suddenly so fraught.

"Lord Daggar," she replies, her words containing just enough deference to take the sting out of them, but not so much as to convey any warmth at her homecoming. "Well met."

Daggar shakes himself forcibly, then turns back to Fortiss. "You brought a *councilor* with you, carried by Divhs through the Blessed Plane?"

I grimace, imagining Daggar's reaction when he learns that Miriam has been banded. Fortiss doesn't respond at first, taking his time mounting his own horse. His cape is thrown back to reveal his black and gold tunic, and he looks every inch the lord protector as he wheels his horse around to face Daggar again.

"There's much we both need to learn, Lord Daggar. We should get to it, if you're ready."

Daggar gestures expansively with his hand for Fortiss to begin, then urges his own horse forward until it's even with Fortiss's mount. The two of them head out toward the Eighth House, first at a trot, then at a canter, then at a full gallop, their cloaks flowing back from them to announce the splendor of their respective houses to any who might be looking.

I glance over to Caleb to find him smirking at me. "So there's some use for capes, I guess."

"My lord," the head guard begins, addressing Tennet, who's by far the most lordly of all of us. "If you and your party will follow."

Tennet, however, doesn't respond at first, and I turn to see him peering hard at the thick knot of forest punching down from the mountains, scrambling along the rocky terrain about a quarter hour's ride from the Eighth House. "What's over there?" he gestures. "Who do you have watching us?"

The guard turns, scowls. "We've positioned no one there, Lord Tennet. Doesn't mean there aren't hunters or worse in the forest, though, and if any saw your brace of Divhs the way we did from the Eighth, they'd be curious."

"Hunters," I murmur, and I squint as well, wondering if we're being watched by the Savasci. Syril and her band made no secret to me about their unsanctioned home near the grand Eighth House, but how exactly did that work in practice? Lord Daggar clearly isn't a fool, and the Eighth House looks well-fortified. It wouldn't be all that hard to assemble a troop of soldiers whose only job was to rout out the marauders from their nest and either return them to the Eighth or disperse them.

But disperse them to where? Unlike the First House, there's no village here at the base of the mountains that I can locate, just the walled fortress. I peer along the mountain range, but the terrain is too jagged for me to see far.

Tennet seems to be tracking my thoughts. "You've a village nearby, then, outside the walls of the Eighth?" he asks, gesturing to the fortress. "If there are hunters not affiliated with your house, they have to get their supplies from somewhere."

"There is." The guard gives up the information easier than the mountain will. "The village of Merrivale is a hard day's ride along the Meridians to there, where the range bumps out." He gestures to the north, where I can easily see the bulging curve of the range —dark green in the afternoon sunlight. "The forest along the path hides a wealth of natural caves. It makes for easy lodging for those not looking for the protection of the Eighth or the rule of the village magistrate. But as long as you ride farther away from the forest, out into the plains, it's a safe enough journey. The hunters, for the most part, are simply that—men looking for game to feed their family or to sell in the village. But for anyone willing to get their food honorably, there are others happy to steal it. Lord Daggar keeps his own safe, but if you choose to roam the forest, you take what chances you must."

Tennet grunts a short laugh. "Then things aren't so different here as they are anywhere in the Protectorate."

He nods to the guard who turns and shouts orders to his men, while the four of us fall into line behind him. The men form a loose net around us, not close enough to keep any of us from breaking away if we chose, but an official protective escort. I glance back to the mountains. If the Savasci are out there watching, how much did they see? I hadn't thought about the message the arrival of so many Divhs might send. Would they guess I was here, marking Fortiss and his bold colors as a party of the First House? Would they know why we're here?

The forest isn't willing to give up its secrets yet, so we strike out across the open plains toward the Eighth House. As we near it, the guards angle to the right, closer to the heavy canopy of trees, until we reach an established road with low stone walls to either side, deep troughs flanking it. The road rises gradually toward the Eighth House, which I realize as we approach is elevated higher against the mountainous cliffs than I first though. It's an impressive fortress, about half the size of the First House, but easily three times as big as the modest manor house of the Tenth.

How does it compare to the Twelfth? I frown as the errant

thought skates through my mind. Tennet's home is buried even deeper in the mountains than mine is, hemmed in by thick forest and rocky terrain. Does he yearn for a larger holding—more power? Or is he content to serve as sentinel for the Protectorate, casting a wary eye in all directions?

"Lady Talia." Nazar's quiet voice, little more than a sigh, draws my attention, and he nods almost casually to the right. I squint up into the trees, not seeing what he's clearly trying to point out...and then I do, as a fluttering shift of movement against the darker branches draws my eye.

Three of the hummerlets are perched there, squinting down at me with an inquisitive tilt to their heads. They all appear far too satisfied with themselves—and one of them is displaying a belly that's full-on *glowing* in the shadows of the branches.

"But..." I glance back at Nazar, startled, and his grimace tells me everything I need to know.

"It appears Kreya is concerned for our safety and has left her sentinels behind. And it appears these particular sentinels offer more than just eyes to help us see. A warrior takes the gifts he is given, and fashions them for war."

CHAPTER 25

I t takes us another easy quarter hour to reach the gates of the Eighth House, which stand open to welcome us, flanked on either side with more guards. Once we're inside the gates, I blink to make sense of the place. It's bustling with as much activity as the village leading up to the First House, just in miniature.

"Everyone lives inside the walls?" Caleb asks, craning around to peer at the two-story shops. "Like, they just live above their storefronts and stables?"

The guard continues to prove a willing guide. "If they work here, they live here. Either above their shops or within the caverns below the castle, deep in the mountain."

We all pin our gazes to the man. "Caverns?" Tennet prompts, and the man nods, gesturing to where the Eighth House rises up like a bulky fist from the stone of the mountain, thrusting out of a sheer rock base.

"It looks solid—and it is, solid enough. But there's a reason the ancients chose to build here. The rainy season is mild enough now, but long before we ever arrived on the doorstep of the Meridians, violent storms pounded this area, filling up every natural crevice with driving rivers. Gouges became corridors, small depressions grew, shallow caves deepened. What nature wouldn't extend or connect, the settlers at the dawn of the Protectorate did—building on whatever they found. There's water below, and minerals to mine, and great open spaces lit from fissures high above. It's a protected space for those who live within the walls, and Merrivale isn't so far away that anyone with an itch to leave can do so. Lord Daggar's rule extends to Merrivale officially, though its magistrate runs the village as he sees fit, for the most part."

I frown at the soldier. His explanation seems perfectly reasonable and provides far more information than I would expect from a house guard—which ordinarily should simply please me. Instead, it doesn't feel quite right. I'd expect this level of detail from a councilor, not a fighting man.

Perhaps the soldiers of the Eighth receive more history training because they were stuck out here so far from anyone? Or maybe we just got lucky with a well-educated man at arms? Either way, I find myself growing uneasy as we stop before the steps leading up to the doors of the main manor building.

The primary structure of the Eighth is far less ornate than the First House. It's a building built for protection, not show, but it still displays fine stonework in its carved grand stairway and bannisters. The bedrock is the same flat red I see everywhere, but the stairway is lined with sturdy, squat statues carved from every color of stone imaginable.

I peer closer and see that the statues are all manner of Divhs, some of them carved out of granite and quartz, some poured in ash-colored cement. They're beautiful in their miniaturized form, and clearly old—maybe as old as the first few generations of the Protectorate? It wouldn't surprise me.

Then I stiffen. One of the statues moves—then another. Two of the hummerlets have lined up in the empty spaces between the stone statues, puffing out their downy chests, their beaks arching up in cocky salute as we ride by. I clamp my mouth shut tight to keep from laughing and pray that Kreya's other representatives are more discreet.

The ground level of the Eighth House boasts doors that extend the height of two men cut into its walls, and these stand open to reveal a large stable. As we approach, several workers rush out to assist, once again stopping short of touching us. They grab our horses' bridles once we're on the ground and lead them away, and within only a few moments the talkative guard directs us up the wide steps of the Eighth House. With each new stair, I'm weighed down with a fatigue that nearly takes my breath away.

"You'll want to rest after your journey," the guard announces, and I peer at him again. Maybe he is a seneschal of some sort, just one who's...very well armed. Or maybe every member of the Eighth House needs to be ready to protect the fortress at a moment's notice. This far out on the western border, there'd be no help coming in a hurry in the event of an unexpected attack. "Dinner will be served in Lord Daggar's inner chambers; you'll be summoned. For now, we've rooms for you as delegates to the Eighth."

He turns us down a long corridor, and I note the uncanny darkness inside the Eighth House. The way is lit by occasional torches set into the walls, but not too many of them. This is a people used to the shadows, I think, their fortress set into the mountain itself. Similar to the First House, but more deeply entrenched.

That changes when we reach the delegates' section, at least. The guard steers us into a wide, airy chamber that boasts a sitting area lined with doors leading to multiple sleeping rooms. It's such a relief after the unrelenting gloom of the inner corridors of the Eighth House that it catches me up short. What would it be like living in this fortress day in and day out? I frown as I retrace our steps mentally through the Eighth House, trying to recall any of the household staff that we passed along the way, but I can't. No doubt, Lord Daggar ordered them to stay out of our way, but the guard is helpful enough, pointing out the rooms and inviting us to take our ease. Within moments of his departure, Miriam retires into one of the sleeping rooms. Nazar and Caleb disappear into two others while Tennet eyes me critically.

"You should sleep," he announces. "You're more tired than you're willing to let the others know."

"Mm. And you know me so well you can make that assessment more easily?"

"I have eyes."

He glances to the sleeping chambers, then back to me, but I ignore him as I move toward the large doors cut into the far wall, paned with heavy glass to let in the sunlight. I expect them to be heavy, but they shift open at the slightest touch, and a moment later I'm out on a wide veranda, not unlike the overlook at the First House. "Impressive, for delegates' chambers," I comment as I step out onto the stone plaza. There's a low wall and several carved chairs that gleam with fresh wood polish. "I wouldn't have thought the Eighth House entertained delegates that often. I don't think Rihad made it a habit to come this far."

"The edge of civilization," Tennet agrees, looking up at the great mountain that rises around us. "Undoubtedly, when the Protectorate was first formed, this would have been a place of great celebration and also great vigilance, holding fast against the dire enemy on the other side of the walls. That threat diminished as the years passed, but the house's reputation likely only grew. We've lost a lot of that history, it seems, all of us becoming more separated as the generations have gone on." He shrugs. "The privilege of peace."

His words hit me oddly, and a chill slips along my skin, as light as feathers. "You fear that war is coming? Real war?"

"There's an unrest I feel, but it's not war, not exactly," Tennet says, surprising me. "There's too much we don't know, too much that Rihad planned. He wasn't looking for the Protectorate to fight back, if everything that Caleb has been telling me is true. He was expecting his allies from beyond the western borders to sweep through the Protectorate on their way to the Imperium, barely slowing down to dispatch all of us and our Divhs. What he planned for them to do after that, I can't guess. Did he expect to overthrow the Imperator himself? To set himself up as the new Imperator? What was his end goal?"

They're good questions and echo the ones that Fortiss has been demanding without success of the councilors. "Rihad operated according to his own counsel, from everything I can tell," I say, dropping heavily into a chair. It's shaped oddly, angled into a position that forces me to half recline. Comfortable, but not conducive to serious conversation. Still, once I sink down into its embrace, I know immediately that I don't plan on moving again anytime soon. I lean back. "He didn't bring anyone into his confidence."

"I didn't know the man, but I have a hard time believing that. He had to trust someone." Tennet pulls a nearby stool into place and sits beside me, perching easily and seeming far more alert than I am. His gaze searches the face of the building behind us, then shifts out over the broad vista of the open plains, but his mind is clearly elsewhere. "Rihad got as far as he did, did as much as he did, because people allowed him to. Anyone he came in contact with, from all accounts, simply bowed to the man, allowing him to take complete control. Even Fortiss bowed and scraped to him, by his own admission."

I bristle at the characterization. "Rihad was the lord protector. He demanded and deserved that level of fealty from his people."

"Fealty yes. But blind trust? That sort of behavior only makes sense in the midst of a crisis. If we were actually at war, we'd want a leader that would instill in us such loyalty that we would follow him to the ends of the Protectorate and beyond. But we're not. We haven't had a major crisis of any sort in the Protectorate other than the seasonal devastation of the storms, the following challenge of drought, and, of course, the endless round of marauders. But these are all issues that we deal with and move on from, year in, year out. Yet here we have Rihad taking a leadership role twenty years ago, then quietly and slowly hatching his plans and building...what? By your own account, he didn't have a private army that was privy to his plans. The councilors, for the most part, seem like worthless old fools, not even skilled in the one job they have, which is maintaining the history of the Protectorate. No. Rihad has no confidantes and even fewer friends—and here he's planning a bold campaign to harness the evil of the Western Realms, burn through the Protectorate, and attack the Imperium? All by himself? It just doesn't make sense."

I scowl. "We don't know anything about his internal network. He's been in some sort of trance since the Tournament of Gold. And lest you forget, that tournament was barely a month ago. It's not like we've had a lot of time to unravel twenty years and more of his machinations."

"Fair," Tennet says, the capitulation unexpected as he twists to pull another of the heavy chairs near him. Rather than sink into it properly, though, he keeps his seat on the stool and simply leans his back against the chair's headrest. He then lifts up a booted heel, and balances it on the edge of my chair, a warrior relaxed but still at the ready. All the while, he stares out over the open plains of the Eighth House lands.

"A man has to have friends," he murmurs. "That type of person thrives on the glory of secret cabals. They mock the average person while celebrating their superiority with fawning sycophants who have their own perceived power."

"Perceived," I echo, following his train of thought. "A group of men, and they'd mostly be men with Rihad, if not all of them, who think that they have some measure of control, some place of value in his power structure. Maybe they do, maybe they don't. But chances are, they have nowhere near the power they think they have even in the best of circumstances."

"Exactly. But he miscalculated." Tennet lifts a hand to rub it against his jaw. "Fortiss was a miscalculation. He didn't bring him into his confidence, because he felt like he didn't need to. He felt like he had him so firmly under his control that he could flip him at a moment's notice. That he simply had to crook his finger and Fortiss would come running. He miscalculated there. Or he didn't, and the situation merely changed through outside forces that he couldn't predict."

He glances over at me. "That would be you, in this scenario. You certainly didn't figure into Rihad's plans, for sure. And your arrival had the unanticipated effect of undermining his control not only over Fortiss but, again, if Caleb's accounting is accurate, over several of the other house warriors as well."

I grimace. "You and Caleb seem to have had a great deal of time to get acquainted."

"He likes to talk, and I like to listen, especially when it's someone whose accounting is both fresh and unvarnished. But you're the important piece here. You turned into more of an enemy of Rihad than everyone before you, combined. And even when he knew the danger you represented, he didn't finish you off. He should have. I would have."

"You'd make the same mistake," I mumble, my eyelids suddenly heavy. "You dismiss me at every turn."

"Not every one," he corrects me, and his voice is suddenly closer, not louder, but—

I blink my eyes open, to realize Tennet is barely a breath away from my face, his blue eyes startling with their intensity as he leans close. "You play a dangerous game, Lady Talia, more dangerous by far because you don't realize you're playing it. I would protect you from all who would seek to destroy you, and I'd protect you from your own misjudgment."

I smirk at him, most of his words running off me like rainwater off a roof. But I still can't resist getting in a jab of my own. "But who would protect me from you?"

Somehow from the place where the words formed deep in my mind to how they sound as they slip past my tongue, the tone and intention of my dig changes dramatically. The question comes out too intimate, too intense, and when Tennet's gaze locks with mine, my heart thuds roughly against my ribcage, so loud he can't help but hear it.

His lips curl into a teasing smile. "No one," he says simply, and leans forward, capturing my mouth with his.

The heat of Tennet's kiss drives straight through me, eliminating every trace of fatigue and languor in an instant. Everything inside me leaps to total attention—fear, excitement, desire, and curiosity fusing together with the abrupt sensation of being plunged into an icy lake on a miserably hot and clammy day. I am suddenly and unutterably *alive* once more, and my hand comes up without any conscious direction of my own, flailing at Tennet's tunic.

I don't know if I'm trying to pull him closer or push him away, but he has no such hesitation. His own hands come up to cradle my face, his large fingers tangling in my still too short hair as he leans down over me, pressing me into the trap of my reclining chair. His tongue snakes out and, finding my lips parted, dips into my mouth, hungrily seeking, tasting...as if he's trying to take anything that I might give, to conquer any part of me I'm willing to cede. I reach up and wrap my fingers around the broad palm of his right hand, peeling it away from my face so I can shift, I can breathe.

The movement seems to recall him to himself, and he leans back from me, but only the barest inch. "You and I were promised to each other, Lady Talia," he murmurs to me, his words like a blade between us. "And I am a man who believes in keeping his promises."

I draw in an unsteady breath, feeling the danger here, but for once, not wanting to run away from it. "That promise wasn't made between us; it was made between our fathers. Maybe yours involved you in the discussion, but mine didn't."

"Not all traditions are bad," he murmurs, and somehow he's leaning forward again, drawing his lips across mine in a move so much more devastating because it is gentle. He traces a soft and intimate trail across my cheek, up my jaw, resting softly at my ear. "We might have been brought together by decree, but we could stay together by choice and be stronger for it."

His teeth scrape against globe of my ear, the pressure sending whirls of sensation shooting through my belly, my blood, compromising both my resolve and my wits at once. Then his fingers are twining through my hair again, the soft pressure tugging my lips toward his once more.

This time I'm the one who reaches for him, who leans up to capture his mouth, to take and to plunder. He tenses for an instant, then the battle renews again and within seconds it seems he's pulled me out of the chair and up. His arms around me as my feet barely shift to ensure I don't stumble. His embrace is hard and demanding, and arms surround me with strength, just as he promised.

Just as he promised.

The indignant squawk of a trio of hummerlets bursting out of the sleeping rooms and onto the overlook is all that saves me from utter disaster.

We pull apart and have fully two chairs between us before Fortiss's voice rolls out over the stone overlook.

"Oh good, you're both here. I could use the counsel of someone who isn't a thousand years old."

CHAPTER 26

"**I**s he mad?"

Tennet's question is a reasonable one, and a distinct possibility given Fortiss's terse accounting of his just-completed conversation with Lord Daggar. I stare stonily at Fortiss as if I, too, am wondering about the sanity of this house lord stuck all the way at the end of forever, defending the Protectorate's borders against utter evil.

In truth, my thoughts are a jumbled mass of conflicting sensations, pinging back and forth between Fortiss and Tennet like weevishes about to molt.

What in the blighted path had I been *thinking*? Yes, I'm exhausted—maybe even damaged by our sojourn in the Blessed Plane. Yes, this House has seemed to twist me around and turn me inside out since the moment we dropped onto the wide, grassy plains before it. But what madness consumed me to think kissing Tennet was a good idea? *Tennet!* I'm no more promised to Fortiss than I am to the Light—there's no real agreement between us—but I don't want to give the Twelfth House lord the wrong idea, either. He's not my future—he's not even my past. And while he's been more than clear that he'd happily be my present, that's a madness any warrior of worth would run far away from.

I am an idiot—a fool.

The more so for how my heart still is galloping madly, standing between these two men who are so different from each other—yet who both distract me nearly to madness.

I draw in an unsteady breath and try to focus as Fortiss dismisses Tennet's assessment about Lord Daggar's state of mind.

"I don't think so. I simply think he's been the lord of this holding for a long time, and that he suffered great losses in the tournament. None of the Eighth House warriors have returned from the Tournament of Gold—their injuries have forced them to tide over in middle plains for now, and Daggar's concerned they may die there. He's bitter, and he has every right to be. If he chooses to place his belief in artifacts over me, I can't blame him."

We're back in the main sitting room, standing close together, the doors to the outside shut fast. A fire roars in the hearth though the day isn't cold. Fortiss looks cold, though, his cloak still hanging heavily over his shoulders, his arms folded tightly across his torso. He looks like a man who's seen some things he would rather forget —done some things he probably now regrets.

Does he know he's not alone in that feeling?

I firmly don't look at Tennet lounging beside me.

"You can't seriously believe he has an actual chamber of prophecies somewhere in this manor house," Tennet protests, giving me another few moments to collect my skittering, chittering thoughts. "Seems to me, he would've attained a higher profile if he held that sort of arcane power."

"Not if he's only held it for a few weeks," I counter, finally finding my voice. "He said he's only gotten visions in that chamber —what, in the last month?"

"Since the melee, yes." Fortiss makes a face. "Apparently, that shook something loose in the Eighth House, some dark, buried power that's existed for maybe as long as this house has stood."

"Well, you never want to leave dark, buried power lying around," Tennet mutters, and Fortiss gives him a wry smile.

"Honestly...I don't know what to think. All these years that

Rihad's led the Protectorate, I paid very little attention to his movements outside the First House unless I was with him—which often wasn't the case. He'd give some order that I was to be nominally in control while he was traveling, and I took it with all the puffed-up importance of a total puppet. But the councilors were there, and his guards were deferent to me. I could practice the art of warcraft, eat his food, and resolve the various troubles of the village as they were brought before me, giving me the illusion of normalcy, of an eventual path to the real responsibility I craved. I wasn't only a fool, but worse—I was blind to what was going on around me."

"You think Rihad was building a coalition?" Tennet prompts when Fortiss's gaze flickers toward the fire.

Fortiss shakes his head, surprising me. "Not in the way you're thinking. I know you find it impossible to believe that Rihad didn't have his supporters, and I'd agree with you. I think there are still truths we have yet to uncover in all this, truths that will implicate even those who remain close. Not Miriam," he answers my unspoken question with a wave. "She's a woman, and Rihad wouldn't trust her with his most intimate confidences."

Tennet humphs in agreement beside me, while I tighten my lips with annoyance. Tennet may be beautiful, but he's still, well... Tennet.

"So, the other councilors, you think," I say to cool my own reaction.

"At least one of them, yes, but even still, I don't think they know anything more than what Rihad was willing to dole out just to keep them on the hook. I think he shared deeper confidences with some of the other lords, but notably not here at the Eighth House. From here, he simply took what he needed. Lord Daggar shared with him all the information about this holding that's due to the lord protector, much as he's shared it with me. Then Rihad left with assurances that he would return soon to deepen his understanding and knowledge of all that the Eighth House held. He never once returned, though, not officially."

"In twenty years," Tennet scoffs. "He never once made it back here."

"No. I suspect quite sincerely, though Miriam will disagree with this, that there were traveling parties that set out for the Eighth over the years. But wherever Rihad went on those journeys, it wasn't to visit Lord Daggar in this mountain keep. It wasn't to explore the mysteries that were held here."

"But you think he did explore them," I challenge. "Just in a way that Daggar wouldn't suspect?"

"Yes, and here's why—that creature you saw in Rihad's fireplace, the man covered in snakes? Daggar described it today to me, calling it the fabled leader of the skrill—the Sahktar."

I stiffen, remembering that word. First from Tennet's ravings after the skrill had chewed on him during the attack over the coliseum, then when Fortiss whispered it to Rihad, back in the caverns of the First House. "So that's a real creature."

"It's real, and it's stirring. He's seen visions of it in his prophecy chamber—which he says he'll show me at dawn tomorrow. Apparently, the visions are most powerful in the morning."

"Or, you know, he's insane," counters Tennet.

Fortiss doesn't honor that with a response. "There are a few references to the Sahktar in some of the archived books here as well, he says, but remarkably few. All *those* books are now held in Daggar's personal chambers for his private use, however, because some of them had gone missing over the years."

"Missing," humphs Tennet. "Stolen, you mean."

"It's the only thing that makes sense. Daggar gave Rihad some books—those they'd already made many copies of—but not the ones most precious to the Eighth House. Through the books he could get his hands on, Rihad must have figured out how to communicate with the dark powers on the other side of these mountains, and they told him what the other books contained. Most likely, Rihad commissioned others over the years to collect the ones he decided he couldn't access magically. The chamber where those most precious books were originally kept was visited by no one other than Lord Daggar—only him, and only to perform the rituals of cleansing at the appointed times four times a year. It's a ritual that falls to the house lord and has since the dawn of the Protectorate. According to Daggar, the vault where all these books were originally held has been disturbed a handful of times over the decades, books misplaced or disturbed, so eventually, he moved the most important ones. But there are other things he left in that chamber, too—talonstones. So many of them that if one or two went missing, he wouldn't know or care."

At the word talonstones, I go still. "What are they?" I ask sharply.

Fortiss's lips twist. "I thought you'd be interested in that term."

"The what?" Tennet looks at both of us blankly, and Fortiss leans toward him, balancing an elbow on one knee.

"You really don't remember anything you said to Talia that night after the skrill attack, do you?"

Tennet scowls. "I—"

"Don't worry—it's probably better that you don't. In your delirium, you mentioned talonstones, specifically the phrase 'from talonstone to grounding stone', indicating a path could be formed between the two. And apparently, in the bowels of this castle—in a chamber Daggar practically gave me a map to, so vivid was his description—there's an entire crate of these talonstone things."

"But what are they, specifically?" I press. "Where did they come from?"

"He didn't say, and I didn't ask." He shoots me a wry grin. "But you can bet I want to find out. Still, that's when my conversation with Daggar turned...more fraught. Apparently, about a month ago, at a time that seems to coincide with the closing days of the tournament, a storm broke over the Meridians, blocking the Unlit Pass from sight. Pressure built, so strong it drove the weak and the sick into deeper illness and caused powerful headaches in the warriors. That lasted for days, and then it was abruptly gone, as if a dam had finally broken or a door burst open from a constant assault. And that's when they started hearing about attacks along the mountain road."

"Attacks," Tennet echoes, rubbing his jaw. "Snake attacks? You're saying the skrill got loose?"

Fortiss shrugs. "Maybe skrill, maybe not. But something was on the move. At first the attacks were easy to ignore, marauders killed at night on the road between the Eighth House and Merrivale. Deaths that were unwitnessed and unremarked upon. Mostly, the villagers and Eighth House residents alike attributed it to the acts of the Savasci. They're known to the point of legend around here, and Daggar treats them as a rumor unsubstantiated. Something to be avoided, but handy in the case of dead bodies that he doesn't want to explain. But there have definitely been more deaths than usual—enough that Daggar is now officially concerned."

"But the Savasci were at the First House, or at least a solid chunk of their party were," I say. "Were they somehow able to get word to the women here? How?"

He grimaces. "That's something I don't yet know, and something else I need to find out."

"What do you mean, women?" Tennet asks. "Who are these Savasci?"

I smirk at him. "What, you mean there's something that Caleb hasn't told you?"

"They're not our focus right now," Fortiss insists. "I'm willing to concede that this prophecy chamber may simply be an old man seeing things in the dark, but the rest of his tale needs investigating. We've got to get into Daggar's inner chambers and read the books we're missing—and we need to find these talonstones."

Tennet shrugs. "Unless Rihad already took everything of value. If there was any book in Daggar's inner chambers or in this secret vault of talonstones that was a threat to him, he would have destroyed it."

"Maybe—but maybe not," I say. "If there was a book that was truly valuable, but too noticeable to be moved, Rihad would simply ignore it until he needed it. Especially if he could somehow access it through magical means. Better to keep it here, locked up tight under the very nose of someone who doesn't know enough to understand when it's being accessed, until he was ready."

Fortiss nods. "I think so too. Rihad thought he would have plenty of time. I suspect he fully planned to return to here after the Tournament of Gold, officially breaking down the borders between the Protectorate and the Western Realms and drawing a dark army of skrill to him to sweep back east."

"Uh-huh. Have you told Lord Daggar any of this?" Tennet asks.

"I have, yes. I've told him everything. Rihad laid the foundation of his actions through secrecy and cunning, but that's not how we're going to overthrow him. If anything, we need to be more forthcoming among the houses, more honest about everything that we do, everything that we're thinking."

As Fortiss speaks, he swings his gaze to me, holds my eyes as if we are the best of friends and he can trust me with anything. I'm sure my cheeks would burn with uneasy self- awareness if I wasn't already reeling from the idea of Rihad using the Eighth House as his personal treasure chest for all things dark magic. "He said something else about you, Talia. You really set him off—first in a way that he seemed to fear, and then...I don't know. He asked a lot of questions about your role in the tournament."

I grimace. "Look, I didn't—"

"'The dark shall draw the dark.'" Fortiss cuts me off, narrowing his eyes at me. "You ever hear that before? I don't think Tennet said it."

"I..." I wave my hand, at a loss. "I don't remember that, no. He said that about *me*?"

"I don't care what he said, we need to lock Daggar down—whether through fear or camaraderie, whatever works," Tennet announces. He's moved closer to me without me realizing it, which sets off an entirely new spurt of panic. But he doesn't seem to notice as he continues speaking. "You should recruit him to your cause, Fortiss, recruit all the houses to your cause if you can. Those that were attacked in Trilion certainly would be willing to listen, I should think. Beyond all that, there are settlements along the western border that would understand the threat that's long loomed over the Meridians and certainly agree to fight on your side to keep it knocked back. With every house you visit, you'll get more followers. And if the time it takes to travel to each of those houses merely requires a tour through the Blessed Plane...you could reach them all quickly enough."

"But we've already tried that." I sigh. "Our Divhs can't just hop from house to house like traveling bards. Warriors need to summon them or Divhs need to be returning a warrior home. "

Tennet turns to me, his brows lifted in challenge. "Do they, though? Before this morning, I wouldn't have thought it possible to travel to the Blessed Plane for any other purpose than banding to or training with a Divh. Maybe we simply haven't figured out the right way to travel through their plane easily."

"You've asked Ayne?" Fortiss asks, but Tennet dismisses that with a frustrated wave of his hand.

"I've tried, and he's tried to answer me. But he speaks in riddles and half statements that seem perfectly obvious to him. What about your Divh—any of them?" He redirects his intense gaze on me, and there's no strange and dangerous intimacy in his expression, no recognition at all of what we just shared—whatever that was. Clearly, he's moved past it, and so should I. "You have a different bond with yours, and a newer one. A changed one, yes? Gent was banded to Merritt and by all accounts was nowhere near the size he became after he banded with you. You're a woman; you shouldn't even be able to band with Divhs according to all our laws—and no, don't bother arguing with me. A month ago you wouldn't have thought it possible either. But it was. It is. Light, today you banded a Divh to a woman—*another* woman—who's not even a warrior. She's a learned, respected sage, but sages don't band to Divhs, or so we thought."

Fortiss grunts in agreement. "Unfortunately, Miriam's not taking to her banding so well as you did, Talia. She's pretty ill."

I frown at that. "She just needs time. Caleb and I were both sick for days after we first connected to our Divhs, we just had the space to work through it. Miriam will recover quickly enough—maybe more quickly, since she's not banded to a battle Divh."

Tennet makes a face. "You make the assumption that they're not all battle Divhs. Too many assumptions, when what we need are answers."

He says this last as a muttered aside, and Fortiss piles on. "Tennet's right, though. Your connection with Gent is the key factor in all of this. You were able to succeed in the Tournament of Gold due to that connection, and you were able to do things that none of us even considered because of it as well. What does *he* have to say about travel, connecting with the other houses, and drawing the other Divhs to our cause?"

"I mean, we did it once before, right?" Tennet turns to me, his mood finally shifting to real interest. His eyes have widened slightly, his mouth cutting into a grin as he rolls up on the balls of his feet. "Back during the Great Conflict, at the dawn of the Protectorate? It's not like the Imperial army came marching in to find the Divhs propped up against these mountains, waiting for them. There had to be that moment of first connection, the point at which the Divhs agreed to lend their aid to the Imperium. How did we manage that?"

I lift my hands in defeat. "I have no idea. To your point, I was never trained formally as a warrior. I never thought I was going to *be* a warrior until a few weeks ago. And it's not like that sort of training was given to the women of our house as a courtesy. You two should be the ones to know it, not me."

"Well, my father wasn't big on fairy tales," Tennet says wryly. "To him, Divhs were less a sacred mystery and more a self-contained army that could be summoned at a moment's notice—a big club to wield if and as necessary, for a very specific purpose, and then relegated back to their magic box until they were needed again."

"At the First House, it almost went too far the other way,"

Fortiss says. His voice takes on a distant, contemplative tone, as he replays decades of memory and finally sees them for what they truly are. "To us, the Divhs are creatures of power and legend, but more than that, they're a sacred trust. Other than in the visceral and bloody pageantry of the Tournament of Gold, they're spoken of only by bards and priests, not by soldiers. We know, of course, that there are common men banded to Divhs of lower station, but there's always a condescension to that acknowledgement, that this was a sop that we long ago provided to the masses to give them a hint of why they should treat us all with veneration. Because we're the ones with the powerful connection, we're the ones with the warrior-level Divhs. But it's both too much and not enough. Rihad could have taken a stand on this, and he didn't—no one has."

I shoot Tennet a confused glance, but his eyes are trained on Fortiss. "Rihad didn't go far enough in either direction. He didn't push to understand more," Tennet says, as if he and Fortiss are having a conversation I'm not privy to. "He did just enough to cement his role as leader, but not enough to actually lead the Protectorate forward."

"He didn't have to do anything more," Fortiss agrees. "And he didn't want to—probably the same as every lord protector before him."

Understanding finally hits me. "Rihad has the ability to band Divhs. That means he could have banded the Divhs as easily as I just did to someone other than a warrior. I mean, the Divhs that he's banded to house soldiers are every bit as capable as Kreya—and she's every bit as capable as them. So, he *could* have chosen to band lower-level Divhs to other leaders in other trades. He didn't. Why? Did he think it would have cheapened the connection?"

"It certainly would have made it harder to control the Divhs, sure. Warriors understand the process of command," Fortiss says. "A scholar? Maybe not so much. That could be a problem."

"Well, maybe—but why not try it out? Why did it take me trying to save Miriam's life to come up with this idea?"

"Don't look at me," Fortiss returns ruefully. "Like Tennet says, you're the one with the deepest connection to your Divh, a pathway already forged. Use it. Ask Gent."

"But I..."

"Here." Tennet reaches for my hand and pulls me back through the large doors and out onto the stone overlook. I should be panicked again, but it's as if Tennet's already forgotten what happened out here, moved on like a galloping horse to a new adventure. Between that and the view before me, a wide vista of dwindling forest leading down to open plains, I find myself no longer worrying about him but about what he wants me to do—which he explains in short order. "Summon your Divh and let's see. Caleb said you could call him on a moment's notice, no rituals or pageantry required."

"It's broad daylight," I protest, chewing on my bottom lip. I feel unreasonably nervous about performing this simple task, like I'm on the edge of a discovery I don't particularly want to make. "Everyone will see."

"Then you go to him," Fortiss prompts. "You've done it before."

I swing my gaze from Tennet to Fortiss, irritation finally sparking within me. I no longer want to talk to either one of them. I no longer want to do anything other than reconnect with Gent to unravel this mystery. To stop with the questions and the wondering and just *know*.

I pull away from Tennet and move out into the center of the overlook. I open my mind, my thoughts, and reach out—straining without straining, reaching without yearning, connecting without the need to touch. Far off in the distance, I hear the delighted howl of my Divh, awakening to my murmured request as if he were born into the Blessed Plane for only that purpose.

"Gent," I murmur, and then I'm moving. Distantly, vaguely, I hear Tennet's startled shout, register Fortiss's sharp command, but they are nothing to me, not anymore, not in this moment. I race forward, leaping up onto a chair, and then onto the low wall framing the overlook. Then I'm in the air, soaring over open space, reaching out my hands as my vision blurs and my eyelids droop and breath is stolen from my throat.

I leap because it's easier than standing still. Easier than waiting and wondering what's possible. And, blood and stone, easier than arguing another moment with two men who value different pieces of me—but who may never be able to accept me in full.

I leap.

And...then I start to fall.

For a terrifying, paralyzing half-second, I feel my trajectory shift, my ascent arc into descent, and for the first time I notice the sun playing across the slithering, shivering grass, the wide empty plain of sun-warmed earth. I'm falling, falling—

With a heart thudding wrench, I'm ripped sideways and thrown into the air. Only it's a different air, a different world. I'm surrounded by the blue, blue sky and distant deep emerald hills of Gent's home territory, the water glistening off the shore like liquid emeralds, everything rich, vibrant, verdant with promise.

Giants roar all around me as I'm swept back into Gent's embrace, my enormous Divh clutching me close as he plummets down to carry me to the safety of the rolling hills of his beautiful home...only...

We're heading straight for the lake.

CHAPTER 27

The shock of our crash into the water blanks all my senses until a moment later we're out again, and Gent opens his great palm to the sky. He beams down happily as I splutter, bedraggled and sodden.

"Did I look like I wanted a bath?" I demand. He throws his head back and howls with simple joy, then grins down at me like a proud parent as I scramble back in his palm, bracing myself on the leathery hide.

"You know why I'm here? You know what I need to know?"

He huffs contentedly.

I widen my eyes. "You do, don't you?" My mind actually starts hurting inside my skull. Not the muscle and blood and skin and sinew, but actual thoughts giving me real pain. "But how? How do you know what I need before I even know how to ask for it?"

He doesn't have an answer for this, just continues beaming at me. His glance slides off to the right as if he's contemplating another impromptu dive into the depths of the lake. "No! No," I say hurriedly. "I need to know, to understand..."

Words fail me once again, so I just create images in my mind, imagining me at the Eighth House, then at the First, and then at the Tenth, as if I'm literally walking out of one chamber in one house and into a second chamber in the next. Gent cocks head at me, and I sigh. So much for him knowing what I need to understand.

"House to house," I say, scrubbing my hands over my face as I try to make him understand. "I need to travel house to house. Like...how did you find us? How did you know all the way back in the beginning where we were when we needed you? How did you know to come to us before any of us were banded to you?"

Gent squints at me as if I'm an idiot, then lifts his other mighty paw and draws it close. With the softest, most delicate movement, he taps the claw of his smallest finger in the center of my forehead. Never mind it's like being hit by the broad side of a pony, I don't stagger back—it's that gentle of a touch.

For a moment, there's no Fortiss, no Tennet, no crown or prophecy. Just me, and the one creature who always comes when I call.

Gent huffs again in hooting encouragement, and I gasp as my mind fills with images of great vistas, mountains, the wide bowl of the open plains, bands of riderless horses—and a million sunsets and sunrises, with trees growing from sapling to towering sentinels the only indication that time's rolling on. Then, over the mountains and through the rich forests of the east, an army comes —not a great army, not a powerful force, but thirty ragtag men and women on powerful steeds, packhorses trailing behind. It's an exploratory party of some sort, their Imperial standards flying boldly as they ride.

They flow across the wide plains, stopping at broken ruins of castles and keeps, plundering and powering on. They ride all the way to the west, but their energy also extends back the way they came. It stretches in a curious starlit trail eastward toward the rising sun, through mountains and endless forests, beside a wide and tumultuous sea to a glorious city of gold where there are books, people, and learned men—soldiers, a room laden with maps, and another dominated by a throne of gold...

And I see it all.

"But how..." My mind balks at the barrage of imagery, bouncing from one scene to the next as I struggle to understand. Above me, Gent huffs again, the roll of his warm, chuffing breath sweeping over me. I know in my heart that he intends to ease my stress, but it only serves to drive me to a heightened frustration. It's all right *here*, right in front of me. And somehow, I can recognize—everything. People I've never met, moments I've never experienced, events that I have no connection to that I have no way of understanding. But how is that possible? Because I *don't* know these people, I wasn't there, I'm not part of...

Then I see it. The man at the head of the troop of Imperial riders—grinning, laughing, every inch the conquering warrior enjoying the spoils of his search. He pulls out a circlet of gold with jutting decorations on either side, and he places it on his head.

Everything in the timeline leaps into brilliant focus. The flow to the west as well as the flow to the east, the memories of a land destroyed long, long ago. And in every stop along the way, small, curved beacons buried in the walls and foundations of buildings large and small light up like a million crescent stars, each of them connected to the others by a thin filament of light. *Talonstones.*

I stare in absolute wonder, my breath stilling in my throat.

These thirty men and women from the Imperium are little more than marauders, but there's nothing for them to conquer but ruins of long-ago holdings. Holdings that I now see in split view through the eyes of a man who wears a winged crown—General Mirador. I hear his thoughts as if they're my own—there was a people here once, and there would be again, all for the glory of the Imperium.

I think of the Shattered City trapped between the Tenth and the Twelfth Houses, a place so full of dread that when the Protectorate had formed the holdings that would support its great families, they hadn't based one there. The houses to the east were small, nimble, and the Shattered City was too much to try and protect and contain. There were too many places for marauders to hide, for animals to shelter, for rumors to build.

But in the plains and the west, the ruins were merely long-ago castles and manor houses, as well as remains of villages next to thriving waterways and verdant fields. Even along the Meridian mountains, the terrain is so much more beautiful in my vision than it is now—a wide valley of trees and thick green grass, a deep lake. Nothing like the yellow, waving, grass-covered plains here now. And the location of the Eighth House is a good place for a manor house—the first of several that would lead this land, all for the glory of the Imperium.

Mirador looks up at the sky, a frown marring his brow beneath his golden crown, and I strain to see what he sees as he lifts his left hand into the sky. Divhs, I think...but not only Divhs. Something else.

Something worse.

"Talia?"

The sound seems to be coming from far away, but it's not Gent speaking my name, prodding and shaking me. Still, it *is* Gent whose gentle poke is growing worse now, so much worse, as in my mind Mirador's eyes snap wide, fixing on an unknown threat. A sense of profound, unutterable loss blasts through me, the driving spike of Gent's talon shoving through my mind, skewering me with a pain so great that I screech out—

"Talia!"

I wake up choking, a stream of water pouring over my face, into my mouth, as powerful arms hold me tight to something warm and firm, my legs kicking out violently, my arms flailing.

"*Talia,*" Fortiss yells again, upending another carafe of water over me, soaking me and Tennet behind me, who grunts with effort as I pitch and writhe.

"I saw—saw it! I saw it," I splutter, struggling for breath, for sanity.

If anything, Tennet holds me tighter, while Fortiss grabs my thrashing arms at the wrists and pulls them in tight. The three of us are so close we could fit into our own grave, and the combined pressure of them finally quiets me. I meet Fortiss's golden eyes, feel them searching mine as if he can somehow pry the answers out of my mind. I open my mouth to speak, but no words come out.

"Tell me what you saw," he urges, and a wave of panic overtakes me again, images pouring through me, drowning me.

It's too much, though, and I shake my head violently, trying to shove it all away. "What...what happened?" I finally manage. "T-tell me what happened to me."

Some silent communication passes between Fortiss and Tennet, and Tennet's pressure eases on my shoulders while Fortiss steps away, pulling me with him with a gentle hold on my wrists until we reach the long benches. I blink around, confused. We're back on the stone overlook of the Eighth House, and I'm drenched to the skin.

"How much water did you dump on me?" I grumble as Fortiss slowly eases me into a seated position.

"Barely two cups worth," he lies as he drags up a stool and sits close to me. Tennet stands at my side, legs braced wide, as if he expects me to tumble over into a faint. "You agreed to summon Gent, and then you seemed to shift into almost a running motion, but you never moved. Your right hand swept out, your left arm cocked, you leaned forward...and then you convulsed, your skin turning nearly blue, your hair, clothes, all of you suddenly drenched. Hardly any time had passed at all, but you started gasping and flailing, and I didn't want to smack you awake. Water seemed the better choice."

"I guess I should be grateful for that," I say, then feel the gorge rising inside me. I lean forward, my elbows on my knees, as Fortiss scoots back—but he doesn't leave me. He won't leave me, I think —just as Gent won't.

Nausea rocks me again.

"I'm fine," I gasp, and I feel his sure touch as he smooths my hair back, slicking its still too-short length into place behind my ears. I spend a few moments dry heaving before finally regaining my breath again.

I squint up toward them both, not trusting myself yet to sit up straight. "I saw...I understand how the Divhs found us. Mirador summoned them, yes, but they were ready to be summoned. They've always been ready. They're tied to this land and to the people who occupy it—whoever they may be. That's where it all begins and ends, with the people who take ownership of the land. We are their anchor and connection to the Fated Plane. There was another society that lived here well before us, who made their homes in the same places where we eventually founded our current houses, at least in the middle of the Protectorate and to the north, south, and west."

I swing my gaze to Tennet. "Our houses are newer, up in the mountains of the east, but there were people there before us, in the Shattered City."

"That was destroyed in the Great Conflict." He nods, but I shake my head.

"I don't think so. I think it was destroyed long before then. The explorers of the Imperium may have gone through that city, or they may never have seen it at all, at least not until after they began building the Protectorate. But there was a reason why no one rebuilt there. It had been ruined long before our original arrival in this place, its treasures lost or buried, waiting for someone to find them."

"Well, the army of the Imperium should have, surely."

"Except they weren't even an army." I shake my head, seeing it all again in my mind's eye. "The scouting party that the Imperium sent out was maybe only thirty riders. Some men, some women. It wasn't the grand army that we were led to believe. It wasn't an army at all, and some died along the way—though most of them survived, I think. They kept pushing west, exploring, raiding, but it wasn't like they were stealing from anybody who was going to object. There was nobody here. Whoever had lived in this land before us had died out centuries before. Maybe millennia. All that they had left behind were a few simple treasures."

I straighten a little more, scrubbing my face to order my thoughts. "One of those treasures was a crown with two flaring sides. It's got to be the crown of wings, Fortiss. It did exist, a relic of some bygone civilization. It existed and the Imperial party found it." I draw in an unsteady breath. "And once their leader put it on his head—that's when they realized there was more to this land than they expected. I think that's what gave them the ability to call their first Divhs."

Tennet stares at me. "The crown of wings—that doesn't actually exist."

"Yeah, well...maybe it did at one point?"

"That's not right, though." Fortiss scowls. "All the old records are consistent on this point. There were people here when the Imperial army rode in to conquer this territory—actual *people*, not some lost civilization. Holdings and villages that welcomed them and let them pass. There was no obstruction at all until the creatures of the Western Realms stopped them in their tracks. Then the Great Conflict took place, and our army protected those who were here and defeated their enemies, and power was gratefully, easily transferred."

He grimaces as he finishes the recitation of history that's been taught to all of us, even me, reaching up to rub his jaw. "It doesn't really hold up when you think about it, does it? Even if Imperial riders were allowed to pass peaceably by, even if we did prove instrumental in protecting the locals from some enormous threat, that doesn't translate into a small army suddenly being granted the right to rule the entire land. There has to be more to it than that."

"More...or, more likely less," Tennet agrees. "If this traveling band was able to somehow connect with the Divhs and conquer the skrill or whatever in the blighted path they are, how much easier for them to do that if it was just a small band of warriors and a mighty army of Divhs? Nobody to protect, nobody to defend, nobody to corral into doing things your way. It's literally like the Tournament of Gold all over again. An exhibition match between two foes off in some separate space. Whatever happens in that battle after it is done is a matter for the bards and historians to craft, because there's nobody around to gainsay them."

"And if there's only thirty people whose stories have to stay straight, then that's easier too." I squint off into the empty plains that my mind keeps wanting to plant with grass and trees, a glimmering lake in the distance. "But how could that be possible? How could we have grown so much so quickly? We are an enormous thriving country—all of that grew from thirty people?"

"That's at least easier to explain." Fortiss waves that away. "We have well-documented accounts of the Imperium sending more settlers after they learned of the threat to the west and the need to create a Protectorate to ensure the safety of the Imperium. It wouldn't take many settlers to build—a few hundred here, another hundred there, and so on, all of them loyal to the Imperium, all of them routinely sending back tithes and tribute. Self-sufficient but loyal."

"And they would be loyal too," Tennet says. "It would serve no one for the Imperium to explore too closely how good we had it here—or to learn that the crown of wings was real. Because if it was, it should have been sent to the Imperator at the beginning."

"Well, fair," I agree. "But the Divhs could have shared all of this a long time ago. They are the keepers of the Protectorate's past; all we had to do is ask for them to explain it."

"You say that, but not every Divh is as easily understood as yours," Fortiss says with a wry smile.

"I..." I blow out a breath, but he's not wrong. "I think it's because I won the tournament. I, um, earned the winged crown. Because the things I saw..." I blink, suddenly recalling another image.

"There's more, Fortiss," I say, straightening, and his focus trains on me, sharp and earnest. He trusts me, I suddenly realize, maybe more than anyone he's ever trusted in his life. "Those talon-stones that Daggar mentioned. They're a real thing. Each of the warriors had them, and each buried them in the bedrock of their new houses, from the First all the way to the Twelfth—in the villages, too. We never use them this way, but in the beginning, they were sort of homing points for the Divhs, separate of their warriors. And there's a *lot* of them—or there were, anyway—"

"From talonstone to grounding stone," he murmurs. "They're the same thing. One you carry, one you bury in the ground or in a building. Rihad didn't have to put them anywhere to direct the skrill—they already exist in each of the great houses—and probably the cornerstones of the villages surrounding them as well. All the skrill needed was for him to summon them...which he did, it seems, though they took their time in answering."

"Or maybe they stole some of the talonstones from Daggar's vault," I point out.

Fortiss winces. "Or that. But for them to come to the First House, to attack the lords of the other houses...Rihad had to have been behind that somehow. Even if he never woke to do it."

"You really think Rihad is that far ahead of us?" Tennet protests. "That he knows this much about what's buried here at the Eighth?"

"Not all of it," says Fortiss. "Not the Divhs' part in all this, I don't think. Rihad never considered the Divhs to be any sort of partner in his path to glory, only an army of beasts to lead gloriously into battle. This link between the talonstones, Divhs, and the crown—that's true partnership. It's connection and communication, not domination. Rihad may have figured out the piece with the talonstones as a directional tool for the skrill, but how Mirador originally used the crown to summon the Divhs? I don't think so. And if he doesn't know that, there's probably more about the crown he doesn't know."

"The crown that doesn't exist anymore," I say, a little bitterly.

Fortiss's gaze swings to me. "The Divhs would never have told us this if we didn't ask. That rule seems inviolate. Yet nobody thought to ask. Nobody thought to rise up and challenge everything we thought we knew, not realizing that there was so much more out there than we could even grasp."

"Some tried," I counter, thinking of the Savasci. "But they

couldn't get far. We're the ones with the army of giant Divhs. That would tend to shut down a lot of conversation."

Fortiss nods. "Tennet—go wake up Nazar and Caleb. If we can find some of these talonstones and use them to help us travel, those two will be the ones make the attempt. Talia, come with me. Lord Daggar was pretty remarkably clear on where the vault was that houses those stones and some of the ancient books. We need to go there, now."

I squint at him. "You really think he's going to allow us to go roam around his house unaccompanied in broad daylight? Even if they don't know exactly what they have?"

Fortiss blows out a heavy breath. "Well...fair. But we need to act soon. Tonight, I think. Something's felt off since the moment we hit the plains in front of this house. And if it's simply this supply of talonstones and maybe the actual crown of wings sitting buried in a chamber somewhere, waiting for its rightful owner to claim it..."

He meets our gazes steadily—first Tennet's and then, for a longer beat, mine. "Then tonight, we begin a new dawn for the Protectorate."

CHAPTER 28

Dinner with Lord Daggar is nothing like what I expect. Then again, little has been what I expected in the Eighth House.

First off, we dine in a room that's only slightly bigger than the bedchamber that Miriam and I have been assigned. Secondly, our dining party is conspicuously small. I'm told by Caleb that Lord Daggar is married and has grown children who serve as magistrates and functionaries in the mountain villages that spread out from the Eighth House, ensuring the protection of the border remains constant and fierce.

Caleb also learned that The Eighth House has its own set of priests of the Light, a true luxury this far away from the heart of the Imperium but another sign that the house hues to old ways. Nazar was keenly excited to meet these worthy men, the first true priests that he's encountered in the Protectorate, and throughout the long walk to this inner sanctum, he practically buzzed with inquisitive energy, rivaling only Caleb in his interest in everything around him.

But none of those priests are here tonight. Neither is Lord Daggar's family. No one is here tonight but Daggar and a couple of the same stone-faced guards whom we'd met out on the open plain.

A faint scuffling noise sounds beneath Miriam's feet as she seats herself, and I give her a sharp look, wincing inwardly at her grimace. At least we're not completely alone. Though I'm not sure if hummerlets are considered decent dinner company.

I don't mind having Divhs on hand, though, even very small ones. Because this private dining room of the Eighth House is buried so deep inside the keep, it almost feels like we're celebrating inside a tomb. The walls are paneled with a deep, dark wood, intricately inlaid with stone in a swirling, sinuous pattern that evokes snakes so powerfully it feels as if they're going to crawl right off the walls.

Lord Daggar waits until we're all served wine, then he stares around at us, flagon in hand. "Tonight, we welcome the return of the lord protector and his interest in preserving the safety of the Protectorate—a visit we've waited patiently for these past twenty years," he says, raising his cup high. "It's been far too long since I've told the story of this house and our place in it. Such stories were meant to be celebrated by those who hand them down directly, not buried in books or twisted on the lips of dilettante bards. We are a proud house, the first to rise up after the Great Conflict."

"We honor you, your house, your family, and your priests," Fortiss says, lifting his cup as well. "I apologize that our unexpected arrival is happening while so many of your people are away. Light willing, we'll have the opportunity to break bread with them in the coming days."

"Light willing," Daggar agrees. He lifts his cup, then drinks deeply. I glance over at Fortiss, accepting his slight nod as all the approval I need to drink as well. If Daggar wanted us dead, he could easily accomplish it in this room where none could reach us. Yet the same could have been true of any room in this keep, built as it is against the mountain. It's the perfect stronghold for a defensive lord.

Is that why Rihad never returned here? Did he sense that this was a place built for war, not for peace—a war that perhaps never truly ended?

I set down my cup, and my next words are out of my mouth before I can stop them.

"Lord Daggar, your holding is as far west as the Tenth is east in the Protectorate, yet they couldn't be more different. Ours was built to sustain a small set of families, giving them support and protection as we watched over the pass that joined our land with the Imperium. But your house is not only larger, it's far more fierce. If the former lord protector didn't visit more often, perhaps it's simply because he knew he had nothing to fear with you standing at the ready with sword and shield."

Daggar eyes me with cool disinterest, as if my observation had been offered up by a passing scullery maid. Then his lips twitch into a condescending smile. "Lady Talia." His nod is perfunctory. "By 'ours' I assume you mean the house of your father, Lord Lemille or perhaps your betrothed, Lord Tennet, as both of those holdings cleave to the far eastern border. In either case, you're right. The Eighth House rose up out of the ashes of the Great Conflict, sustaining itself on a steady need to defend our great land. Lord Protector Rihad saw that with his own eyes. Why he never chose to return is someone else's story to tell, not mine."

He swings his gaze to Nazar as I clench my hands into fists, twin daggers of embarrassment and fury piercing me to the quick. Both my anger and my shame are heightened by the simple fact that he's right. I have no house of my own. It will take years, if not decades, to build a house that is anything like this one, along with men and supplies I have no way of paying for. Talia of the Thirteenth house, bearer of the winged crown—that all has a nice ring to it, but it's no more accurate than the romances spun by the traveling bards that Daggar so clearly disdains.

He's not wrong about them. Is he wrong about me?

"Priest Nazar, you honor both your party and this holding by your presence. It's been some years since I have spoken to a priest trained in the heart of the Imperium. It's rare that they travel so deeply into the Protectorate. But ours is a story all should know, from the humblest stableboy to the Imperator himself. To allow it to fall into obscurity is to invite disaster."

"I confess, I haven't heard this tale, certainly not in any detail," Nazar says diplomatically, giving Daggar the opening he so plainly seeks.

"Then listen well," the man declares, thunking his heavy goblet down on the table. Somewhere near my right ankle, I hear a querulous humph at the noise. Biting my lip, I glance almost furtively to Fortiss, only to find him staring at me, as if waiting for the opportunity to meet my gaze. As Daggar leans into what will undoubtedly be a long-winded tale, Fortiss lifts his fist to his chest and holds it there, his golden eyes fierce in the dimly lit room. I hear the message as clearly as if he speaks in my mind. Daggar can think what he wants. To Fortiss, I am a warrior, a lord. With Fortiss, the lord protector of our great land, I have nothing more to prove.

Well...not quite nothing. I'm all too aware of Tennet sprawling on the other side of the table, eyeing us both. With amusement? With annoyance? I'm losing my patience for not knowing where I stand. I bow to Fortiss swiftly and shoot Tennet a glare, only to meet his gaze, hot and smug, as he sips the Eighth House wine. My stomach tightens at his scrutiny, but my heart doesn't twist, my pulse doesn't race.

Something happened on that overlook between us, but it sure as the Light isn't going to mean anything more than what I want it to, I decide. I'm a lord and a warrior, after all. I make my own rules.

Oblivious to my racing thoughts, Daggar swaggers on. "The delegation from the Imperium had swept in a more-or-less straight line across the heart of the Protectorate, taking note of its riches and its ruins. This clearly had been a land of great wealth at one time, but there were no people anymore—anywhere. They explored uncontested, all the way to the jewel-like foothills of the Meridians, the entryway to the Western Realms."

"Jewel-like?" Fortiss murmurs, his voice rich with curiosity, and Daggar turns hard eyes on him.

"Jewel-like, Lord Protector Fortiss, by all accounts. The Great Conflict devastated these lands, and their luster never returned. But the spirit of the mountains still feeds us and makes us strong."

"Well, that is definitely true." Fortiss waves for Daggar to continue, and he does, after taking another long drink of his wine.

"At that time, the delegation was led by General Mirador, the future founder of the Eighth House." He glances around, his smile turning a shade more self-satisfied. "You don't know much more than his name because he didn't want you to know much more. At the close of the Great Conflict, he deferred all leadership to other members of the party, two warriors whose loyalty to each other was unmatched. One of them, warrior Lanark, was gifted in diplomacy. The other, warrior Bertrand, excelled in warcraft. The diplomat took the lead and became the first lord protector we so venerate today. To him, Mirador gave the winged crown."

"He did?" Caleb pipes up, drawing Daggar's gaze. "Forgive me, Lord Daggar. I've made a study of the history of the First House—there's no record of that crown, anywhere. All the accounts just say it's been lost."

"It was a sacred trust," humphs Daggar. "Not the stuff for idle chatter. There wouldn't be record of it."

He turns back to Fortiss, while Caleb and I exchange eyerolls. "Lord Lanark's family has continued to rule all the way to present day, while his faithful second built a legacy of strength and skill to support him all these generations since. All the while Mirador and his children faded into quiet obscurity, content with the role of serving as the protector no one knew."

I take another sip of my wine. Clearly, Daggar isn't as content as he's trying so hard to convince us, given how he's brought this point up at least a hundred times already today. But I school my face into polite interest as he continues.

"But before all of that happened, the Great Conflict occurred." He exhales a heavy sigh. "None of the Imperial delegation could have predicted what awaited them in the shadows of the Meridians. They rode into the mountains fully expecting to continue their journey west, but three quarters of the way up those slopes they encountered sheer stone walls blocking the path. Walls that looked poured, not natural, the stone forged from water, ash, and limestone but as pure and unblemished as snow on a crisp winter's day. They couldn't go around these walls, they couldn't go over them. So, they decided to go through them."

"None of these men would have been stonemasons," Tennet points out. "How did they have the tools to make any sort of tunnel?"

"They were determined to use whatever they could to keep their journey moving forward. Understand, these were men—and women too—who had accepted a commission from the Imperium and who set out on a journey where they were not under anyone's control but their own. They answered to no one while they were on this journey and were completely independent except for the order of their own leadership. The moment they had to turn around and go back home would have been the beginning of the end of that freedom."

I grimace, but it's Miriam who puts my thoughts out in the open this time. "From what I know of Imperium history, this adventure would have allowed a highly unusual level of freedom particularly for the women in the group too. But they wouldn't have been warriors in this delegation. They would have been cooks and healers, seamstresses—and maybe scouts? But not warriors, correct?"

I blink at her direct question and am a little shocked when Daggar answers her.

"Pressing women into battle was as bad an idea then as it is now," he says, his mouth settling in a hard line that I desperately want to punch off his face. "General Mirador saw the truth of that in the end and ensured the future of the Protectorate would remain in the care of those who could defend it. But every member of that delegation who could fight—did. However they knew how.

Because with the first chip into the wall that barred the way into the Western Realms, the warriors awoke the creatures on the other side. By the time they had forged an opening, the enemy was ready. Snakes poured through the fissure and into the mountains. Frightening enough, to be sure, but nothing compared to the beasts that climbed over the walls next. Shadow monsters as tall as any Divh, terrifying to behold. The Sahktar."

"Climbed over," Fortiss echoes, leaning forward. "They could have done that at any time then. Why didn't they?"

Daggar points at him, clearly satisfied that he's captured the lord protector's interest. "No one's ever determined that." He grins. "Perhaps they needed to be asked."

He continues on, but I no longer hear Daggar's droning recitation of what happens next, which does follow the history as I've heard it so many times. The attack of great evil on the delegation, the desperation of the warriors. Only thirty—not three hundred or even three thousand as the legend eventually grew—"A legend we at the Eighth House have always known is wrong but held our tongue," Daggar says proudly, recalling my focus.

He leans in, staring hard at Fortiss. "But the horror of the attack was real and the threat plain. If these monsters continued across the wide, verdant lands and reached the Imperium, the delegation that had been sent to expand the Imperium's borders would have essentially destroyed it instead. In their pain and despair, they donned the garb of the ancient rulers of this land and cried out to the Light, and the Light responded in a way no one could have imagined. By sending the Divhs."

All this I know, all this at least has been shared even with me, an unwanted female of a royal house. But I can't unhear Daggar's flippant assessment of why the skrill and shadow monsters attacked in the first place. I can't help recalling my own words to Fortiss. Skrill and Divh alike responded to the warriors of the Fated Plane because they were *asked*.

"You said all this to Lord Protector Rihad twenty years ago?" My words don't even sound like myself. I'm quiet, deferent, almost meek, but a warrior uses the best strategy for the moment, and what I want more than anything is answers. "Surely he was amazed."

"He seemed to be, yes." Daggar nods, addressing me with far more civility this time. "Asked me to take him up to where the wall was eventually rebuilt to the sheen of smoothest glass, as strong as ever through ways we still have not replicated all these years since. Walls that stood stable and solid for hundreds of years until Rihad stood before them."

"What happened then?" Tennet asks.

"Then he left," Daggar forms a fist to gently tap the table, as if for luck. "And now you are here, you will want to see them as well I assume? To reassure yourselves that all is well in the Eighth House? Because all is as it ever should be, and we are ready to serve."

"We would be honored." Fortiss nods. "With the events of these past several days, I'd like to simply see with my own eyes that the wall remains sturdy and true. You have performed the highest service in the Protectorate for generations upon generations here at the Eighth House. But if that threat is no longer sleeping..."

"You'll see the truth. We are ready to serve." Daggar says all this resolutely, then his gaze turns hard as he stares at Fortiss. "And then, Lord Protector Fortiss, you will repay me the men I have lost in your foolish tournament games, or I'll take my complaints straight to the Imperium."

CHAPTER 29

The meal ends without much more in the way of conversation, and we're returned to our rooms, all of us hungry enough despite all the food and drink we consumed to raid Miriam's rations another time. Shortly afterward, our entire party retires to their bedchambers—even Tennet and Fortiss—and I content myself with perching on the edge of my bed, waiting for Fortiss's signal.

After what seems like several weeks but is probably only an hour or so, I hear a small, huffing chirp from the main chamber. A moment later, a hummerlet pokes her head around the edge of my still-open door and fluffs her feathers at me.

I scramble off the bed and follow her to where Fortiss is waiting at the entry door of our rooms. He doesn't need to remind me to be silent, but when I look around questioningly, and mouth Tennet's name, he shakes his head. Then he presses his palms together and mimics Tennet sleeping peacefully.

I blink, and my face must clearly transmit my surprise, because Fortiss grins—grins! Not an expression I'm used to seeing on his stern, careful face. Then he reaches for my hand. I take his, and he pulls me close—so close I can feel the measured cadence of his heart, so slow and steady when mine feels like a bunch of cats trapped in a bag. For a long moment, he merely stares at me, his golden eyes searching mine. Then a smile flickers across his face. "We must be quiet and fast," he murmurs, and his fingers close mine, holding them tight in an iron grip. "That's not really Tennet's skill set."

My eyes go wide—Fortiss spelled Tennet to sleep somehow? Drugged him? Or just told him to stand down? Somehow, I can't see Tennet accepting this last idea, and curiosity burns through me. "But how?" I mouth, only to see Fortiss's grin deepen.

He leans in closer still, so close his mouth brushes mine, and when he speaks, I feel the tremor of his moving lips, twisting my stomach into knots. "He was *very* tired," he whispers, the words like a fluttering kiss. I stand rooted in place, my eyes locked on his as he leans back again, and in that moment, I know—he was—is —fully aware of the kiss I shared with Tennet, fully willing to accept it...

And fully willing to fight for me, even on the cusp of a clandestine mission through the halls of the Eighth House.

"Fortiss," I begin, but he lifts a finger to caress the lips he'd just almost kissed, trailing them with an unexpectedly sensual swipe. His grin has softened now to a look of tender, almost fierce longing.

"Talia." The word is firm and certain, but he says nothing more...and when he turns my still-linked hand in his and drops a soft, burning kiss to the inside of my wrist that sends my pulse into a frantic thrumming, I find I've completely lost the ability to speak.

Straightening and shooting me another quick grin, Fortiss releases his hold on me and turns toward the door. He pulls it wide, the movement quick and sure, as if it's perfectly natural for him to want to wander around his host's holding in the middle of the night.

I gape at him for only a second, wondering what story he has for the guards that are surely stationed outside—but there's no murmur of surprise from the hallway, no shuffling of feat.

Instead, Fortiss steps out, gestures me forward, and immediately sets off down the long, silent hallway.

I hurry to join him, matching his long strides and peering around wildly as a pair of hummerlets bounce along behind us. I long for him to hold my hand again, which is the height of stupidity, so I content myself with tightening both hands into fists. "Um...where'd all the guards go?" I finally manage.

"No idea," Fortiss says, his voice low enough that I wonder if I actually hear him or if he's speaking in my mind. How *did* he manage to lull Tennet to sleep, after all? "Do you remember the faces of the ones at dinner? They kind of blended together to me."

I think back, but I don't have much luck either. "Not really. Nobody said a word except Daggar, I don't think." I hesitate, but I've been running over Daggar's conversation in my mind almost constantly since dinner and keep tripping on one line. "Remember what he said about the delegation calling for help, and the Divhs showed up? He said 'they put on the garb of the ancients.'"

"I caught that," he nods, peering down a corridor, then moving on. "That's got to be the winged crown. There couldn't have been anything left in those ruins but stone and metal."

"Yeah, but—who's 'they'?"

Fortiss scoffs a laugh. "Just Mirador, I'd bet. In Daggar's mind, he may as well have been the right hand of the Light."

He squints down another hallway as we come to an intersection. "We're close. He said the vault was...this way, I think."

Fortiss breaks off into distracted mumbling as he leads me along the corridors, and I find their lingering gloom disconcerting. It's because there are no windows, I decide. There's only the occasional lit sconce.

In truth, the only sense of time I have since we came to the Eighth House is that I watched the darkness creep across the wide plains as the sun set behind us—and behind the mountains—hours earlier. After having watched the sun set in the west for so long, it seems almost unreasonable to not have a vantage point to watch it slip over the horizon. I console myself with the idea that sunrise must be glorious here, but it somehow doesn't feel the same...mostly because there's somewhere I could always go near the Tenth House to watch the sun rise *and* set. As flush as the Eighth House is against the mountains, I suspect that most rooms in this manor have never seen the sun. It's one of the most impregnable fortresses I've ever walked through.

Apparently, however, Lord Daggar's concern over ensuring the Protectorate's safety doesn't extend to keeping an eye on his guests at night. The corridors are eerily empty as we move deeper into the keep.

"Turn here," Fortiss whispers, and his hand touches my elbow, then holds it as he steers me down another corridor. The sconces are still lit here, but they're nearly guttered out, and I wonder how the staff will be able to see to relight them if they all go out at once. Though maybe they'll carry a torch?

These thoughts swirl around in my head long enough to carry us through two more turns and down a long corridor that terminates at a closed door. No one guards this one, either.

"Hmm." Fortiss huffs out a breath as he reaches out and touches the handle. The door opens easily. "Not locked."

"Trap?"

He steps inside the door and draws me in, waiting until our hummerlet escort enters as well before he closes it shut. The room plunges into full darkness, and he waits another ten full breaths before I hear him rustling in his pockets. I expect to hear a flint strike signaling him working up a flame to light one of the torches that must line this room...but instead I hear his low, quiet voice ease out in the darkness.

"Shine bright, little ones," he murmurs. "Show the way."

A chirruping sigh is accompanied by a sudden, quickly brightening glow, so unexpected I have to avert my eyes to keep them from being seared into blindness.

"Softly, softly," Fortiss continues, and I look up to see him grinning from ear to ear, one of Kreya's hummerlets now perches on his shoulder, looking half asleep as her head nods down over her softly glowing belly. Another equally glowing one rests on a nearby table.

"What are you doing? What's wrong with fire?" I hiss at him, my eyes going wide as I get used to the illumination. "And how did you make them *do* that?"

"I asked." He grins, gesturing at the long-guttered torches. "I didn't want to risk leaving a trace that we were here, and after Nazar told me about what he saw the hummerlet do in the forest, I decided we might need them. They certainly don't seem interested in returning to Kreya in the Blessed Plane. Miriam had three hummerlets hanging from her curtains all afternoon, and another one snuck into her cape on the way to dinner."

Now it's my turn to grin. "I thought I heard that." Then I swivel around, trying to pick out the details of the room. "I still can't understand how he'd leave this room open if the crown and talon-stones were here."

"Not the crown, I think." Fortiss shakes his head. "If it still exists, it would almost have to be guarded. But these..." He leads me over to a wall where a heavy chest sits, its lid propped open. I stare at what's inside.

"But...how can they just be *sitting* here?"

"Because Daggar doesn't fully realize what they can do, that's how," Fortiss says. He scoops his hand into the box and comes up with a handful of polished stones, each of them shaped like curved talons. "Think of how many decorations we have in the First House that look exactly like this. Made out of every type of stone and metal imaginable. They're *everywhere*."

"Well, they don't look like these," I say, holding one up to the hummerlet's belly. It glints in the light, deep blue shot through with gold. "I don't even know what this stone is."

"Daggar told me that the Imperial delegation hauled thousands of these across the open plains on their way west, to the point where they stopped even collecting them, there were so many. After your vision, their purpose makes so much more sense." He grimaces. "I've seen these at the coliseum too—and you can bet they're in some of the oldest houses in Trilion. Nowhere near as beautiful as these, but they clearly got the job done."

"Do you think Daggar knows the truth about these stones, though? Did he only tell you about them so that you could make an attempt for them, and he could, what, arrest you for stealing? You're the lord protector—literally the law of the land. Only the Imperium is higher. What's his game?"

"I don't know if he has a game." Fortiss sighs. "He's definitely skittish, but his men seemed loyal enough out on the plains, for all that most of them didn't follow him into the Eighth House. Did you notice that? Other than a few guards and his generals—the rest didn't get close. The whole place seems empty."

"We didn't let them know we were coming, and they've been through a lot recently," I point out. "Perhaps they really are patrolling up and down the border. I would be, if people kept showing up dead."

"Fair..." Fortiss reaches into his pocket and pulls out a silken pouch that smells of aromatic tobacco. "Nazar offered this up for our search when I told him what we were looking to do, and why. He didn't want me to draw any attention by trying to steal anything, And the scent could throw off any casual search."

"Not for very long if these talonstones don't clink together," I point out, but dutifully we fill the pouch with enough stones to visit all twelve houses of the Protectorate three times over. Then Fortiss tucks it back in his belt. He glances at the hummerlets, then back to me. "I'm, ah, going to let them go dark now. With the torches guttering outside, we should have enough light to see by."

"I mean, I guess...?" I bite my lip as Fortiss whispers something comfortingly to the hummerlets, then opens the door of the room. He peers out and seems to come to a decision.

"Here you go." He pulls one of the talonstones out of the pouch and hands one each to the tiny birds. With delicate fingers, the hummerlets grab the talonstones as Fortiss murmurs "Kreya."

The hummerlets disappear.

"What?" My jaw drops in surprise as Fortiss shuts the door

again firmly—this time locking it from the inside. The room descends into utter darkness.

"What are you doing?" I squeak, hearing him breathe out a long, shuddering exhale. I stick my hands out into the darkness, grateful when I brush the table beside me. This much blackness is disorienting.

"Do you trust me, Talia?"

"What?" I blink, but before I can recover, I hear him step toward me. A moment later, he wraps his arms around me, pulling me close. Naturally, instinctively, my body melts toward him and his lips come down on mine.

Our kiss is nothing like the stolen, aggressive embrace I shared with Tennet. That was a battle, I realize—this feels more like a war —of wits, of twining hearts, of kindred souls, a war that might be fought over years, decades, generations to come. And I want that war—*need* it. I have fought with and against this man, I have trusted and been betrayed by him...and I've betrayed him as well, yet here he is, holding me—kissing me.

It's...glorious.

In that moment, that breath, I know in the deepest, secret places of my heart, the world will never, ever be right if Fortiss is not with me. We barely know each other, but I know enough to want to learn and grow with him, to explore and lead with him. To rise and fall and face every new danger by his side. I want to see him at his pinnacles and depths—I want to cheer him and heal him, I want to hold him in my arms and soothe away his nightmares when he can do no more than sleep. Fortiss is everything the Protectorate has been and everything it will be. Like me, he was held down, discounted and ignored by those who had no interest in letting him soar. Like me, he turned himself into something entirely different, built himself into a leader and dared to explore a magic that had been left dormant and lost for centuries except for Rihad's corrupt dabblings. The Protectorate will be remade because of him. Because of me, too.

And I *want* this—want it all. More than anything I think I've ever craved in my life. More than everything I thought I could be allowed to even dream.

"Fortiss..." I manage against his mouth, even as something cracks inside me, the glass-thin hold I had on my emotions, my fears, my identity, myself. I sway a little more into his body and he growls against my lips, then wrenches himself away from me.

And shocks me to my toes.

"Do you want him?" he gasps, the question making my heart seize up. Though I can't see anything in the utter darkness, I can feel the desperation coming off him in sudden waves. "If you want him, Talia, if you want to be Tennet's wife—if you want him to take you away and be your partner in anything you do, I can make it so. I can ensure that you get whatever you want. You deserve to get whatever you want."

I gape wordlessly as he huffs in frustration, then paces across the room. I can't even pick him out in the darkness, so how he can see I have no idea, but I turn my head to follow the sound of his footsteps.

"I thought I'd have more time," he mutters. "But I don't. Everything is happening too fast, too fast! But this, if this is what is decreed and you want it, if you want it—"

I suck in a shaky breath, but before I can even say anything, he's back in front of me. His hands come up to either side of my face and he pulls me to him once again. When he hesitates, I lean into him, giving my tacit consent. This time when he kisses me, it's a long, searching, and needful embrace, leaving me breathless by the time he finally drags his mouth away from mine.

He leans his forehead against mine. "But you *can't* leave me, Talia," he whispers. "You can't. You're like nobody I've ever met before, nobody I ever will meet again. I felt an instant kinship to you even when I knew—knew!—you were off to be married, that first day near the Shattered City. And when I met you as Talia...I was lost. Even when I saw you as Merritt, I knew there would be no warrior I'd rather ride into battle with—I just didn't fully understand why. Now I do...by the Light, I do. I saw you fight, I saw you rage, I saw you cry—and I saw your eyes when you looked at me, doing everything you could to get me to see Szonja, to understand. I've seen—Light, *everything*—and I still barely know you. So he can't have you, Talia. He can't." He draws in a shuddering breath, his whole body quivering with emotion. "Unless...unless you want it."

I sense more than hear his mind crashing against the walls of his own prison, and my heart shatters all over again. Tennet and Fortiss aren't so different after all. They've both been brought up in a world where women have a certain place to occupy, even—especially—if you loved them. Fortiss's heart is pounding so loudly I can hear it, feel it against my own chest, thudding in a cadence with my own rushing pulse. He wants so desperately to claim me for his own, I know...but even more than that, he wants me to have a choice.

A choice.

That makes him unlike any man I've ever met in the Protectorate...and this is who will be our leader. This is a man worth giving everything to, knowing he will pour back into me his energy, his fire...his love.

This is a choice I can easily make.

"*Fortiss*," I whisper.

I don't know if it's the darkness surrounding us like a second embrace, or simply the fact that we have been here and done this before, but Fortiss and I are suddenly matched action to action, thought to thought. Like lovers who've known each other for decades, not weeks, we pull at each other's clothes, unlacing and untying, shimmying out of tunics and breeches until there is nothing between us but the cool close air of Daggar's vault.

"No," Fortiss announces grimly, and I blink, swaying uneasily in the open air as he dives for our discarded clothes. *No?* Then a second later I hear the telltale scratch of flint and the smell of sulfur—and light leaps high from his cupped hands.

"What are you doing?" I squeak. "I thought you didn't want anyone to realize we were here." I stare at him, weirdly flummoxed as he stalks over to a torch and lights it. The thin flame provides more than enough illumination to fill the room.

He turns to me, a new smile creasing his lips as his gaze roams over my body, hot and fierce. "I couldn't stand another moment without seeing you with my own eyes, Talia. I've imagined you for so blighted long."

We stare at each other for a long moment, and I drink in every disparate image of this beautiful man—his broad chest heaving, his shoulders taut and muscled, his long, sculpted arms, the left now heavily banded. His waist arrows down to narrow hips, and his heavily muscled thighs ripple as he strides back over to me, pulling me to him.

This time he doesn't ask my permission. I shudder against him as his broad palm slides down my rib cage and rests against my waist, while his other curls around the back of my head and draws me in for a long, lingering kiss.

I press back and give as good as I get, touching him, tasting him, my fingers splaying over his chest, down his rippled abs, circling his hips as he shifts against me. His breath is coming faster now, harder, and he hooks his hand into my breeches and drags them down—

A door crashes open at the far end of the hallway.

Fortiss and I spring apart like we've been lashed with a whip, staring at each other, then at the door, then back at each other. As one, we lurch toward our clothes. It's a testament to our skill as warriors, how quickly we recover. We move in one timing, with each hard-charging thud of the runner outside coinciding with another article yanked onto our body—breeches, tunic, boots. Whatever we can't throw on in time is stuffed into pockets, and by the time someone tries the door, we're dressed.

"The light!" I hiss, but Fortiss doesn't attempt to snuff out the torch. Instead, he yanks it from the wall, holding it high in one hand as he draws his knife in the other. Then he gestures to me to pull the door wide.

I do and jerk back in utter surprise. "Syril!"

Her eyes snap wide in horror. "Talia—what are you doing here? This is a house of *death*."

"But—"

"Follow me—bring the fire!" She turns and hisses something, then throws her torch back up the corridor. Fortiss and I pile in behind her, and only then do I see it.

The hallway is filled with snakes.

CHAPTER 30

The mass of serpents scatter as Syril's torch hits the ground, but Fortiss shouts at me—I don't hear his command, but I don't need to. I sprint past Syril and scoop up the guttering torch, then jam it into the thickest knot of skrill I can find.

"No!" Syril's cry of horror is lost in a rushing *whump*! of sound as the snakes explode into sparks. Within moments, the entire hallway has become a writhing inferno, but Fortiss doesn't stop. He races up behind me, and throws his arm around me, another one already clasping Syril close.

With us all tangled up like this, there's no way he should still be able to move, yet he seems to pick up speed. He shouts out something I can't quite understand. His voice is low and guttural, but his words do the trick—a hole opens up ahead. We flee through a tunnel of flame and poisonous snakes, around the turns and up the stairs. Once again, I see that Fortiss doesn't just fight through fire, doesn't just batter back the danger. He clears paths through chaos, hauling us all along with him. Even when we don't ask him to.

. . .

We finally burst out into one of the main corridors of the castle, and stagger to a halt sucking wind—just in time to hear another warrior's light feet upon the corridor floor.

"Syril! You're hurt!"

"Report, Greta." Syril pulls herself upright, shoving her soot-streaked hair out of her face.

"There's four recovered from the main floor—no one harmed. Still no sign of Daggar or Nemeth."

"What?" Fortiss rounds on Syril, but she's regained her focus, and she glares at him, then me.

"You're not hurt? You can run?" She screws her face up in concentration and stares up at the ceiling. "With you setting their scouts ablaze, the skrill will hit this place in less than a quarter hour. We'd better be under cover by then, but the fastest way is out the front doors. That'll run us right into the teeth of them if we're not fast.

"Go—get your people out. Talia, with me," Fortiss orders, but he doesn't take off for the front doors. Instead, he heads back toward our rooms.

"What are you *doing*?" I demand as Syril shouts out after us, then barks orders to her subordinate. A moment later I hear her hard charge on the stone floor behind us.

"There are books in this keep—records! They're all in Daggar's inner chambers. We can't just leave them here."

"You're a *fool*," Syril roars at us as we pound up the stairs, but I can only grin. If there's one other thing I've learned these past few weeks, Fortiss will do just about anything to preserve knowledge, even run headlong into a fire he created.

But there's still more that we don't understand. Syril gasps out her next words as she nears us down the long corridor. "Daggar's been dead for weeks—they've all—been dead."

Fortiss stops, whirling around, and she inhales deeply and rushes on.

"We saw the lights in the windows tonight and thought maybe the Eighth House warriors from Trilion had finally returned, and we set out immediately to warn them away. No one has breathed air in this keep for a full fortnight. Those who could, fled to the villages down the range, but most—" she draws in another huge breath. "Most of them died in the first skrill attack."

He glares at her. "Then who is it we've been talking to since we've gotten here? Who *are* these people?"

She winces. "They're not people at all, Lord Protector Fortiss. The best we can tell, we believe they're skillful illusions created by the skrill to lure you to your death."

"*What?*" Fortiss's face flushes with outrage as I gape at her. "Why didn't you *tell* us?"

Syril bristles with equal anger. "I didn't even know you were *here* until a bare hour—"

"Save it." Fortiss turns again and takes off, not stopping until he reaches Daggar's inner chambers. He races through the sitting area and flings open the door to the sleeping room. No guards rush out to block his way, but I can hear the slip and whisper of snakes in the walls.

Here, the room looks remarkably like Fortiss's own chambers —like any sleeping chambers I've ever seen—a desk, a few shelves, and a large bed, curtained against the cold and damp. But the similarity stops there.

Because here, there are books. Large and small, thick and thin, stacked high on every shelf and scattered across the floor. Some aren't even books, but rolled up maps and scrolls, strewn about with a madman's sense of organization. Fortiss holds his torch up high, illuminating the room, then jams the torch into the nearest sconce. Then he darts forward and pulls a cloth hanging from the wall, muttering something at it as we stare. It zips around the room as books tumble from the shelves into it, weighing it down until full.

I stare in wonder at what's happening, unable to fully process it. How is it that Fortiss has so much power—and what's behind this magic? Could Rihad wield it so easily? Can he still?

Those thoughts converge into a chaotic howl in my mind as

one cloth, then another fill in the same way. Finally, Fortiss whirls toward us. "Don't just stand there. *Haul*."

We plow back out of the room, staggering and straining under the weight of Daggar's books, and the building roar of the skrill is louder now. The walls of the place are practically vibrating, when the first snake slithers across the floor, it's all I can do not to chase after it to stamp it dead. Instead, we race down to the stairs to the visitor's chamber and out to the overlook.

Fortiss howls into the night sky and with a mighty heave, he hurls the first bag of books into the air. He rips my burden from me and tosses it next, then Syril's.

The cloth bundles barely clear the low stone wall before they plummet into darkness.

"*Go!*" He shouts. I turn to grab Syril, who's already backing up, but Fortiss beats me to her. He grabs her around the waist and, spinning, hurls her into the open air with what seems like the strength of ten men.

A burst of flame rips across the sky, and I hear Syril's scream, but the urgency of Fortiss's command reverberates through my blood. I race across the platform, taking three great strides, and launch myself out into the open space as I open my mind and heart to my great and mighty Divh.

I crest my low arc all too quickly then drop as heavily as Fortiss's stolen books, dropping into a tight fissure. The Eighth House is tucked too tightly against the mountains, I realize too late —there's no way Gent can swipe his mighty fist—

A scream rips from my throat as my back is pierced with what feels like twin daggers as long as my body. In three bone-breaking heaves I'm wrenched skyward, the pain swamping me until a familiar thick-fingered paw plucks me off the hummerbill's talons like a vintner plucking a grape. I tumble back, exhausted in Gent's palm. He curls his claws around me, his howl of outrage turning my bones to milk.

Kreya screams back at him as she swoops off, her indignation clear. If I wasn't in so much pain, I'd laugh.

Instead, I loll to the side of his palm, fading in and out of awareness as Gent strides once, twice, then drops me to the ground, directly into the midst of a crowd of shouting people. I think I hear my name called—no, I'm sure I do—but my hold on this world is feather light. Instead, in my mind, I race along with my Divh, feeling every stride as he pounds up to the crest of the Meridians and leaps into the stars.

Then Gent turns, and though his eyesight is nowhere near keen, for just a moment, I see what he sees over that wild mountain range—the land of the Western Realms.

It's a blighted wasteland.

I've never had the privilege of viewing the Protectorate from the shoulders of Fortiss's or Tennet's dragon, or even Nazar's winged lion. But I've leaned out over the grasp of my beautiful goliath, and seen the wide plains before me, lush and full, waves of yellow and green grasses stretching to the far horizon. I have marveled at the bluish gray mountains surging high, punching up out of the earth like children eager to burst into a new world and call it their own. I've witnessed marshlands and rivers, even wide lakes—to say nothing of the Blessed Plane with its sun-bright sky and heavy air, its lush green hillsides and the extraordinary lake that fills its center.

None of that awaits us in the Western Realms. Even with Gent's poor vision, I can see an endless vista of stark, moonlit mountains and valleys filled with dull gray sand. Nothing seems to move in this barren hellscape, nothing breathes, nothing—

A light flickers on.

Gent's mournful cry reverberates through my blood and bones, but there is something *there*, I think, a tiny speck of gold glittering against the relentless expanse of shadow. As I study it, stare at it, it flares even brighter, almost as if it recognizes me, reaches out to me. I yearn to reach out to it as well, to grasp it and hold it in my hand, as if this tiny speck is my birthright, my own peace of sunshine to claim and call my own.

All this happens in barely a blink, but with that desire, I experience a lifetime's worth of agony as Gent forcibly turns his head away from the barren landscape and fixes his gaze on the white canopy of stars. Because he's *not* carrying me, because I'm only seeing what he can see, I can no longer glimpse that tiny burst of light. I can only sense his abject misery at the fact that it even exists, a sorrow so great, it sinks into my bones and renders me hollow on the inside, with endless tears pouring down.

Gent continues on to the Blessed Plane, leaving me behind, and I fall back into to my own body, in my own plane, still reverberating with his pain. I was pierced through by Kreya's talons as she strived to rescue me from the Eighth House, I know that clearly—and yet, I've been damaged worse by that tiny yellow speck against a boundless sea of ashen sand.

And that wound...I may not recover from.

I huddle into my cloak, weeping in harsh, shuddering sobs without really knowing why. Then the sounds of shouting men and women overtake me, and I collapse to the ground, my blood seeping into the earth of the Fated Plane.

CHAPTER 31

I stare out at the sky as it lightens over the distant eastern horizon—dawn breaking across the wide plains. It's even more beautiful than I expected it to be. I munch on thick bread and shift under my bandages, willing myself to spontaneously heal from Kreya's talon punctures. I don't have time to feel this bad. I certainly don't have time to have bled so much.

The smell of cooking meat wafts toward me, reminding me of how long it's been since I've eaten. I glance over to where Tennet lies collapsed beside me, his face clean, his shoulder bandaged, his long dark lashes soft against his sunburned face, a warrior in repose.

He's totally awake, of course. He has been for a while. But awake and stretched out under heavy blankets is better than awake and functional, and I've let him "sleep' for another quarter hour past what he should have. If I have to be upright and suffering, he should be too.

"Yo." I reach out to poke him, wincing at the stretchy ache in my shoulders. "What happened to you? Did the skrill decide to return for a second course of tasty lord?"

He cocks one eye open, then serves up a self-satisfied grin, which is effective even from his reclined position. "Could you blame them?"

"Only if they were starving. And had seriously low standards."

His chuckle dissolves into a groan as he hauls himself up to a seated position. "They were only part of the issue. I also nearly got my own arm dislocated hauling that Savasci woman, Syril, up onto Ayne. It seems she's the type to punch first and ask questions later. I can see why you two get along."

"I'm surprised she didn't knock you right off your dragon."

"At least I didn't drop so fast that only a long-beaked death monster with pincers of doom could catch me. I'm surprised you still have any blood in your body. It took three Savasci healers to patch you up—I think one of them may have sacrificed a goat."

Fortiss's loud command from the front of the cave draws our attention, and my eyes widen as I focus on him. He's gotten cleaned up since the night before and changed his clothes. But there's no great stock of lord protector black and gold silks sitting amongst the storehouses of the Eighth House, of course, especially since the Eighth House is now apparently overrun with death.

Instead, Fortiss is wearing head-to-toe leathers, suitable for fast horse rides over harsh territory. He looks like the male equivalent of a Savasci.

It's...a good look. Good enough that my mouth goes a little dry. Blight him for looking like that right when I'm trying to regain my sense of equilibrium.

"Try not to drool." Tennet smirks at me. "Speaking of low standards."

"Everyone, look sharp," Fortiss begins, saving me from a response. "We don't have much time, and we all need to understand what's happening here in case one or more of us fall to the wayside. The plan has to continue. Who can fight?"

Every one of the Savasci stands tall and pounds her fist to her chest. Tennet grunts his way off our makeshift bed and pulls me to my feet as well, then we echo the move. Nazar, Caleb and Miriam are all present and accounted for at the far end of the gathering, though I don't see any of the hummerlets. Hopefully, they all made it back to the Blessed Plane when the skrill first attacked.

There are some male guards as well, all of them dressed as Savasci. None of them look like any of the men who accompanied us to the Eighth House, though. My head is swimming with questions, but for once I hold my tongue as Fortiss continues.

"Nazar, Caleb and Miriam, you'll take the talonstones I recovered from Daggar's vault and travel to all houses along the western border, as well as those along the southern border that allied with us during the melee in the Tournament of Gold. Speak to the house lords, recruit any soldiers they can spare with Divhs, and return. Horses won't help us here, and we've got more than enough along with skilled riders already. If the men are willing to fight on their feet and there's a Divh that can carry them, we welcome them. Otherwise, no. They should stay behind and prepare to defend their own houses."

He turns to Syril. "If you can spare a delegate, it would be good to have a first-hand account of what they need to expect should we fail. Plus, they can describe the locations to Nazar, so he can ask our Divhs to travel there."

"I'll give you two," she says. "One of our own and one of the guards of the Eighth House. Where a woman's words may fail, a man's won't, and these guards have lost good men. They've also lost their leader."

I jolt, Syril's revelations from last night flooding back to me. Was it all true? Could we seriously have walked into a nest of skrill without realizing it?

Fortiss just nods, then looks to Nazar.

"I can carry two additional riders on Wrath, and Marsh can harness a second in," Nazar says. "Miriam's hummerbill would love nothing more than to pinion any traveler who needs a lift, but as we've already seen, she's not so careful with her claws."

He nods to the Savasci hunter, a slender woman with sharp features and hard eyes. "If you can stomach a rougher ride, you ride with Caleb and Marsh."

She swings her gaze to Caleb, and if she notices the fact that he has only one arm, you can't see it in her face. "I fought in the melee," she says instead. "I have seen his Divh and understand its movements. I will keep my seat."

Fortiss nods again. "Then it's done. Everyone, summon your Divhs."

The five travelers turn toward the open sky, and Caleb, Nazar, and a slightly less certain Miriam curl their right fists to their chest. Shoulders straighten, and all three lift their chins and murmur the names of their Divhs. The sky pulls tight, as if the very wind holds its breath, and a moment later the three great Divhs burst into view, Wrath taking the lead. They charge toward the earth, then pull up at the last second, landing on the grassy plains with remarkable grace—except Marsh, who tumbles end over end in three cart-wheels before leaping to his feet, his arms flinging out along with his wings in pure, unfettered celebration. I can practically feel Caleb's pride radiating out, and even the Savasci woman smiles.

Fortiss steps forward and gives each of the traveling party a small, curved stone. "I have blessed these with the Light and limned them with the darkness," he says, his voice resonating with a strange timbre. "They'll guide you to each new house at Nazar's lead. Nazar then has a supply for any who would come to our aid. We have no time for negotiations or discussion, only action. Whoever's here by nightfall will stand ready to fight for the Protectorate. Even if we die, we cannot fail."

The warriors, the Eighth House guards, and Savasci all tap their fists to their heart, then they turn toward the Divhs in the wide plain. Hurriedly I scan the mountains and the distant Eighth House to see if any other ghost warriors might be riding out to meet us, but there are none.

"Syril told me a little when she wasn't railing at me," Tennet says quietly beside me. "The illusion magic of the skrill is strong enough to fool man or beast, she says. It has both weight and heft in the very narrow corridor of its focus, which in this case, includes the Eighth House and the plain before it. If you're not the target of the skrill's focus, you can't see the illusions. You don't see any actual snakes, either, until darkness falls. By then, of course, it's far too late."

"It wasn't too late for us," I point out.

Tennet grins at me. "Well, we're more stubborn than most."

We watch the five travelers reach the Divhs. Caleb and the Savasci warrior climb into their harness supervised by a thoroughly delighted Marsh, while Miriam and the Eighth House guard take their places between Wrath's mighty wings, and Nazar tucks in behind his neck. Then Fortiss extends his arm, murmurs something else, and drops it.

The Divhs leap up into the sky, the wind snapping tight—and they're gone.

I stagger back slightly, and Tennet's hand shoots out to grasp my elbow. Fortiss turns, his gaze sweeping over the small company, then it rests on me and Tennet. And my elbow.

"Good, you're up," he says to us both. "You can fight? We can't count on anyone returning."

I open my mouth to speak, then shut it.

"We can fight," Tennet answers for us both. "But what exactly are we fighting if we can't believe what we see?"

"We're getting to that. We have exactly twelve hours to prepare," he says gruffly, his wave encompassing our entire thirty-odd company. "Everyone—get food, water, whatever you need, and draw close. Then Syril will tell us what we're looking for...and explain the dangers we face."

The small company becomes a hive of activity, and Fortiss strides toward Tennet and me, singling us out for private conversation. I pull my elbow out of Tennet's grasp as discreetly as possible, but not discreetly enough. His snicker grates along my nerves as Fortiss skewers me with a look.

"How much do you remember of the Western Realms?" Fortiss asks. "Szonja was connected to you, but she shut that connection down hard and fast at whatever Gent saw. She was pretty disturbed."

This immediately draws the attention of Tennet. Any hope that I harbor of him sidling off to find food is dashed as he squares himself up. His gaze goes from Fortiss's scowl to my set jaw, and his eyes alight with interest. "What did I miss? I clearly missed something. And here I was thinking it—"

Fortiss cuts him off, his gaze still hard on me. "Why did Gent venture into the Western Realms, even briefly? I didn't know he could do that. You'd like to think that if traveling into enemy territory was something so easily done, we could have made that attempt any time over the last five hundred years and routed out these creatures for good. But we didn't. Why not? What did you see?"

"You act as if I had anything to do with it," I snap back, fully irritated. "He leapt, and my mind leapt with him. And as to what's over there—there's nothing, Fortiss. Absolutely nothing. It's as barren as a graveyard, without even the bones to indicate that anything once lived there. As far as I could see—as far as Gent could see, anyway—there was nothing but gray sand. I couldn't even see the skrill, but they would have been tough to spot from that height. I certainly didn't see the shadow creatures like the one I saw in Rihad's fireplace, the Sahktar. There just—was nothing."

I decide to omit any mention of the golden spark in the midst of all that desolation. Now, thinking back, I realize it's possible I never really saw it.

Tennet makes a face. "Why would anyone want to go there?"

"Because there's a mighty power buried in that sand," Fortiss says grimly. "Or at least...that's what I'm getting from Daggar's books. It's hidden, but it's there. It can be drawn upon by any who know the ancient ways. Neither Divh nor human can survive in the realm for long, because neither of us can live in total darkness, but—"

"Except we do." Tennet scratches his jaw, waving a negligent hand as we turn toward him. "We live in darkness every night. And just look at the way these Savasci have been living. They've tunneled into the mountains to protect themselves. It's *dark* inside their caves. I've checked. And yes, they've got fire, but all around that tiny island of light is darkness. We focus so much on living in the Light, maybe there's something to be said for adding a little more of the shadow."

"You're speaking sacrilege," Fortiss reminds him, and Tennet shrugs.

"I had dinner with illusions last night that told me stories that I believed. I watched them eat and drink—and I ate and drank alongside them, even though now, I couldn't tell you a single thing I ate last night until we broke into councilor Miriam's supplies. They put us on real, live horses that somehow didn't balk at this abomination and rode us to our doom. Magic is also sacrilege, but that doesn't make it any less powerful—as you yourself have already proven."

He rocks back on his heels, dropping his hands to his belt. *One day, I will master this move,* I promise myself. "Besides, you can't ignore an enemy forever, Fortiss. You either kill it or you control it, and we're not doing either here."

"For now, I'd be happy if you just helped us contain it." Syril's words interrupt us, and Tennet shifts to the right to let her into our group, even as he folds his arms over his heavy chest in clear disapproval. I'm not sure what he's disapproving of, but there's no denying his attitude.

Syril squares against her shoulders and confronts Fortiss. "If we don't remove the skrill from the Eighth House and destroy them completely—chasing them back through the Unlit Pass and into the Western Realms, and sealing off the wall again—they'll eventually adapt to life in the sun. Even now, we find more carcasses every morning, snakes trying to see how far they can survive in the sunlight. Each morning, they get a little farther before they succumb, and sometimes we find none at all."

"Where do they go?" Tennet has instinctively shifted forward as if he's about to be called into battle.

"We don't know, but we suspect that those are the winged ones. They've certainly shown they can travel along the edges of the Blessed Plane for long enough to reach the houses in the center of the Protectorate. How much farther they can get is anyone's guess, but they're out, and they're exploring."

"But how can they do that?" I ask. "I thought they had to be summoned?"

"From talonstone to grounding stone," Fortiss says, and I make a face. He's right. Of course he's right.

Syril nods. "It doesn't matter how, in the end. If we don't return them beyond the barrier, we won't have the luxury of figuring out how to destroy them entirely."

"From the looks of things, we tried the barrier approach once before," Tennet puts in. "Yet here we are."

She shoots Tennet a scornful glance. "Here we are fully five hundred years later, yes. I'm willing to wait another six months with them safely shut away, so we can find a permanent solution born of wisdom and not of crisis."

Tennet flushes, but says nothing more, and Fortiss gestures to the larger group. There's no disputing his quiet command, and I struggle to keep my emotions in check, my face neutral. "You know what's been happening here, Syril. Tell us what we need to know."

CHAPTER 32

Those closest to us don't take long to come closer as she begins to speak. This history is not so ingrained among them that the tale has lost its impact.

"Anyone standing here today didn't see the first attack of the skrill, not firsthand," Syril says. "Even those among the Savasci who weren't directly attacked but who saw it occurring have left this place, at least for now, giving aid at the houses and villages along the border. They're uniquely suited to the task because of what they saw during the attack on the Eighth House, because of what they now know and cannot unknow."

She stares around at the group. "We believe that should a similar attack come again, our people will be ready, hardened, able to shepherd those they protect to safety in the mountains until sunlight comes again. But even that may be hopeful thinking. The warriors of the Eighth House and their Divhs were good, solid fighters. While it's true that the best of them were given leave to travel to the Tournament of Gold, those who were left behind were well trained. They just weren't well trained for this."

There's a murmuring through the group, which Syril waits out before she continues.

"First came the snakes, through and around and over the wall, which still looks solid, in case you're wondering—at least to us. Maybe not to you."

"What?" Fortiss demands, clearly surprised at this piece of news. "It has to have been breached."

She shrugs. "I agree with you. As soon as I returned and understood what happened here, I organized a small team to investigate, but the wall appears to stand firm—the way it always has, to us. Like I said, skrill illusion magic can be directed at anyone who specifically needs to be deceived."

"Blood and stone," mutters Tennet.

"The wall was most likely compromised some twenty years back, we suspect, the only time that Lord Protector Rihad visited this house," Syril continues. "He never came again and nothing ever happened, so his actions that day slipped into obscurity, not even worth being remarked upon five, ten years later. Only when we cast a view backward in the wake of the skrill attack, did we recall he'd even traveled up to the wall, and even then, there was only the slightest aside about it, the stuff of children's tales."

Fortiss leans in a little. "Lord Daggar...or the illusion we thought was Lord Daggar, spoke of that visit."

"Lord Daggar." Her lips twist. "There's more you need to know about him and the warrior Nemeth. They were the only two who spoke to you, right? The only men who guided you into the Eighth House with actual words? There's a reason for that."

She exhales a gusting sigh. "The skrill didn't just kill those two —we think they've been feeding on them."

Beside me, Tennet goes very still. "What do you mean?"

"I mean exactly what it sounds like. When we reached the Eighth House, bodies were everywhere—none of them scarred with more than a few teeth marks and stripes of burned skin. The poison of the skrill can cause hallucinations in small doses, but in large enough doses, it's clearly deadly. Over the next few days, working fast and only in daylight, we emptied the Eighth of all its souls and burned them in a pyre. But there were two men we couldn't find. Two men who had either been spared or, we quickly realized when a banded soldier came down from Merrivale to help us, were turned in some way. The banded warrior saw Nemeth and Daggar on the ramparts of the Eighth, even when a whole company of Savasci could not. It was only when he witnessed all the other bodies on the pyre that he accepted that what he saw couldn't have been real."

Fortiss rubs his hand over his face. "You think Daggar and this other warrior, Nemeth...they're still in there? Somewhere in the Eighth?"

He studiously doesn't look at me, but he doesn't have to. There's only one place the men could be, I think. Daggar's prophecy chamber.

But Syril merely shrugs. "We don't know. We didn't search too deeply, for obvious reasons—but they were the only ones whose bodies we couldn't recover. The only ones the warrior saw, and who you've now seen and spoken to. We've found no reference to the skrill creating shadow warriors of their victims in the books we've stolen over the years, so there's no help there. Then again, we never could get close enough to raid Daggar's inner chambers."

She says this last to Fortiss, and he smiles grimly in return. "I was uniquely motivated."

"And I'm glad of it. There's doubtless more information in the books you recovered that will keep us alive. But for now, you have to know—while much of what Daggar likely told you was true— some of it may not have been. In the end, that illusion was simply a spider spinning a web to keep you in place until the skrill could attack again, like they did a month ago."

"At the close of the Tournament of Gold," Fortiss says.

"That's what we think." Syril nods. "While the Divhs were busy protecting their warriors at the Tournament of Gold during the melee, the skrill rose up and swept with dark intent to the base of the mountains. The only thing that people at the Eighth House heard the evening of the attack was a mighty screaming up in the mountains and a crash to the earth that rocked the entire region.

Rocks fell, the Eighth House shook, but then—everything quieted. According to the guards who survived—because they left on errands of their own after the first event—there was some talk of going up to the Unlit Pass to ensure the wall held firm, but nobody got the chance. The snakes came later that same night with their poison-oiled bodies. They flowed through the Eighth House as a silent, killing force. Those who slept, died quickly, we think. Those who resisted, fought valiantly, but in the end two hundred men, women, and children were dead. Only the horses remained, along with the men who slept in their guard stations outside the castle walls."

"But why?" I protest, drawing everyone's attention. "Why devastate an entire house in one night and do nothing more? We had no idea this had happened and that was a *month* ago."

"Because they were awaiting orders, I suspect," Fortiss says grimly. "I think Rihad fully planned to call the skrill to his side after taking out all the Divhs at the tournament. He just didn't plan on not still being upright. Maybe...maybe that's why it took so long for the skrill to show up to the First. He started the call to arms for these creatures but never completed it."

"So now, they wait." I surprise even myself by speaking up, but the enormity of what Rihad has done staggers me. "He opened up the Unlit Pass. He invited the skrill into the Protectorate, but he's no longer here to command them. Do they think he's coming? Do they think *we* will give them direction?"

Fortiss and Syril lock eyes, then she turns to me. "After that first killing sweep, there was only silence. No one remained in the Eighth House to kill—except for the horses—and the skrill returned to the mountains. They only came back last night, after you arrived. We found them stirring in the courtyard of the Eighth, and the farther we got into the house, well—you saw them. So yes, I think they are waiting for that direction, and they believe you're here to give it."

I make a face. "But if they wanted us to serve as their leader, why did they attack us?"

"They didn't, though," Fortiss points out, reasonably enough. "They were in the house, but it's not like any of them tried to stop us. They didn't even stop Syril and her team, not at first. Then we opened the door to Daggar's vault and immediately set them on fire. I'm thinking we've got some pretty confused snakes right now, but they won't remain that way for long. They'll figure it out."

"The dark shall draw the dark," Syril murmurs, and Tennet, Fortiss and I all look at her sharply. She would have had no idea that Daggar had said those words to Fortiss less than a day ago. But something in the words pricks my attention in a way it didn't before.

"If the dark draws the dark, then anything that's not dark *won't* draw it, won't order it forward," I say slowly. "And anything that can't or won't draw the dark, is the enemy. They just assumed we were what they were waiting for. We show up directly in front of them, blithely follow them back to the Eighth House, accept their hospitality, and break bread with them. Maybe they just assumed we understood who and what they were."

"While all along, we simply were idiots," Tennet says. He winces and reaches up to pinch the bridge over his nose.

"Not idiots," Syril protests quickly, then pauses. "Well, some-what idiots. But you learned something important too. The Savasci would never have gone into that house again. To us, there's been nothing left alive in that house but snakes since Daggar and his family, staff and servants were all massacred. Outside the house, there was nothing living except the horses in the stable—which we kept there since there was food aplenty for them and the skrill didn't seem to mind us feeding them and leading a few off a bit at a time. Then you landed in front of the Eighth House and saw a robust company of men and horses galloping out to greet you. You believed what your eyes showed you, just as the horses did."

"Honestly, we really do sound like idiots," I mutter.

Syril shakes her head. "Again, you're missing the point. The skrill illusion magic works against a specific target. In the case of the wall—anyone around here, who knows the history of the place and what they should expect—sees an unbroken wall. Fortiss, you may well see a crumbled one. In the case of the Eighth House, the skrill needed to draw banded warriors into their midst to receive their direction. For that they needed you and the horses of the Eighth to perceive them as real...but no one else. That's important. Maybe because the energy is so focused, the illusion holds more firmly for their targeted enemies."

"But not you?" Tennet asks. "Why? You've clearly proven your-selves to be a threat."

"Maybe we're neither enough of a threat or a tool to be worth their energy." She shrugs. "I don't know. What I do know is that banded warriors can't see what's real at the Eighth House. And given that the only people who are coming to help us tonight are banded warriors, you'll need to keep some members of the Savasci with you in every fighting unit. Someone needs to see clearly."

I grimace. "I was kind of hoping that I could band you and your warriors to Divhs before night falls. We'll need all the help we can get. But if you need to see clearly in order to keep us from blun-dering into another illusion..."

Syril turns to me, her eyes widening. "You would band us? Just like that? Without..."

"Well, *I'm* the lord protector," Fortiss puts in, his wry smile taking the arrogance out of his words. "And so, I'm the ultimate arbiter of who gets banded, but Lady Talia has authority over her own Divhs by my decree. That said, I understand both sides of this discussion. You should be banded, yet we need your sight to keep us aligned. But if you could choose, say, half your group to receive the band, and Talia's willing, we could use the help. We don't know who if any of the other houses will be able to supply assistance."

I don't miss Tennet's grim expression, and intriguingly enough, neither does Syril. "You disagree," she prompts him.

"The bands of the Divhs have been passed down from father to son for five hundred years," Tennet says gruffly. "We've been taught that that was the tradition of our forebears. Now that tradition lays in ruins. We've also learned that the original delegation from the Imperium wasn't made up entirely of warriors, but each to a one was banded to become warriors to fight in the Great Conflict. That much we know is true, and that much explains why Talia could become a warrior with a Divh so mighty. Fair enough."

"Your enthusiasm is breathtaking," I comment, but he ignores me and barrels on.

"That said, should we not have some measure of decorum when it comes to awarding the band going forward? All in your company are worthy, undoubtedly," he says to Syril, who regards him with a baleful eye. "But is this a precedent we truly want to set, linking those who are not warriors to Divhs? I confess I don't know. And it seems that we don't have the luxury of knowing. So, perhaps I should hold my own counsel."

"Never that," I murmur. drawing Tennet's attention as Fortiss scowls at me. "Warriors fight not only with their sword and staff, but with their minds. Still, you're right enough—we don't have the luxury of picking and choosing who our allies are. And I know from previous experience that we could do far worse than banding the warriors of the Savasci."

I turn to Syril. "If they're willing, I'll band half your troop today and the guards among our number. Anyone with any battle skill, honestly. Those who remain as lookouts should know that their time will come if we survive this. For now, though, we need their clear eyes as much, if not more, than we need pairings with Divhs."

"We'll need your healers too," Fortiss says grimly. "There's always a reaction to banding, and there's no way to tell how severe it will be. We've got less than twelve hours before nightfall. That's not a lot of time to band your people or help them recover from the shock of the experience."

"I can take on the training of your warriors these next several hours," Tennet says stoutly. Even if he doesn't love this plan, he's clearly committing to it. "That training, I'm afraid, will be simply honing your people's willingness to command their Divhs into a battle none of us have ever fought before these past few days. But from what I've seen, your people can handle that."

Syril smiles at him, the first real smile I think I've ever seen her share. "Then I will lead the sighted Savasci, Lord Tennet, and you will lead my warriors."

CHAPTER 33

"They'll work out their conflict over you before nightfall, if you're wondering. I've watched this particular battle worked out too many times not to know the signs."

"What?" I look up to see Syril at the top of the path. She's looking between me and the far edge of the encampment. A small smile plays at the corner of her mouth, but she doesn't seem particularly happy. I roll to my feet, suddenly alert. "What are you talking about?"

"The two men circling around you like dogs before the hunt." She gives a short, curt wave to still my objection as I draw up alongside her. She shifts to the side just enough to give me an eyeful of Fortiss and Tennet squaring off near the sleeping cave, their manners tense. She's right—they do look like they're about to fight. "They've tried to play it civil enough, but that can only work for so long, and Fortiss is no fool. He can't guide a lion in battle if he thinks it might chew off his foot."

"Oh, please." I roll my eyes. Just what I need before a battle—two powerful men deciding who gets to bleed for me first. But on this, I think Syril is wrong. "They're not going to fight over me, if that's what you're getting at. They've both made it clear that it's my choice."

I wave off Syril's scoff. "Well, Fortiss has, anyway. And he's who matters."

"Is he?" Syril's question is soft, oddly neutral, but I keep going.

"And they're certainly not going to hurt each other. Their swords are more valuable than that and so are their Divhs. They won't do anything to jeopardize their ability to ride into battle against a real enemy."

"Mmm." She eyes me with new interest. "You won't ride alongside one of them?"

"Well, I won't be in the air, if that's what you mean. Gent doesn't fly, but he's half again as big as either one of their Divhs. He can do plenty of damage from the ground. Together, we can take on whatever the skrill want to throw at us, and attack or defend, depending on what our best strategy is. Probably a little bit of both. The Divhs with wings will go on the offensive while Gent and I will protect the mounted warriors from below—as well as the healers who remain in camp."

"So who will protect you?"

I curl my lip, watching as Tennet drops his hands to his belt, his stance wide as he rocks back on his heels. "Well, not them. I don't need their protection."

She huffs a derisive cough. "Spoken like a woman who's been protected all her life."

"I didn't have a choice in that," I shoot back, unreasonably annoyed. "It's not like the Savasci had an encampment outside the Tenth House, welcoming in women tired of being crushed under their father's bootheels."

"We don't do that at the Eighth House either." Her words are low, even, but her gaze remains on the quarreling men. "No woman joins the Savasci because they want to—and certainly not because they seek it out. They do it because they have no other choice. We're known in the Eighth—well, we *were* known in that house—the way we have to be known. As marauders and outlaws, living off the land and the hard work of other people. And among those who would do us harm, we're also known as being a band of both men and women."

"Really?" That surprises me enough to take my attention off Fortiss and Tennet. "You cultivate that belief? Why? And why even draw attention to yourselves at all?"

"The belief would be there whether we cultivated it or not. It's to our advantage to control it, so that we understand our enemy. Or our ally, which Daggar was on occasion. But men fear what they don't understand, Talia. Everyone does. It's a challenging thing to accept the idea of a band of women working together happily and successfully all on their own without the existence of men among them, especially when we also have the reputation of being thieves and cutthroats." She smiles, the expression darkly satisfied. "Never mind that the throats we cut richly deserved it, or that I can count on the fingers of one hand those unfortunates who actually fell beneath our blade, never mind the tales. Daggar knew that truth, at least."

"That you fought to protect your own," I clarify. "But you really think he didn't know that there were no men among the Savasci?"

"I know for a fact he didn't, because we still exist. A troop of self-sufficient marauders who can be used to further your own ends on occasion is one thing. A troop of women successfully living outside the walls of any keep is a threat to established society. If he knew about it, he would have to do something about it."

"You mean dismantle you." I stare at her, baffled. "But somehow the mere idea of you having men among your number afforded you protection from that?"

She gestures to the arguing men. "Wouldn't you worry less if you knew that men like these were among the women, ensuring their safety?"

"Oh, please." I roll my eyes. "I'd worry more." I glance down the path as the first of Tennet's words reach me. "—Not your decision to *make*. It's mine."

"Blood and stone," I groan, glancing back at Syril. What I see in her face stops me short. She's watching the men not with derision, or even smug condescension, but with the open curiosity of a woman unused to anyone bristling for the honor to defend her. For a moment, I think about what it must be like to be her—working for the safety of her women, teaching them, nurturing them, protecting them. And yes, the Savasci have been very successful at it for many years, but Syril won't be young forever, and there will always be more women to protect.

She seems to realize that I'm watching her, and her face blanks of all expression as Fortiss lifts his voice. "—and you will *respect* that."

"Blighted path I will," Tennet shoots back, and I know I can't watch this any longer. Never mind that as I turn to strike down the path, I catch the renewed flare of interest in Syril's eyes.

I don't have time to wonder about what she's thinking as I swing away, moving fast. I'm almost to the clearing when I hear the hiss of metal clearing scabbards—Tennet and Fortiss have drawn their swords.

"Blood and *stone!*" I scramble the last of the distance to where they're fighting, then draw up short, just out of view but with a clear vantage point allowing me to see them. In truth, I don't know the meaning of their fight, or if it's actually about me, only that they're fighting. And while I know I should rush in and somehow put a stop to it before either one of them is injured, I...well, I don't.

Because now that I'm up close like this, I've never seen anything more beautiful then these two warriors slashing at each other.

I stare with open surprise as I watch Fortiss fend off the bigger, bulkier Tennet with a series of slashing thrusts that drive the taller warrior back, clearly catching him off guard. I realize I've never seen Fortiss fight, not up close. Though he directed Rihad's mighty Divh in battle during the Tournament of Gold, and I've seen him performing aerobatics on the back of his mighty dragon, simple swordplay was never part it.

He moves with a ferocity I wouldn't have predicted, every cut, every slash timed perfectly—not simply for defense but for pressing the advantage, for harrying and driving and keeping Tennet on his heels.

Tennet is even more of a revelation. Once he overcomes his initial surprise at Fortiss's attack, he regroups and moves forward efficiently, strategically. His strength is impressive, and Fortiss clearly respects it. Fortiss works hard to ensure that Tennet never lands more than a glancing blow, shifting to the left or the right to go with the force of his sword and then coming around again with his own blade to prevent Tennet's advance.

The men are no longer shouting at each other, wholly absorbed in their swordplay, but they're evenly matched. Where Fortiss wins on exposing more opportunities to bloody Tennet, Tennet dominates in moving as if driven from within, spurred on by the heat of passion. Fortiss is like water, but Tennet is like fire. They battle back and forth across the open space thirty, forty times, showing no sign of fatigue until at last, Tennet takes a wild, uneven stroke at Fortiss's shoulder, and Fortiss ducks away, barely avoiding the blade.

The two fall away from each other to regroup, and I take my opportunity to redirect them.

"Lord Protector Fortiss! Lord Tennet!" I deliberately pitch my voice low and keep my manner brisk as I stride into the clearing, as if I've only just now come upon them. Warriors in the midst of battle might as well be wild animals, focused so intently that startling them is unwise except from a distance.

They both wheel around and stare at me as if I'm a sandworm suddenly erupted in their midst. I stand and place my legs wide, dropping my hands to my belt. "Syril reports that the healers have assembled additional provisions against tonight's battle, though we don't know exactly what to expect. She awaits further orders for spreading word down to the villages of Merrivale and Kirk."

"Syril?" Tennet asks, and he turns and searches the rocky outcroppings above the cave, as if he might find an audience there. Fortiss, meanwhile, stares at me. The force of that stare is like a punch to the gut, his energy leaping across the open field like a roar of triumph. I hold his gaze, return it glare for glare, and he grins wide and sure. A breeze suddenly whips up around me, strong enough to lift my hair and dance across my lips, and I blink at Fortiss, shocked anew.

Was that real? Did he just stir the very wind?

It dies away as quickly, and my sight clears to take in both warriors again. Both of them are blowing hard, their chests rising and falling, and this close, I can see that the battle has taken a toll on both of them, even if they don't bleed heavily from their few cuts.

Sweat streams from Fortiss's brow, and Tennet's tunic is dark with it across his back, his hair plastered to his head. They both keep their swords in their hands as they turn back to each other, then Fortiss scowls down at his blade.

He sheaths it roughly, turning to Tennet. "I won."

"Did you?" Tennet challenges, though he sheaths his blade as well. He turns to me and grins. "You saw it, Lady Talia," he drawls. "Who would you say won?"

"I'd say the fact that you're both still standing and haven't completely exhausted yourselves is about as much of a win as I can take away from this. You expect to do a lot of hand-to-hand battle on your feet tonight, taking out snakes one by one?"

"Sometimes that's the best way to make them pay attention," he shoots back, but he's still grinning, and Fortiss laughs and shakes his head.

"If you weren't so bullheaded, you'd make an excellent councilor, Lord Tennet. I've never met anyone who is more ready with an answer, no matter how ill advised."

"That's because the people who you surround yourself with didn't grow up in the mountains. If you don't talk back to yourself, you never hear any conversation at all."

Even I burst out laughing at that, and both men look hard at me, as if I somehow just showed some favor I never intended. I feel a headache coming on, and I turn squarely toward Fortiss. "Have you learned anything that we can use from Daggar's library?"

"Not enough." He frowns. "I know there's more information in there, more information that we need, but time is running short. What I have learned so far is this—the skrill haven't come through the mountains in generations, but attacks across the western borders definitely continued for the first few hundred years after the Great Conflict. To the point that it feels like maybe they weren't all entirely attacks...as in, maybe they were attempts to make connections that the Eighth House strongly rebuffed, time after time."

"Connections?" rumbles Tennet. He pulls off his tunic and uses it to wipe his face, a move that Fortiss copies, leaving me staring at two bare-chested warriors, both of them glorious in their own ways and equally exasperating. Where Fortiss's muscles are wrapped around a lean, sinewy frame that speaks of horse riding and fast climbing or cutting through the endless waters of the lake in the Blessed Plane, Tennet is built like he could take out a bear and then carry a small pony to safety. I give up trying to look at either one of them without ogling and stare at a point over Fortiss's shoulder as Tennet continues.

"What kind of connections would the skrill be seeking to make? They're mindless snakes. All they seem capable of doing is screaming. I never got anything coherent out of them, did you?" He folds his arms across his chest as he turns to me, and once again, I'm forced to laugh. But I quickly switch my gaze to Fortiss who's tucked his tunic into his trousers, dragging the belt down a little.

"I haven't," I say, determinedly keeping my gaze on Fortiss's face. "But I don't know their language, and it's something it seems like we'll need to learn. Something maybe you already have started?"

"The books in Daggar's library are quite descriptive," he says nodding. "They all describe the Western Realms with the harshest terms possible, a land of ash and fire, sudden storms and endless gray mountains."

"No wonder the Imperium didn't push to continue exploring it," Tennet puts in.

"And that tails with what I saw—but is that all there is?" I ask. "To Tennet's point, if anyone wanted to discourage someone making the attempt to cross the borders, accounts like this would do it. And then there's the wall that stretches across the Unlit Pass, not to mention the clear antagonism of the skrill and their deadly nature. Daggar's entire house was taken out by these things in a *day*. They're definitely the enemy, but why are they doing this?"

"They are a mighty force that is being used as an enemy, yes," Fortiss agrees. "And I have to agree with Tennet—I don't think they need a reason why."

He breaks off to grin at him. "Don't get used to it."

"I won't." Tennet snorts as Fortiss continues.

"The skrill don't impress me as having the ability to reason through their actions. They go where they're told to go. But someone is doing the telling, I think. Why? And who will we combat tonight? Just the skrill, or the Sahktar too?"

I shudder involuntarily, thinking of the creature that I saw in Rihad's fireplace—and can barely imagine it being as tall as a Divh. "If we're facing the Sahktar, will you be able to talk to them? Will we be able to understand should they try to speak to us? Based on what happened to Lord Daggar, I can't believe it's going to be a very fruitful conversation."

"No. I don't think it'll be much of a conversation at all," agrees Fortiss. "And I don't know that it will be beneficial for us to betray any understanding we have of their language, for that matter. But it might be wise to keep our ears sharp and see what we do under-stand, and how it may change during the tide of battle. We may not get the advantage of that surprise again."

He looks up at the sun, still high in the sky. "For now, all we can do is prepare for the fight—and for whatever may happen after."

CHAPTER 34

We spend another few hours packing up the Savasci's home, but it's obvious from the start that Syril has seen this day coming for some time. While there's plenty of evidence of children—clothes, dolls and well-used toys—only warriors remain in this camp. There's little else to move other than food and a few provisions for each of the women. Everything else Syril orders to be added to a growing pile destined to become a pyre.

Tennet lends his back to the effort, but his face grows stormier with each new addition. Finally, he's had enough.

"Why burn it all?" he confronts Syril as she throws another small pile of children's clothes onto what will soon become a pyre. "Are these children and their mothers all dead?"

She recoils a little, startled out of wherever her thoughts had taken her. "Of course they're not dead. They were sent to safety. Some of them as much as six months ago, others after the first attack and the destruction of the Eighth House. It wasn't safe for them here. And we have gone through too many cycles of privation not to know the signs. There are places where they can blend into the villages, and we've amassed enough wealth over the years that we don't need to go empty handed anywhere."

My lips twitch. The Savasci are some of the most skilled thieves the First House has ever experienced. If they did show up someplace empty handed, they certainly didn't leave it that way. I glance over to see if Fortiss shares my reaction, but he's standing at the far edge of the Savasci camp, his gaze hard on the Eighth House rising silently in the distance. He's up on his toes, his fingers twitching.

That's not good.

"Then why not simply hide these goods until you reunite with them?" Tennet persists.

Syril sighs. "Because we may not reunite with them, Lord Tennet, and I won't let their belongings be used by the skrill to fool others with their illusion magic. Besides, if we do survive this night, *when* we do, we'll be forever changed. They will be forever changed. And the trappings of our past, especially bits of clothing and toys they are even now outgrowing have no place in the lives we will forge. We'll keep our tools and our weapons, the food we can carry and the clothes that can serve us in the weeks ahead. The rest we will make or buy when the time comes."

"But this—" he holds up an intricately carved comb, sized for a young girl, almost like it's a weapon, but there's nothing but sorrow in his voice. For a man made of fire and fury, Tennet burns strangely soft for the innocent. "This is fine work."

Syril's eyes fall upon it, and her mouth falters a bit, her gaze going a little soft. "You've had the luxury of having a place to call your own, a place of safety and certainty. We have that luxury, too, as the Savasci—but only here." She taps between her breasts with two fingers. "Anything of value that cannot be carried here doesn't truly serve you, not when you're both hunted and hunter."

Tennet looks like he's about to object but merely sets his jaw. Gently, Syril takes the comb out of his hand and tosses it high upon the pile.

Glancing back to the edge of the camp, I stiffen. Fortiss is gone. *Blood and stone.* "Syril, I'll be back in just a—"

"Lady Talia!" A tall, lean Savasci calls me from the opening of the great cave, and I wheel toward her, blinking as she leads a row of more than a dozen women out of the shadows, all of them in tunics and breeches, their well-muscled arms bared. Some of them I've seen before, some I haven't—but they all could be sisters in the way they move. Stern-faced, sharp-eyed, and as fluid as the wind through the trees, they follow the first woman until she stops in front of me. Tennet and Syril have turned as well.

"These are the women you will band—with no training?" he begins, blustering, but Syril places a hand on his shoulder, staying his complaint.

"Arrant, Johl! Report with your men," she calls out. A few moments later, a small knot of guards appear as well, the soldiers who'd managed to survive the first attack of the skrill and remained to serve the Savasci. They line up with the women, a group of nearly twenty souls.

"These are the best warriors I can offer you, Lord Tennet." She hasn't removed her hand from his shoulder. "I trust them with my life. I have trained most of them myself. They will follow your lead wherever it may take them, even into the Light itself. But if you can't accept them, I'll release them now. It's your decision."

I bite my lip to keep myself from smiling, though no one is looking at me. Still, Syril has caught Tennet well and truly in her trap. He grits his teeth so hard I can hear them grind together, but he nods. "Then we shall fight," he says.

By the time he turns back to me, I've schooled my face into stoic indifference...but I don't miss the fact that Syril's hand is *still* on Tennet's shoulder. She's easily ten years his senior, I think—but only ten. Could there be a connection there?

Not a possibility we have time to consider today, of course. The Savasci and guards now stare at me with a mixture of hope, anxiety, and wonder...and I can't say that I blame them. I don't know what I'm doing either.

The warrior acts first with the mind, then with the body.

I square my shoulders and lift my voice.

"I've been blessed with a battalion of Divhs who need warriors, and you have been chosen to meet that need." My words carry out boldly across the open space and into the plains. Before I can even wonder if Gent is listening, I hear his hooting laugh of pleasure, equal parts commentary and call to arms of Divhs I've barely met. But their buzzing energy builds within me, and I gesture to the wide plain. "To take the band is a swift and painful experience, but the pain is fleeting and the connection life-long. The best advice I can give you is to surrender to it. To leap, knowing you'll be caught."

Gent's howl is louder now, and it's joined by the keening cries of twenty-some additional beasts, their roars pounding through my blood so loudly I can barely hear Tennet's question.

"How will they know whose Divh is whose? Do they just pick?"

"No." I shake my head, sudden clarity laying out the way in front of me. "I do."

I point at the woman closest to me, the oldest of the group of warriors. Gray streaks her hair, and deep lines bracket her mouth and eyes, but they tell the tale of a woman who not only fights with ferocity but laughs with all her spirit. As I focus on her image, an answering call screams across the Blessed Plane, and I see the creature in its full, magnificent glory before it bursts into view.

The group collectively gasps, and they should. A bird almost as large as Wrath soars over us, breathing fire. Though she only has one set of taloned legs, the talons are that of a raptor and the glint of steel at the end of her orange wings indicate that her wings are every bit as vicious weapons as her claws. She screams and the woman I've designated as her match shocks me by screaming back, a wild and vibrant howl that has the winged phoenix banking back sharply, searching the ground where we stand. Wind whips off the plains and around us, drawing our unit more tightly together.

I command the woman forward and extend my left arm as she approaches, palm up. At my direction, she places her left hand in mine, barely flinching as I squeeze our hands into a tight grip.

What happens next does make her flinch, of course. As I hold her gaze steadily with mine, I can feel the lowest strand of my segmented warrior band break away and carve its path down my bicep, into the crook of my elbow, and along my forearm, leaving a bloody welt in its path. It spins around both our hands and cuts into the warrior's wrist, burning its way up her arm until it burrows deep into her bicep, circling it in a ferocious clamp.

Her eyes widen, and she falls back. But she doesn't falter from there. Her chin comes up, her jaw sets, and her hand redoubles its strength as she grips mine.

"What's your name?"

"Selena," she shouts, And I realize the wind hasn't died down, and that the phoenix is not the only Divh that has entered this plane. The sky is choked with flying creatures, while furred beasts pound the earth as far as the eye can see.

"Go and fight, warrior Selena," I command her. The scream of the phoenix fills the air as Selena turns toward the open plain. She breaks into a run, arms pumping, legs churning, and her phoenix sees her as of course only she can, the beacon of her warrior partner lit up like the sun. She swoops down with her talons bared, and moments later, the two of them vanish into the Blessed Plane to complete their bonding.

I turn to the next soldier nearest me, a guard whose face is a mass of scars and long-ago broken bones. His Divh appears in my mind's eye, a mountain of a landed creature that looks like a fall of boulders taken physical form. We grasp left hands, the warrior's massive paw dwarfing mine, and he proves himself to be a quick study. "I am Rud," he shouts—and he still has to shout, as the screaming all around us has only gotten worse. Rud's grip nearly crushes my bones as the band leaps from my arm to his, but his eyes glitter with ferocity and pride as his rock-boulder Divh roars ebulliently and pounds its way to him, running with both hands and feet connecting with the earth.

Rud turns and, as Selena did before him, shouts in pure, unfettered joy at the breathtakingly ungainly creature galloping our way. In that moment, he doesn't look like a guard of nearly five decades in age. He may as well have been my own brother, seventeen years old, wild and free, racing toward his Divh and hurling himself forward, knowing that he would be caught.

The two practically collide before they vanish to the Blessed Plane.

The banding goes quickly after that. In less than a few hours, the full company of warriors has disappeared, and the wide plains before the Savasci's camp have fallen quiet. Both Tennet and Syril search the heavens, him with something approaching shock on his face, her with pure wonder.

"What a gift you have given them, helping them become warriors, Lady Talia," she murmurs.

To my surprise, Tennet turns on me, his eyes gone hard and fierce.

"She should be banded as well. You know that. If you're going to band all these..."

I shake my head even as Syril scoffs at him. "You'll all be as blind as newborn babes without my eyes to show you how the skrill play you for fools. Banding with the Divhs is not a prize to be awarded to the best at playing warrior games, not here, not now. We may as well be thrust back into that first Great Conflict, thirty horsemen facing a mountain spilling over with evil, seeking the aid of the most unlikely allies. We will fight in the way that we must."

"Then *afterwards*," he stresses, not willing to cede the point.

In this at least, I fully agree with him. "Afterward you will have a Divh so fierce, it will give Tennet's dragon pause," I promise her.

She barks a laugh. "Done."

We turn our attention to the far horizon. "Will they be ready to fight?" Syril asks quietly, though there's no one left to hear but the healers standing at the ready for when the warriors return.

I shrug. "Most of them will. Some may be overcome with sickness and need to be tended, but they'll join as soon as they can stand. Their bond with their Divhs will demand it. And if the Light blesses us with any luck at all, we'll have the warriors from the other houses up and down the borders to aid us as well. We've seen only a little of what the skrill have to offer. We'll need all the help we can get."

Tennet glances around. "Where's Fortiss?"

Syril sighs. "He's gone back to the Eighth House to find what he may. Lord protector or not, he's like every man in that regard. They're never content to leave well enough alone, but the Eighth House holds on to its secrets tightly. If he's not careful, it may hold on to him too."

I look at her sharply. "What are you talking about? There's nothing in the Eighth House anymore but illusions."

"But what are illusions but shadows of what we expect to see?" Syril grimaces. "If there's anything that can haunt the lord protector, he'll find it. And when he finds it, he'll learn truths he may not wish to know."

"Blighted *path*," I mutter. "Tennet—"

"I'll take care of the warriors," he booms, as I take off toward the horses. "You go bring our leader home."

CHAPTER 35

Approaching the Eighth House feels exactly like riding into a graveyard—for all that I know this one is technically empty of the souls the skrill have claimed. I'm slightly surprised that my horse doesn't balk as we approach, the mare's strides long and sure as we gallop up the slow-rising grade to the main gate, which remains open, and into the grand courtyard. The horse that Fortiss commandeered is standing at the ready, though her bit has been loosened enough to allow her to enjoy the open bag of grain he's left for her.

Dismounting quickly, I scan the courtyard. Is this the last place he stood? Is the warmth in the air still his? What if he's already dead and ash in this house of horrors, lost to me?

No. That's not an outcome I'll ever allow.

I tie off my horse next to his and choke down my fear long enough to run up the stairs and into the front doors of the Eighth House, which has been opened wide. Now I see the foyer more clearly—the leaves scattered through it not the result of a sudden gust upon our arrival, but the first signs of a house falling into decay without the constant upkeep from an army of servants. I smell the staleness of the air that I simply didn't notice yesterday and wonder how I could have missed it.

"Fortiss?" I call out. I have to make a second effort when my first attempt is little more than a whisper. "Fortiss!"

When there's no response, I weather a wave of panic that roots my feet to the stone floor and force myself not to just tear off running through the keep. Yesterday, this place was filled with illusions—perhaps it still is. If this house is hiding Fortiss from me, no matter how many rooms I storm through...

I blow out a hard breath and reach out to Gent, imagining Fortiss lost in some shadowy chamber in this place. "How am I going to find him?" I whisper and receive his hooting reassurance in return.

Still, Gent can't help in this, not really—unless I want him to pummel the Eighth House with his mighty fists until he shakes Fortiss loose. And if I don't find Fortiss before too long, that's exactly what I'll ask him to do.

I'm halfway down the main corridor by the time I receive Gent's full response. With an earsplitting cacophony of coos and chirps, a gaggle of hummerlets explodes through the front door and sweep toward me down the hall. I gape, then force myself to imagine Fortiss while shouting his name aloud. The fluttering, twittering creatures look at me questioningly as if I'm a fool, then dart off through the castle, their bellies lighting up as the way darkens.

I follow them as best as I can, almost crying out with relief when I round a corner and realize a torch has been lit and placed into a sconce on the wall. Not willing to trust my own eyes, I dash up to it, lifting the torch free and drawing it close to my face. I can smell the burning wood, feel the heat of the flame, and my heart thuds with new hope. This is real, I think. Fortiss was here.

A hummerlet pops out of a side chamber, nearly scaring me to death, then trills at me with an attitude of clear irritation as she bobs up and down, belly glowing. She darts off down the corridor. Emboldened by my torch, I dash off after her, and together we wind our way deeper into the castle, heading up, not down. Not returning to the talonstone vault, then, but...where?

We reach the floor where our sleeping chambers were, but the hummerlets draw me away from those rooms and up a second set of stairs. I'm heartened to see another torch lit, and after pausing briefly to make sure that it, too, is real, I dash along the corridor, moving swiftly until the hummerlet in front of me suddenly stops midflight and poofs into nothingness. She's gone.

I stare, mutely for a long second more, with nothing but the soft crackling of the torch for company, and then I hear it.

Weeping.

Swallowing hard, I move forward toward the large open door at the end of the corridor. Light plays out in a rosy glow from the chamber, and when I peek my head around the door, I'm hit with the eye-wateringly awful smell of rotting meat. Then I see a large grate with an oddly red flame, walls lined with books, a bulky pile of blankets stacked in a corner...

And Fortiss kneeling over a body.

"Fortiss!" I gasp, shoving my own torch into a holder just inside the door and rushing toward him. A large pool of dark liquid has stained the rug around the body, and the scent of death in the room is as thick as winter fog. "What are you doing?"

"It's my father." He hunches over the corpse, shielding the man's face from my view. "Daggar said the truth was made plain to him in this chamber of prophecies, that all who entered would see what they couldn't face. I had to see."

"Fortiss..." I try again, edging closer to him. His shoulders are shaking, and the sight of his abject sorrow is nearly my undoing. I've never seen him so distraught.

I draw in a steadying breath. "That wasn't actually Lord Daggar talking to you. It was an illusion created by the skrill to deceive us into spending the night in this place of death. Where they could kill us in the middle of the night, when our guards were down."

"But he said—I—would know the truth," Fortiss manages, his voice cracking. "And he was right."

I bite my lip as he doubles over again, but he's making no sense to me. I don't want to startle him into attacking me, though, so I drop into a crouch, edging toward him bit by bit. "All right, so you came here to learn what you needed to learn. That's good, then. That can help us."

"My father didn't die in a fall," Fortiss moans. "Rihad killed him. He's been planning this so much longer than we even realize."

He pulls away from the body, and I see the telltale gray-flanged arrow sticking up out of the chest of what is clearly a great warrior —or was. Now the man is soaked in his own sticky blood. I reach out a shaky hand and grip Fortiss's arm, gritting my teeth as I realize how violently he's shivering. "He—he said Rihad needed Szonja for...for the winged crown, the one that was l-lost."

Fortiss gasps, clearly struggling for breath. His gaze swings to mine, eyes ravaged by tears, and I jolt as something—magic? Emotion? Some combination of the two?—leaps between us, a cord that winds around my heart and binds me fast. In that moment, I am one thought with Fortiss, one breath, his aching well of sorrow so deep we both may drown in it. I feel his pain as surely as it is my own, the loss and devastation of a betrayal that has stretched from an orphaned boy to the man I hold today. "That's why—Rihad kept her all those years in the caverns. My father told me that. And then he d-died in front of me."

"Oh, Fortiss," I whisper. I lean in even closer, wrapping my arm around him, intending only to draw him away. But I can't resist the ghoulish urge to glance toward the face of the corpse in front of me —even though I know it's an illusion, even though I know it's...

My breath dies in my throat.

The man lying in the pool of blood hasn't been pierced through with a flat gray arrow, but with an arrow of pure silver, whose feathers gleam with dyed flanges of silver struck through with the faintest brush of green. And the man whose mouth sags open, his eyes staring up sightlessly at the ceiling, isn't some dead, hallowed warrior I've never met. It isn't even Merritt—who, I realize, is what I most expected to find. Merritt, who I failed.

It's Fortiss. A mirror image of the man trembling beside me, one whose eyes are filled with the past, and one who's dead by my own hand.

He's wearing the crown of wings.

"Stop it." I yank Fortiss back so hard that we both go sprawling, and the image vanishes at my feet. I shake Fortiss roughly, slapping at him when he stares at me dumbly.

"*Stop* it," I yell again in his face. "You came in here for a reason. What was it? What did you think you would find in these chambers? What was worth being trapped by an illusion?"

"Not trapped," Fortiss insists, still dazed. "Not trapped." But he's shaking his head now, peering around wildly.

I haul myself to my feet and pull him up as well. "You looked trapped to me. What did you think was going to be in here?"

"The reason the Divhs came here in the first place. The crown of wings."

I stare at him, hard, then back to where the illusion of his own dead father had so ensnared his attention. Now there's nothing there, of course. No father, no Fortiss. Had I truly seen the crown of wings on Fortiss's head? If so—what did that mean? I had won the winged crown, not him.

"I thought you said Daggar never indicated that the crown was here," I say carefully. "Only the talonstones."

"But it *has* to be here." Fortiss shakes me off him, finally seeming to come back to himself as he turns to glare at the walls of books. "Rihad can't have been hiding it all these years. He's too proud. He would never have missed an opportunity to display it at the First House. He would have wanted to study it, delve into its powers. You forget, in the past month since the tournament, I've read his books, I've memorized his notes. I know more about his research than I ever wanted to. Rihad wasn't just looking to control Divhs. He was looking to command an army capable of helping him take over the Imperium. He wanted every scrap of power he could bend to his will. And he's been planning this for far longer than I even realized, and at a much higher level than I would have thought possible."

"Maybe—but maybe not," I counter. "You don't know if what you saw just now is anything but what the skrill wanted you to believe."

"No." He grimaces. "That's not how they're made, Talia. They don't lie, they don't think. They don't read minds and then manipulate what they learn to greatest effect. Divhs are summoned, not pushed, right? Well, skrill are drawn to darkness. They see it and they reveal it—that's all. We see what we're meant to see."

He's still scanning the walls, moving around the room, apparently oblivious to how much it still smells like a slaughterhouse. "Do we? Think about what happened here, Fortiss. Daggar and his entire family were killed. His guards. His staff. Now we're the ones being manipulated by the skrill—singled out specifically and manipulated, because of our connection to our Divhs."

"But how is that even possible?" he complains, sounding genuinely aggrieved. "How can the glory of being connected to a Divh be a worthwhile target? There's so few people that are connected to Divhs."

"Today, yes. Five hundred years ago? The only people alive, certainly the only people attacking the skrill, were those affiliated with Divhs. Maybe that's the only way they know how to connect with us now. The only reason why we succeeded in batting them back last night was because we caught them by surprise. They couldn't manipulate us. Tonight might be a different story, depending on what Syril sees."

"We're blinded by the only thing that can save us," he mutters, while I lean back against the wall of books.

"You've read Daggar's accounts. How is it the skrill have gone so long without attacking?"

He waves that question away. "Because no one has been able to summon them until Rihad. And even then, because he's no longer connected to them, they haven't moved with any sort of speed. If we find the crown of wings, we can control them. I'm sure of it. And I'm beginning to think they want to be controlled, Talia. Just like the Divhs want to be banded, the skrill want to be allowed into this plane."

He glances around. "There just has to be something here."

"I mean..." I watch him a little helplessly as he moves around the room, opening drawers, sifting through parchment pages. I slant my own gaze to the far corner of the room where the blankets are stacked and head that way. Maybe there's a crate beneath them, filled with more books—or even the crown of wings? Maybe that's...

I stop in my tracks.

"Fortiss," I croak, though the words die in my throat, barely loud enough to make a soft, gusting huff. I force my feet to lurch forward one step, then another. "Fortiss," I try again, my eyes peeling so wide, I feel like they must take up my whole skull. "*For—*"

"*Light*, Talia, what?"

I hear him turning, but I can't hear anything else. The horror in front of me is so loud, so terrible, it consumes all my senses. My ears, eyes, mouth, nose, hands are weighted down with the sight of the hand that flops out underneath the red-soaked blankets stacked against the wall, the thinnest curl of a tail slipping out between the gnarled fingers.

It's still moving.

"Blood and stone!" Fortiss rushes by me in a whoosh of air, so fast it almost feels like I'm falling backward. I see the blankets peel away, the den of fat snakes flopping and undulating—too gorged on the guts of their victims to do more than ooze out of Fortiss's way. The two men's faces that gradually emerge as the serpents depart are little more than gore-covered skulls, but there's no doubt in my mind who they are. If Syril's warnings weren't still ringing in my mind, the fact that the snakes' skins are now a luminescent orange would demonstrate their unholy link with the defenders of the Eighth House.

"Let's go."

Fortiss is in front of me again, yanking me away from the

lolling snakes, pulling me around to face him. His voice is hard as granite. He shakes me, hard, and I come back to my senses.

"We've got to *go*, Talia. You're right. There's nothing else here, but they'll be coming now. They'll find us, kill us, and use us to fool the others, so we've got to *go*!"

"Go..." I finally manage, but any more words than that fail me. I let him drag me out of the room. I stumble a little until I can get my feet underneath me—then I match him stride for stride.

We race back through the Eighth House and out into the courtyard, and I'm more relieved than I expect that the horses are still there. The sun has dropped behind the Meridians and shadows even now are lengthening across the open ground, which only spurs us on. We tighten the horses' tack and swiftly mount up, then turn them toward the gates...

That are now shut tight, a broad bolt clamped in place across thick, unyielding metal doors.

We're trapped.

CHAPTER 36

"It's an illusion—it has to be!" I practically scream, but the horses balk as we approach the gates and shy away, leaving Fortiss and me no choice but to dismount and approach the gates on foot. We race right up to them, then slow, and extend our hands outward. Sure enough, the heavy metal gates won't let us pass. When we reach out, we encounter smooth metal.

"It's our eyes," Fortiss realizes. "Our eyes won't allow it."

"Fine," I snap. "Then we don't use our eyes."

I stride out from the gates a good dozen steps, turn and square my shoulders. "We're going to have to run right through it. If we have enough momentum, and we don't open our eyes, and we don't run into any actual walls, it could work. Twenty strides should do it."

"Are you serious?" Fortiss shakes his head, but he quickly joins me, and we turn and face the gate. He reaches out and grabs my hand and we lock our fingers tight. "What if we're wrong?"

"Well, we should keep one arm in front of our faces, like this," I tell him, demonstrating. "If we're wrong, we'll break our momentum without smashing our faces too much. Hopefully." I grimace. "What happens if we open our eyes in the middle of the door?"

"*Light*, let's not even think about what could happen then." He draws in a deep breath and squeezes my hand. "Ready?" he asks, closing his eyes and turning his face forward again.

I shut my eyes tight, then swallow. "Ready." I mean the word to come out like a defiant shout, but it's barely a murmur.

Fortiss huffs a short laugh. "Let's go."

We take off at a dead run, never let going of each other's hands. Five steps, ten—fifteen. Twenty. At twenty-five, something hard clips me in the shins at the same time I suspect that it hits Fortiss, judging by his startled 'oof.' Despite my best efforts to keep my eyes closed, they pop open as I sprawl forward.

My hand rips out of Fortiss's as I find myself windmilling in the open air. We've gone over the side of the causeway.

"Gent!" I scream, but before the word is even fully formed, I hear his cry. A massive hand reaches down and swoops me out of the air, then to my utter shock he chucks me high in the air. I scream in terror for one breath, two—then all the wind is knocked out of me as he catches me again. Is he playing some kind of game?

Gent roars with delight as a burst of flame erupts next to me, and I watch, dizzily, as he drops a dazed Fortiss onto Szonja's back as she hovers midair. As my heart leaps with transcendent joy—*he's safe! Fortiss is safe*—my mind puts it together, two of us falling and Gent snatching me first, but needing to get rid of me long enough for him to capture Fortiss as well.

Dizzy, half-delirious with relief, I stagger back, bracing myself in Gent's palm. I watch Fortiss grip Szonja's neck and want to weep, to laugh, to shout—but all I can do is give thanks to the Light with every shaky breath. Seeing him like that in that accursed room, weeping and shaking with love and loss, vulnerable and broken...and then having him pull me out of a similar thrall, the two of us racing together to free ourselves from the twisting lies that loom all around us...

It's changed me, I think, and I manage a weak smile, watching

Szonja swoop around in a low, lazy arc. Every time I think I can't be changed any more, I discover how wrong I am.

With this crisis solved, Szonja banks off to the right with a defiant scream, while Gent wheels around toward the Eighth House—and, more specifically, the mountains that jut up behind it.

As the night draws down over the mountains, a storm is crashing toward us from the Western Realms.

"Report!" I scream, clamping my hands over my ears and hunkering into the rough, leathery skin of Gent's palm as he holds me against his chest, his farsighted gaze on the approaching lightning storm. And, with the strength of my bond to the Divhs and their warriors...a bond I suspect has only been strengthened by my exposure to Fortiss's magic and the ancient pull of this house...I instantly make the connection I need.

We've got everyone away, Tennet's voice pummels my mind with quick, percussive strikes. *Whoever isn't banded to a Divh is with the horses. We'd wanted them all the way to the village by now, but we've had our hands full. These people were not trained for this kind of connection, Talia. More than half of them are still too sick to ride.*

His rebuke drives a knife through my wooziness, and I lash out, the fire going a long way toward making me feel normal again. *All they needed was to be banded. With a band, they can ground the Divhs in this plane—and here they are. We can do the rest until they get on their feet.*

Gent swings around to show me the army that we've assembled, and I am immediately reminded of the melee.

The rising moon bathes the plains before the Eighth House in spectral light, its eerie magnificence heightened further by the bursts of fire emitted by the chaotic mass of monsters that fills the sky around it.

If I hadn't seen it once before, I'd be mesmerized by the vision of so many Divhs gathered at once, bristling for battle. As it is, I'm filled with an almost suffocating pride.

A towering griffin, three times as tall as the Eighth House and five times as broad, unfurls its magnificent wings, casting a shadow over the howling, hooting Divhs stamping beneath it on the ground. Beside it, a scarlet-scaled flying lizard snarls, smoke curling from its nostrils as its dozen short, stubby legs churn in the air. A full pride of green-furred lions race up and down in front of the Eighth House, each of them as large as Miriam's hummerbill, but bristling with horns that jut out from heads and hindquarters. They roar in unison as an ape-like colossus slams its massive fists into the ground, sending tremors through the wide plains.

To their left, a massive bull with a shimmering bronze hide paws at the earth, its horns arching up to wicked points. Its snorts release twin bursts of steam, and the ground beneath its hooves seems to shrink away with every furious stamp.

Above them, a pair of golden falcons circle, each with a wing-span stretching nearly as broad as the griffins', their sharp eyes scanning the battlefield. Their feathers gleam like polished metal, and their talons slash the air. They let out piercing cries, rallying their allies below.

I stretch forward for a closer look. Only about half of the flying creatures hold warriors tucked into place high upon their necks. None of them look too comfortable with their seats, judging from their wide eyes and strained mouths, not to mention their deathly grip on scales or feathers or buried into fur. I know they're terrified, but I'm not worried for them. Their Divhs will do anything to protect them. Even if I were to order them onto the blighted path itself, I sense that somehow the Divhs would find a way to stow their warrior cargo in some nearby rock or tree before fulfilling my command.

No. These warriors have never been safer. There's just not nearly enough of them to carry the standard if Tennet falters.

A roar catches my attention as another lion-like creature with six legs and a mane of black spikes prowls forward. Its eyes burn with an intense orange glow, and every step leaves smoldering paw prints in its wake. I blink in surprise. This creature goes beyond simply breathing fire. The heat radiating from its body distorts the air around it, making it appear as if it were wrapped in a shimmering mirage.

Beside it, a serpentine colossus rears up high, its scaled body glinting like obsidian. With all the snakes we're about to face, I only wonder for a moment about the wisdom of having snakes on our side too. Then I see who's riding this creature—a red-haired, wild-eyed Savasci, bound with ropes to keep her in place, directly behind the snake's head. A huge longbow spikes up behind her, and quivers of arrows hang from the tightly lashed rope.

She's definitely one of us. With glacial movements, the serpent coils its massive tail, its golden eyes glowing with a predatory intelligence. As it hisses, the sound reverberates like distant thunder, and its forked tongue flicks out, tasting the air for the approaching enemy. It's almost as if the massive Divh is taunting the unknown darkness to show us its worst—

And it does.

A sudden sucking sound rips through the plains, loud enough to drown out the roars of the Divhs. Through the breach pours a churning, hissing tide—snakes the size of pigs, ponies, and even caravan wagons, both grounded and winged, their slick scales glinting like oil. *Poison*, I remind myself, and send the message out again to all the warriors and Divhs linked to me. *Don't let the skrill touch your skin if you can help it. If they get hold of you for long enough, their poison can turn your mind to mush. Stay clear.*

The snakes rush down the pass out of the mountain and, in a gut-churning vision of horror, overtake the Eighth House in a mere space of breaths. One moment the Eighth House stands tall, lit up by flickering blasts of exhaled fire, a beacon of strength in the night —and the next it's almost as if it's become a living thing, shivering and writhing with fury.

The initial wave hits hard. Flying snakes dart in like arrows, aiming for vulnerable eyes and throats, while ground snakes coil around the legs of the smaller Divhs, striking at weak spots in armor-like scales. The open plain becomes a soup of twisting bodies, and the griffins take to the skies, raking the air with their talons, snatching up serpents and hurling them into the jagged rocks. Led by Ayne, the dragons and other fire breathers unleash a torrent of flame, incinerating dozens of snakes at once. The saber-toothed cat roars as it leaps into the fray, crushing serpents under its paws and snapping flying snakes out of the air with precision.

Gent tucks me against his chest as he dives into the next mass of snakes, crushing and scattering them so violently that they flow away from him in a shattered tide. But that tide seems endless. For every snake crushed or burned, a hundred more slither forward and the night wears on with the growing certainty that this well of slithering death might never be exhausted.

Then, the air turns cold.

One of the griffins screams in outrage, and Gent wheels around to face the mountain range, giving me full view of the newest nightmare to beset us. Three immense figures, built like men but practically dripping with snakes as big as a manor house, loom over the broken wall, their movements eerily smooth for beings nearly as tall as the mountain. Their faces are masked with what look like metal faceplates, but they don't seem to be wearing any clothes. They don't need to. Their forms are obscured by shifting masses of snakes that coil and writhe like living armor. Where the snakes part, however, there's no flesh, no bone—only an abyss of smoke, black and swirling.

The Sahktar.

The defenders falter. Whatever they hold in their collective memory of the Great Conflict all those centuries ago, it apparently didn't include this.

One of the winged lizards, its emerald wings flapping furiously, roars and launches itself at the nearest masked figure. The claws of its powerful front four sets of legs rip through the writhing armor of serpents, scattering them like leaves. For a moment, it sems the Divh might succeed. Then the Sahktar moves.

Its snake-covered arm lashes out, and as the serpents part, a jet of deathly vapor strikes the lizard's chest. The great beast's roar becomes a gurgle as its emerald scales turn gray, its massive body decaying mid-flight. In seconds, it crumples, plummeting to the ground—then winks out of this plane completely.

The defenders freeze for just a moment. Divhs have battled each other in the pageantry of the Tournament of Gold for centuries now—and some were injured, yes. Sometimes badly enough that they, too, had to flee to the Blessed Plane. Their enemies in those battles were their own kind, though, not this abomination. The griffin lets out a mournful cry as the tide of skrill surges forward, emboldened by the death of their foe.

But the way of the warrior is death.

The ape-like colossus suddenly bellows, scooping up a massive shaled rock from the ground and swinging it like a club. Snakes explode into bursts of gore and spitting poison as the massive weapon sweeps through their ranks. The saber-toothed cats leap into action, their claws ripping through sinewy flesh. Above me, Ayne and Tennet lead a formation of fire-breathing falcons, raining down fury on the flying snakes.

"What does Syril see?" I demand of Tennet.

"Only about a third of the snakes I do, I can tell you that. These bastards are putting on a show."

I lean forward in Gent's grip, forming the order in my mind as I vainly try to scream it over the wind— *Fire!*

From every corner of the battlefield, flame erupts. Dragons spew torrents of fire, bulls snort burning embers, and the phoenix ignites its wings in a blazing dive, carving through the swarm like a fiery spear. The snakes writhe and shriek, their numbers thinning under the relentless assault, even to our duped eyes.

But the Sahktar remain.

One of the colossal ape-like Divhs charges, hurling a boulder at the nearest sentinel. The stone smashes into the snake-armored chest, scattering the slithering creatures. The figure staggers but doesn't fall. Another defender, a bull-like behemoth, follows up with a fiery charge, its horns blazing spears of flame. The impact tears through the snake armor, exposing the roiling smoke beneath. For a moment, we all see a flicker of vulnerability.

Then the bull disappears to the Blessed Plane, lost to the deadly vapor.

I scan the battlefield desperately. With this most recent attack, the Sahktar are retreating toward the mountains, their movements slow and deliberate. But they aren't defeated, I think—merely regrouping. We've bought time, but the cost to the skrill has already been far too high. The bodies of their fallen litter the pass, and the air is thick with smoke and the acrid stench of decay.

Prepare another surge— Fortiss begins his voice pounding in my mind.

The mountains explode with flying snakes.

The screeching cacophony takes us all by surprise, and the fighting begins anew, only now it's taken on a breathless, desperate urgency. For all that I know that way is certain death, I can't do anything about it. I urge my great goliath around, and Gent punches and pummels his way toward the Eighth House—

Another scream rips through the air. A familiar one.

I look up, stunned to see the sky has been split anew, and Nazar's mighty griffin soars into view followed by the windmilling Marsh, and fully a dozen more Divhs of all descriptions—some I remember from the tournament. Reinforcements! They unleash fresh terror on the skrill while I resolutely turn Gent back toward the Meridian mountains.

The mountains, and the unholy blight that lies on the other side.

"Fortiss!" I shout and he's there in my mind and in my sight-line, Szonja racing forward as Gent lurches toward the mountains. Gent flinches away from the wall as if the very nearness of it burns him, and Szonja banks away as well. She screeches in indignation and flies close enough to Gent that I can see Fortiss clearly—and

witness his startled expression as Gent plucks him from Szonja's back and drops my beautiful warrior right next to me.

Gent throws his head back and roars with—not joy, certainly, not delight...but with resolute, unmistakable purpose.

Drawing back his arm, he swings around—

And hurls us over the great wall of the Unlit Pass.

CHAPTER 37

We land in a lake of powder, surrounded by utter silence. Whether Gent had known our landing would be so soft before he threw us here is anyone's guess, but I come up coughing and spitting, my nose, my eyes, my mouth filled with the soft, heavy texture of...whatever this is.

"It's not even sand," Fortiss grunts, plowing his hands through it. He's kneeling on the far edge of this shallow basin, looking far tidier than me. "It's like the accumulated molt of centuries."

"Not helping," I cough, dragging myself across the depression as if I'm slogging through a silty sea. I finally reach the other side, and he hands me up—then helps me shuck the worst of the ash from my hair and face.

I narrow my eyes at him as I wipe the back of my hand across my mouth. "How did you manage to miss all this?"

He grins and cocks a thumb toward the rocky shelf above us— where his cape is hanging. "It got twisted up around my face, and I didn't have time to fight it off. Then I hit and rolled, and I was glad for it. You just landed a little short." He makes a face. "Had a bad moment when I couldn't get the thing off me, but at least once I could, I could see."

"Uh huh." I continue dusting myself off as he squints around him.

"It's so quiet," he murmurs, and it's true. There's no indication at all of the full-on war happening just over the mountains. "If this is everything that the Western Realms has to offer, then I'm not sure Tennet was wrong. Maybe that wall was just built to keep *them* from coming to *us*. Who would ever want to live here on purpose? It's hot here, too, you notice that? Far hotter than the other side of the wall. That can't be good for growing things."

He has a point. Whereas the mountains leading up to the Unlit Pass are craggy and perilous, they're also filled with ravines of vines and trees, cheery waterways, birds and animals. But there's nothing here. It's a kingdom of stone and ash. Beyond the wide landing pit that could have been a small lake at one time, there's rocky shale broken by several passageways that look like they were naturally formed that way. Everything is heaped with dust, scree, and ash, and though the moon shines as brightly and the sky is as clear, it seems like we've been dropped into an empty dreamscape —as if nothing ever grew here and nothing ever would.

"Is it some sort of prison?" I brush my hand through a pile of dust from the ledge beside me, aimlessly creating a small, conical tree on the shelf of rock. Beneath the thick layer of silt is grooved stone. My fingers catch on the rough edges, and I pull my hand back sharply. I don't need my fingers lacerated.

"Yeah, I'd glove up again," Fortiss says as if he's reading my mind. "If we can get to some water we can clean you up more, but you look fine as long as you can breathe."

Together we stand but hesitate even still. "Why did Gent want us to come here?" Fortiss asks. "There's nothing here."

I grimace. "Well, there's *something* here, I think..."

My words are cut off as a boom of thunder sounds overhead, startling me. I search the sky. It has the heaviness of an imminent rainstorm, but there are no clouds—at least no clouds that I can see. Still, I can't say that I mind the opportunity for an impromptu bath. I pull my gloves off again and shake more dust out of my hair, turning my head up as the first drops of water spatter the rock beside me.

A hail of fiery, glowing projectiles hurtles out of the darkness and plows into the lake of dust, whirling, churning, and bursting back out without hardly slowing down.

"Watch out!" Fortiss shouts, but the half-dozen hummerlets barrel toward us like wild dogs who have spotted their next meal, knocking us backward into the shallow impression of our cave. They hurry, harry, and bully us back as the skies officially open up and rain sheets down with sudden, violent fury.

"I need to get cleaned *off*!" I insist, but the moment I try to push my way past the hummerlets and out to the open rainstorm, I set off another flurry of rejection, and I'm forced to watch, bitterly, as the rain pours down, the hummerlets keeping raucous guard as they hover and hop in the entryway of the cave.

"Hey, there's fresh air back here," Fortiss says, his voice floating towards me from the gloom. "I think there's a way through."

"Or we could wait until this rain passes and climb to the top of the ridge and actually get a good view," I grumble. "And maybe there'll be some actual water there, after this rain."

"We could, but we could also go a little bit of a distance underneath the mountain with one of these hummerlets showing us the way? In case we need the light?"

He asks the question hopefully, and the nearest two hummerlets bounce up and down with clear approval. They dart up to the ceiling of our small cave, showing that it's actually arched in a smooth bowl, and down into the entryway. There they hover, glowing brightly, clearly happy to be of service. Fortiss and I, however, can do little more than stare.

"What is this place?" he murmurs.

The back of our shallow cavern doesn't simply boast a rude passageway cut by time into the rock, but a rounded archway framed with intricate symbols of no language I've ever read. "Is this the language of the Western Realms?" I ask. "Can you read it?"

"It is, and I can't, not really. I've barely had time to open the few books I kept back from the supply we sent into the Blessed Plane." He makes a face. "How confident are we that we can find those books again?"

"About as confident as we are that we can get out of here in one piece. But the Divhs can come and go apparently, so...that gives me hope. Still, this isn't some random cave, Fortiss. This is—or *was*—somebody's home. I don't think they're still here, though."

He snorts. "I suspect that's highly unlikely."

One of the hummerlets scoots by us and darts down the passageway. Other than piles of silt, there's nothing there. No hangings, no wood, nothing but stone walls. But Fortiss isn't wrong. The air is fresh here, or as fresh as I imagine it ever gets in this land of rock and dust.

A chirping flutter draws our attention back to the mouth of the cave, or not a cave at all, I see now, as the hummerlets swirl around the space. The walls are smooth and there are more painted inscriptions, and soft grooves frame the doorway. I think about the grooved stone outside. Was that some kind of ledge? A bench?

"The rain stopped. That was quick." Fortiss takes a step towards the cave door, then back towards the interior opening. "Which way?"

I blink at him, realizing the question is an honest one. Fortiss wants my opinion—honors it, depends on it. His gaze sharpens when I don't answer right away, then his mouth flickers into a grin. "You wear your emotions on your face, Lady Talia. You know that, right?"

"Fortiss..." I don't need to say anything more. He moves to me in three short strides, folding me in his arms. With just that simple gesture, the muck and chaos of battle seem to fall away from me, spinning into the air like another fine coating of ash.

I chuckle a little grimly against his chest, reveling for another second more in the thrum of our matching heartbeats. Then I lean back and narrow my eyes at him. "Just how much magic are you wielding right now?"

"None." He looks down at me, then leans forward, brushing his lips over mine as a flare of energy zips along my skin. "Okay, maybe a little. Is it working?"

"It's...yeah." I push him away, and he rocks back on his feet, his smile seeming like the only bright thing that could possibly exist in this kingdom of gray. I shake my head, not willing to think too much on my own luck quite yet, given how quickly that luck can change. "We should get our bearings, I think. Let's see what's out there."

This time, the hummerlets offer no complaint as we head to the opening of the cave. We step out into the moon-swept plain and everything seems...far cleaner. The dust has settled, the lake smooth and slightly cupped, as if it was subtly drained during the quick rainstorm. I frown, heading toward it, when Fortiss's hand snaps out and grabs me by the bicep.

"Talia," he whispers. I glance at him sharply, then turn to see what has so captured his attention.

The cone of dust that I had so carefully formed on the ledge is still there, which ordinarily wouldn't be much of a surprise...except for how it's changed.

"That can't be right." Never taking his hand from my arm, Fortiss moves us across the entryway to the cave until we're right next to the small cone, no larger than the size of my palm. When we reach it, he leans forward and plucks it up off the ledge with his gloved hand, turning it over in his palm before offering it to me. I hurriedly replace my own glove and take it from him. It's solid stone.

"What is this?" I whisper.

Fortiss doesn't reply, but strides toward the edge of the ash lake, hesitating only briefly before stepping out onto it. I can hear the clunk of his boots on its hard surface.

"It's solid. Solid stone. Like cement." He taps his boot experimentally, and a dull thud echoes around the shallow bowl. "All that ash and dust in this basin...you add the slightest bit of water, and, with this heat, it turned to solid cement in barely a quarter hour."

I stare down at the cone, weighing it in my hand. "We were covered in that dust, especially me. If I'd been outside when it started raining..."

Both of us turn to watch the gamboling hummerlets as they bob and weave near the front of the cave. I look up, but no, we didn't miss some grand manor house when we stumbled in the first time. There's nothing but the craggy side of the mountain facing us with one rude cave-like opening.

"You think it's going to rain again?" I ask nervously.

"Probably, yes. I think we should get up to the top of the ridge as fast as we can and see what we can see. Then we can explore the caves without worrying so much."

"Fair."

The wind picks up as we mount the craggy trail, and every chance I get, I brush more of the rock dust from my clothes, my hair. I tuck my gloves into my belt and spit into my hands to clear yet more of it from my face. Fortunately, my saliva isn't enough for the ash to harden into stone. I'd never thought I'd be terrified of getting caught in a rainstorm, but now I think it'd mean certain death.

Finally, we reach the top of the ridge, and Fortiss lets out a startled cry. I scramble up beside him, then take a sharp step back.

"*No*," I whisper.

A massive heap of a Divh lays curled up in a circle in a basin not dissimilar to the one where we crash landed. It looks like it's been here for easily a century, its enormous body covered over with a thick layer of cement, the ebony sections of its carapace barely visible now.

But it hasn't been here a century. Wings that once allowed the mighty creature to soar high above the Protectorate all the way to the Blessed Plane are now caked in rock, and its long slender tail spiked at the end curls almost to its head. The creature is almost as large as Gent, and I know it to be one of the deadliest, most fearsome Divhs I've ever encountered.

The great scorpion Divh commanded by Lord Protector Rihad.

We stare, dumbstruck at the sight...

And then it moves.

"Talia! No!"

I barely hear Fortiss's cry as a sudden anguished wail of pain and loss unleashes in my mind. I can't think—I can hardly breathe—but I know this cry isn't coming from Gent or from any of the Divhs that are bonded to me. It's coming from Zhang.

Zhang. I never knew the name of Rihad's scorpion. I never wanted to ask, especially once my gender became known. Warriors could speak of their Divhs among themselves, but a woman in the Protectorate could be killed if she so much as sounded the name of one of these great creatures out loud.

How many centuries have we lived under such lies? And for what? For *what*? Because women were better connecting with Divhs? That was our big crime? Not that we were better warriors, not that we were stronger, braver, or better at strategy. But because we could *connect* to these mighty creatures and understand what they need...

What they need.

Another blast of despair washes over me, and I slip, tumble, and fall down the mountainside until I reach Zhang's head. The hummerlets race up to me and spin around in noisy celebration as Fortiss trails behind me. He stops short as I drop to my knees, coming level to Zhang's half shut eye.

"Why are you here?" I whisper, lifting a hand as Zhang exhales heavily.

"Talia! Careful." Fortiss bounds up to me, pulling me forcefully away as a burst of fluid coats the ashy bowl before me. The rock dust burns away.

"Everything about Rihad's scorpion is death," he warns. "Its very breath is poison. So is its blood, and so is its skin."

"Him," I say quietly, straightening. "His name is Zhang, and he breathes poison because it burns away the rock dust in front of his eyes and doesn't let it harden to stone. He's been trapped here, unable to leave, unable to return to the Blessed Plane, Fortiss.

When Rihad went down a month ago, he didn't send his Divh home. He sent him *here*. Zhang crashed into this basin, just like we did, but he didn't recover in time before the rains came. He's been trapped here ever since."

"But why here?" Fortiss demands. "Why would Rihad send him..." He breaks off, his eyes going wide. "It has to be the crown of wings," he whispers. "*This* is where it is."

Zhang's reaction to Fortiss's words is a massive convulsion. A new wave of panic rolls through me, but when I turn, Fortiss is already backing away from the scorpion's head, heading toward the center of the basin. He shuffles his feet, kicking up dust.

"There's no way it's here," I call out, though I eye the ashy bowl with concern. Clearly, the recent storm we barely escaped didn't reach this far, if all this ash is still here.

"Oh, come on. Why do you think Gent threw us both over the wall? He had to want us over here for something."

I think about Gent's mournful howl when he and I had spied into this barren, blighted land—had he known Zhang was here? I hadn't noticed anything but the tiny glimmer of light...but had Gent known more than he let on?

Fortiss exhales an excited breath. "It's here—we both know it is," he mutters. "Can't you hear it humming?"

I jolt in surprise, and a flicker beside me has me glancing back to the trapped scorpion's eyes. The shiny black surface shivers as Zhang's eyes practically spin in their sockets, but there's no denying the image burned into my mind. The crown is here, Fortiss is right. But I don't hear any humming, and frankly—I should. I won the tournament, after all. I earned the winged crown. Not Fortiss.

"How is it connecting to him?" I mutter, and another image surfaces in my mind— Rihad in his chambers, the fire leaping high in the grate. I'm watching Rihad as if I'm the one standing in the fire, I'm the mighty Sahktar and skrill, all bound up as one.

I jolt, curling my lip in disgust. I need Rihad, I realize. I...I *yearn* for him to free me, desire it with a desperation that vibrates in my very bones. I will promise him *anything*—any power, any service, any treasure. *Anything* to set my people free.

Even the long-lost crown of wings.

What was sundered shall be—

"I found it!" Fortiss's shout explodes my vision, and I gape at him as he turns toward me, holding something high in his fist.

The image of him wearing that golden circlet, collapsed on the floor of the Eighth House with my arrow through his heart, stabs through my mind.

A teeth-rattling *boom!* rips across the sky as the skies betray us once again.

And this time, the screeching cries of the hummerlets can't save us.

CHAPTER 38

I dive under Zhang's head as the storm breaks open above us, leaving Fortiss trapped in the dust sea. I lunge out to grab him even as I feel the sheeting rain connect with the dust in my hair, instantly dragging me down. The myriad howls of "*No!*" surge in my brain—equal parts Zhang, Gent, Szonja and Kreya—but with an echo that seems to travel all the way to the Blessed Plane and back.

I jerk back with a scream of frustration, ripping at my hair. I succeed in pulling out smallest pebble of cement but take out a good chunk of my scalp as well. Angrily, I shove aside the trickle of blood that drips down my forehead.

The storm passes and I peek out, my heart practically pounding. Fortiss is caught in half-run, as if he's trying to make his way back to cover. His hand is outstretched, and dangling from it is a plain circlet of gold with a jagged triangular flourish.

Otherwise, he's covered in cement.

Fear rips through me. I think of Fortiss laughing—running—fighting—leaping—kissing and touching me with fire in his eyes. Now those eyes are stone, his breath choked out, his beautiful body frozen, locked in place like a statue formed by the Light itself.

A statue that looks like it may crumble down to ash at any moment.

"*Fortiss!*" I don't think anymore, I don't even breathe. I surge out into the basin, my boots slamming hard on the newly hardened surface. I reach him and yank the crown out of his hands and slam it onto my head.

"*Free him!*" I scream, and my eyes pin wide, my mind filling suddenly with the same vision I'd seen before when Mirador flung his hands wide and commanded the Light to deliver their delegation from the attack of the skrill. Only what I'm seeing now is completely different. Meridor doesn't stand alone with his hands outstretched to the heavens. While the rest of his troop is hip deep in writhing snakes, a *woman* stands beside him now. A fierce, clear-eyed warrior with long, flowing hair, her arms outstretched, her chin tilted up, a longbow lashed to her back.

But that's not the most shocking part. A *second* crown of wings atop her head, what looks to be a perfect mirror to Mirador's own. *Ehlyn*, I think. Her name is Ehlyn.

Then the image shifts and I'm surrounded by a seething wall of skrill, while the three immense figures of smoky death rise high behind them—the Sahktar. The Divhs roar, and I roar back; the skrill hiss, and I snarl and thrust my hands up in the air—

Then I feel as if my body's ripped in two, and all I've ever wanted, all I've ever loved, is ripped away from me with a brutal, devastating surge, and—

"*No,*" I gasp, ripping the crown from my head as I refocus on what is and not the fever dream pounding through my head. The vision disappears, but the shattering sense of wrongness remains.

I drop to my knees beside Fortiss, who has collapsed to the ground, now freed from his cement trap. Chunks of rock lie in a pile of scree all around him.

Behind me, the great Divh Zhang screeches in triumph as he surges up, but my focus can only be Fortiss—my friend, my leader, my heart...I can't lose him! Not now—not when I've finally come to understand what he's become to me.

"*Fortiss,*" I lean over him, using all my strength to haul him upright, but no sooner do I stagger backward under his weight than I hear an unearthly, blood-curdling scream.

Zhang! I fling my arms around Fortiss, winding my hands into his cloak as I tie it around us, unable to protect him any other way.

I crouch down, keeping his sagging body beneath me as Zhang races low toward us across the stony basin. Rihad's great scorpion lashes out at us—and strikes me full in the back, his tail raking along my spine. I gasp, falter, but everything is moving in slow motion. I can't get Fortiss to safety, I can't do anything but clutch him tightly—and he barely breathes. I've faced down warriors and skrill and centuries of lies. But it's Fortiss's stillness now that terrifies me. If I die here—if he does—I'll lose more than the fight. I'll have failed the man who's the truest possible future of the Protectorate...and my future too.

Add to that, my back is on *fire*. Have I been stung by Zhang's scorpion tail? Is his venom even now working its way through my blood stream?

I can't move, I can't think.

Moments later—too fast, too *fast*!—another scream assaults us, and Zhang swoops down again. This time, aided by my complete inability to move, he grabs us in his talons and soars up—up—then flings us over the Unlit Pass and back into the battle at the base of the Eighth House.

I have soared through the sky so many times, fully expecting to land roughly, happily in the palm of my glorious Divh, that it takes me a few moments to realize I haven't been caught. I strain to hold onto Fortiss, but there's no way I would accomplish it without his knotted cloak. We plummet to the ground, closer—closer—

At the last minute, I'm hauled up by my shoulders, mercifully spared another piercing as my own cloak is yanked upright. I jerk involuntarily as Szonja swoops down, down. She drops us roughly to the ground, both of us somersaulting to a stop, tumbling end over end. Our tangled cloaks keep Fortiss and me together—and by extension, the crown—until we slow to a sprawled stop.

I blink my eyes open and realize something is still terribly wrong. The sky is filled with Divhs shooting fire in front of the Eighth House; the ground is overrun with Divhs stamping, trampling, and clearing great hordes of snakes with a sweep of mighty paws. But Gent isn't here.

He isn't *here*.

I roll myself up to my feet, pulling what's left of Fortiss's cloak with me while he remains collapsed on the ground. With one hand still wrapped in that cloak, I slam my palms to my ears, which are ringing with the roars and shouts of the Divhs and their riders. They're all crying out—some in battle lust, some in fear, and some trying to reach me—but I can't hear Gent anymore, can't pick out his words in any of the screeching assault.

I've lost my connection to him.

"*Gent!*" I try again, dropping one fist to my heart, and lifting my left arm high, but there's nothing. I may as well be shouting into a storm.

"*Talia.*" Fortiss's shout isn't panicked, isn't particularly strained, but it pulls me around all the same, my eyes wild, my mind racing. Then I stop, my arm still punched aloft in the sky like a scarecrow off its crossbar, grief and loss swamping me in waves.

My Divh may not hear me anymore, but that doesn't mean I'm not connecting.

A wall of snakes easily eight feet high surrounds Fortiss and me in a perfect circle—but they're not surging forward to bite us with their razor teeth or smear their poison into our skin. They've stopped, sort of, an undulating mass that has lost all forward motion and is swaying, staring...their shining obsidian eyes fixed solely on me.

"Talia," Fortiss says again, and now his voice is almost absurdly calm, his manner one of exaggerated care. He rolls himself up to his feet and takes a long, measured step toward me, never mind the combined hiss of approximately a million snakes and the sudden updraft of their winged cousins to hover above us in the sky. "Something important happened on the other side of the wall, Talia, something I have no memory of. You need to tell me what it was."

"What are they doing?" I ask, or try to ask, but the words are like glue in my mouth.

"Look at me, Talia. I don't want to touch you, but I need to see your eyes. Don't drop your arm, don't do anything but turn to me. Everything is right and good."

He says that, but I don't know that I believe him. I don't know that anything will be right and good ever again—except he's safe. He's alive. I hold on to that though everything else feels like it's fallen to ruin.

"What are they doing?" I ask again, and I shift minutely in Fortiss's direction, only to set off a sea of hisses. Something else is wrong too, but I can't quite place it. I can't focus on anything other than Fortiss to the right of me, still not in full view, and the wall of snakes writhing less than a few horse length's away, wrapped in a tight circle around us.

"Shift again...again...good. You're doing this exactly right, Talia. Shift again. Hello, there." His eyes lock on mine as he gives me a reassuring smile, and I drink in the sight of him—his angular face, his full lips, his dark eyes. His hair is no longer caked with cement, but blows across his forehead in a stiff breeze, wavy light curls against moon-bright skin.

Moon bright...

"There's no more fire in the sky," I say shakily. "The Divhs have stopped fighting."

"Everybody has stopped fighting," he agrees good naturedly, almost as if we're talking about what we might have for breakfast tomorrow. "They faltered once we hit the ground, and when your arm went up, everything stopped. Szonja says the smoke warriors —her words, not mine—exploded into mist, and all the snakes on the ground and in the air turned away from the battle and headed for you."

"Not me." I want to deny this, but I'm afraid to so much as

shake my head. The undulating wall of snakes is starting to speed up its rhythm, their hisses rising in volume.

Fortiss doesn't move either, but his gaze is steady and supportive as I raise my eyes to meet his again. "I think we can assume you," he counters. "About two-thirds of our battle party disappeared too. Those warriors who were riding those Divhs left with them."

"Left," I echo, but my eyes slide past Fortiss, onto the snakes surrounding us. Have they edged forward? Are they going to over-run us?

"Returned to the Blessed Plane," he confirms, causing me to jerk my gaze back to him. "All the ones banded to you at the close of the melee. Gent, too, Talia. Szonja says he's not hurt, not physically. But he's no longer with us."

Not hurt. Not physically. I want to throw up. "He's not here."

Without my intense attention on it, my arm falters, and the snakes convulse forward, tightening their circle around us.

"Careful there, careful," Fortiss says, his orders almost cheerful. When I refocus on him, though, his face looks like it's been set back into the cement shell I just freed him from. "The skrill are tied to you the way all your Divhs are."

I lick my lips. "They're...they're not anymore. The Divhs. Connected to me."

"Then the way all your Divhs *were*," he nods, his tone still light. "I don't remember anything after pulling the crown out of the dust. It was buried in cement, and I thought there was no way I'd be able to yank it out without damaging it or dislocating my shoulder, but it came up easily. Almost like it was waiting for me. Then —the next thing I knew, we were being hauled up into the sky by Rihad's scorpion and flung back into battle." He smiles at me, and pride radiates from him to fill the space between us. "Szonja caught us."

"She did," I say evenly while everything inside me cries out at the injustice of that. Szonja, beautiful Szonja, wasn't the one who was supposed to catch us. Gent was supposed to catch us. Gent would always catch us—catch me. Catch Merritt.

But Gent isn't here.

"What happened, Talia?" Fortiss prompts again.

I blow out an unsteady breath, trying to keep from screaming. "You pulled the crown out of the stone, and Zhang, um, reacted."

"Zhang."

"Rihad's scorpion." I want to meet Fortiss's gaze, but my own sight falters. For a moment, I'm back in the land of dust and ash, standing beside the head of the great scorpion Divh, the ground scorched with his poison clearing away enough of the powder from his belly to ensure that he isn't completely encased in cement, that he can still breathe. And not just breathe, I realize. His six enormous pairs of eyes seem to be able to focus far better than Gent's. He truly *sees* me. He understands who I am...or at least what I am. And he still tries to warn me.

I lick lips that have now gone as dry as the ash that surrounds us. "I don't know why Zhang was there, but that has to be where he crashed after the Tournament of Gold. Rihad must've sent him over the border."

"But why? Zhang was pretty damaged after that battle, and Rihad needed him to be strong, presumably. Why keep him from the Blessed Plane and risk him not recovering? Because he definitely wasn't recovering where he was."

I shake my head. "I don't know. Maybe he wanted him to guard the crown. Maybe he knew where it was, and he was content to leave it where it was until he needed it. But something happened after Zhang crashed down. He found the crown, but he could only guard it so well when he was trapped in cement."

Fortiss blinks at me. "I freed him?" he asks, the blood draining out of his face. "By picking up the crown, I freed him?"

I offer him a weak smile. "Not exactly. He reacted strongly when you lifted it up, but it wasn't relief or any sort of joy at being freed, though that should have been there. He was panic stricken. He said 'no.' He was trying to warn us about...something."

"Well...that's good, I guess." Fortiss nods. "But—"

I rush on before it he can interrupt again. "But then the skies opened up with another storm just as quick as the first one. I tried to run out, to get you to safety, but the rain struck me and turned the ash in my hair to stone."

Fortiss visibly jerks, and his agitation contributes to my own unease. The snakes surrounding us start keening. "The crown did that? It called down the rain?"

"I don't *know*, Fortiss," I answer, my voice too shrill, too panicked. "All I know is that the rain came and coated you and I ducked under Zhang to stay protected. By the time it ended and I could get out again, you still held the crown, but the rest of you was rooted in place, and you were covered in a layer of cement. I ran out. I didn't know what else to do, so I took the crown from you and put it on."

His eyes flash wide, anger and indignation warring with shock. "You *what?*"

"I didn't know what to *do*," I repeat, rounding on him. This sets the snakes into a roiling frenzy, and I hear the distant scream of Divhs over the cacophony of the skrill's cries. Of Divhs, but not of Gent. The arrowing loss of him adds more heat to my words. "You were totally covered in that ashy cement. You might as well have been a statue. Rihad's Divh was now half-buried in another layer of the same blighted stone. I had to do something to *fix* that. This stupid crown has been the stuff of legends for the last five hundred years, it seemed reasonable that it might—I don't now—*help*. I didn't know what else to do!"

Fortiss grimaces in what looks like actual pain, whether at my words or my tone, I don't know, and I don't care. I barrel on. "And it worked. It *worked*, Fortiss. I saw visions of the Imperial delegation summoning the Divhs. The sky seemed to open up and this time not with more rain. Instead, the energy shifted, the Divhs showed up and rained fire on the skrill and everything was good but—but in the midst of that, I lost my connection to Gent—my other banded Divhs, too, I think." I swallow. "I lost connection.

Zhang roared again, and I wrenched the crown off. I swear I only had it on my head for a breath, but everything was different, suddenly. You'd fallen to the ground, but you were no longer covered in stone. Zhang shot straight up into the sky. and I..." I shake my head furiously, willing the tears not to come.

Fortiss is staring at me now. "Zhang picked us up," he says, sounding strangled. "He flew us over the wall. Dropped us. Did he hurt you?"

"Some. His tail hit me in the back, hard—I don't know if it was on purpose. That still hurts. But he saved us too. And he *tried* to stop me from putting the crown on in the first place." I search his gaze. "What have I done by doing that, Fortiss? How is the crown tied to the skrill? They're of the blighted path! They are nothing but darkness."

"And they apparently cleave to whoever claims the crown, if what's happening here is any indication." He gestures down with his chin at the crown still attached to me, snarled up in the folds of his cloak. "The dark shall draw the dark. Right now, that's you. Rihad may have somehow channeled its power from afar at one point, but not anymore. Your proximity overrides his claim."

"I only wore it for a few *moments!*" It's all I can do not to shriek.

"And you carry it still, warrior Talia," he says gently. "So why don't you send your battle party home?"

I turn, barely enough to see over Fortiss's shoulder, and I can't think anymore. The crushing weight of losing Gent, losing all my Divhs, threatens to press down on me, flattening me like so many layers of cement.

Slowly, so slowly, I drop my left arm and cross it over my right, making an X over my heart. I lift my chin, and channeling my thoughts and my words into one single focus, I do as Fortiss asks.

"Retreat," I say aloud to the wall of skrill. "Return. Reclaim your home in the Western Realms and be at peace." Shakily, I speak that last word as it bubbles up within me, a word I can't understand, let alone sanction, but it's what I must say, what I'm driven to say, in fact, so I say it. "Thank you for your gifts. For now, we are at peace."

While the snakes had seemed largely unimpressed with my speech up to that point, the repetition of the word *peace* seems to startle them into action. They rise up, an oily black wall swirling high, and even I can hear the startled screams of the Divhs circling at a safe distance.

Then the wall breaks. As one, the snakes surge back toward the Eighth House, back toward the mountains. The rushing, undulating tide of them parts around Fortiss and me, and I realize I've collapsed against him, his arms holding me tight but also positioning me so that the crown is clearly visible to any snake with eyes to see. I watch in stunned silence as the flood of snakes completely consumes the Eighth House once more, making it a writhing, sinuous blightscape, and belatedly I remember the horses trapped behind the gates. Had they escaped once we had begun fighting in earnest? Could they see that the gates were open even though they appeared closed?

"What are they doing to the Eighth House?" Fortiss murmurs.

I turn in confusion and see a new silhouette that now stands high in front of the Eighth House, nearly as tall as the manor house itself. I can't make out what it is at this distance, but Fortiss is right. There's definitely something there. But for now, I'm happy just to see the black oily mass continue its furious scramble over the Eighth House and up into the mountains, eventually disappearing from view.

Fortiss looks up, then pivots in a half-circle, peering at the eastern sky. "Is it daybreak already?"

We reel around and stare as our battalion of Divhs swoop toward us once again, by air and by land, the Divhs stopping well away, the warriors dismounting and rushing forth. Another company of horsemen rush up but also dismount at some distance. They join the others on foot as the first rays of sunlight streak across the wide plains before the Eighth House.

"Talia!" Caleb's cry surfaces above the rest, and he breaks out from the crowd, running hard, his ungainly stride pulling right with the strength of his pumping right arm. But he reaches Fortiss and me in a few more breaths and practically bowls us over. "Talia, we were fighting—fighting—and we'd no sooner make some gains than we were struck down again. Those things, those smoke warriors, Marsh called them, they just had to split open their snake covering and we were goners. Marsh got hit early, I sent him back. He said, he said..." He shakes his head hard. "The poison made it more difficult for us to communicate. Anyone connected to a Divh, if they got hit with that skrill slime, the things we saw..."

He trails off, and I blink up to see Nazar before me, striding forth unevenly. The entire left side of his robes have been burned away, leaving tattered cloth that looks like it's been permanently seared into his arm.

"Lady Talia." He stops and bows to me, but his gaze drops to the crown, and I can feel his attention on it like a living touch. "You have found the winged crown, then. You can command the darkness and the light."

"Yeah, well, mostly the darkness right now." I shake my head, forcing a grim smile as his eyebrows wing up. "I only put it on to free Fortiss, not—" I wave my hand ineffectually at the distant Eighth House, the mountains standing tall behind it. "To do all this."

"Where's Tennet?" Fortiss asks, and another woman steps out from the crowd. Syril. Blood cakes her face and soot streaks her clothes into an oily black smear.

"He's back with the healers," she says. "He doesn't know the battle has ended yet."

Fortiss frowns. "Doesn't know?"

Syril doesn't respond right away, just looks from me to Fortiss. Caleb casts his gaze down, and Nazar grimaces.

"The way of the warrior is death," he reminds us all quietly. "It's up to the Light if it's the way Tennet follows today."

CHAPTER 39

"Everyone—off the plains. We need to get out of sight," Fortiss announces.

"We're ready for you." Syril steps up as Fortiss steps into full lord protector mode, issuing orders for us all to follow her. We take no more than a half-dozen strides before I falter, and Caleb yells something about my back.

Then darkness rushes over me like the skrill, and I'm gone.

I awake to find Tennet staring at me through one bloodshot eye, the rest of his face covered in bandages. Both of us are sprawled on low pallets separated off from the rest of what looks like a dozen sickbeds.

"You just can't help wanting to crawl into bed with me, can you?" He grins at me.

If I had the energy to throw something at him, I would. Instead, I grimace, and struggle to pull myself into a sitting position. The pain in my right shoulder is intense enough to make my sight go white for a moment, and when I refocus again, Nazar is at my side. One gentle palm is on my left shoulder, another is gripping my right bicep, and he's staring me keenly in the eyes as I refocus.

"What do you see, Lady Talia?" he asks, and I barely keep from giggling, which I know is not the right reaction at all. Still, this is Nazar, a high priest of the Imperium and a banded warrior to one of the fiercest Divhs I've ever met. I stare at him, not truly seeing his face as I try to capture the images assaulting my mind.

"I see the Blessed Plane," I murmur, and my voice sounds as wrong as the vision feels. "I can see them all—even Gent. I can't connect to him, hear him. But I can see him with the rest of them. They're healing, Nazar. They are well."

I frown over in what I think is Tennet's direction. "Ayne is injured more than he should be, more than even he expects to be," I tell him. "He's submerged in the great lake up to his nostrils."

Tennet's response is a short, percussive curse. "Ayne took it into his head that he needed to protect everyone, everywhere, all at once—most especially the fire-breathing Divhs who weren't prepared for battle. The fire falcon was—young. And stubborn. She wouldn't band with anyone but Syril, and Syril couldn't, not yet. When she set herself aflame in self-defense after getting weighed down by skrill, Ayne decided he'd save her."

He grunts and I can almost picture him flopping back on his blankets. "He's an idiot."

But my mind is already wandering down distant shores, searching, searching...but not finding. "So much is lost to me," I murmur. "I can see, but I can't connect. And Gent..."

Nazar taps my right shoulder, sending a blinding shot of white-hot pain through me. My gaze sharpens again, and his face snaps back into focus. "You were stung by Rihad's scorpion, in its first pass before it picked up you and Fortiss."

"His," I correct him through the pain. "Zhang."

He nods, giving me the briefest of smiles. "Scorpions don't usually leave anything but poison behind when they sting. But in this case, Zhang did. A pebble the size of your thumb, shaped almost like a talonstone but not of any stone that I can identify. It was more like cement. Fortiss said you'd understand it but offered no other explanation."

"Because I didn't have an explanation to offer," Fortiss says. I turn, blearily, as he moves toward me. Pain blankets his expression, but centers in his eyes as he stares at me—worry, I realize. He's worried about me, and that realization kindles a small rush of warmth in me, though he's not looking so well, himself. He's not injured like Tennet, but his movement is off, too slow, too awkward. He holds up a small stone object, offering it to me. I stare down at it, dumbly.

"That's what was inside me?"

"Part of it. We don't know if it broke off the tip of Zhang's tail, but that seems the most likely explanation. There's a second piece as well, buried in your shoulder blade. When we attempted to remove it—"

"No," I cut him off short, a wash of agony ripping through me, a memory I cannot fully understand. "No. Leave it there. I can move my shoulder."

I make the attempt at it to prove my point. The pain is sharp, but manageable, while the idea of them wresting that piece out of my bone the way Fortiss ripped the crown free of its cement prison makes me want to faint. "So this was around the barb on his tail? And it split off when he stung me?"

"That's my thinking." Fortiss grimaces. "I wanted to see if you had a different idea."

I snort, rolling the tiny piece around in my hand. "I don't. And I was *helping* him, by the Light. It seems like if he had wanted to do me harm, he could've just left us there. He didn't. None of the other bits of cement remained on me, right? Why did this survive?"

"It was wrapped around his tail," Fortiss suggests. "Maybe his poison..." he sighs. "I don't know. I suspect only Zhang does, since he broke it off deliberately, wedging it into your bone."

I wince at the image, and Nazar turns to me.

"Do you see him in the Blessed Plane?"

"I..." I break off, frowning, then I shake my head. "No. If he's there, I can't connect to him. Honestly, I can't really connect to any of them." I refocus on Nazar. "Is that the price of wearing the winged crown, then? It breaks apart the connection between warrior and Divh?"

His brows go up. "You've lost all connection?"

"I mean..." I shift uncomfortably. "No. I can still hear and speak to all of them at once but—I mean Gent. The ones I'm banded to. Those—they're gone from me."

"Mmm." He nods. "It's telling that the leader of the Imperial delegation, the first great warrior, found the crown first, and used it to clear success in the Great Conflict, then immediately gave it away. It's also telling that it was banished to the Western Realms at some point over the centuries. I suspect that to wear the winged crown gives the bearer the power over both Light and darkness, without true connection to either. That power would allow you to draw the darkness from the blighted path, command it, and return it at will. It might also allow you to draw all the Divhs to your service, command them, and return them at will as well. Should you truly wish to cleave to one or the other in real partnership, however, the crown won't allow it."

"But I only had it on my head for an *instant*," I moan. "I wasn't trying to rule the world, Nazar. I was trying to free Fortiss and Zhang too. Even Zhang seemed terrified of the thing, but I had to get them out. I had to get them free. Besides all that, how am I still able to talk to the skrill if I don't have the thing on my head?"

Nazar holds my gaze. "Can you hear them now? From their home in the Western Realms?"

I feel the blood punch out of my face at his question, but I reach out with my mind...

A chorus of eager hissing swamps me.

"I can. Just...like the Divhs. I'm not connected to any one of them but..." I swallow. "They can hear me. They're all just right there waiting for me to put the crown on again."

Fortiss folds his arms over his chest. "We need to understand this better. There has to be something about the crown in the great books that we recovered here, and maybe more than we realize in the volumes we have back at the First House. But we can't return there through the Blessed Plane, Talia. We must ride across the open plains."

"But why?" I asked, though I already know the answer to my own question. I shake my head fiercely. "I'm not that injured, Fortiss, no matter what Zhang stuck into my shoulder. I'll be fine. I won't slow you down."

His mouth sets into a firm line. "I won't risk it, and I won't risk you. You're too important."

"All right, fine." I wave at him, suddenly exhausted though I stiffen my spine so as not to betray myself. "Then I can ride across the open plains with a small company, and you can go back to the First House as fast as you can—with the crown. *Someone* should go back."

"I won't return without you," Fortiss says, with such hard certainty that I blink. "And Tennet is too damaged to fly, even if Ayne did return to this plane."

"I can ride," Tennet assures him, but his voice sounds different, and I look back to see him collapsed back on his pallet, Syril scowling down at him.

"He'll be strong enough to attempt it in another day," she says quietly. "And stubborn enough to stay tied into the saddle. But it will take another few days for him to be able to move with any speed."

"Since when does a woman want speed over skill..." Tennet mutters, but Fortiss turns to Nazar.

"Talia's not wrong, though. We should send a delegation back through the Blessed Plane ahead of us, to learn what we may about the skrill with the books I've left there and to prepare for our return. Right now, the darkness sleeps. But until we fully understand it, it'll remain a threat. To us, to the Protectorate as a whole, and eventually to the Imperium. We can't afford to let the skrill wake again without being ready."

"But they remained sleeping for a long time before, right?"

Caleb gestures at the collection of the sick and injured. "They made their stand, and they definitely proved that they could hold their own with us in open combat. Maybe that's all they wanted to prove."

"They made their stand, and in the course of the battle, the crown of wings was wrested from its holding place and returned to the Protectorate," Fortiss counters. "That may change things, it may not. I don't worry so much about the skrill acting on their own, though. There was something guiding them until Talia donned the crown."

"The shadow monsters?"

"I think so. Frankly, I hope so. The idea of there being something else behind the Sahktar, some greater power yet unseen, doesn't sit well with me. But now that we know what we're looking for, there may be new interpretations of the old texts that can help us understand what we're looking for."

He turns to Nazar. "I'd like you go to go back to the First House."

"No," Nazar says, surprising me. "I'm not of this land, Lord Protector Fortiss. I'm a priest of the Light but also a warrior. I should remain with you."

"And I need someone I can trust." Fortiss gives Nazar a grim smile. "And someone who can provide balance to whatever readings the ancient councilors come up with."

"Yet I'm older than some of them," Nazar points out.

"In years, maybe. In wisdom, most definitely. But not in your heart. And your heart is what I need."

The two exchange a long glance. Then Nazar looks skyward. "I haven't fully connected with Wrath since the battle," he says, sounding hopeful. "He also was injured but...he's recovering, I think."

"Then it's settled. Take Miriam and maybe two or three lords from the houses who fought here this day. Their insights will be valuable not only to tell the tale of what happened here, but to give us the background of what's been happening these past months, years—decades even since Rihad first visited the borders. With the right person asking questions, and the right people answering them, I suspect we'll learn a great deal."

"I shouldn't return to the First House as a banded warrior." Miriam's voice startles me, and I swing to see her with less precision than I would prefer. Exactly how injured am I?

"Explain," Fortiss says, bracing his hands on his belt. But as I study him more closely, I see the telltale indications of his physical state as well. His feet are braced too wide, the grip on his belt is too firm. As if he can single- or I guess double-handedly hold himself up under his own power. If he had a staff, I suspect he'd be leaning on it. Heavily. As it is, he can only rely on the solidity of the earth beneath him. He looks like a man alone, but he's not alone. He still has his Divh.

A bloom of emptiness erupts in my belly as Miriam steps forward. "You made the decision to band me to a Divh in the Blessed Plane, Lady Talia. You did it to save my life," she continues, raising a hand when Fortiss bristles. "And I thank you for it. The experience is nothing like I ever dreamed it would be, and of course I never dreamed to attain such a bond. It wasn't my place, and in the eyes of the Protectorate it still isn't my place. I'll need to re-enter the First House as if I am unbanded and reconnect with the other councilors. Together, we'll bend ourselves to the task of understanding what just happened here and what may happen next. We'll have to pore over the contents of the books that you were able to recover from the Eighth House and reinterpret the books that we still have in the First House against the information we now have. You've seen the monument at the Eighth House. That will need to be explained as well. Not right away, arguably as there's no one to see it but us right now. Still, the lords of the border houses have eyes, and they undoubtedly have questions. We'll have to manage that. However, none of them saw me fighting alongside the other battle Divhs. They don't know my secret. That's to our advantage."

Fortiss continues to hesitate, then looks to Nazar. "It's a deception," he points out. "I have no desire to build power based on a house of lies. Rihad did that, and it served no one but himself."

Nazar favors him with a small smile. "The way of the warrior is sometimes to draw the eye with one hand while striking with the other. It's the way of the statesman even more frequently. Councilor Miriam raises fair concerns. She has been banded to a Divh, and is neither male, nor a warrior. It's one thing for Talia to have proven herself on the battlefield as a warrior before her true nature was revealed. Miriam being banded might be seen as an act of recklessness, an affront to traditions that have served the Protectorate well these many years. We can afford to be discreet until you arrive."

He turns and nods to Miriam. "I'd be honored to carry you on Wrath, councilor Miriam."

She nods, though still looks a little green at the idea. I feel a surge of pride for her bravery—for everyone's bravery—taking on this foe and now taking on those who will have to face that same foe eventually. We've won a victory, yes, but that victory may be fleeting.

"Thank you," she says, and returns the bow. I see something... indefinable arc between them, a shift of energy, like a fine filament cast out to test the air, or a line dropped into a lake to see what fish may be drawn to it.

Then Fortiss speaks, and my thoughts scatter anew. "It's decided then," he says, rocking back on his heels. "Leave as soon as you are rested and able. We can't say for certain how much time it will take you to pass through the Blessed Plane to return to the First House. Probably only a brace of hours, while for us it will take a good ten days to reach you, and that's pushing hard."

"Perhaps too hard," Syril puts in, from her position beside the sprawled Tennet.

"Maybe for you," his irritated response drifts up, though he never opens his eyes.

"A fortnight, then, no more," Fortiss says. He curls his right hand to his heart, and Nazar does the same.

Nazar glances to the sky again, then drops his gaze—not to Fortiss, but to me. "The warrior shall anticipate everything and expect nothing, Talia. It is the only way."

Then he turns and stalks off.

CHAPTER 40

I'm not awake when the delegation back to the First House leaves. I sleep for another several hours, and when I wake, the sun has chased its way beyond the Meridian mountains. I'm alone, with no other pallets filled around me, not even Tennet's.

"I was beginning to wonder if you were ever going to wake up."

I jerk up and around to see Fortiss watching me from a ledge, his feet dangling over the rock. I blink in surprise. I've never seen him looking quite...like this. Relaxed, almost. Like he's just a man about to set out on a leisurely journey, not a warrior or a leader. He's changed into a tunic and breeches, with only a slim leather satchel slung over his shoulder, and his long, flowing cape is packed away for the moment.

"How are you feeling?" he asks, as the moment stretches awkwardly between us.

"Good," I say, my voice sounding like rocks. I clear my throat. "Better, anyway."

"You can stand?"

"I can try." I swing my legs over the side of the pallet, grimacing as my head starts to swim. Fortiss jumps lightly off the ledge and strides over to me. I'm so focused on my own challenges I don't try to gauge how steady he is on his feet. Clearly, he's in better shape than I am. Then again, he still has his connection to his Divh.

I glance quickly, almost reflexively to his head as he helps me stand. "Where's the crown?"

"Here." He pats the satchel at his side, and I exhale in relief that the crown is so close but still safely packed away. "When the others left there was some question about sending it back with them—"

"No," I say hurriedly, and he laughs at my outburst but lays a hand on my shoulder. It might be to reassure me, it might be simply to steady me, but I accept it all the same.

"Don't worry. While Miriam argued that the safety of the artifact was paramount, and so speed in getting it under lock and key at the First House was potentially ideal, she agreed that, once again, it would cause more questions than it was worth, especially without me there to answer them. We will ride with it, maybe test it to some degree. Not by putting it on." Once again he squeezes my shoulder, and I realize I've started trembling. "Just by holding it. Maybe if you held it, you could find your way back to your center, and Gent could find his way to you."

I grimace. "I don't think it works like that."

"Talia." Fortiss's voice changes, and I blink up at him, surprised at how much taller he suddenly seems to me. Granted, he's wearing boots and I'm still barefoot from the sick bed, but it's more than just simple height. Fortiss has changed subtly, or perhaps I have. Either way, it makes me uneasy.

But there's no disguising the expression on his face, equal parts remorse and wonder—and even a little curiosity. "I forced you to take an unthinkable action by my own rash foolishness. You acted without hesitation, without any question or thought to your own safety. You ripped that crown out of my hands and placed it on your own head. What were you thinking?"

"I wasn't thinking." I sigh. "I just wanted you freed."

A smile flickers across his lips as he shakes his head. "You're a gift I'll need to work a lifetime to be worthy of," he murmurs. And before I can move, before I can think, he reaches up a light finger to my chin and tilts it higher.

Then his mouth comes down on mine.

I don't know if it is the profound sadness that I feel, the loneliness at the loss of my connection with Gent, or the residuals of my body being battered and blown across the Protectorate these past several days, but I don't want to fight the feelings that wash over me when Fortiss kisses me. I don't want to do anything but collapse in his arms and allow this to be. I sag a little, and Fortiss's arms come around me, holding me tight. His kiss deepens, his tongue pressing against my lips until I open them, then dipping in to touch me, taste me, meld my body to his. My pulse pounds in my head, my blood fairly sings, and I'm—warm, I realize. Warm, safe, and whole, in a way I never would have thought possible.

Maybe Fortiss really is pure magic.

He hums against my lips as if he somehow can read my thoughts, and my mind goes spinning off again in sheer, delirious wonder. His arm drops down to cradle my waist, his right hand lifts to cup my chin, my cheek, and his mouth moves, though the words he speaks make no sense to me. It's a language, but no language that I know. It has the rushing sinuous seduction of bodies sliding over each other, slick and wet and—

We both freeze.

"What...were you...just saying?" I ask haltingly, my words barely a whisper against his lips.

He lifts his head back from me, sucking in a heavy breath. "I don't know," he admits shakily. "I don't know. I knew I wanted to kiss you, wanted to hold you, wanted more than anything to connect with you. When I realized you were here without a guard, at first I was angry and then just relieved. When I finally touched you, kissed you, all I wanted to do was heal you and make you whole. And then—just now—the words came to me on how to make that happen."

He pulls back farther from me, eyeing me with curiosity. "Ahh... so. How are you feeling?"

I laugh shakily and push him away, but when he steps back, I blink. "Actually, I'm feeling pretty good. I feel almost myself." I cast my mind out, seeking, searching, hoping for some sense of Gent, some connection or spark, but that is still a bridge too far. I shake my head at Fortiss's questioning glance, but there's no denying how much better I feel.

"You did all that with a *kiss*?" I demand. "Is that something you've been working on with the healers?"

He grins at me. "If it is, you can bet we're going to need to have more female warriors among our troop. I don't think Tennet would necessarily appreciate that particular form of healing. But come on." He holds out a hand to me, and I take it, feeling lighter and easier in my own skin than I have in longer than I can remember. Perhaps not since that day in the forest near the Shattered City, what feels like years but wasn't even two months ago, when I first saw Fortiss of the First House, and didn't know who he was. He was merely a traveling lord on a mountain path, a brief adventure for me to enjoy before I took my rightful place in Lord Orlof's house.

So much has changed since then.

Fortiss pulls me along, but while before I thought he'd probably have to drag me away from my bed, now I move easily, almost comfortably. I squeeze his hand, and he looks back at me and lifts his brows.

"Whatever it is you're about to ask me, hold that thought," he says. "I have horses ready. I wasn't sure you'd be upright this quickly, but there's something you really need to see before the sun goes down, especially since we're going to be moving out at first light."

I stuff down my questions, bemused as he leads me out to two saddled horses, then helps me up onto one of them. Even that is far easier than I would have expected. If I hadn't known how badly I felt just a few hours ago, I wouldn't have believed such a transformation was possible. Now I feel...almost normal.

Fortiss mounts his own horse with smooth and easy precision, then turns us both out of the Savasci encampment. There's no one around, and before I have a chance to ask, he fills in those blanks as well. "Only about a dozen of us will be heading to the First House on horseback. The rest are off to give aid up and down the border. Nazar helped return some of the warriors and their lords to their houses via the Blessed Plane, while others preferred to discharge their Divhs and return on horseback."

"Seriously?" I ask, not even bothering to try to hide my surprise.

He laughs, and once again the sound strikes me as oddly joyous, making my bones shiver. "Believe me, I share your reaction. But the habits of five hundred years have been instilled in these men, and they won't shake easily. We can afford to be gracious as they come to terms with the possibilities of what these Divhs can do—and not only the Divhs we know."

With that last cryptic comment, he urges his horse faster, and the two of us gallop around the rocky point that marks the separation between the Savasci encampment and the Eighth House. I marvel again at the protected enclave that Lord Daggar suffered to exist on the periphery of his awareness—content that if he didn't have to look at the Savasci, he didn't have to worry about them. Still, he had to have known they were there, he *had to*. And he let them live.

He didn't deserve to die at Rihad's command.

Those thoughts trouble me for another several minutes as we pound around the rocky outcropping of the mountain and then press on to the Eighth House, for that's surely where I'm going. The mountain is already shrouding the manor in gloom as we approach, and I squint up at it, my eyes affronted by the strange,

JENNIFER CHANCE

misshapen form that I vaguely remember from the night before. "What is—"

"Eyes straight ahead," Fortiss orders. "Don't look at it full-on until I tell you."

He sounds so happy that I'm willing to do what he asks—really, anything he asks in this moment, if it keeps that lightness in his tone. And I don't have long to wait. Fortiss leads me all the way up the graded causeway, which I notice with some surprise looks different as well. "There's no way these walls were this high," I point out. The walls that border the long path up to the Eighth House are now easily as tall as a man, with wide, cut-out holes allowing easy sightlines to either side—or access to arrows if a bowmen was particularly skilled. But they didn't exist before. I know they didn't. "They couldn't have been here," I insist.

Then I realize— "They're illusions. Blood and *stone,* the illusions of the skrill are still this vivid? Are you seeing this?" I turn in my saddle to stare at him. "You see it too, right? It's not just me?"

He grins at me. "It's not just you. Look up, Talia."

Belatedly, I recall the oddly bulky form I'd glimpsed from a distance, and I turn again to look at the gates of the Eighth House.

My mouth gapes open. "What is *this*?"

A statue now stands before the open gates, as tall as the keep's mighty wall—easily the size of ten men standing on each other's shoulders. But it's not a man depicted here, but a woman. She stands with her left arm held high, her right hand curled at her chest. Her cloak billows around her, and she's dressed in a long tunic, breeches and boots. But that's not the most distinctive feature.

On her brow sits a heavy circlet, flanked on either side with jagged flourishes. Even from this distance, there's no mistaking it.

"It's the winged crown."

It takes me a moment to register that Fortiss is speaking again, and I wheel toward him, my wide eyes searching his face in complete and utter disbelief.

He only grins at me. "It's you, Lady Talia, and you're wearing the crown of wings."

"But, Fortiss..." I shake my head, equal parts horrified and amazed. "This isn't real, right? This can't be real. This—this is an illusion we see because we're bonded to our Divhs—even if I broke that bond for myself?"

He turns to stare up at the intricately carved stature. "Ordinarily, I'd be the first to agree with you on all counts. Both about the wall and the statue. But I'm not the only person who sees it, Talia. Everyone does, the Savasci who are banded and those who were not. Miriam and Nazar, and the other banded warriors."

"But this...This is bad," I say, turning my gaze back to the statue. "What is this even made of?" I know the answer of course before he even responds. It's the only answer that would be possible.

The ashen cement of the Western Realms, grooved with the sinuous bodies of the skrill.

"It rained at the Eighth House as they passed through," Fortiss says, as if tracking my thoughts. "Not for very long. We both know it doesn't need to be for long. But I think the skrill reinforced the short walls along the causeway because we nearly died going over the edge of them, remember? We went flying."

"I remember," I say, my voice shaky, "but..."

"And they somehow pushed enough ash together and built this statue as a testament to who you are to them now. You wore the crown of wings, you connected with their realm, and you balanced the light and the darkness."

"I *didn't* though," I protest. "As soon as I put that crown on, I lost my connection to Gent, to my other Divhs. And then I turned on the skrill. I fought them, I burned them, I pushed them *back*. I'm no leader to these creatures—I tried to *destroy* them."

"I said as much to Nazar. I figured as a priest of the Light, even if he came to that path as a warrior, he would have the answers perhaps when no one else would."

I wince. "Let me guess. He told you that the way of the warrior was to flow like water."

He barks a laugh. "To flow like water and adapt your strategy for the battle that *is*, not the battle that you wish to be. He was very clear on that point."

"He always is." I squint up at the statue. "We're going to have to knock this down, though. Get a Divh if we need to but knock this down. The last thing we need is for people to think that you have some sort of sorceress among your warriors, commanding an army of darkness."

Fortiss tilts his head, looking up at the statue as well. "I'm not so sure. Are you willing to set up your house here, Lady Talia, replacing the Eighth with the Thirteenth? We can build another Eighth House—I doubt quite sincerely any of their holding would want to return to this place."

I stare at him, aghast. "And you think I would? This is a place of horror, Fortiss. People *died* here."

"It's also the guardian of the great pass into the Western Realms. It needs to be defended by someone the skrill respect."

"No," I say definitively. My heart has turned to lead. "No. Absolutely not. And even if I did—that statue has to go. Knock it down."

"Mm." Fortiss continues looking up at the statue. "As unobtrusively as you can, turn and glance through those cutouts the skrill have so generously provided us in the border walls of the Thirteenth House causeway and tell me what you see."

I exhale in disgust and shift slightly right, glancing through the walls. And then I stop.

Standing out in the wide plain before the Eighth House—or the Thirteenth House, as Fortiss would have it—is a group of thirty-odd women—from long-legged girls to bent crones, broad-shouldered warriors to mothers with babes in arms. "What are they doing?" I ask below my breath.

"Syril told them about the statue. Told them to come see what magic a strong woman can wield."

I shoot him a hard glance. "You're making that up."

"They're here, aren't they? And they see a testament to the strongest woman I've ever met, the bravest and the fiercest." He glances back at me with a smile filled with pride and maybe even wonder, a smile like nothing I've ever received before. It makes my heart feel too big in my chest, too full of emotions to work right—and then he keeps going.

"You can knock it down when you take ownership of the Thirteenth House, Lady Talia. But for now, the statue stays."

CHAPTER 41

We make remarkably good time heading across the wide plains, taking advantage of the skill and experience of the Savasci to follow trade routes that lead us along meandering streams and the occasional thriving town. We stop only long enough to gather food and supplies and pitch our camp early the first few days, to allow those who are still injured more time to sleep under the wide sky.

The first night, I'm dead to the world. The second night, I realize that while so many of the sick are sleeping, Fortiss isn't. He moves from pallet to pallet, standing over each of the wounded, murmuring words I can't quite catch. They sound both musical and foreign to me, and I think about the books that he spirited out of Lord Daggar's inner chambers, the ones he didn't send into the Blessed Plane. I'm once more drifting off to sleep, lulled by the odd cadence of words that he speaks over the still gravely burned Tennet, when I hear a murmur to my left.

"He walks too close to the darkness, even now," murmurs Syril.

I glance up at her with some surprise, but her eyes are on Fortiss, her manner taut and high energy. I want to ask her what she means, but I already know. "He's carrying the winged crown with him, isn't he?"

"He never puts it down. He knows enough not to put the thing on his head, at least. Whatever happened on the other side of the border wall convinced him *that* isn't a good idea, but he told me he feels connected to it. He found it after all, he liberated it. And even though he nearly was trapped by it, he felt its power —and has used it to heal." She grimaces. "The dark shall draw the dark."

"And what exactly is this particular darkness capable of, Syril?" The time has come for me to ask this question. It's something that has been niggling in the back of my brain since nearly the moment we arrived at the Eighth House...and everything I've experienced after that moment has only deepened my certainty that the Savasci know far more than they've shared so far. "I've seen the fortifications of the Eighth, I've met...well, I've met the ghost of Lord Daggar, anyway. There's no way that Daggar in any form would've allowed you to live, suffered you to exist unless you had some advantage that he couldn't combat. At first, I thought you'd simply entered into some arrangement to ensure his protection, but if so, you didn't do a very good job?"

She snorts. "Lord Daggar would have sooner died than accept the protection of the Savasci, but as it turns out, we couldn't have saved him from his doom. It was put into motion twenty years ago and more when he opened his doors to a new lord protector, one who had him preening with pride and spilling his secrets like a child. I had already left the Eighth House by then, joining ranks with the Savasci. We are a house unto ourselves, Lady Talia, as I suspect you've figured out. We, alone, hold the sacred story of the Protectorate's birth."

I shift on my pallet, staring at her. "You're talking about the warrior Ehlyn. The woman who stood with Mirador."

Her brows drift up, her eyes cool and inscrutable in the dark. "So you saw the truth when you put on the winged crown."

"I saw something, for sure. I don't even begin to understand it. Explain it to me."

Syril settles more comfortably on her ledge, like a woman

setting down a heavy burden. She's quiet for so long that I begin to wonder if she's drifted to sleep.

Then she speaks. "The tale of warrior Ehlyn is something every woman of the Savasci is told and commanded to memorize, for we can't dare allow any record of it to be found. We can't dare allow any suspicion of it to be formed. And we can't share it unless we are directly and specifically asked by a friend who may never be a foe."

I grimace, shifting my gaze back to Fortiss. "Then I'm not sure that you can tell me, Syril. I don't know what will come of the darkness that still dogs our heels. I've worn the winged crown; I've touched the energy of the skrill and the aching depths of the Sahktar. How has that damaged me? What might happen if I get captured and am interrogated? Maybe it's better if you don't tell me what you know, not yet."

She chuckles softly.

"You should have thought of that before the skrill erected a statue in your honor, and Lord Protector Fortiss gave you the keys to what will now be the Thirteenth House. The Savasci *are* your people, Lady Talia, whether you wish to command us or not, whether you're able to protect us or not. We will protect you. You are the sign we have awaited after nearly five hundred years of darkness. You command both the darkness and the light."

"Well, maybe, but I've lost connection with Gent, with all the Divhs who promised themselves to me." My words are stony, and they hover in the air before me, damning and stark. "I may never recover it."

She smiles. "All the more reason why you should know the story of your house, the house that has waited for you all these long years. Light willing, you'll one day be able to share the full story in peace with the rest of the Protectorate—but for now, what you need to know is...you're right. The great, exalted Mirador didn't stand alone as leader of the Imperial delegation that faced down the skrill and commanded the Divh to their aid. A second warrior also bore a winged crown that day—Ehlyn the bow mistress. Though a woman and smaller than most of the men in the delegation, she had grown up apprenticing under her father, who shaped, strung, and maintained bows for the Imperial army. She was a skilled marksman and a master fletcher. Those skills kept the company fed when food ran low, earning her the respect of all. The history goes that Mirador discovered two crowns, not one, in some abandoned holding as the delegation pushed their way west. A wise tactician, he had no interest in stoking a competition between him and the other warriors in the troop. He gave the second crown to Ehlyn for safekeeping, swearing her to secrecy. As a skilled fighter, she would keep it safe. As a woman, she was no threat."

I make a face. "Of course she wasn't."

"When Mirador breeched the borders of the Unlit Pass and drew the skrill into the Protectorate, Mirador beseeched the Light for aid. Nothing happened. The skrill were attacking, the delegation was overrun by snakes of every description, and Ehlyn did the only thing she could think of. She pulled the crown out of her pack, slammed it onto her head, and added her voice to Mirador's. That's when the sky opened and the Divhs appeared. Her connection was simply stronger with the Divhs until they banded with warriors on their own." She smiles, a little bitterly, and doesn't say anything more for a moment. "Before that day was done, she rode a falcon and shot flaming brands into the heart of the skrill."

"So she saved us," I fill in for her. "But—"

"Ah, but did she?" Syril lifts a hand to stop me. "Remember, it was chaos that day. No one saw what she did but Mirador and a few of the women in the troop who were fighting off a pocket of skrill nearby, hidden from Mirador's view. In the midst of that chaos, with the Divhs holding strong and victory certain, Ehlyn was struck down."

I stare at her. "By Mirador?"

She shrugs. "That's never been proven, but by all accounts, the skrill attacked neither Mirador nor Ehlyn directly—they gave them both wide berth. So who attacked her? Confusing matters more, by the time the serpents left this plain, a several foot-thick layer of ash covered the earth. We believe Ehlyn and her crown were buried in that ash—or perhaps carried off by the skrill. Either way, no one ever mentioned the second crown again, while Ehlyn was hailed a martyr for the cause—honored by Mirador and quickly forgotten. The women who knew the truth never betrayed it to any but their own daughters, who in turn told it to their daughters from that point forward. And so, the Savasci were born."

"But…"

"There's more," Syril says, lifting a hand. "All the warriors but Mirador successfully banded to Divhs that day until he took off the crown. Only then could he band to a Divh, and he understood that the crown gave him rule, but not connection. For reasons of his own, he chose connection."

I stare at her. "That's why he gave his crown to the First House. And why no warrior—ever—has worn that crown since…if it even still exists. But how is it that no one *knows* any of this, how is it…" I fall silent then, once again answering my own question. While Mirador had managed to call the skrill to him, it was Ehlyn, not Mirador, who'd successfully summoned the Divhs. By all accounts, it was the Divhs who saved the Protectorate. Whether another man *could* have summoned them doesn't matter—a woman had.

Syril nods as she sees awareness darken my expression. "So now you understand. This is a story only outcasts can tell, Lady Talia. And even then…we whisper."

Before she can continue, her gaze sharpens. Without another word, she nods to me, then dissolves into the shadows.

"Lady Talia." I look up to see Fortiss striding toward me, concern etched over his face. "You should be sleeping. Above all the others, you need to conserve your strength."

I smile as he hunkers down beside me. "How's Tennet? His burns are healed, but he doesn't seem to be improving as fast as he should."

"He's…getting there. But Tennet's connection with Ayne is more powerful than mine with Szonja. In many ways, I've made a study of it, as I hope to achieve that same link with Szonja one day. For now, however, it's serving to keep him in a constant loop of fury and fire, as he fights to save those who are already dead. Not only those who died the night of this most-recent attack, but all who have died at the mercy of the skrill and the Sahktar, all the waves of darkness that have tumbled over the mountains for centuries. The site of the Eighth House is an ancient, ancient place. A city reborn on itself time over time, swallowed by the mountains and reborn again. Something is tying Tennet to it as a protector, and with Ayne as his Divh, he sees not only the failed protections of the moment, but of centuries."

He eyes me with a bemused smile. "If I didn't know better, I would say it was because you and he were fated mates, with a tie that binds you both to protect this great land. But, as I've already said, I don't want to accept that, Talia. I really don't." He sighs, glancing away from me, as if making an admission to the Light itself. "I can't."

His possessiveness stirs something warm in my chest, a feeling I'd never expected to welcome. With most men, such a claim would feel stifling, but with Fortiss...it simply feels honest and true.

The firelight catches on his features, illuminating a strength that isn't just physical, and that doesn't need to diminish others to prove itself. When Fortiss looks at me, I don't feel like a trophy to be won or a position to be claimed. I feel seen—simply seen—for exactly who I am.

What a wonder that is.

Still, I regard him with a bald, hopeful curiosity I work hard to hide. Something has shifted in Fortiss. The man I met a month ago wouldn't have laid claim so boldly over anything—least of all me. And I want that claim, I realize. I want him. I want *this*, and only this. Nothing and no one else matters.

A warrior should make her decision in seven breaths.

CHAPTER 42

*O*ne. "Walk with me?" I ask, sitting up. I try not to look at him directly, instead focusing somewhere vaguely over his shoulder while my heart gallops forward all fists and feet, like Gent racing across a distant ridge.

Fortiss shakes his head, his expression immediately turning to one of concern. "Talia, no. You should rest."

Two. I push my hair out of my face, straightening my clothes, and rake my gaze across his face. He's worried over me—ordinarily, I'd welcome that, but I don't need him to think of me as some injured warrior. Not tonight.

I offer him a casual, easy smile. *Three.* "I'm done with resting, Fortiss. There's a river here, and I, for one, need a bath." *Four.* "This far from the Eighth House, I can only pray I've cleared enough of the ash of the Western Realms to take advantage of it."

"A bath?" He blinks at me.

Five. Before he can object, I roll off the pallet and stand, shoving down the dizziness that I feel at the sudden elevation change. I brush by him, but he easily falls into step as I lead him away from where the sick beds are clustered. There are fewer of those beds tonight, I see, and my heart skips a little in relief.

Then it skips some more as I realize Fortiss has quickened his step, drawing up close behind me. *Six.*

"It's off to the right," he murmurs, taking my hand. "This way. We should stay together."

Seven, and it's done.

I swallow down another rush of emotion, so intense it borders on hysteria. What's wrong with me? It's not like Fortiss and I are strangers to each other. And yet in many ways, we are. We've gone through so much in such a short time that every day it's as if we've been forged in fire all over again.

Will he want me the way he did before the great battle? Before I saved him and lost my connection to Gent? Am I just a warrior to him now, not a woman?

I blow all these fears out in a quick exhale. "No one will be looking for us, will they?" I ask quietly as we step into the woods.

Fortiss squeezes my hand, and my heart nearly surges straight out of my chest.

"Not until morning," he murmurs back. "Thank the Light."

It takes us no more than a quarter hour to reach the river, far enough away from the camp for privacy, but not so much that should danger come we would be useless to help defend our party. If anything, at least for Fortiss, the distance would allow him to call upon his Divh and she would help carry him into the fight.

With an intuition I don't know whether to credit to him or to the books of magic he's been consulting, Fortiss speaks to me in the darkness, spinning tales of possibility. "You will regain your connection to Gent, you know," he murmurs. "You had the crown on your head for mere breaths, just enough to free Zhang and me and to forge your connection with the skrill. You can't be punished for a lifetime for such a brief action. Light, I can't even call it a mistake. It wasn't a mistake, as far as I'm concerned. It saved my life. It restored Zhang's freedom. It gave us a glimpse of what the skrill can truly do."

"I know," I say, and I think of Syril's story. Mirador was able to band with a Divh after he removed the crown. Could I reband to Gent? Would my beautiful goliath even want that?

I send up silent prayers to the Light as we walk.

Eventually, the path opens up to a soft, loamy space, edged with boulders that line the riverbank. Without hesitating, I pull away from Fortiss and in a few, efficient motions, strip down to the skin.

"Talia—" He practically chokes with surprise, but I don't give him time to think. I step toward him and reach up, placing my hands on either side of his head and pulling him in for a sharp, greedy kiss, as if this is something I do all the time. My heart leaps again, pounding frantically, and he gasps as I turn away and sprint toward the river.

It's a testament to Fortiss's skill as a warrior that he's out of his clothes and on me before I've even waded more than five long strides into the bracing chill of the river. He lifts me up then dives with me into the deep, cool water, pulling me up a few breaths later and holding me apart from him as his legs scissor through the slow-moving water to keep us afloat.

He searches my hair, my face, his expression taking on an air of severity. "How are you feeling? You don't seem like you weigh any more than usual. I think you would if there were cement chunks weighing you down."

"I think I'm—oh!" Fortiss doesn't allow me to finish. He pulls me close, wrapping his arms around me tightly as his lips meet mine. We turn in the water, our legs treading easily beneath the surface, keeping us afloat.

"Talia," he murmurs between kisses, but the time is long past for talking. In this moment, there's merely him and me and a time carved away from everything else. He breaks away and pulls me across the water to the far side of the bank, the two of us matching each other's movements. I've never swum across a body of water like this, but there were enough mountain lakes near the Tenth— whose waters were far colder—that I can keep up with him easily.

When we reach the far edge of the embankment, he exits first, holding his arm out and leading me along the rocky shale, picking out a path that won't lacerate our heels. He's rewarded when the rocks give way to a soft, grassy embankment, and he pulls me down with him. Through a break in the rocks, we can see the campfires in the distance that mark our presence, and we watch the flickering flames for a few moments without speaking, our arms wrapped tight around each other.

"You know, if we were any other two people, we could walk the other way," he murmurs. "We could make a life or travel beyond the borders of the Protectorate and see what the wide world holds, never having to fight another battle or face another wall of skrill."

I smile. "Then I thank the Light we're not," I whisper as he turns to me.

He reaches out and draws my face to him, leaning in for a long, lingering kiss. His fingers thread through my hair, now almost down to my shoulders, slicking the river water away and continuing down to caress my shoulder, my arms, trailing lightly across the band.

When he does, something deep and needful shifts within me, a door opening where before it was clamped shut. But I can't focus entirely on it as his fingers continue their quest across my body and he cups my breasts, my breath growing ragged as he draws his thumb over the tight, pebbling flesh at their tips.

He groans and says another word, something I can't make out and the door within me expands, a light kindling in its depths, as his hands draw down my waist and flare out over my hips. Slowly, intently, he kneads his palms into the aching muscles of my legs, his nimble fingers picking out every knot. I groan with a soft, guttural release I didn't know I was capable of as something unbends within me, a surrender that goes far beyond the unclenching of muscles and release of control.

His chuckle is warm and knowing, and it undoes me even more. I sigh, whispering inarticulately as he lays me back in the grass. "Just relax," he murmurs, his hands continuing their slow, rhythmic movement over me, as if he's somehow memorized my body so well that he knows what still hurts, what has ever hurt, and he alone can make it right again. I realize my eyes have drifted shut. When I flicker them open, he's staring at me, his eyes hard, intent, his jaw set.

"If you ask my permission again—" I warn him and he grins at me with wild, fierce abandon, then leans in and captures my mouth with his as his body covers me. I revel in the weight of him, pressing me down, covering me. Covering, not smothering. Protecting, not imprisoning.

Who is this warrior who was taught the creed of the Protectorate virtually from birth, but is still willing to accept me, to want me, to give to me all of this? Every touch feels like a revelation—not just of pleasure, but understanding. Every sigh feels like a benediction. Every murmur another twist of soaring energy that binds us closer together, our breaths flowing like water, our hearts beating as one.

I arch up into him, and it's my turn to brand his body with my hands, my skin, to press into his warmth and surround myself with it. In one moment, I feel incredibly frail and weak, as ephemeral as a feather on the wind, able to be swept away by the merest puff of air...and in the next, I feel as mighty as a Divh pounding across the earth, surging into the sky. Fortiss makes me weak, he makes me strong. And in the racing of our thudding heartbeats, I hear the music I've been missing my whole life, never knowing it was even possible.

I slide my hands down his waist until I lock onto his hips, our gazes meeting with fierce resolve as I draw him into me. The pressure builds almost to the point of pain—past the point of pain, but I grip him tight when he would shift to ease it. I want this. I want him. The moment he sinks into me, fully joining our bodies as one, all other thoughts go out of my mind. Twin spires of pain and pleasure intertwine, and I can no sooner stop the tide of my need than I can the gasp that escapes my lips, the groan of pleasure that chases it.

After that, all sense of time and place slips away from me. He thrusts into me, and I press back, our bodies flowing together like water and racing like fire, our breath as one between us.

Then slowly, slowly, just when I thought that there could be nothing but the inevitable rush to reach the pinnacle of sensation and crash over the top, the dance falters and eases back, and Fortiss and I are staring at each other almost in wonder, as if we're seeing each other for the first time. We whisper and smile, we laugh and play, we drift and explore and revel in the magic of our bodies and our minds and this perfect moment on this perfect night. When his intensity builds anew, the air snaps tight around us—only this time, no Divhs break through to this plane. If anything, it's as if we break through to theirs, leaping higher—higher—soaring through a starlit sky.

The fire that has kindled within me grows to a burning crescendo, and all that was empty is filled, all that was lost is found, and the sharp, fierce scream of a dragon sings through my mind—joyful, triumphant, and bold.

And over it, so far distant it seems like little more than a memory of a long-ago dream, is a long, ululating howl of pure, transcendent joy.

CHAPTER 43

I t's nearly dawn by the time we pick our way back down to the river, swim leisurely across the water, and stagger back out onto the shore to collect our clothes—which I'm not surprised to find that Fortiss hid thoroughly out of sight. Walking beside him in the pre-dawn light, I feel different, changed in ways I can't fully articulate. The connection we forged by the river feels like a thread binding us together, invisible but unbreakable, even as we return to our roles as warriors with responsibilities beyond ourselves.

My limbs feel languorous, heavy, but not in the way that I feared with the weight of hardened cement anchoring me to the bottom of the river. Instead, everything flows easily, slowly, almost like a dance.

"We head out at daybreak?" I ask, turning to see Fortiss simply staring at me. The sky has lightened enough that everything is soft and lush, and I glanced down at my body, suddenly concerned that he can see an injury I have not fully accounted for. "What?"

"You're beautiful," he says simply, and there's something vulnerable in his honesty, as if he's offering up some secret, sacred truth. "I always think it, but I don't always say it. And perhaps if I say it enough, you'll believe it."

"Probably not." I roll my eyes, but my hands are shaking as I pull on my clothes. In some ways, nothing has changed between us. In some ways, everything that came after that moment by the Shattered City was simply part of a single stroke of the sword. And yet every moment, every breath I draw with Fortiss seems like it opens up new possibilities—and new dangers.

Unbidden, the image from the Eighth House prophecy chamber surges forth in my mind, Fortiss's mouth slack, his eyes dead beneath the weight of the crown of wings.

A crown he now carries with him everywhere, according to Syril. I glance sideways and note the leather satchel even now, bouncing against his hip.

I draw in an uneasy breath. "I think—I think I should carry the crown, Fortiss. I've already lost my connection to Gent. If I have to use it again, if the skrill return—I can...I will. I don't want you to have to make that choice."

"I..." Fortiss breaks off, and for a long time he says nothing, the two of us walking more slowly now toward the sick beds where my gear is stowed. But before we draw too close to the lights of camp, he stops and turns to me. Without a word, he lifts the satchel over his shoulder, then drapes it almost formally over mine.

"You *will* regain your connection to Gent," he says fiercely, leaning forward until our foreheads touch. The simple point of connection makes me want to cry, and I press my lips together firmly to forestall the urge. "You will."

This simple contact—forehead to forehead, breath mingling with breath—feels more intimate than even our precious hours by the river. It's a promise without words, a connection that transcends the physical. In this moment, I understand that what's grown between us is more than desire or convenience. It's something I've never allowed myself to imagine possible. Something I can't imagine living without.

"I hope so," I whisper, and then his arms come around me, and we embrace a long moment in the dark, stronger together though we must, in this, stand apart.

At length he shudders, then steps back again. He glances up toward the sky. "I think we'll head out at a sharper clip this morning," he says, and then a soft, quick smile plays at the corners of his mouth. "I think we need Tennet to get back on his feet officially too. He's milked his injuries long enough."

I straighten my tunic. "Syril's worried about him," I point out, and Fortiss snorts.

"And that's why he's played the fainting flower. But—"

"Woohoooo!" The sky snaps tight, and I look up to see Caleb's Divh, Marsh, burst into view, the plumage on his birdlike head sticking straight up, his powerful arms thrashing the air, his small wings and legs churning violently, as if he needs every appendage to gain the speed he needed to land.

"What the—what is he *doing*?"

"His job." Fortiss laughs, but he's already heading that way, and I scramble to catch up with him. "We talked about this last night. Enough of the Savasci warriors have improved or are on the cusp of improving that we need to start making better time across the plains. Even if we can cut off our trip by a few days, we should try to do so. We still need our warriors to heal, but I begin to think that they would heal more easily in connection with their Divhs."

I consider that, but I see the value in what he's saying. Even the memory of my connection to Gent with Fortiss wrapped in my arms is enough to make me feel stronger, more whole. And maybe, if all these Divhs connect with their warriors...maybe Gent will be able to find his way back to me too.

Another scream sounds across the heavens, and this one, I know even better. Szonja, Fortiss's beautiful dragon, arrives and soars low across the plains before banking toward the forest and the riverbed. She knows where Fortiss is, and he raises up a shout then takes off at a run for our campsite.

I let him dash ahead, though I keep even with him enough that I can watch the furious scramble of the dozen or so warriors as they all head out to where they can reunite with their Divhs. Girls and women join battle-scarred guards as they spread out across the field, and one by one their Divhs appear—griffins and raptors, flying lizards and soaring eagles, even the glorious phoenix. To a one, these Divhs can fly, and I blink as that realization strikes me. Had Fortiss chosen this party intentionally with flight in mind? But what of the horses? What of—

Another scream cuts across my thoughts as Tennet's glorious golden dragon appears in the sky, his head darting around as he works to locate Tennet. I see him the same time Ayne does, and I'm almost lifted off my feet at the sound of Ayne's triumphant roar.

But Tennet isn't alone. He's leaning heavily on Syril at the edge of the campsite, so heavily that I frown at him.

He's fine. I don't know what startles me more, Fortiss's assessment of Tennet's legitimate injuries or the fact that I can hear him so easily in my mind. I can hear him! For one wild breath, I cast my mind out farther, searching, searching for Gent in my awareness, my beautiful Gent, his powerful arms outstretched, his massive paws pounding the ground, his head thrown back in a fiercely joyful howl.

But my Divh does not respond. Our connection remains broken.

Punching down the desperate emptiness that rises inside me, I focus intently on Tennet. He's half-leaning on, half-dragging Syril away from the camp, out into the open territory. She's shaking her head, trying unsuccessfully to pull away from him, but a moment later, the decision is taken from her. Ayne skims over the grassy plains and plucks them both up off the ground, tossing them high. My stomach churns, but they don't break apart. If anything, Tennet twists midair, clutching Syril tight as Ayne swoops out and away, then drops beneath them just in time for them both to sprawl on his back between his wings. The two of them scramble for purchase, and their voices break through my mind as well.

—*idiot*, Syril rages, while Tennet laughs with unbridled glee.

Talia—look! At Caleb's shout, I swing around to see Marsh standing at the edge of the plains with his great arms folded, his bird head tilted quizzically as he surveys the progress of the makeshift battalion. I follow the trajectory of his gaze, and I can well understand the pride in Caleb's voice.

Of the dozen freshly banded warriors, ten are in the air, and the two most injured who remain on the ground are sheltered beneath the wings of their Divhs, leaning against both talons and paw, drawing strength. If Gent were here, this isn't a sight I might even see, so consumed would I be with connecting with my own Divh, riding high clasped in his great paw, clinging for dear life as the wind rushes around us, and he races forward laughing at the sun.

But Gent isn't here, so I draw what joy I may from this army I have helped bring into being, their bands once part of my band, but now unequivocally their own. And as I watch, their voices surface in my mind as well. Their laughter and fear, exhilaration and joy. I hear Fortiss shouting a command, and I mouth the words as well, startled to see the reactions among the troops. They can still hear me. They can still talk to me. Only Gent can't.

And Gent, of course, is all I care about.

They continue their maneuvers for another hour, and as I watch, I find myself drifting farther and farther along the camp, eventually coming to rest beside a large boulder that juts out at the edge of the woods. It's just big enough for me to scramble up and seat myself with an almost royal view of the proceedings.

With every pass, the Divhs seem to grow more certain of the skill of their riders, and the riders seem to strengthen their hold and their seat on their mighty creatures. They swoop and dive, roll in the air, soar straight up and then plummet down, and all of them are buzzing and chattering in my mind. I relay Fortiss's orders as they come, and the Divhs respond with breathtaking speed. It's a joyful, relaxed training, and I recognize it as a healing one as well. The bonds between these warriors and their Divhs were forged in the cauldron of battle, but despite five hundred years of Protectorate lore claiming otherwise, battle isn't the only reason for Divhs and warriors to connect.

I settle back, once again trying to stuff down my despair and confusion over my broken connection with Gent. Perhaps my role in this new order is to serve as Fortiss's first general, helping direct this battalion of Divhs, connecting them together, reporting back. It will never be the same, of course, but perhaps it will be enough.

Talia—look up— Fortiss's voice shakes me out of my reverie, and I strain up, hoping without any real hope to see Gent's mighty form galloping across the plane. Instead, I see only Szonja banking toward me. She's coming in far too fast, and I leap to my feet, waving my arms to signal where I am. Like so many of the Divhs, her sight is not her strongest asset, unless it comes to finding her own warrior. But it's a bright day, and I'm garbed in our dark traveling gear. Surely, she can see me.

She doesn't slow, though. Instead, her wings stretch wide and her powerful hind legs curl under her, and I gasp with shock as her talons bear down on me. At the last second, I turn my back to her, hunching down, just in time for her to wrap her claws around me and lift me high. She screams again with pure, unfettered ferocity, and wings up-up-up. Blearily, I wonder if this is some new training attempt of Fortiss's, some battle formation he learned in one of Daggar's history books or conjured up in his own fevered imagination, but we swiftly leave the other Divhs behind. We soar up even higher, and I finally understand what Fortiss is trying to do—enter the Blessed Plane with me as a passenger—or at the very least, fling me forward into it, like Gent flung us over the border to the Western Realms.

It could work, I think; it should work. We successfully brought Miriam into the Blessed Plane before she was even banded, and though my connection has been severed to my Divh, surely I can travel in a similar fashion. Surely the crime of wearing the winged crown won't keep me from that.

And if I could travel this way, so could horses, so could anything that we chose to move from space to space, plane to plane. The Blessed Plane could be an extension of the Protectorate, a byway for travel in times of war, if nothing else, and maybe in times of peace as well. If we could travel this way, if we could connect—

Pain rips through me with such agonizing force I feel as if my muscle and sinew are being wrenched off my bones. I scream in utter agony out to all the Divhs and warriors, my mind blanking with the horror of it, and I'm not surprised when a shocked Szonja drops me straight out into open air. I vaguely register Fortiss's howl of dismay and urgency as he realizes something has gone terribly wrong, but I blank in and out of consciousness as I plummet down, down, down—my mind teetering on the brink of madness.

Still, in the back of my thoughts, a certainty grows within me. Gent will catch me. Gent will always catch me. My connection with Gent was forged at the dawn of the Protectorate to protect my long-ago ancestor, and he will protect me as well. He will *catch* me.

He doesn't.

CHAPTER 44

Consciousness doesn't ease upon me gently; it slams into me with the force of a Divh's mighty paw.

I awake with a violent convulsion, air bursting into my lungs and rushing back out on a scream. I jerk upright and instantly wish I hadn't, as every muscle and joint shriek in agony.

Wildly, I get the impression of lush green grass and blue and white flowers and a distant vista of sparkling water hurtling toward me, then I pass out again.

The second time I open my eyes I can taste dirt and blood. My ears are pounding with the sound of my own pulse, and everything on my body hurts. But if it hurts, it means I'm still living, so at least that's something.

I shove myself up on one arm, blinking around. My sight isn't quite working right. I can see the green hills and the mist in the air, so thick that it should be rain and yet isn't, the sunlight arching through the sky, shimmering in bands of color. I remain still for a moment, my hands braced on the earth, my legs crumpled beneath me, and try to take stock.

I can breathe. My legs move when I twitch them, my hands are sturdy upon the ground, my elbows locked. I can feel the earth beneath my fingers, the soft dew of the grass. I can smell a combination of loamy soil and fragrant flowers that I recognize...I recognize.

Hands shaking, I dig my fingers into the earth, scraping up the rich soil as I breathe in a shuddery breath, then exhale. I look up, but there is no Gent staring down at me, there are no mighty Divhs at all. But that doesn't mean I'm fully alone.

With a chirruping pop and whirl, a small clutch of hummerlets flutter at the edge of the hill, at least four horse lengths from me. I blink at them, still fully dazed. They bubble over with enthusiastic chirping as I focus on them but don't move toward me while I'm too exhausted and in pain to stand. We face off like this for two breaths, then three, then I collapse into darkness again.

The next time I wake, they've moved closer. I can tell because their whirring and chirping sounds like they're practically breathing into my ear. I slowly, carefully open my eyes, not wanting to scare them away.

"Hey there," I manage, but my voice comes out as a throaty croak and the words are more in my mind than spoken aloud.

The hummerlets predictably wheel back, but not so far this time—just out of arm's reach. I huff a strained cough, then work my arms beneath me again, pushing myself up to an almost seated position.

"Where's Kreya?" I ask, and from the chorus of coos and murmurs, I get only sadness, loss, and separation.

I smile a little. "It's not your fault, Miriam had to go to the First House alone. People don't understand that—mmph." I sit up a little straighter, drawing in a heavier breath. There's no one besides me and the hummerlets on the mountainside, not that I can tell. I wonder for a moment about Fortiss and Szonja. His thinking hadn't been flawed. He thought that Gent was simply waiting on the other side of the separation between the planes, ready to catch me and make everything right again. But why hadn't he and Szonja come to find me? How much time has actually passed since I landed on this grassy ridge? Has the battle party moved on, pushing inexorably towards the First House?

The hummerlets offer no opinion on this last, but they've moved closer to me now. "I'm sorry you were left behind," I murmur, and whether it's my words or the emotion behind them, this elicits a chittering whirl of dismay. "But you'll be reunited soon, okay? You'll be..."

A strange, foreign smell wafts up to me, making my nostrils twitch. It almost...it almost smells like burning flesh, but of course that can't be possible. I've never seen Divhs eat, on this plane or any other, but if they did eat, it wouldn't be the charred carcass of one of their own. That just doesn't make sense.

I shudder again, aware that the hummerlets are now spinning around in anxious concern. "I know, I know," I mutter, as I get my feet beneath me and push myself up to a standing position. I wobble a little, my stance going wide as my hands go to my belt. The stance of the proud warrior, only now it's all that serves to keep me upright.

I take an awkward step, then another, my hands twitching for the edges of my cloak to wrap around me. I'm so cold. Unreasonably cold. I don't remember it being cold last time. As if in sympathy, the hummerlets duck and weave around me, a living cloak of tiny Divhs. With no particular direction, I trudge up the ridge, my heart beginning to pound with both excitement and a little fear as I near the top. Maybe Gent is waiting for me on the other side, ready to snatch me up and dive into the great lake? Or, far worse, maybe he's hurt—broken somehow—needing me, and I never knew it?

I pick up speed. By the time I reach the top of the hill I'm gasping, but as I dash forward, trying to see everywhere at once, there's no denying it. Gent isn't here.

Disappointment squeezes my heart in my chest, and I stop abruptly, then stagger forward as the brightly colored hummerlets crash into me—first one, then another, their chirruping chorus growing more frenzied as I wave them away.

"He's not *here*." My words come out in a wail, but surely they don't need me to tell them that. I glare at them, suddenly furious that I can't connect to them like proper Divhs, can't pierce through their chirruping pips, hums, and squeaks. "Where *is* he?"

They dance back and gyrate, their wings flapping frantically, but as I conjure up an image of Gent and try and press it toward them, they whoop and jitter, only growing more agitated. The images that flood my mind are pure chaos. Divhs soaring through the air, plunging into the water and out of them, Gent among them —but clearly this is from happier times, because sometimes I'm with Gent, sometimes I'm not. Sometimes Gent is the mighty creature that I know him to be as my Divh, sometimes he's far shorter, stumpier and more furry but still gloriously joyful—the Divh that he was for the long line of Tenth House warriors, ending with my brother. But even as I implore the hummerlets to slow down, to focus and go back, they're on to other images. A mighty phoenix, winged lions, cats and lizards, everything we've seen over these past several days since Kreya burst into—

Kreya!

The moment I form the name of their core Divh in my mind, the hummerlets explode in a frenzy of screaming dismay. They shoot straight up, dart across the top of the ridge, then drop out of sight, only to rise again and hurtle back toward me, so frantically I end up crouching away from them, my hands raised over my head to protect myself.

"What are you doing?" I screech at them as they zip around me in dizzying circles and then crash into me, shoving me toward the edge of the ridge. I duck and try to twist away, but two of them slam into me at once, grabbing my cloak at the neckline and dragging it forward, nearly strangling me. "You can't carry me, you idiots. Kreya can't even—"

Kreya.

They burst away from me, a tiny, mad flock, and dart over the ridge then up again, whirling back as they bob and jitter just off the range.

All thoughts of Gent slip away as I suck in a breath and head out after them, striding, then running across the grassy hill. I can't see over the ridge, but I remember this terrain from when Gent and I were here. The hill drops away into a basin lined with trees and craggy rocks, until it opens into a wide curving bay. It's too small an opening for Gent to ever have fit into—at least not now. Maybe Gent before he'd made the switch to me, but not...

I reach the edge of the ridge and finally see what the hummerlets have been trying to show me, then pick up the pace and launch myself over the other side of the ridge, toward the broken mass of trees and shattered rocks. The hummerlets explode in a frenzy of movement as I half-scramble, half-fall down the hillside, barely able to breathe by the time I reach the fallen Divh.

"Blood and *stone*," I whisper as I reach Kreya's tailfeathers, my heart in my throat as I take in the awkwardly broken wings, their soot-streaked tips. "What happened?"

The screeching of the hummerlets fades into the background as I come around her head, and I see her long, beautiful bill... wrapped tight with a leather thong.

Rage blasts through me, and I give up any pretense of caring. I scramble onto the snapped-off tree trunk and run as far as it extends, then leap onto Kreya's neck. Her body shudders beneath me, and I realize she still lives. She lives! Wincing at the pain I'm no doubt causing her, I grab handfuls of her feathers and pull myself over to where I can slide down her head and off to the right, crashing into the bushes near where the trailing edge of the leather strap is.

When I reach for it, I'm shocked anew as it wrenches away from me—then dives for my hand, spinning around my wrist in a living coil. It's a warrior band, stretched beyond all recognition.

I gape, not even fully registering the pain as it shoots up my forearm to join the thick, multi-layered sentient band now pulsing around my left bicep. "Miriam's band?" I stare in shock from the band to the hummerbill as it opens its mighty beak and caws. "She took it off *completely*?"

The hummerlets screech and yammer in unison, and the

hummerbill attempts to flap its wings, but its crash landing into the trees has trapped it.

"Wait! Wait—we can do this together. Just wait."

I concentrate my rabbiting thoughts into an image of the hummerbill lying still, very still, while her hummerlets and I clear the debris crashed over her. She's quivering with fear, rage, and an emotion I can't fully identify, but she stops thrashing around. Better still, with her back in connection with her flock of hummerlets, she can focus them as well...somewhat.

It takes what feels like hours to finally free her from the debris, and when she finally pulls herself aloft, her left wing is badly skewed. Her hummerlets race to her aid as she shakily soars over the water of the lake, and I'm left to trudge out of the wooded cove and haul myself over the rocks until the deep, thick grasses of the ridgeline greet my questing fingers.

More exhausted than I feel like I've been in my entire life, I turn myself over on the hillside, and stare into the clear blue sky. Kreya yodels a cry of cautious joy, and I feel a burst of relief—half from me, half from her hummerlets—but that doesn't stop the dread from taking hold within me, seeping through my chest.

Miriam is no longer banded to her Divh.

Did *I* do that to her, somehow? By allowing her to return through the Blessed Plane without her Divh, did I break some sort of contract, some bond that I had no idea even existed? The protocols of warrior and Divhs may be written in the books of Lord Daggar's library, but even there, I doubt they ever recorded the proper ways to ensure the connection between Divhs and non-warriors. Or even if such bonds were meant to last.

And what of Miriam? *Is* she hurt? To hear Nazar explain it, the forced unbanding of Divh and warrior outside the Light-blessed handoff between family members is always absolutely devastating to the warrior. But this band didn't go to anyone, nor did it remain wedged in Miriam's wrist like Nazar's had, unwilling to let go. It returned to the Blessed Plane scorched and stretched, wrapped around Kreya's beautiful bill.

I reach out with my mind to Kreya, searching her memories, but everything beyond the screech of her own hummerlets and her first sight of me is only blackness. I watch her fly roughly, awkwardly across the lake, her hummerlets propping up her wings and adding what limited power they can to her flight, and grimace.

There's no way for me to get back to Fortiss on Kreya's back. She might—possibly—be able to make the trek on her own, but she can't carry a rider. Still, I'm connected to her, at least. I may not be able to call Gent to me, but I could hear the other Divhs as they practiced...when was that? Just this morning?

I frown, staring across the waters of the great lake. From this vantage point, I can see the small island in the middle of the placid blue water, both it and the nearby rough outcropping that I now know as a mirror of the coliseum serving as the only visible inter- ruptions from here to the far horizon. I wonder what's going on at the First House right now.

Had I underestimated Miriam's fear at returning to the council with her band? Had she begged Nazar to officially unband her here in the Blessed Plane, before she even returned home? I could see that, honestly, though I can hardly countenance it. Even though Kreya is nowhere near as large or fierce as the other battle Divhs, she gave Miriam the gift of flight, of travel—of connection.

Who wants to live without connection?

Not me.

"Gent," I whisper, almost desperately this time. I clench my eyes shut, focusing on his immense, beautiful bulk—the parade of heavy horns that stick out from his head and trail down his shoul- ders. His massive, gorgeous, protective paws. His mighty onyx talons, glinting like jeweled spikes from a sea of green scales. I do everything I can to will our connection to be reformed, but there's nothing but the distant howl of the hummerbill and the buoyant cries of her flock.

Frustrated, I lift my left arm high, forming a fist. "*Enough* with this, Gent," I groan. "I need to *see* you! We need to return to the First House or to Fortiss—but we can't stay here!"

But Gent doesn't respond.

Scowling, I think again about Fortiss. Is he searching for me—frantically wondering what happened when Szonja threw me into the sky and I left the Fated Plane? Or does he somehow know I'm alive, feel it through whatever connection has grown between us?

Even if he does, this place has no use for me, not anymore. The moment Tennet is well enough to make the journey through the Blessed Plane, Fortiss and the entire battle party will transition to the First House. That could be a matter of hours—but not days, I don't think. If I don't return immediately, I can't imagine Fortiss would go so long without knowing for sure I was safe. He probably thinks I'm already at the First House safely with Gent.

That thought makes me smile, even if a little sadly. My connection with Gent may still be broken, but with Fortiss? That bond has been forged in fire, magic, blood—and pure, visceral need. It will hold, I think. It will hold.

Far out over the lake, Kreya banks in a wide, lazy arc, her movement finally catching my eye. As she turns toward me, flapping her wings in ungainly swoops, my gaze shifts to the far western horizon beyond her. I frown, dropping my arm so that my hand shades my eyes. Has it grown darker on the horizon?

I back farther up the ridge, trying vainly to see more, but the approaching hummerbill obstructs my view. I reach out to her, imagining the skrill, the shadow monsters, but her focus is intent, her flight only seeming to pick up speed as she nears me. Too late, I hear the burst of chittering chirps and squawking excitement as I realize what's happening here.

Gent may not have heard my cry for help, but Kreya did. And she's going to try to answer my call.

"*Light*—no—no!" I hold my arms up, stumbling back, but there's no stopping her as she screams with utter joy and shoots across the top of the ridge, her claws out, her wings flapping surprisingly well. I don't think she'll be able to build up the momentum for another run, and at the last breath, I turn and start running ahead of her, my cape flowing in the wind, giving her as big a target as I can—and praying she doesn't rip me to shreds.

I wince with blinding pain as her raptor-like talons skewer my right shoulder yet *again*, my head jerking to the side as her left foot tangles in my cape. Then we're off the ledge and she's soaring up —up—but I already know we're too slow even to reach the limits of the Blessed Plane, and far too slow to break through. We're too *slow*!

We'll never make it.

And once again, Gent won't be there to catch me.

CHAPTER 45

For the second time in what seems like only a few hours, I'm dropped unceremoniously to the earth, the wind completely knocked out of me as I land on a patch of turf that's thick, lush, and endlessly green.

Only this time...it's breathing.

If I could breathe, I would shout—scream—howl with joy. But I've clearly re-entered the Fated Plane with its harsh, dry air and shimmering heat, and my lungs aren't reacting well. My breath squeezes tight in my throat, and I'm also buried in what feels like four feet worth of fur that doesn't at all seem right for the creature I know has to have caught me, the creature whose broad back I'm sprawled over, next to a wide swath of skin that's smeared with...

I freeze.

Blood?

Slowly, carefully, I sink down deeper into the thick fur that was never a part of my glorious Divh, but which I know must be his all the same, and desperately try to take stock of my surroundings.

Kreya has done the task she endeavored to do. Blue sky stretches out above me, and I'm lying on top of Gent against a wall that stretches up—up. I know where we have to be. The coliseum at Trilion. I can hear a distant roar, though it's impossible to understand with my ears still ringing from the force of my fall. I flop over on my belly and move over Gent's bulky body until I can peer through his fur to see...

What in the Light?

I stare in absolute confusion as I pick out the scene in the center of the coliseum. A platform has been set up there, almost rivaling the ornate battle stages of the Tournament of Gold. But while those were tall, functional towers intended to support warriors guiding their Divhs into battle, this platform seems entirely created for show. As if a famous bard might be holding forth there, or perhaps a priest of the Light.

Despite my high vantage point, I can't take the risk of sneaking a true look at what's going on across the tournament field, because to do so I would have to lift myself out of the thick fur that's hiding me, and I'm too bleary and confused to do that quite yet.

But without question, there's something intensely wrong with everything that's happening here.

For one, it's broad daylight, and I'm lying on top of a giant Divh, but no one is paying any attention to me—or, more importantly, to Gent. Secondly, though I'm still struggling to breathe while grasping the long, flowing hair of my Divh's back...Gent *doesn't* have hair like this. There's too much of it and it's a pale sage green. My mighty goliath is also at least twice as big as the creature I'm currently laying on, though admittedly, from what I can tell, this version of Gent is still as big as three manor houses stacked on top of each other. Worse, though Gent is alive and breathing, he's desperately damaged, his back sliced open to allow thick green blood to ooze out.

Also—damningly—I can see one of his mighty legs stretched out behind him...chained to the coliseum wall.

What in the Light has happened here?

I collapse back down over Gent's body, taking comfort in his warmth even though there remains no connection between us. He may as well be a shaggy green mountain for all the awareness he has of me, but at least he breathes. At least he lives.

I close my eyes tightly, willing the tears that are now leaking through my lids to slow, to stop, even as I futilely attempt to make a connection again with my Divh. The sentient band that's wrapped around my arm is still active and vibrant. The heat pouring out of it is real. But as I desperately search in my mind for a link to the giant beneath me, I get nothing in return. It's as if he isn't there—as if I'm sprawled on the back of some other warrior's Divh.

I choke back a sob and Gent ripples beneath me, his broad back shifting as he groans in his slumber. How did they manage to restrain him with a chain? How had they even caught him in the first place? The only time I've seen anything like this was when I crept down from the banquet hall in the First House to see the fabled beast being held in the caves beneath the castle. That fearsome monster turned out to be Szonja, the glorious Divh destined for Fortiss, yet stolen from him by Rihad. Rather than shifting the band from father to son according to the tradition of the Protectorate, Rihad had taken Szonja for his own. Taken her and imprisoned her for no real reason other than, I'd supposed at the time, he could.

But if Fortiss's vision in the Eighth House prophecy chamber was to be believed, there'd been a definite purpose behind Rihad's horrific imprisonment of Szonja. Rihad had needed a Divh to enter the Western Realms and locate the crown of wings—never mind the cost that might entail. He'd chosen Szonja as his victim, and then, when she had escaped his clutches, had sacrificed his own mighty Zhang to find the crown.

But why? Rihad clearly already had command over the skrill. He didn't need the crown to call them to Trilion.

Besides that, had he known what awaited his Divh in the Western Realms? The desolation and danger of the entrapping ash? Surely not. There's no way he would have ever risked the Divh who had protected his line for *generations* by sending him to an almost certain death—

A blast of trumpets scatters my fevered thoughts into cartwheeling frenzy. I scrub my eyes, shoving my tears away. Then slowly, carefully, I crawl farther up the steep rise of Gent's back and peek over his shoulder, gaping at the view.

There are easily three hundred spectators gathered around the broad base of the stage. Torches as thick as tree trunks stand at the four corners of the pavilion. They're lit to a full blaze, never mind that it's mid-afternoon here. On the pavilion, a familiar man stands dressed in the splendid robes of his former position and holding his arms out to the adulation of the crowd. *Rihad.*

Despite my sinking horror, I'm not surprised to see him. It's the only possibility, really. Rihad has been preparing for his triumph for more than twenty years. The fact that Fortiss bested him in the tournament melee surprised the lord protector, clearly, but he wasn't left completely without his defenses. Somehow, he was able to call the skrill to attack Trilion, and now, after we left to go battle the skrill at the western border, he's come to life again.

Could we have stopped that from happening? Even as I stare at him, hatred welling up within me, I don't think so. The image of Daggar's and his guard Nemeth's dead bodies, covered over with snakes, shows just how far Rihad's reach extends. If we'd remained in Trilion, we wouldn't have battled the skrill and at least delayed their future attacks. We wouldn't know the truth about Rihad... and we wouldn't have found the winged crown.

I reach down to grab the strap of my satchel, holding on to it as a talisman as I feel the weight of the crown against my belly. I don't know what I might do with the crown at this point, but just having it makes me feel better. I know I'll sooner die than let it drop into Rihad's hands, that's for sure.

My momentary spurt of strengthened resolve shatters in the next breath, as Rihad shifts to the side. He's not alone on the platform.

A man stands beside the former lord protector, his cloak tossed back over his shoulder and his burly hands resting heavily on his belt. With his fierce glower and aggressive stance I can feel all the way across the coliseum, he looks every inch the brave warrior of the realm. Only it's no ordinary warrior standing there. It's Lord Lemille of the Tenth.

My father.

My gaze swims as I try to make sense of everything I'm seeing. How long have we been gone? And more importantly, where is Miriam...and *Nazar*?

Gent shifts again beneath me, his deep sonorous rumble setting off ripples across his flesh that toss me around like an angry sea. I try to swallow my fear, but none of this makes any sense. If Rihad summoned Gent to reband him to my father, why is he knocked out cold and chained to the wall of the coliseum? Why did someone feel it necessary to slice open his back and leave the wound untended, a sticky mass of blood and gore?

And for that matter...

"How is it no one's over here gawking at you?" I murmur aloud, though Gent remains deeply asleep. I mean, yes, we're in the corner of the coliseum, and Gent is chained to the wall and not out in the middle of everyone, but the crowd surrounding the pavilion seem oblivious to the fact that a mighty Divh is in their midst. It's like Szonja all over again, but why?

I blow out a long breath, glancing back to the center stage. There's a strange sort of energy in the coliseum this day, frantic and wild, like a mob about to be unleashed.

Rihad strides forward and holds up both arms. The crowd goes fully silent. When he cries out, his voice reverberates across the walls of the coliseum. "Men and women of Trilion, I salute you! Long have we worked to ensure the success and prosperity of our land, and we have succeeded!"

A wild cheer goes up, and I sweep my gaze over the crowd of people. Then I—finally—notice something else.

Thirty riders stand off to the side of the stage, all of them dressed in heavy, ornate armor that looks nothing like anything I've ever seen from any of the houses of the Protectorate. It's bright silver and glints in the sun, and they all, to a man, are wearing large, plumed helmets with golden ribbons cascading down. Were they in full gallop, with their bright armor and streaming helmets, they would look like fire itself riding across the plane. I've never seen anything like it—not even in paintings—but I know what and who these soldiers must be.

Rihad's next words confirm it. "We are honored to receive this delegation from the Imperium and to reaffirm our dedication to the Imperator and the Light. Blessed are we that they come at such a critical time to help us defend ourselves against *all* threats—not only to the Protectorate but from those who would attack the Imperium and the Light itself!"

The crowd cheers wildly, and I shimmy forward a little farther to peer at the men gathered before the platform. They remain stoic, but something indefinable has changed in their manner. The three men at their head are no longer watching Rihad, but they've angled their horses so that they can get a better view of the crowd—as if the threat that Rihad's warning of will come from there. None of them look my way, however, or to the enormous Divh chained and hidden from them with magic that Rihad could only have borrowed from the skrill. There's no other way he could convince so many people to see only whatever the bearer of such spells most wanted them to see.

But these are ordinary citizens and Imperial soldiers, not banded warriors. How had he managed to twist the skrill's illusion spell to affect them?

Just how powerful is Rihad?

And once again, *where is Nazar and Miriam in all this?*

As if responding to my unspoken demand, Rihad shifts forward, and I jolt to see the long-robed men of the council standing next to the two border lords from the west and Nazar... but not Miriam, and certainly not the Savasci. Had they realized what was happening here and split up? And if so...what has happened to Nazar?

I stare at the warrior-turned priest-turned warrior again in wonder. He looks nothing like I remember. Now he's dressed in long, silver robes, gold plumes at his shoulders draping down, echoing not Rihad's ostentatious gold and black attire, but more closely resembling the armor of the Imperial soldiers. I squint, but I can't find anyone else that I recognize on the platform—no other house lords other than Lemille, and none of the other councilors. Are they back at the First House—imprisoned, or worse? Have they been struck down in Trilion?

There's too much I don't know, and I can't remain here, safe and protected, for another moment. I have to understand.

But beyond that...I need Fortiss here. No matter how injured Tennet is, no matter who they can bring and who they leave behind, they have to come to the defense of the Protectorate, before there's no Protectorate left to defend.

Slowly, carefully, I bring my hands together around the talon-stone. I am not Fortiss; I have no innate magic within me, and I certainly have not studied the ancient texts. But I can reach him, I think. I can imagine him with all my heart, all my love, and will him into being beside me. I can summon him, like I've summoned my own Divh...because he is mine.

"Fortiss..." I whisper, closing my eyes and praying to the Light, through the Light, and all the way across the wide Protectorate. I pray for Fortiss—and for us. I pray for the Protectorate.

But most of all, I pray that my love is enough to cross through the Blessed Plane, and find him wherever he may be.

Moments stretch and spin, my heart pounds, and tears slip from my eyes, but when it's finally done, I slide down Gent's shoulder and stop for a precious moment to lay my hand on his skin. He's still spectacular, of course. But chained the way he is, injured, and definitely sized more as he was when he guarded the Tenth House, he seems so...diminished.

"You're still mine," I murmur as I press my hand against his warm skin. "Even if I can't connect to you anymore, know that I'll always be yours and you'll always be mine. Nothing will ever change that."

He doesn't respond. Not even a flicker of awareness stirs in my mind, and I press my lips tight together, willing myself not to cry as I pat his side roughly. "I love you, Gent."

Turning away before I lose my nerve, I move as quickly as I can beside his long, sprawled arm. There are a few stragglers of the crowd only a few steps distant, and I push forward as if I have somewhere to go, hastening toward them. As I stride quickly away from Gent, I can feel the pulse of magic, like a curtain being pushed away from me as I pass. I turn back, startled...

Gent has disappeared.

CHAPTER 46

"What's this?" I whisper, reaching out my hand to test the air. It gives way like a fine netting, then allows my hand through. I pull my hand back hastily as I see a guard moving along the perimeter of the magical barrier. Behind it, I'd been as hidden as Gent currently is, but now, in full daylight...

Twisting away, I hurry into the crowd, moving toward the main stage, where Rihad continues to whip the spectators into a frenzy.

"We shall stand together as we have ever pledged to do," he declares. "The Protectorate stands with the Imperium and the Light!"

"The Imperium and the Light!" the crowd roars back. "The Imperium and the Light!"

"Talia!"

A spindly hand snakes out from the crowd at the periphery of my vision, and a moment later I'm jerked awkwardly around—to stare into the heavily hooded face of Miriam. But it's a Miriam I barely recognize. She's stooped over like an old woman, her eyes blackened, her left arm hanging strangely awkward at her side as her right clutches her robes close. "Miriam! What's happening here? How is Rihad—"

"There's no time!" she hisses. She yanks me deeper into the crowd. "Where are the others—are they coming? Are they on their way?"

"What?" I blink at her. The cocoon of chanting spectators gives us enough cover to speak, but I have to bend almost double to hear her, two women huddled against the howling mob. At least we shouldn't draw attention this way. Still, I push her cowl back enough to see the bruising at the side of her face, the long-dried tracks of her tears.

Something very wrong has happened here.

"They may be coming—but they may not, Miriam," I inform her sharply. "I've done my best, but they may still have no idea what's happening here."

The harshness of my tone seems to cut through her delirium. She blinks up at me, her eyes more lucid but no less desperate. She clutches my hands as I continue speaking. "I'm here alone. I don't know if they have any sense of me, but we have to assume they don't. I've lost connection with Gent—and you've lost your connection with Kreya too, haven't you? I saw her—"

"You saw her?" she asks, the words almost a cry. She shoves aside the neckline of her cloak, and I see the bloodied stains, now dried and scabbed over, that have soaked through the cloth at her left shoulder.

"When we got here, Rihad...Rihad had awakened," she whispers fiercely as I pull her cloak back in place. "It'd been a full week since we left the First House, and much had happened. He'd met with the house lords—and poisoned some of them, blaming it on the attack of the skrill. Others he quietly imprisoned in the First House, along with those few councilors who remained loyal to Rihad. Lemille stands with Rihad."

"I figured that." I don't want to believe her, but it's the only thing that makes sense. Especially given how easily Lemille stands on the stage beside Rihad, exhorting the crowds to ever more delirious shouting.

Her wandering eyes find mine. "Lemille returned to the First House not to re-pledge his allegiance to Fortiss, but to complete the mission that Rihad had set for him. He left the First House after the tournament with one further task—to intercept the delegation that Fortiss had sent out to the Imperium, then to impound them or kill them at the Tenth House and send men in their stead who would report to the Imperium all that had transpired, only flavored with Rihad's interpretation. If I understand it correctly, Lemille was only partially successful. A delegation from the Imperium was already headed this way, with the belief that they would be able to finally witness the Tournament of Gold. Apparently, Rihad's work in the darkness had somehow disrupted the meditations of the high priests of the Imperium. They were concerned and set out this delegation months ago. Delays kept them from our borders until a few days after Lemille sent out his own men, who dutifully relayed the story, then led them back to the Blessed Pass and the Tenth. A runner warned Lemille of the coming delegation, and that's when he set out to the First...to warn Rihad."

"*Traitor*," I say bitterly. "And here we treated him with respect as an honored house lord. No wonder he expressed no concern about us heading out to take on the skrill at the western borders."

"He's beholden to Rihad, and those obligations stretch far into the past." Miriam shrugs. "Plus, Rihad promised him the return of Gent when it first became clear what had happened with you and your brother."

I curl my lip. "And this is how he proposes to band himself to Gent?" I practically snarl. "By wounding him and chaining him to a wall?"

"Lemille doesn't know that part," Miriam says, surprising me. "Rihad summoned Gent the same night he forcibly unbanded me, but...Lemille couldn't see that he'd done so. He has no idea that your Divh lies chained and wounded. I can, because—well, I think because of you. I'm tied to your line, just like Kreya is. I see clearly, where all others do not." She stares at me with haunted eyes. "Rihad wears the winged crown."

"*What?*" I rear back in shock, my hand slapping down against the satchel, still heavy with the weight of the crown I recovered from its sea of ash and stone. But there's no doubting the truth in Miriam's words. It's the only possible explanation, really...and what I had secretly feared without understanding.

There were two crowns the day that Mirador turned back the darkness at the edge of the western border, calling down the Divhs from the Blessed Plane. One of those crowns was lost across the border, but the other...

"He's had it all this time," I murmur. "Fortiss thought Rihad would never have kept it hidden away, but—he was wrong. No wonder he could call the skrill so easily, once he decided to act."

When Miriam doesn't speak, I set my jaw, casting all doubts away. It doesn't matter how the enemy lands at a warrior's door, I remind myself. At that point, the only thing that matters is how well you stand against him.

"What happened to you?" I demand of her roughly, jolting her to refocus on me. "How do you know all this? And why in the blighted path is Nazar up there on that platform with Rihad?"

"Nazar brought us to the Trilion under cover of night three nights ago, then bade us to release our Divhs back to the Blessed Plane. When day broke, we set out for the First House as ordinary travelers...only to see the army of the Imperium ride through. He recognized them immediately for what they were, but there was no time to get out ahead of them. When we learned in Trilion that no one had seen the other house lords for several days, we knew something wasn't right. We set off in the wake of the Imperial army and arrived to see Rihad welcoming them to the First House. Though we tried to shrink back, Rihad saw Nazar in the crowd of spectators and announced with great and pompous fanfare that Nazar was his closest advisor in the wake of the betrayal of his councilors—and he welcomed the lords from the western realms as if they were boon companions. At Nazar's earnest order, we played along."

"Betrayal of..."

But Miriam pushes on. "When Rihad saw me, he summarily had me arrested. Nazar..." She shudders. "He told me that the way of the warrior was death, but that I would live if I stayed strong. He seemed very certain of that, and I took some solace in it. Then he strode away and left me to face my fate."

I curl my lip. "He does that."

She gives a short, huffing laugh. "It sounds harsh, but it was the only way. The Imperial delegation needed to be shown that Rihad still followed the Light, and Nazar is a priest—so Rihad needs him. I'm sure Rihad will have him executed the moment he no longer has a use for him, but for now...he lives."

My lips twist in a cruel smile. "Which means Rihad, for all his great powers, remains a fool. But Rihad hurt you. Why?"

"I have no such value to him, and he needed an example." She waves a tired hand. "Rihad demanded to know how I came to be banded as a woman, and I told him it was through the dark arts."

I snort. "Well, that had to give him pause."

"Not enough. He had me forcibly unbanded and scorched with fire—I think he believed he would get my band himself, but it disappeared the moment it slid from my arm. I was thrown into a cell until I could be killed with due dishonor. Fortunately, I still have some friends in the First House, and I made my escape easily enough, hoping to live long enough to see him dead. But I haven't been idle—my spies remain loyal too, and they have shared the predicament facing Rihad now. The Imperial army, this delegation you see here, is just an advance party to scout out our loyalty to the Imperium. If they don't return with a positive report, more soldiers will come. Even if they do return with a positive report, our time as a Protectorate is likely coming to an end. It's apparently been too long since we have impressed the Imperium with the dangers we're keeping away from them."

"So Rihad needs an attack that he can protect everyone from, doesn't he?" I can see it now, a solution that's at once elegant and brutal. "And since he's had the crown of wings all this time, he can summon the skrill at will. He's planning another attack here today."

She nods. "He announced that there would be a demonstration to honor our guests, and he brought everyone here—along with the house lords from the western borders and Nazar. So far, the soldiers of the Imperium have been treated with absolute respect. Now, I fear they'll all die—the delegation, the house lords, Nazar."

"And Gent?"

She grimaces. "Rihad still can't summon his Divh, but once he subdued Gent, he seemed to stop trying. I think—I think he's lost connection to his Divh entirely."

"Yeah, I bet he has," I mutter, thinking about the crown on his head. Miriam doesn't know that I freed Zhang...I wonder if Rihad does. "But Rihad brought Gent here, what—to be sacrificed? He's *bleeding*. He's been hurt!"

"He'll unleash him if the skrill get out of hand, I suspect." She sighs. "Like I said, Lemille can't see your Divh, but I can. And I could see what Rihad's soldiers did to him, weakening him through blood loss and holding him in place with spelled chains. It's an abomination, but...Gent did let it happen, I think. He didn't fight it."

I grimace, my heart quailing in my chest. Did he think I broke my connection with him willingly? Does he think I abandoned him?

These thoughts fracture as Miriam fixes her bloodshot eyes on me again. "Rihad did the same to Szonja, and she was able to break her bonds. Maybe you can help Gent break free?"

"I...I don't think so. But maybe." I shove a hand through my hair, but my words are only meant to soothe Miriam, not because I believe them. "Is there anything else I should know before we...do something? Because we can't let this continue, Miriam. We can't let Rihad do anything more."

She nods. "Apparently, when the Imperator leveled the order

for all Divhs to be severed from their warriors outside the Protectorate, we received orders too—we are now only able to summon the Divhs for the Tournament of Gold. So, Rihad told the head of their delegation that, by order of the Imperator, he couldn't summon the Divhs otherwise unless we needed them in true battle. I think he's got several warriors planted in this crowd for that purpose, depending on what happens with the skrill."

"That's it?" I ask roughly. "That's his plan?"

She gives me a wry smile. "That's it."

"Then we act." I shake my head firmly and hold her gaze. "Miriam, Nazar was right. You may not have been born a warrior, and you may not have been trained as one, but you have become one, nonetheless. And we need all the fighters we can get."

I hold out my left hand to her. Her gaze drops to my bicep where my sentient band is already alive with movement beneath my sleeve, and she physically recoils—but for only a step. Then she raises her bloodied, shaking left arm, and puts her hand in mine.

The band bursts to life around my arm, and the familiar searing pain rips down my forearm and palm, then leaps onto her wrist. Miriam gasps and staggers, but her eyes are steady on mine, her mouth breaking into a smile so full of wonder that my own heart surges with joy.

"Kreya," she whispers, but I place a firm hand on her shoulder, holding her in place.

"We will need her—and we'll need every Divh she can summon to come with her, across the Blessed Plane. I can't summon Gent anymore, but you—Nazar—even the western lords...I can connect to you. And together, we will fight."

She nods and I grimace, hearing an answer that Fortiss gave me so long ago it seems to be another lifetime.

Together, we cannot fail.

But even as I think those words, a cloud passes over the sun, thick enough that even with the searing heat of Miriam's band still sizzling on my skin, it feels like we have entered into a chilling frost. I stumble away from her as she clutches her cloak around her again, both of us peering up to the sky.

All the breath dies in my throat.

The cloud that covers the sun is a writhing, twisting mass.

Though my own warriors still haven't answered my call, the skrill have answered Rihad's. And now they're here...

In broad daylight.

CHAPTER 47

"To Safety! To Trilion!" Rihad's roar is so loud, I practically vibrate with it, and this time I know for sure that it's not simply the weight of his voice carrying forth, but the amplification of dark magic.

It has the desired effect, though. The skrill attack on Trilion is still fresh enough in everyone's mind that they don't need this assault to actually begin before they respond to the danger. As Rihad's shout dies away, the crowd breaks as one and starts racing for the giant doors of the coliseum, while the only mounted horsemen—the Imperial soldiers—wheel around in sudden confusion. Some of them are looking to the sky, others have pulled their swords, then they all, belatedly, join in the stampede for the doors.

Miriam and I move along with the throng, keeping our heads down as the skrill surge closer. I lose sight of Nazar and the house lords almost immediately, but I don't think Rihad has such control over his men that they will take out the priest of the Light or the savvy westerners so quickly. At least, I pray to the Light for that to be the case.

We all eventually clear the great doors of the coliseum, and the racing villagers gain speed as they spread out across the plains, barreling toward Trilion. I've lost Miriam, but I keep a keen eye on the horsemen of the Imperium—the more they wheel around in utter confusion, the more they draw other eyes too—especially with Rihad no longer leading anyone, anywhere. It's as if the plains have opened up and swallowed the traitorous former lord protector whole.

"It's the Imperium!" someone shouts in the middle of the melee, the bold, booming shout of one of the First House guards. "We're being attacked by the Imperium! Betrayed—we're being betrayed!"

A new cry goes up from the fleeing villagers, and a burst of fighting men surges back toward us, moving fast. I recognize them at once as the men that Caleb had been training in the coliseum, the newly banded soldiers of the First House. They're too new to the politics of the Protectorate to follow anyone but their lord protector, no matter who wears the black and gold. And they're more than eager to prove their mettle. These new warriors barge through the crowd, and I watch with horror as they tap their fists to their hearts, their arms surging high...

The air around us snaps tight, and suddenly the space between the fighting men and the retreating townspeople is filled with Divhs.

These Divhs are nowhere near as big as the mighty goliaths who had battled so fiercely in the Tournament of Gold, but they're impressive all the same. Most are the size of manor houses, some stretching three stories high, they take a moment to roar with unbridled battle lust, then go swinging about, looking for something to crush. Unlike the great Divhs who fought largely separate from their human counterparts, the men guiding these smaller Divhs stay close, swinging up on to their backs and shoulders depending on where the greatest purchase is. I can only imagine what this looks like to the Imperial soldiers—a horde of ravening beasts, carrying men brandishing swords, and heading straight for them.

The army of the Imperium doesn't shrink away, however, their confusion disappearing like shadows beneath a brilliant sun. And with the skrill still boiling toward us across the sky, the only enemy they can focus on are the newly banded soldiers of the First House.

"No!" I race forward as Rihad's fuller plan reveals itself to me. First, he'll kill as many soldiers as he can, both the unsanctioned banded ones not fully allied to him as well as the Imperial soldiers who would otherwise bear the tale of a Protectorate fully able to defend itself against all comers, including Imperial ones. That's not a message that Rihad wants to get out. It's also why he's called on the strength of the skrill to swell his army of loyal soldiers and Divhs.

He no doubt sees all this as little more than a practice run.

But I can't let it stand. I can't let these Divhs, many of whom came into this plane at my behest, be used as executioners. I also can't let the soldiers of the Imperium be slaughtered.

I may not be able to summon Gent to my aid, but I still have my band...and there's a soldier in need of a Divh in this melee who may yet prove valuable to the cause.

A warrior uses all the weapons at her disposal, no matter who has forged them.

I break out into a run to where Rihad's men are watching the churn of battle at a safe remove, but my father isn't mounted. He's standing there with his hands balled into fists, his legs braced—a man eager to fight anyone, barely restrained. For all his flaws, for all his issues, I know he would sooner die than see Gent the way Rihad has prostrated him. And only with full vision can he ever understand the treachery of the man he follows.

I give him someone to focus his rage on.

"Father!" I shriek as I draw near.

"*You!*" He whips around, his face mottling as soon as he recognizes me. "Why can't you stay dead?"

"Because you keep needing my *help*," I snarl back. Without hesitating even a moment, I grab his left forearm in a tight grip, bearing down.

The innate nature of my sentient band takes over. Here is a warrior that I have chosen, a man who not only can fight with a mighty Divh but who *has* fought with a mighty Divh. A slender tendril of my band rips free and burns its way down my arm, but the greater mass of my band stays intact. It stays! I pray to the Light that means that I haven't lost my connection to Gent forever, but for this moment, I can only stare into the startled face of my father and see the wonder that washes over it as he realizes what's happening.

Reflexively he jerks back, no doubt wanting to reject this gift, considering who's giving it to him. But as a one-time warrior with a Divh of his own, put off by the one man who he thought could reband him, he can no sooner reject this connection then he can reject breath itself. When the band seats itself tight around his bicep, I release him, allowing him to stumble back. Lord Lemille of the Tenth now has a Divh of his own again, and that Divh is of my line, not his. Light willing, that will make a difference.

The guards near me shift, and I finally see Rihad—who's staring straight at my father, as if realizing something important has changed. "Lemille!" he roars, but I'm off again and running, diving into the fray of mounted warriors on their Divhs and horsemen. The skrill are nearly upon us.

For all the might and bulk of the Divhs, the soldiers of the Imperium are clearly well trained, and equipped with both long sword, short sword, and spears. The plain is littered with men— but *only* men so far—their Divhs flashing away back into the Blessed Plane as confusion reigns.

I barely avoid getting trampled in the churn of horsemen. I shift at the last moment to allow the next warhorse to pass, scrambling to haul up a thrown spear that's one of dozens littering the killing field. The spear is heavier than I expect, its shaft rough against my palms, but I have no time to think—only act.

I swing around with a shout as the next member of Rihad's personal guard bears down on me, his horse's hooves punishing the earth. He's not looking at me, though, but at some other unfortunate villager, and his face breaks into a blighted grin as he raises his blade high. Heart hammering, I lunge forward and swing the blunt end of the spear upward as he races by me. The impact cracks against his armor just below the ribcage. He saws on the reins, bringing the horse around sharply, but the force of my desperate shove is too much, and he topples to the side.

I try to grab the reins of the horse, but it rears away from me, and I barely miss getting trampled again. *Light!* If I don't improve my position, I'm not going to get off this field alive.

As focused as I am dodging horses and blades, I almost don't notice when the first skrill drops out of the sky. Then the second hits my back and bounces away. Then I see fully a dozen glistening snakes cover a horse and rider in front of me, draping over them like a cloak. They so unnerve the rider that he drops his sword and shield. He flails, waving wildly enough that he falls clean off his horse—while his mount shucks the snakes with a furious convulsion—then stands still as if momentarily dazed.

"Hey!" I gasp, and without stopping to think about what I'm stepping in, I lurch my way toward the abandoned horse and catch its reins, swinging myself up into the saddle. I turn the horse around just as the field erupts in terror.

Snakes are everywhere. Falling from the sky in an oily sheet, or flying in bristling knots of terror, the skrill swoop across the plain to harry both villager and Imperial horseman alike. Where they strike, men start screaming, and though the horses are far more stalwart, even they start bucking and rearing to shake the creatures off them, unseating their panicked riders in the process.

I gallop back across the open field, angling for the coliseum as more snakes drop out of the sky or fly into the faces of the fighting men. Right now, they're causing equal terror in both the villagers and the soldiers, but the only men falling are the ones on horses—and once they hit the ground, both panicked villagers and skrill alike swarm over them. I race through the chaos, my eyes trained on the opening to the coliseum and whatever blightscape awaits me there.

I can't think of what I was or what I will be, but only the now —only the movement through the madness of the field, shifting and leaning, leaping and pressing on, until I gradually become aware of something else.

The snakes aren't slowing me down.

I grimace as I lean low against my horse's neck, urging it on, but even the occasional snake that whips through the air and strikes me, bounces off so quickly it's almost comical.

No longer able to remain fully present in the moment, my mind lashes furiously at this question. *Why?* Is it because I still carry the winged crown in a pouch at my waist? It almost has to be.

I wheel around at the mouth of the coliseum and see the carnage as it lays out in front of me. Men down—maybe dead, maybe dying—as the serpentine horde of the skrill sear the field with their poison.

And I have the power to stop it, I think. I must stop it—all of it. Even if it means I break my bond with Gent forever, I must.

The thought of never connecting with Gent again is agonizing…but even worse is the realization I might never see Fortiss again. Never feel his steady presence beside me, never look into his eyes and see that quiet certainty that somehow makes me feel protected and powerful at once. If I die on this battlefield without giving my all—or if the Protectorate is crushed because of my own weakness…no. I owe Fortiss more than that. I owe myself more than that.

After all the times I've been asked to put the greater good ahead of my own interests and rebelled against it, deciding not to step up and step out for the greater good, this isn't something I can rebel against.

This is the way of the warrior, a kind of death I had never expected to face.

I want to scream—to rage. But instead, I draw in a shaky breath. If this is to be my last act as myself, before I lose everything I've come to cherish, I allow myself one moment more to remember Fortiss's touch, the warmth of his smile, the certainty I feel when we stand together. Whatever comes next, no one can take that from me.

I pull the winged crown out of the pouch at my waist, and before I can decide otherwise, I jam it over my head.

Even as I do, the sky snaps tight. And on the far horizon now stands three enormous, implacable beings—a fell wind rushing toward us as they spread their arms wide. The Sahktar.

Deep on the other side of the battlefield, Rihad roars with joy —his voice so loud, I hear it pound against my skull.

"No, no, no!" I gasp.

Rihad turns sharply toward me.

No! Panic suddenly swamping me, I wheel my horse around and ride like mad into the coliseum, where with the added strength of the crown, I pray that I can release Gent to fight with us and for us—and, if I'm being honest, with and for me.

But I can see at a moment's glance that Gent isn't there. And it's not simply a matter of a magic I can't fight through. The chains are there, the blood still staining the fields of the coliseum, but my mighty Divh is gone.

"Gent," I gasp, a pit of despair opening inside me.

A hundred possibilities assault me, each worse than the last. By putting on the crown of wings, did I just lose him forever? Did I free him to serve my father once more—is that even possible? I lift my face toward the heavens and cry out with all the rage, despair, and loss that fills me up and flows out from me, but this battle is not done. I can feel the presence of the Sahktar as they rush across the open plains, swooping toward the coliseum.

Then I'm through the doorway and out again, my left arm punching into the sky as I shout for any and all Divhs who would come to fight, by the power of the winged crown.

For a long second, nothing happens.

Then the skies open up and there is only screaming.

CHAPTER 48

A battalion of Divhs screech across the skies, either barreling into the flying skrill or searing them out of the air with gouts of flame. More great beasts drop to the earth, but as they land heavily, the ground seems to break into pieces below them, and an entirely new wellspring of snakes erupt, shooting skyward and spinning out in a furious mass.

Meanwhile, the Sahktar press toward us, blackening the earth. Any Divhs that get close enough to them to be a threat immediately fall, victim to the killing vapor that fills the shadow creatures.

Men, horses, and Divhs are overrun for a moment in this swarm, and I wheel around in horror to see Rihad standing now separate from the others, his arms lifted high as his mouth extends into a grotesque howl of obscene joy. On the opposite edges of the battlefield, the Sahktar raise their arms as if in solidarity, and a new horde of skrill emerge from their depths—larger and more horrible than any that have come before, winged and fanged.

Then a cluster of spinning balls of light burst out of the depths of the coliseum and race past me, angling toward Rihad. They wink out of view and appear again half a battlefield away, repeating the move once more until they appear directly in front of the former lord protector. They smash into him unceremoniously, and I don't know who's more surprised—him or the hummerlets.

As he falters, though, the first wave of the new horde shatters into nothingness, simply disappearing. Then Rihad rights his stance and the hummerlets scatter.

The moment Rihad raises his hands again, the screaming fury of the skrill mounts anew, but that brief break is all I need to understand my course.

I need to get to Rihad.

No sooner do I press forward then a lumbering Divh, some sort of half-bear, half-bull creature, roars into my path and swings around, completely covered in the glistening bodies of the skrill. There's no way for me to avoid the punishing blow of his fist, and I'm lifted bodily out of the saddle as my horse scrambles away. I crash into the ground so hard, my sight flashes away to utter blackness, then roars back again with fire and pain.

Literally fire and pain, as a blanket of heat scorches the air above me, and fire dissolves the curtain of snakes that shower over me. The snakes that still live fall to either side. I'm protected that way at least, but there are still so many of them, too many. I'll never reach Rihad in time on my own.

Talia! Syril's voice rips across my senses, and I look up, stumbling back. She's riding low, her waist clamped in Tennet's grip, and she gestures me back, away from the mound of snakes as the glorious golden Ayne drops another line of fire in front of me, clearing the path. I stagger forward, then gain speed, but I know I'm still too slow. Too slow!

Still, if Ayne and Tennet are here, that means they heard my call—heard my summons across the Blessed Plane. I did it! I called and they heard, never mind that I wasn't bound to Gent, never mind that I hadn't yet put on the crown. And if they're here, then...

"Fortiss?" I call out with all my might, both inside my mind and through my bloodied lips, and I hear his voice in return but it's still too far. Is he making his way through the Blessed Plane? If so, what's taking him so long?

I see Marsh then, all bird head, winged shoulders, and man-like body barreling through the sky to hit the ground in his usual awkward gallop, Caleb brandishing an enormous torch as the Savasci woman beside him shoots flaming arrows into knots of skrill. From the corner of my eye, I see Nazar's great winged lion swoop across the sky, plucking skrill-covered guards from their mounts and tossing them to the ground.

A scream has me turning around in the middle of the field, and I see my father on the ground, stumbling forward and covered over with a pile of snakes. They've pinioned his arms wide, and in his newly banded delirium, he can't get up.

I hadn't thought the sickness would come on him so harshly, but he hasn't been banded in nearly a decade. I didn't think!

Gent! I shout in my mind, willing my Divh to hear me with every fiber of my being. *The Lord of the Tenth house is fallen! The house you have stood for and fought for since the dawn of the Protectorate is in peril. Please come!*

But Gent doesn't come, and only chaos reigns. I fight my way toward my father, slashing my hands to the right and left, clearing a path based on little else than the sheer force of the winged crown. It's not enough, it can never be enough, but if I can just get through them fast enough to free my father, get him to call his Divh...

I finally reach him, and with a mighty heave, I sweep the snakes from his hands, his arm. His face is covered in glistening goo, the poison of the snakes creating a thick, sticky mass that turns my stomach. But we have no time for him to recover. I jerk his left arm forward and up as his bleary, poison-addled eyes meet mine...

A glorious green fire raptor bursts into the sky above us, talons out. I only have enough time to register my father's startled gasp as he's snatched up and away from me—and tossed into the sky. Then the raptor spirals around him, coming up and under his limp form, and somehow my father has the wherewithal to clutch onto her showy green plumage as she lets forth a burst of fire to blast another fall of skrill into ashes.

I grin in a moment of sheer, undiluted joy at the sight, but then realize how much my distraction is going to cost me.

A veritable wall of the bigger, stronger skrill drop out of the sky, circling me and pressing close—close—and then cover me completely.

I collapse to the ground. The skrill can't outright kill or even poison me, but as Rihad is clearly demonstrating, they *can* imprison me. And whether they intend to or not, I understand as I gasp for air beneath them...they can kill me. By the sheer pressure of their bodies, I can feel the breath leaching out of me, my heart starting to hammer with real fear.

Talia. I hear Fortiss's voice finally break through my own panic, and I almost burst into tears. His voice in my mind feels like coming home after being lost in the darkness. Even separated across the battlefield, my body broken and dying, our connection remains unbroken—something deeper than magic or duty.

I don't have the strength to answer him back, I don't think, not with words. He can't see me, and if he's riding Szonja high above the battlefield, there will be no way to pick me out of the undulating sea of skrill. Instead, I picture Rihad in my mind, the imposter lord protector with his gleaming golden crown.

A responding tide of fury washes over me, Fortiss's protective instinct surging not just for the Protectorate, but for me specifically. Despite my dire condition, I smile. For Fortiss, it's always personal.

My shoulders weaken, and I somehow sink farther into the dirt, as the slithering pile of snakes press me down. Despite the horror I fully feel, I don't fear the snakes themselves. The skrill were, as always, simply tools to be used by the warriors who claimed the crown. They're deadly weapons, yes, but also stone masons capable of incredible feats of creation. The mighty fortress of the Eighth House, the great wall that cut off the Western Realms —neither of these would've been possible without them. The poison that drops from their body, the fear they incite, the hallucinations...these are a part of who they are, yes. But only part. They are creatures of the darkness, but they're not evil.

Only the warriors who use them with evil intent can truly claim that mantle.

Still, I wish they weren't so *heavy*.

I hear a scream that sounds...almost familiar in the distance. Not Gent's hooting, ululating howl, but the high-pitched, chittering screech that once upon forever ago during the Tournament of Gold turned my bones to milk. Now, I can barely recall the mighty creature it belongs to. Now...I only wish to sleep.

A scorch of heat slashes above me, and I blink up at it, blearily. There's no pain, though. The poison of the snakes may have worked enough for me that much, numbing me to the truth of my situation. It's nice, almost. It's quiet, and my sight is dimming, weakening with each strangled gasp. Then another wave of blistering hot wind rushes over me, and I can almost believe I see daylight, and the flare of a sapphire dragon zipping by. I sigh, and with what little breath I have, I murmur my last, most important words.

"I love you, beautiful Gent," I whisper. "I hope you're back among the hills of the Blessed Plane, running—"

A blow of incredible force knocks words—breath—even thought, from me as I'm swept aside amid the pile of skrill, like winter leaves cleared from a mountain pass. I go tumbling end over end, bouncing hard against the ground before another blow sends me flying in the other direction. Before I can catch my breath, I'm slammed again, this time into a dark, thick wall of warm, smooth hide—

Hide?

I suck in a huge lungful of air and fling my arms out, my eyes unseeing as I'm lifted high into the sky and cradled tight against an immense barrel chest. Gent's howl lifts up to the heavens as he swings me around, his right arm sweeping out from side to side as his left paw curls around me protectively.

But how—*why*? Practically incoherent with joy, I reach out to Gent and glory in his transcendent energy, battering him with questions that make no sense even to me as I dive deep into our renewed connection. As devastating as the loss of it was, the reconnection is so much more powerful than I would have expected, as if a new constellation of stars has been added to the night sky that I've never seen before and never knew I'd missed.

How? I demand again.

His response is as cryptic as ever, since we're outside the Blessed Plane, but I understand it well enough—two spinning, winged crowns—one battered and weathered, the other shiny gold. Could it have been as simple as that? Two crowns bringing balance, while one brought power but devastating separation?

I don't know—and at this moment, I don't care. I just never want to be separated from my beautiful monster again.

Fighting my way up the tips of his fingers, I peer out from my vantage point in time to see him lifting me up, up...and onto the back of Zhang.

"Gent!" I gasp, but he happily turns away and continues smashing skrill as Rihad's scorpion...no, *my* scorpion swoops down to where Fortiss and Rihad are squaring off.

What are you doing? I demand, but Zhang doesn't speak to me, just fills my mind with images of the battle far below. Unlike any other Divh I've ever experienced, he can see perfectly, and my eyes snap wide to see Fortiss and Rihad fighting hand to hand. Zhang replays the battle to this point, the images punching through my mind. It started with swords, but Fortiss quickly dropped his to pile bodily into the former lord protector. He isn't trying to kill Rihad, I realize, just take his crown from him.

"No!" I scream into the wind, but of course Fortiss can't hear me, and my mind may be too addled to convey my fear coherently to him. But even if he's able to snag the crown from Rihad—he can't put it on. He can't.

Let me down, let me help!

Zhang swoops around in another great arc and shows me a

new image, him skewering Rihad with his vicious tail, but I know that won't work. Divhs were never intended to kill humans, not intentionally, but only at the behest of their connected warrior. Rihad created the path for them to do that, but that was never their intention. And I, by the Light, don't wish anyone dead. The soldiers of the Imperium—whoever among them still live—can't take those images home to their leader. No.

But still, Zhang has given me an idea.

I lean close into his shiny carapace—so different from the gleaming hide of my beautiful Gent, but no less magnificent—and force my mind to concentrate. I conjure up an image as clear as I know how, the two of us soaring through the sky, angling down, distracting Rihad just enough that he breaks away from Fortiss, perhaps glances up. Over and over, I push this image to Zhang, and the scorpion's harsh, chittering scream is as close to an approval as I think I'm going to get.

He makes the arc just as I imagined it, then we're banking sharply towards the skrill-covered field, and the two warriors in gold and black battling at its edge.

Zhang lets loose with his loudest, boldest scream yet, and Rihad looks up as his Divh swoops low, his face alighting with pure joy—

While Fortiss rips the crown from Rihad's head—and jams it on his own.

"No!" I scream desperately...but it's too late.

In the blink of an eye, the sky snaps tight, but there are no new Divhs nor skrill that are called into this battle. On the far edge of the field, the Sahktar explode into a fell wind of death that sweeps across the field, clearing a swath of Divhs and warriors in its wake. But while dozens fall to the earth, so too do the Sahktar disappear, leaving the horizon clear of their monstrous forms. Divhs scream, fire shoots across the sky, and Zhang swoops out across the battlefield, pivoting around to show me the view on the ground.

Which is how I know the exact moment that a mighty swarm

of skrill collapse on top of Rihad, biting and swarming, and he drops to the ground and doesn't get up again.

Several strides away now, Fortiss lifts his left arm high and curls his right arm into his heart, and I feel the pull of energy—so strong I can't possibly ignore it. I urge Zhang to take me down—down—until the scorpion is skimming the ground, deftly performing a barrel roll to send me tumbling toward Fortiss in a mad somersault. Somehow, I gain my feet without plowing into a wall of skrill, and stagger to a stop.

As Fortiss turns toward me, I lift my left arm as well, curl my right hand to my heart, and our gazes connect across the writhing field.

All the Divhs above and below suddenly vanish from the Fated Plane.

All the skrill disappear a moment later.

For a long, blessed moment, utter silence blankets the battle-field...and then the roar of warriors, Imperial soldiers, and villagers alike soars high.

Across the field, Fortiss turns, our gazes meeting as a bolt of pure, wild energy arcs between us. Even amid this chaos and victory, surrounded by hundreds of souls, it feels like we're the only two people truly seeing each other.

For all we have potentially lost—we've gained this.

We've gained this.

CHAPTER 49

The moment shatters a second later, as Fortiss and I move in one timing, both of us adopting a solitary focus—the soldiers of the Imperial delegation.

As we move toward them, he yanks his crown off his head and hands it to me, and I pull mine off as well, stowing the powerful circlets in my pouch. These two extraordinary symbols of power have done their job, but they can't fall into the hands of the Imperium, now or ever. Nor can they be lost or hidden away again, to be used as weapons against our own people.

There is so much we have yet to do...but first we need to assure our safety, maybe even for another five hundred years.

Of the original thirty Imperial soldiers, only twenty remain, most of them wounded and all of them overwhelmed by the riotous attack they just endured. With both word and mental force, Fortiss commandeers guards and random villagers alike to swarm around these men, instructing his recruits to take on the mantle of healers and helpers. Anyone with a tunic of yellow and black is pressed into the cause. Only after that detail is secured does he start moving through the soldiers, helping them to stand, recapturing their horses.

I watch from the sidelines, allowing him to take the lead, and feeling my pride in him brim over. He was meant to rule, while I was meant to fight. I know that now more than ever. I have no interest in making a stand on a stage I care nothing about. Instead, I turn my attention to the horses, realizing with some surprise that none of them appear to have gone missing, despite the chaos of these past hours. Here, as at the Eighth House, no horses died in the skrill attack, a detail that makes me smile, if a little grimly. For all their efficacy in killing warriors and villagers alike, the skrill didn't harm the horses.

I stumble a little as that truth strikes home. There's only one reason for that, of course.

Because the skrill weren't asked to harm them.

There's a mutter and rustle at my side, and I glance over to see Caleb moving through the crowd, his face streaked with ash beneath his wild, tousled hair, his tunic torn. But there's no denying the grin of fierce satisfaction as our gazes meet and he strides up to stand beside me. Today, we have held the line against Rihad—who can no longer command the darkness or the light. Today, we're finally safe.

The moan of a man who looks like a prominent soldier in the Imperial delegation draws my attention sharply as Fortiss helps him to his feet.

"Snakes," the soldier gasps, his voice sounding a little shrill, and Fortiss nods, taking the man's weight as he lists to the side. "Monsters..." The soldier shakes his head, then catches himself, pushing off Fortiss to stand straighter. His face flushes with outrage as he takes in his diminished troops. "Those were the great Divhs of the Protectorate we have been told over and over again still honor and obey the Light. And they attacked us—attacked the Imperial *guard*. "

"Did they?" Fortiss's words carry a strange resonance that makes the man stiffen and stare at him—all his soldiers following suit. Fortiss smiles easily and the warrior blinks several times, then shakes his head.

"They were called to save us," he corrects himself. "And you directed them."

"I did." Fortiss bows stiffly at the waist, a sign of formal deference to a respected ally. Then he reaches out an arm to stabilize the soldier when he falters again. His right hand squeezes the arm of the man as he speaks. "Lord Protector Rihad fell in the melee, and I am his second, and the new lord protector of these lands. You can trust me."

"But..." the man frowns, shaking his head again in clear confusion. Fortiss doesn't remove his hand from his arm but bears down ever so slightly more.

"Lord Protector Rihad fell. All that he said to you before was meant to protect you in the face of a coming attack. Now, all that *I* say is actual truth, and you can believe it not merely for your protection, but because it is that truth."

"We don't want to be *protected*." The soldier curls his lip. "That is not your place."

Another squeeze of the arm, another glance over the men. I feel the power of Fortiss's magic and the hum of the crowns in my satchel. "We honor the Imperium and stand ready to protect and defend you. The Protectorate remains steady in the face of all enemies."

"Steady." The soldier blows out a hard, gusting breath. "Those things...skrill, you called them? What in the blighted path are they?"

Tools, I think to Fortiss, but to my surprise, he pays no attention.

"Agents of darkness," he says succinctly. "Seeking the Light and all that is great and good in the Imperium. But as with the original Great Conflict, the Light prevailed this day. The agents of the Western Realms found a way in after five hundred years of safety, but they were turned back, as they must ever be. We in the Protectorate continue to keep the Imperium safe. As we have for the past five hundred years, as we will for centuries more."

The soldier stands tall. "And the Imperator salutes you, Lord

Protector Fortiss. By the honor of the Imperium, we thank you too. Your valor will be heralded."

"Not my valor, yours," Fortiss corrects him. "You will return to the Imperium with the tale of your strength in standing with us against the fell attackers. You—and all your surviving men—are the heroes as much as any of us here. I will send a sealed letter of my commendation for the Imperator to know the truth of this day, explaining how you honored him and all the Imperium with your acts of courage. Together we have served, for the glory of the Imperium."

"For the glory of the Imperium!" the soldier agrees.

Then he faints dead away.

I press my lips together as Fortiss glances up to me, catching my eye across the fallen soldier. A flicker of wry humor passes between us. Even with the danger past, our bond holds firm.

I pray to the Light it always will.

The process of clearing the battlefield proves almost as grueling as the fight itself. The skrill bodies begin to dissolve within hours of their deaths, leaving behind only dark stains that smell of sulfur and ash. Teams of villagers work to scrub these marks with clay and sand, sweeping them away before the poison can seep into the earth, while others gather the fallen soldiers, separating the dead from those who still draw breath. The air fills with the sounds of mourning mixed with barked orders as healers rush between the wounded, their yellow-and-black tunics stained dark with blood.

Inside the hastily erected medical tents, the soldiers who faced the skrill writhe in their cots, lost in the throes of poison-induced hallucinations. The healers work tirelessly, applying poultices and chanting prayers to the Light, while scribes assigned by Fortiss record every rant and moan that the fallen utter. By now the healers have all heard tales of the skrill's poison, how it corrupts not just the body but the soul—yet none have treated such wounds in living memory, and there is so much we still don't know about the magic these creatures have brought to our lands.

As the sun begins to set, we finally begin the slow procession back to the First House. Those who can walk help support those who can't, while the most grievously wounded are carefully loaded onto wagons padded with straw. The remaining Imperial soldiers cluster together, their earlier bravado replaced by dazed silence as they process what they've witnessed. I notice how they flinch at every rustle in the undergrowth, every shadow that falls across their path. They've seen the truth of what lurks in the darkness beyond the Imperium's borders, and that knowledge has marked them as surely as the skrill's fangs marked their fallen comrades.

There is no victory dinner at the First House this night. Now, simply being alive and safe is celebration enough...and there are still lies to be told, it seems, newly stitched tales to embroider further. Our story is not yet done.

The following day, we set out again for the coliseum.

CHAPTER 50

The funeral procession for the fallen former Lord Protector Rihad, champion of the Protectorate, hero warrior of the Imperium, is a stately masterpiece that will go down in the history books and become a staple of bardic tales for centuries to come.

And perhaps, one day far in the future, it will be footnoted as the total farce it truly is.

I ride stiffly behind Fortiss and my father, struggling vainly to keep Darkwing from prancing at my tension. Despite my impatience, I feel Fortiss's steady presence like a physical touch. Our connection through the crowns has only amplified what was growing between us—this understanding that transcends words, this shared vision of what could be.

Behind me, Lord Tennet and Syril ride silently, and behind them, an honor guard of the surviving delegates of the Imperium ride in a position of honor with the few house lords still in Trilion who we've conscripted for this unlikely pageant.

Following after all these noteworthy souls, Nazar the exalted priest of the Light leads a twin procession of mourners—half dressed in bleached-white robes, half in deeply dyed black. A cluster of white-garbed attendants leads the two lanes, and a final cluster gathers at the end, as the procession snakes its way all the way from the First House to what we've convinced the representatives of the Imperium is our primary holy ground—the coliseum.

Though it's broad daylight, each line of mourners carries braziers billowing forth with smoke. The water-soaked wood of the white-garbed mourners produces thick clouds of white smoke, while the sooty coal of the black-garbed mourners belches out bulky, black plumes.

Nazar's voice soars high above the procession, a melody weaving around us.

We are born in the Light, and we die in the Light.

I listen to the hypnotic cadence of his words, following along as best as I can. The path we tread in between those two exalted states is never fully without the Light, but it's also hung with darkness. Those who learn how to balance both will gain treasures without seeking—at least if Nazar is to be believed. How he's remembered such songs after so many years in the Protectorate, I have no idea, but his voice is loud and clear, reaching all the way up the line to me.

I long to turn around to see the impressive sight of the light and the dark, to be anywhere but here, actually. Instead, I keep my eyes respectfully and stoically on the backs of the two men who have done so much for the Protectorate, according to all who have been told the tale—Fortiss and the head of the Imperial delegation.

It is the only way, Talia.

I sharpen my eyes on Fortiss's back. Since he wrenched Rihad's crown from his head and placed it on his own, our thoughts have been a hopeless tangle of connection, impossible to separate. But at least the answers I so desperately sought have finally come to me. My crown, Ehlyn's crown, was cast into darkness and sank into the rock of the Western Realms for centuries. It's battle hardened and true, and its edges are far rougher than the beautiful, pristine circlet that Rihad claimed for his own, handed down for centuries since Mirador gifted it to the First House at the dawn of the Protectorate.

Though both crowns remain safely in my satchel, their characteristics are echoed in the two warriors who have now claimed them. I am hardened and bitter, rough in my disavowal of the pomp of this ridiculous funeral procession. Fortiss, however, carries himself like the true leader he is...shiny and bright, but also far more polished in the deception of this day than I will ever be.

It's a lie, I remind him harshly, hating every plodding step of this false procession. *The way of the warrior is truth.*

No. It is strategy. And with this strategy, we secure all that we honor in the Protectorate.

I accept his assessment mulishly, my lips turning down at the corners, though I know he's not wrong. And, for all our differences, I also realize anew how we balance each other perfectly—my rough edges against his polish, my impulsiveness against his strategy. Where I would burn bridges, he builds them; where he might hesitate, I charge ahead. Together, maybe we can make something stronger than either of us could alone.

We continue along the path for another full hour at this stately pace until we reach the coliseum. We ride into the fabled space, and even I can't stop my gasp of surprise and admiration. There, where barely a day before bodies of warriors and carcasses of snakes littered the ground, the space has been transformed.

A sea of silken carpets has been rolled out in a luxurious, overlapping blanket, leaving only a wide corridor for our procession, until, about a quarter of the way into the great space, the great warrior's pyre awaits Rihad. Scattered across the carpets, some standing, some sitting, some weeping, some staring with wide-eyed interest, are the residents of Trilion, as well as many spectators from farther afield, I suspect. To gain entry in this space and to the feast that will follow in Trilion, all they had to do was give their names and troth to follow the lead of Fortiss, the new lord protector.

The pageant continues, and Nazar announces to all who will listen the tale of the First House's glorious defense of the realm.

Rihad was a testament to the Protectorate and the Imperium, Fortiss his rightful successor. Both contributed equally to protecting the First House and, by extension, all of the Protectorate from the loathsome threat of the twisted powers of the Western Realms. At Rihad's tragic death, the transfer of power between him and his beloved nephew was peaceful and blessed by the Light.

Nothing to look at here.

A chorus of singers finally lapse into silence as we reach the great pyre. We draw our horses to the side, but only Fortiss dismounts to accompany the bearers of Rihad's heavily wrapped and draped body to the pyre. Together, he and Nazar shoulder the body of Rihad alongside the other carriers. They mount the pyre, then lay the body to rest atop it.

Idly, I wonder what poor structure had been sacrificed to provide the great stack of wood, and I catch Fortiss's dark mutter as the thought slips through my mind.

Look closer.

Frowning, I edge my horse slightly to the side to see past my father, and blink. Behind the thinnest layer of stacked wood, the interior of the pyre is filled with snake carcasses.

"Fitting, I should think, that he burn with the darkness he cultivated." I stiffen as my father angles his horse back to be even with mine, his gaze also resting on the snake carcasses as he speaks his words in low tones that only I can here. He glances over to me, and I see in his eyes a weariness I'd never marked before. "I should have died too in that battle. Deservedly so. And yet, you not only spared me, you..."

He tightens his mouth, looking away as his eyes shine mirror bright. Then he turns back to glare at me. "Why?" he asks tightly. "I gave you no reason to treat me so fairly. I gave you no grace or compassion, not once. Why did you trust me?"

I hold his gaze steadily, my own heart thudding, as a faraway hooting call sounds deep in my mind—a call of pure, undiluted joy. "Because you gave me Gent," I say simply. "He would never have been mine if he had not been yours, first."

We stare a moment longer, and a tear does slip from his eye then—maybe mine too. Neither of us wipes it away.

"Today we send a warrior into the Light!"

Fortiss's shout echoes off the walls of the coliseum, and I jerk my glance up again as the attendants descend the pyre, leaving only Fortiss and Nazar atop it. They both lift their arms high as a chant lifts all around me, so loud it seems to shake the walls.

"To the Light! To the Light!"

I watch as they both heft the braziers of white-and-black smoke and pull lit tapers out—setting the platform around Rihad aflame. They step back as the fire licks and curls around the structure, then move with stately grace down the stairs as the fire gains momentum. The cheering continues around them, lusty and full-throated, and I finally get my horse angled enough to see the faces of the Imperial delegates as they watch the conflagration.

They look...satisfied, I think.

Satisfied is good. They will carry this story back to the Imperium and hopefully never return—or at least not for generations to come. That is enough, this day. Because all I want is to stay here in the Protectorate—with Fortiss, our people...and my beautiful, powerful goliath, who even now is singing far away in the Blessed Plane, so close but still so far away. I haven't dared to summon him directly yet, but...I can, I think. I can. I will.

By the time we reach the First House again, the celebration in Trilion is already reaching a crescendo. It's as if the collective breath of villagers has been let out, a burden unshouldered and allowed to crash to the ground. I know this celebration will continue for days, and I'm glad to leave them to it—but there are hours yet of celebrations I still must endure before I can finally break free.

Later that evening, the great hall of the First House buzzes with voices and music, the celebration reaching fever pitch as more and more villagers crowd in to toast their new lord protector. I watch as Fortiss moves through the crowd with practiced grace, accepting condolences for his uncle's death even as he receives a second round of congratulations for his ascension. The duality of it all makes my head spin—or perhaps that's the weight of the two crowns still hidden in my satchel, their power humming against my hip like a half-remembered song.

I close my eyes for a moment, letting the noise of the celebration fade as I reach out to Gent with my mind. The connection that was merely a whisper during the ending moments of the attack on the plains and this morning's funeral procession is stronger now, and I can feel my mighty Divh's presence with a familiar warmth that belies his monstrous form. It's all I can do not to leave this crowd of celebrating people—even though my heart fills to nearly overflowing to watch Nazar and Caleb, Syril and Tennet, laughing and talking together. These are my people; these are my friends. But their song is not the one that calls me. Not tonight.

Still, I bide my time, understanding more with every passing hour how right Fortiss is. The Imperial delegation is still here, still watching. And the way of the warrior must be one of strategy as well as joy.

When I finally manage to slip away from the feast, my feet carry me toward the eastern overlook—the highest point of the First House grounds, where the cliffs fall away to reveal the vastness of the Protectorate stretching out below. The night air still carries traces of smoke from Rihad's pyre, but even that is fading away, replaced by the winds of change. The world has been remade, and I'm still standing, no longer alone.

Never again alone.

I stride out on the overlook as I lift my hand high, reaching to the heavens. I reach for myself and for the Thirteenth House—I reach for Merritt and his irrepressible joy—but most of all, I reach for my glorious, magical, monstrous Divh, who even now is howling far away in the Blessed Plane, shimmering with joy.

"Gent," I whisper.

Without another moment's thought I race out, leaping up onto a chair—a table—and then launch myself off the edge of the banister to soar into the sky.

And, of course, he catches me.

CHAPTER 51

B y the time I return to First House and collapse in near exhaustion, everything is quiet and still...so quiet and still that I fall face first into my bed and sink immediately into dreamless sleep.

I awaken in the early morning hours to find that Fortiss has found me. I hear him slip into the door and recognize his energy immediately, as if we're now forged from the same magic that thrums in our twin crowns. His soft, quick footfalls across the floor of my bedroom echo my own rushing pulse, and he slips in beside me easily, as if, again, we've been joined together for years instead of what feels like mere moments. His presence here feels like the most natural thing in the world—as if my body recognizes his before my mind even registers who his is. How swiftly this man has become essential to me, a part of my being as vital as my connection to Gent, yet completely different.

Our words are soft in the darkness as our bodies intertwine, but with each sigh, each brush of our hands, our lips, our bodies, we're writing a new story for the future.

I don't know how this story will end, of course...but it's certainly starting well.

After another full day of impressing the Imperial delegation and vowing our earnest loyalty to the Imperium, Syril, Tennet, Caleb, and I gather the following evening almost by unconscious agreement, warriors drawn together by our common bond. I have no doubt that the others of our small group will join us soon. It's been a day full of so many plans, declarations, and promises, that it's good to be with those who need to say very little to be understood.

This high above the open plains, the air carries the sweet, sharp scent of victory and woodsmoke as I lean against the banister of the First House's eastern overlook. My hands ache from the day's training, but it's a good ache, one that reminds me I'm alive and whole, and that the days to come will hold no challenges so heavy that we can't overcome them. The setting sun paints the wide plains in shades of gold and crimson, while far away in the Blessed Plane, I imagine our mighty Divhs soaring through a twilight sky, their shadows dancing across the waters of a shimmering lake. It's an image I'll never tire of seeing, either in my mind or with my own eyes.

"Our newest warriors are managing well—the ones who are back on their feet already, anyway," Caleb says, sprawled in one of the carved wooden chairs that Fortiss had servants drag out here. His right arm gestures expansively at the vista before us. "They seem sort of stunned, though, and I guess I can't blame them. An army of newly banded warriors and their Divhs, working together on the ground and in the sky, defeating an ancient evil? Rihad's— well, Talia's now—mighty scorpion actually helping us defeat his dark plan to destroy the Protectorate? The Imperial army seeing it all happen and stumbling around wonderstruck a full day later? It's like something out of a bard's tale."

"One that no bard would dare tell," Tennet puts in from his position near the edge of the overlook. He stands with his feet braced, thumbs hooked in his belt, but his usual intensity is softened by the presence of Syril beside him—which is saying something, since the leader of the Savasci remains as fierce as ever. Her shoulder barely brushes his arm, yet I can see how the contact grounds them both. The mighty warrior of the Twelfth House has finally met his match, I think, and I can tell he doesn't quite know what to do with that.

It's all I can do not to grin.

"Oh, they'll tell the tale," Syril says dryly. "They'll just get all the details wrong. In this case, though, it will be a blessing. Speaking of getting details wrong, however..." She casts a meaningful glance at Caleb, who immediately flushes red enough to match the sunset.

"Don't start," he mutters.

"Start what?" I focus more sharply on my friend, only it's Syril who's grinning now, her expression turning even more gleeful as Caleb waves her off.

She pays no attention. "Oh, nothing. Just warrior Dara of the Savasci following our young friend around like a love-struck falcon. She's quite taken with his 'heroic battlefield prowess.'"

Caleb groans and slumps farther in his chair, which only invites more good-natured laughter. "She just wants to learn more about working with Marsh," he protests. "She's fascinated by how we coordinate our attacks."

"Is that what they're calling it these days?" Tennet drawls, earning himself an elbow in the ribs from Syril. The soft grunt he makes at the jab is deeply satisfying to me. Syril has particularly hard elbows.

"Leave him be," Fortiss says, emerging from the doorway with a flagon of wine and several cups balanced carefully on a tray. His eyes meet mine briefly as he moves to set them down, and the warm pride in his gaze makes my heart skip. The fading sunlight catches in his hair, turning it to molten gold. "We've all found unexpected connections through this conflict."

"Indeed, we have," Nazar agrees, following with bread and cheese that fills the air with sharp, homey scents. Miriam completes our party, carrying a stack of leather-bound books that she sets carefully aside before helping to distribute the wine. The leather bindings smell of age and secrets, adding to the air of possibility that weaves around us, drawing us close.

We settle into a comfortable circle, the fellowship of shared battle making formal seating arrangements unnecessary. I find myself between Fortiss and Caleb, their shoulders forming a protective bracket that feels entirely natural. I'd trust either of them with my life and would gladly lay mine down for them—for anyone here, really. The realization fills me with a real and lasting peace. The wine—some of the Twelfth House's finest—is rich and dark, tasting of berries and summer heat.

"I've been reviewing some of the texts we recovered from the Eighth House," Miriam says after we've all taken our first sips. "The accounts of the Western Realms before the Great Conflict are fascinating. There are hints of an entire civilization there, one that worked with both light and shadow. It bears...exploration."

"And now we have the means to do that properly," Nazar adds. The priest's voice remains, as always, even and patient, but there's no denying the glint of interest in his eyes. "The Divhs have shown us that the Blessed Plane connects to all realms. With proper guidance and respect, we could learn so much."

"Proper guidance being the key phrase," Fortiss says. He absently touches the satchel at his hip where his crown now rests, a brighter mirror to the one I carry. Even without seeing them, I can feel their power humming faintly, their connection only drawing Fortiss and I closer. There's still so much we have to learn, and Fortiss's next words echo my own thoughts. "We've seen what happens when that power is misused."

My hand finds his, our fingers intertwining. His skin is warm against mine, callused from sword work but infinitely soft against my own rough palm. "That's why we'll do it together," I say quietly. "All of us. The Divhs, the skrill, the warriors and scholars both. The old ways of separation served no one."

The conversation flows on, but my attention is caught by a familiar hooting call, far away and somewhere else. I imagine Gent floating on his starlit lake. My connection to him hums strong and true in my chest, all the more powerful for having been lost and reclaimed. At my thoughts, a rolling wave of joy floods through me, pure and fierce and perfect.

We fall into comfortable silence as the last rays of sun paint the sky in deeper purples and blues. The night air grows cooler, carrying the promise of stars and a future filled with more discoveries.

"To new beginnings," Miriam says finally, raising her cup. "But may we never forget the past that brought us here."

"To the Light," Nazar adds as Caleb also hefts his cup.

"And to learning." He grins. "Light knows we've got a lot of training ahead of us."

"To the Protectorate and all she has brought us." Fortiss looks around, his shoulder warm against mine. We all fall silent then, drinking deep as we each consider how far we've come—and how far we are so blessed to still be able to go.

I look around at these people who have become my family through fang and fire, trust and even love, then up at the starlit sky, imagining the Divhs who have helped make it possible. In this moment, I can feel it all—the weight of the future, the strength of our bonds, the power of what we've built here in such a short time.

"Together, we will fight," I remind them, and Fortiss turns to me, his eyes glittering with the magic he possesses as well as something deeper, truer, that will bind us together in both Light and darkness, wherever our paths may take us.

"Together," he agrees, "we cannot fail."

EPILOGUE
ONE MONTH LATER.

The day dawns in absolute splendor across the wide, grassy plains, the sun rising over the eastern horizon turning the world into an endless sea of gold.

Off to the right, his great form throwing a monstrous silhouette against the Meridian mountains, Gent tips his head back and howls. The hair on my arms goes up, every nerve pricking to awareness.

In the nearly three months that I've been banded to my colossus, I have heard him howl in many ways, for many reasons. For joy, in excitement, in battle rage, in despair. But this is different. This howl seems to shake the very mountains and make the skies tremble.

Before us on the wide plains, the long sinuous grass shivers and writhes, whipped by an unseen wind. It's not just the elements of this plane that respond, either. The sky snaps tight and suddenly the field before me is filled with Divhs.

Remarkably, none of them have wings. There are enormous four-legged cats, bulky-bodied bears with fists the size of manor houses, and beasts that seem more spikes than body—but all of them heavily muscled, broad—and howling.

"What's this?" Fortiss yells above the cacophony as he joins me on the overlook of the Eighth House...well, what is now *my* house, the Thirteenth. It will take some time for me to get used to that, to everything that's happened since we sent the Imperial delegation back to the heart of the Imperium with spices from the south, precious metals from the northwest—and casks filled to bursting with Twelfth House wine.

Fortiss's shoulder brushes against me as he moves closer, his hand finding mine with that unconscious ease that still makes my heart quicken. Even in the midst of this astonishing display of Divhs around us, I'm acutely aware of him—the clean scent of his skin, the warmth of his palm, the way his breath matches my own without either of us trying. We're together here as in all things, and I may never get over the wonder of that.

Tales from our spies who followed along in the path of the Imperial delegation have also been reassuring, and for that I'm truly thankful. There will be no more soldiers, no more politicians to placate, at least not anytime soon. Instead, we can focus on rebuilding our troops of warriors and Divhs and creating new connections between our finest councilors, artists, and tradesmen and the mighty giants of the Blessed Plane.

Not just the Blessed Plane either, I think, as my gaze strays to the ridiculous statue that yes, still stands of me...or of Ehlyn, as I prefer to believe. A reminder of what's possible for women in the Protectorate, and what's possible in partnership with some of the most extraordinary stone masons and illusionists I've ever encountered, the skrill of the Western Realms.

There's so much ahead of us, but this morning, with Fortiss at my side, my eyes are only for Gent as he whips around, throwing his massive arms wide. He turns his palms up, open to the sky— first the right, then the left. Then he slams his hands together with a percussive *boom!* that proves too much for a section of the Meridians. I hear the rocks explode outward, feel the rumble in the earth. For a moment, I wonder what great caves he's now revealed, what windows into the mountains he's just opened for us, and know the Savasci will probably be exploring just that before the day is done.

Then Gent once more puts his right hand out and his left, palms up. He swings around to stare at me, and in my mind, I see two spinning crowns entangled together.

"He wants us to put them on," I shout to Fortiss, the words lost in the howling wind. But Fortiss hasn't come this far, nor grown so close to me, that he can't hear me when I speak.

"Heart to heart!" he shouts, grinning. He reaches into the pouch slung to his side and pulls out the golden crown—pristine and gleaming as he holds it high. "Plane to plane!"

I follow, though my fingers are far more clumsy, my heart shivering with dread even though I know—*know!*—that the danger of separation is past. Still, I doubt I'll ever forget the moment my tie with Gent was severed without warning, that devastating ache of loss that filled me and emptied me at once. I also know that together, Fortiss and I have overcome the fearsome prophecy of his solitary death foretold in the room of this great house—if only because we returned to that same room, now fully cleaned and cleared with sage and Savasci healing rituals, and saw an entirely different prophecy unfold before us, one I still can't quite process... but which I look forward to with every echoing heartbeat.

Now, however, Gent's howl only increases in urgency and excitement at my hesitation, and I fumble out the second crown of wings, Ehlyn's crown. I hold it up with trembling hands, not missing the difference between the two circlets—Fortiss's polished and loved, mine battered and bent, but both of them shining in the sun, the work of master craftsmen long ago lost to history.

Fortiss catches my eye and in that glance is everything we've endured together—every battle, loss, and triumph. I remember the first time I saw him, a cipher in the forest, and marvel at the man before me now, eyes bright with adventure and possibility. How far we've both come from those first teasing exchanges, from reluctant allies to this—a bond so complete it feels like it's written into my bones.

"Warrior to warrior!" I shout, speaking the last of the words we found—finally—in the ancient books from Daggar's library. There's no clear indication about what they mean, exactly, but they feel right, they feel good. And when we read them and heard the hooting joy of Gent and the triumphant scream of Szonja— echoed by what sounded like every Divh in the Blessed Plane—we knew they were important. This morning feels a fitting time to utter them into life.

I place the crown on my head in perfect timing with Fortiss.

All the Divhs roar with a wild, unbridled joy, then those with paws or powerful forelegs swoop them high—and drive them into the ground. Those built for stamping pound the ground with heavy hoofs, and those with nothing but bulk to recommend them, leap into the air then drop down, jolting the earth with their feet.

It seems like the entire Protectorate must shatter with the force of every blow, and the Divhs continue on and on until Fortiss and I are wrapped in each other's arms, crouched against the wall of the Thirteenth House overlook, wincing and shrinking tighter together as boulders fall all around us and the very mountain seems ready to collapse into the ground.

But it doesn't collapse.

Instead, after a few more mighty thuds, the earth itself falls away beneath the paws of the Divhs. The wide plain before us suddenly darkens in a long, sinuous stain that sweeps out in front of the Thirteenth House as far as I'm able to see. This apparently is the sign the Divhs have been waiting for. They erupt in another wave of mad howls and whoops, and another tide of pounding follows. This one, so fast and rhythmic it seems to take on a vibration all its own.

"They're breaking the plain!" Fortiss gasps. He wheels to me, his eyes suddenly filled with equal parts horror and wonder, and I know my expression echoes his. "What have we—"

Look.

Gent's command can't be ignored, and from far above the mountains, Szonja screams with approval as the stain that darkens the plains erupts with a geyser of water. Similar spouts burst across the wide valley, torrential plumes that shove up from the ground as if an ocean has been lying in wait all this time beneath the grassy plain, waiting for its chance to gust forth. The Divhs scramble back, some of them winking out entirely, others retreating as water fills the space, covering over roads and trees and pushing up towards the Thirteenth House until it laps the causeway that leads up to the great manor building.

Then the water rushes back again, draining away as quickly as it filled, but leaving thick grassy lawn behind it, sapling trees by the thousands, and a wide, lush bank to mark the edge of a crystalline blue lake.

"Talia," Fortiss whispers, and his voice is so shaken that I turn to him, only to see him staring over my shoulder, far up the mountain range. "Look."

And that's when I turn and see that the inhospitable harsh crags surrounding the Thirteenth House stronghold are now filled with trees, strips of tall grass, and thick tumbles of bushes, wildly blooming with blue and white flowers. The carpet of flowers chases its way up the mountain and into the trees until the rocky outcroppings finally emerge far, far up toward the peaks.

Gent's howl has me turning around again, and I blink to see him floating far out in the middle of the water of the huge, glistening lake, his arms waving wide with joy as he sees me watching him.

"What have we done?" Fortiss asks again, but his voice is trembling only with wonder now, not horror. In unspoken synchrony, we reach up and remove the crowns from our heads with shaking hands. I stare down at the two circlets, feeling the weight of power in my grasp...power and possibility.

Fortiss puts into words what I can't bring myself to say. "These gifts were too mighty for us five hundred years ago," he murmurs. "Even if Mirador hadn't struck down Ehlyn, the delegates of the

Imperium would never have survived long with power like this. The contract would have soured, the partnership between the first leaders would've fractured. Better that the second crown was lost to us for so long—and that the price to pay for wielding the one we had left was so high that no lord protector would ever dare attempt it except in direst need, lest he lose the thing he valued most."

He sighs, squinting out over the enormous lake. "Rihad didn't care about any of that. He didn't want the power to heal a broken plane. He wanted only to destroy and rule through chaos."

"Do you think the Imperium knew...about any of this?" I ask. "Do you think those First House lords ever explained what happened here?"

He grimaces, then glances at me. "Do you?"

I shake my head. There may be a time of reckoning, yes, a future battle to be fought, but not here. Not now. For now, we can explore the magic newly returned to our land and can look to see how we might ask the skrill to build—not destroy—homes, cities, and works of intricate beauty like the statue of Ehlyn, proudly reaching out to all who venture this far across the Protectorate.

Fortiss takes my hand again and turns me to him, but no more words are needed. I rise on my toes to press my lips to his, a kiss that carries the weight of all we've survived, all we hope to build.

When we part, he rests his forehead against mine. "Heart to heart," he whispers, echoing the ancient words that feel increasingly like a vow between us.

"Plane to plane," I answer, completing the phrase that now holds so much more meaning than when we first discovered it.

"Warrior to warrior," we finish together, and the words hang in the air between us, a promise as binding as any ceremonial oath.

It's a new dawn, and as the sun continues its soaring ascent over the eastern horizon, my heart spills over with what may come.

Fortiss and I turn again to witness this newest, most glorious gift of the Divh, a gift of twinned connection and power they had given us all those centuries ago when we first called upon their aid...and have been longing to return to us ever since.

The way of the warrior, once more, is life.

Beautiful. Powerful. Fierce.

And never again to be walked alone.

GLOSSARY

Blessed Pass: The primary passage into the Protectorate from the Imperium. The Tenth House is perched in the mountains overlooking it. Creatures called hummerlets may have returned here when the skrill attacked.

Blessed Plane: Home of the Divhs.

Caleb: Formerly a squire for the Second House, now a banded soldier. His Divh is Marsh.

Court of Talons: An honorary designation for warriors who have won the Tournament of Gold.

Crown of Wings (Winged Crown): Artifact(s) believed to pre-date the Protectorate and the Tournament of Gold pageantry. It is associated with Mirador and the ability to rule darkness or command an army. At the opening of the story, it is considered an honorary award given to winners of the Tournament of Gold.

Daggar (Lord Daggar): The lord of the Eighth House.

Darkwing: Talia's mount.

Divh: Mighty creatures bonded to warriors, summoned from the Blessed Plane to assist most their warriors, usually in battle.

Eighth House: One of the twelve great houses, located on the western border of the Protectorate. Lord Daggar is its master. Books and talonstones from this house are important for understanding the threat from the Western Realms. Its color is orange.

Ehlyn: A warrior of the Imperial army who stood with Mirador during the Great Conflict. She is credited with successfully summoning the Divhs.

Eleventh House: One of the twelve great houses, located in the east of the Protectorate. Bertrand of the Eleventh House is named among those killed. Its color is midnight blue.

Exalted Imperium (see Imperium):

Fifth House: One of the twelve great houses, located in the north of the Protectorate. Its color is charcoal gray.

First House: One of the twelve great houses, located in the center of the Protectorate. It's the house of the Lord Protector. Lord Rihad was its master, followed by Fortiss. Its colors are gold and black.

Fortiss: Warrior of the First House who becomes the new Lord Protector after Rihad's defeat.

Fourth House: One of the twelve great houses, located in the northwest of the Protectorate. Its color is sky blue.

Gent: Talia's Divh, a great green-and-silver goliath.

Gamon (Lord Gamon of the Third): Lord of the Third House.

Great Conflict: A major event that occurred at the western border and devastated the land. The Eighth House is said to have been the first to rise after it.

Great Houses: The twelve ruling families of the Protectorate. Their firstborn sons command the mightiest Divhs.

Grounding stones: Stones mentioned in a deluded state by Tennet. They are small, colorful, curved stones buried in the cornerstone of structures, believed to be a beacon for skrill. They are the same as talonstones, with "from talonstone to grounding stone" indicating a path between them. They already exist in the great houses and likely villages.

Hakkir: The capital city in the heart of the Imperium.

Hummerlets: Small Divhs that are offshoots of the hummerbill Divh.

Imperium (also Exalted Imperium): A nation that borders and also rules the Protectorate. The Blessed Pass is the primary passage from the Imperium into the Protectorate.

Kot'lok: The name Imperial soldiers called "evil" creatures from the Western Realms.

Lanark: A warrior from the Imperial party, gifted in diplomacy, who became the first lord protector after the Great Conflict. Mirador gave him the winged crown.

Light (The Light): A guiding force or principle for members of the Imperium and the Protectorate, also called the Way of the Light. Nazar is a priest of the Light.

Lemille (Lord Lemille): Lord of the Tenth House, father of Merritt and Talia. Nazar tutored his son Merritt.

Meridians: Jewel-like mountains that serve as the entryway to the Western Realms.

Merritt (Lord Merritt of the Tenth House): Talia's younger brother, the supposed firstborn of the Tenth House. Originally bonded to Gent.

Mirador: The leader of the Imperial party that came to the Protectorate before the Great Conflict. Mirador is credited with successfully summoning the Divhs. Warrior Ehlyn stood with him.

Miriam (Councilor Miriam): A councilor of the First House. Her Divh is Kreya.

Nazar: A priest of the Light who serves as Talia's closest advisor. He came from the Imperium and was welcomed by Lord Lemille to tutor Merritt. Once and now again a banded warrior, his Divh is Wrath.

Ninth House: One of the twelve great houses, located in the south of the Protectorate. Its color is umber.

Orlof (Lord Orlof): The lord of the Twelfth House. Talia was betrothed to his heir.

Protectorate: The land ruled by the twelve great houses under a Lord Protector. It is bordered by the Imperium to the east and the Western Realms to the west. Divhs are found within the Protectorate.

Rihad (Lord Protector Rihad): The lord of the First House and governor of the Protectorate before Fortiss.

Sahktar: Powerful creatures as tall as Divhs who lead the skrill, made up of snakes and smoke.

Savasci: A group of warrior women who live and hunt with Syril, their leader, and are based near the Eighth House.

Second House: One of the twelve great houses, located to the west of the First House. It's known for its libraries of books about Divhs and warriors. Caleb was formerly a squire for this house. Its colors are red and white.

Seventh House: One of the twelve great houses, located to the south of the Protectorate and known for its riches. Its color is yellow.

Sixth House: One of the twelve great houses, located to the northwest of the Protectorate. Its color is deep purple.

Skrill: Flying snake-like creatures from beyond the western borders linked to the Sahktar. Also known as the Kot'lok.

Syril: The leader of the Savasci, a group of warrior women from the western borders.

Szonja: Toma's and then Fortiss's Divh, a sapphire-blue dragon.

Talia (Lady Talia): The true firstborn and first-blooded warrior of the Tenth House, whose birth is considered a heresy. She was betrothed to the heir of the Twelfth House, but instead became champion of the Tournament of Gold and winner of the winged crown, making her the head of the Thirteenth House.

Talonstones: Stones carried by warriors and also buried in the bedrock of the great houses and likely villages. They were originally used as homing points for Divhs, separate from their warriors. They are blessed with the Light and limned with darkness.

Tennet (Lord Tennet): The lord of the Twelfth House. His Divh is the dragon Ayne.

Tenth House: One of the twelve great houses; its lord is Lemille, father of Merritt and Talia. It is one of the smallest houses in the Protectorate, located on the eastern border of the Protecorate, in the mountains overlooking the Blessed Pass. Nazar was the priest of the Tenth House. Its color is green.

Third House: One of the twelve great houses, located in the south-west of the Protectorate. Kheris is a warrior of this house. Its color is sand.

Thirteenth House: A new house established with Talia as its head after she wins the winged crown. The Savasci are considered its people. Its colors are dark charcoal and silver, though Talia also sometimes wears dark green in deference to her original house.

Toma: The father of Fortiss, considered the greatest warrior in the land. He was called "dragon" in honor of his Divh, Szonja. Bardic tales were written about him and his Divh. His books contained records of battles in the Western Realms.

Tournament of Gold: An extraordinary proving ground for warrior knights and their Divhs, established by the First House. Held yearly, the event includes rank and file competition and warrior/Divh exhibitions. The two-day competition for high-level warriors is at the end. Winners can receive Divhs and banded soldiers.

Trilion: A robust village near the great coliseum of the Tourna-ment of Gold and the First House.

Twelfth House: One of the twelve great houses. It is described as the weakest of the Protectorate's houses and is located in the mountains. Lord Orlof was its lord, and then Lord Tennet. Its color is deep crimson.

Way of the Light: The religious system of the Imperium and Protectorate, associated with priests of the Light like Nazar.

Western Realms: An area located beyond the western borders of the Protectorate. It is associated with dark powers, the Kot'lok, also known as the skrill. Books detailing its history and battles are important, although some were seemingly lost or controlled by Lord Rihad. Its landscape is described harshly in some texts. The Meridians serve as its entryway.

ACKNOWLEDGMENTS

A debt of tremendous thanks to my editor Sally OKeef, who took on this even longer book with grace and skill, and proofreader Rafiqa Young, who was an absolute miracle. Any errors that remain are very much my own. I'm also profoundly grateful to Lizzie Bemis, Sabra Harp, and Judi Soderberg for providing me with a clear view of the story and how I could improve it, and to Geoffrey Girard for his storytelling inspiration. Finally, thank you to Dar Albert for the beautiful artistry of my cover—your work became an integral part of the story. While I'm sad to leave the realm of the Protectorate, I'm so grateful for the chance to have told its tale.

Also by Jennifer Chance

Fang & Fire Series

Court of Talons

Crown of Wings

Gatekeepers of the Gods

Courted

Captured

Claimed

Crowned

Boston Magic Academies

Touch of the Mage

Blood of the Mage

Heart of the Mage

Soul of the Mage

The Hunter's Call

The Hunter's Curse

The Hunter's Snare

The Hunter's Vow

Witchling Academy

Teaching the King

Tempting the King

Taming the King

ABOUT JENNIFER CHANCE

Jennifer Chance is the pen name of Jenn Stark, an award-winning author of paranormal romance, urban fantasy, and contemporary romance. Whether she's writing as Jenn or Jennifer, she loves writing, magic and unconditional love.

Thank you for taking this adventure with her. If you're feeling social, you can find her online at https://www.jenniferchance.com or visit her on Facebook at https://www.facebook.com/authorJenniferChance/!

www.ingramcontent.com/pod-product-compliance
Lightning Source LLC
Chambersburg PA
CBHW020517110726
47899CB00004B/1137